CITY OF LAUGHTER

A NOVEL

CITY OF LAUGHTER

TEMIM FRUCHTER

Grove Press
New York

FIRST EDITION

Published simultaneously in Canada
Printed in the United States of America

The interior of this book was designed by Norman E. Tuttle at Alpha Design & Composition.
This book is set in 11.5-pt. Adobe Caslon by Alpha Design & Composition of Pittsfield, NH.

First Grove Atlantic hardcover edition: January 2024

Library of Congress Cataloging-in-Publication data is available for this title.

ISBN 978-0-8021-6128-4
eISBN 978-0-8021-6129-1

Grove Press
an imprint of Grove Atlantic
154 West 14th Street
New York, NY 10011

Distributed by Publishers Group West

groveatlantic.com

24 25 26 27   10 9 8 7 6 5 4 3 2 1

For Savta and Great-Grandma

CITY OF LAUGHTER

Prologue

I t was the sudden switch in the weather that gave Baruch pause, it is told.

The morning had been usual—the clear air smelled cold as dirt, the empty sky preparing itself to fill with the sounds of the day to come. Baruch was already running late for the wedding, so he quickened his steps to the synagogue, and as he curved around the path where the road tucked into the trees, the sky flipped quick to gray. Not rain-gray, not thunder-gray. Gray that was thick, difficult to see through, like smoke become a solid thing. Baruch craned his neck and looked up through the tree cover, trying to understand the sky's behavior or to find the fire.

The weather in Ropshitz rarely surprised. Summer too hot, winter too cold, and the only variety right in the middle of fall, moon low and golden, and wild winds tearing leaves from the trees so they danced the whole way down to the ground. Baruch looked around. Was anyone nearby? Had anyone noticed what he noticed? No. He was alone on the quietest part of the path to the synagogue. Sky dark as a pocket. Foreboding, approaching; maybe even a warning. Of what, he couldn't know.

Baruch watched upward until his neck hurt, so long that, by the time he turned back down to earth, he realized he would have to run if he had any hope of making the badeken. Baruch, you see, was not quick. He was tall with short legs, which made wedding guests chuckle when he danced for them. Nights, after working some wedding or another, he gazed at his reflection in the mirror, trying to pray himself into someone more even-limbed.

He ran the rest of the way to the wedding, but he was still late. He was still wearing his work pants, still so thoroughly dirty from helping his father with the chickens that morning, it was hard to tell whether they had ever been any color at all. He staked out the synagogue like a crook, looking for the right moment to slip unseen into the crowd and find a private place to change his clothes.

I couldn't help it, he thought, rehearsing excuses. *The sky turned to smoke.*

It is told that Baruch's flights of fancy often made him late but that the lateness was part of his charm. He was a badchan, a holy wedding jester, one of the village's very first, and truth be told, he was middling at it. In his dreams, he turned up in front of some room and reliably stirred frenzied peals of laughter from hordes of forlorn wedding-goers saturated with the week's melancholy. His brother, Yankel, the smart one; his sister, Shaindy, the fearless; and Baruch—how fervently he wished he'd been born with a natural gift for making people laugh. In his fiercest moments of longing, he imagined standing in front of a procession of mourners, for God's sake, and making them sing with a dark laughter, dirt still fresh on their relative's grave. Eventually he would win the crowd over so thoroughly, he'd draw a muffled giggle out of the dead uncle himself.

The truth, it is told, is more regular.

The truth is that, in childhood, Baruch was clear-eyed but distractible. He turned to pranks instead of Torah study and stared out the window instead of at the page of Talmud his father was trying to teach him. So, he was sent into badchanus. Clownery, a rare but viable career path for a Ropshitz boy. *The angels laughed*, said his father. *And Sarah laughed, and Abraham laughed, and even God laughed*, said his mother. *Moses laughed*, said the rebbe, under whose tutelage Baruch began his studies. *The laugh that comes only of weariness, of complicated joy, of holy attention.* To Baruch's parents, the rebbe said, *Perhaps he can be taught.* In this tradition, Baruch learned to sow laughter the best he could at a village wedding. He learned how to make the bride and groom and their tired families laugh, or at least exhaust himself trying. His dearest wish? To charm the sternest rabbi in any room. This, Baruch knew, would prove he had something. That he was someone, or at least might one day be. He scanned the assembled at any wedding until he inevitably found the man, the one hidden under the brim of his humorless hat and scowling in some corner, almost defiantly (*You're at a wedding*, Baruch thought. *Can't you even* smile?), and aimed his best jokes directly at this man. Danced at him, lolled around at him, dropped his drink toward him, swooned and sang in his general direction. It had never worked.

As a practice, Baruch tried to think funny thoughts on his way to a wedding. A cow wearing a crown, a moon made of cheese, a whole synagogue full of praying potatoes. He had tried today, too, to become funnier on his way to the synagogue. But he had failed. The sky, now—it was markedly not funny. Something was wrong. Baruch wanted, inexplicably, to warn someone, but he wasn't sure how or of what.

He hid behind a door, peeled off his soiled clothes, stepped into his clean ones, and emerged right on time for the rituals of the badeken, watching as the groom veiled the bride, the mothers and grandmothers openly weeping. As was his practice, he aimed his opening bit at the sternest rabbi in attendance (Reb Zalman, a devout and somber man who, despite seeming older than the earth itself, had traveled a whole day for the honor of the groom, a pupil of his). Afterward, Baruch took his bow and immediately walked into his father, who had a schnapps in one hand and a handful of nuts in the other.

"Baruchl," he called, voice hoarse from celebration. "Did you see the stranger in the bright blue jacket?"

"Jacket?" This unusual day. "No. Who was he?"

Baruch's father adjusted his hat and looked around the room. Guests feasted on plum cake and drank wine as musicians played, dressed in black and gray and gold and red. No blue jackets. "I don't know," he said. "I wondered whether you might know such a character. He seemed to be looking for someone, maybe a woman. He didn't say who." Baruch's father paused. "He was too clear-eyed to be a drunk. But I heard him say, *I think she might be here,* as though talking to no one." Baruch's father shook his head. "Who did he think he might find here? There are no strangers in Ropshitz. Everyone and everything there is, we already know." A pair of almonds, washed down by a final gulp of schnapps.

Mystery, for Baruch, was seductive, and it was true: where he lived, there was so little of it. But now. The perplexing clotted sky and a visiting stranger no one knew and no one could find. He couldn't wait to tell Bluma. Bluma understood the beauty of a question without an answer. She loved riddles—of which Baruch had plenty, thank God—and preferred wildflowers to any flora more pristine. *But wait,* Bluma said, every time Baruch started to tell her anything—a story, a joke, a secret wish. *I want to guess.*

"Papa, did the man seem sad?" The thought of a strange man looking for a woman at someone else's wedding—*well,* Baruch thought, *how else could he seem?*

"No," Baruch's father said, and he didn't hesitate. "He didn't seem sad. He shone." He thought for a moment. "Either like a vagrant madman or a man who has just glimpsed the face of God."

After the wedding, Baruch headed to the exit at the back of the synagogue. He would go see Bluma, who might still be hanging out the clothes. Baruch had loved Bluma since they were children. "Ask her to marry you already, Baruchl," said his mother. "No tzadik would dally like this." His mother, an efficient woman, was frustrated by her boy's leisurely pace in such an unleisurely world.

And Baruch would ask Bluma one day; he knew this. But not yet. With marriage, Baruch imagined, came a heavier kind of responsibility. He didn't yet want to relinquish the constant feelings of anticipation that animated his days, wondering whether he might catch Bluma for a brief and quiet hello as the sun sank, and walk home nostril-drunk with the faint notes of honey he could always smell on her hair. He didn't want to relinquish romance altogether, worried it would disappear once he and Bluma made such a serious commitment.

Baruch, it is told, was astonished to push open the door out the back of the synagogue to the courtyard, only to be met with a green-eyed man wearing a bright blue jacket.

When people tell the story, they tell of a man.

I, of course, know different.

"It's locked," said the man, whose voice was higher than a man's but deeper than a boy's. He was jaunty, leaning tall against the synagogue's back gate. "And I couldn't get back inside again either, so it would appear I'm stuck right here."

"Hello," said Baruch, self-conscious. *There are no strangers in Ropshitz.* "It's always locked. I work a lot of weddings, so I know how to open it."

"I see," said the man. "I'm just passing through. Maybe you can show me the way to the nearest inn? I'd rather not sleep in the synagogue courtyard." The green in his eyes was alarming, and his wavy hair stood almost straight up.

"Of course," said Baruch. "Reb Nechemiah's. I can walk you." He would see Bluma tomorrow. His curiosity about the blue-jacketed stranger had him by the shoulders.

The stranger's nose was angular and certain. His gait, almost a trot. He wore no skullcap. He had no beard. His cheeks, smooth as Baruch's sister's, shone in the light of dusk.

"So," Baruch said, as though he walked men in clothing brighter than Joseph's coat to the inn after weddings every night. "What brings you to Ropshitz?"

"Well," said the stranger. "It's a long story."

The darkening sky was beginning to reveal the moon, just past three-quarters full. The wind drew the grass gently prostrate toward the dirt. Perhaps the proximity of the divine or perhaps simply the weather.

"I have time," Baruch said. There was at least a mile left until the inn.

"I get the feeling this town doesn't get too many visitors." *Evasive stranger*, Baruch thought. Baruch knew Ropshitz down to every crack in its well-worn walkways, from the synagogue to the market to the woods and back but, blue jacket in the corner of his vision, Baruch felt now like he was walking somewhere he had never been. "Everyone at that wedding looked at me like I was from another world. Which isn't unfair, I suppose. It was someone else's wedding. I wasn't invited."

"You're right, we don't get many visitors," said Baruch. He kicked a pile of pebbles with his scuffed brown wedding shoe, and they sprayed outward. "Not much to see here."

The stranger glanced up. "Well, you do have the moon here, don't you? And it's shining beautifully tonight. So, already, not so bad."

Baruch felt the corners of his mouth tease upward, charmed. He screwed up his courage. "So?" He didn't repeat the question.

"Well, I can't tell you much," said the stranger. "Do you have mail service here in Ropshitz?"

"Of course," said Baruch. "Reb Yankel brings the mail and parcels most Thursdays. Sometimes, when the weather is bad, every other Thursday." Baruch sped his steps. Enough talk about the mail and the weather. "Why?"

"Well," said the stranger. "That's like what I do. I bring deliveries from one place to another. Packages, messages, information." He paused. "Sometimes, more powerful things."

Baruch couldn't imagine what this meant. He knew that a boy on his street had herbs and tinctures sent from afar because the local doctor couldn't cure what he had. He knew that the woman who saw disturbing visions sometimes, the one on whom the rabbi had given up, had scrolls and potions sent to her from a healer in a neighboring village, a last attempt to extract the evil presence from her blood. He didn't like to think about it. "What do you mean, powerful things?"

The stranger looked back up at the sky. "Really beautiful night tonight, isn't it, Baruch?"

Baruch turned sharply. "How do you know my name?"

"Word gets around in a small town."

But you don't live here, thought Baruch. *There are no strangers in Ropshitz. Are there?*

Then, sudden and sure, the stranger took Baruch's hand. Laced his slender fingers through Baruch's thick ones. Baruch dizzied, skin singing. A man didn't take another man's hand. Not unless they were dancing in a circle at a wedding. The stranger's grip was firm.

"Come this way," he said.

"Where?" Baruch asked helplessly, knowing he would follow, no matter the answer.

The stranger walked them off the path, into the woods at the edge of the village. His grip loosened on Baruch's hand, but he didn't let go. Neither did Baruch, whose palm prickled against the warmth of the stranger's. *He held my hand*, he thought over and over again, imagining explaining this moment to anyone else, let alone to himself. *The strange man held my hand.*

"Here," said the stranger. They had arrived at a clearing, and he gestured to the middle of it. Baruch's eyes stung looking. Even under the dark of the evening sky, he could see that the air in the clearing teemed with gray—a gray that roiled and shook like a trapped monster. Like the aftermath of an angry fire, but—no fire. The same smoky silver sheen that had saturated the sky earlier that day. Here, in the clearing of the woods at the edge of Ropshitz. Baruch had never seen anything like it. What was this presence? Godly or ungodly? What was it like to have a story no one else had?

"The weather has been strange all morning." Baruch spoke quietly, entranced. "Is this why?"

"You noticed," said the stranger. "Most people don't notice. They forget to look up, not understanding that weather speaks to us. It gives us information. Most people simply complain about the rain or the snow, but that's because they aren't paying the right kind of attention."

It is told that Baruch had trouble speaking then. "Weather?" he rasped. "This is not the kind of weather I know. What is it?" His words came hot from his throat.

The stranger looked down, as though himself refusing to look at the vision he'd cast before them, one that shouldn't exist, not in any natural world Baruch knew. "This," he said, "is something I was supposed to deliver."

"Here?"

He hesitated. "I was supposed to deliver it to somewhere it was needed."

Baruch had forgotten he was still holding the stranger's hand, even though they were no longer walking. Embarrassed, he dropped it. "And Ropshitz needed it?"

The stranger adjusted his bright jacket and stared ahead. "Let me ask you a question. The people in this village, do they laugh?"

Baruch blinked, conjuring images of the dozens of weddings where he had stood in front of roomfuls of reluctant and haggard guests, bending his body and orating until he was hoarse, just to try to get them to crack a smile. "Laugh?" Baruch paused, wondering whether the stranger already knew. "I'm a badchan. My job is to make the bride and the groom and guests at weddings laugh. Using God's humor, of course," Baruch added quickly. "Nothing unholy."

The stranger nodded, a flash of recognition across his face. "God's humor." He nodded again, looking back at the swirling gray. "Of course this is your job. It's an important job."

"Is it?"

"And do they? Laugh?"

"The people here struggle," said Baruch, as honestly as he could. "It is difficult to make them laugh. I am no magician. I do the best I can."

The stranger looked at Baruch. Then he looked at the dancing weather system, reckless in the clearing. He nodded, as if answering a question no one had asked. "You'll take good care of it."

"Of what?" Baruch no longer recognized the earth or the sky. He forgot to be surprised when the stranger took his hand again.

"Take me to your inn, dear Baruch. I'm tired and I have a long journey in the morning."

They walked then, silently, to Reb Nechemiah's. Baruch brimmed with questions he was certain the stranger wouldn't answer. Every few minutes, he'd try to ask one of them, but staggering wonderment had replaced his powers of speech.

It is told that when Baruch and the stranger parted ways—after the stranger kissed Baruch gently on the temple, assuring him, once again, that he would do a good job—Baruch fell to the ground. The moon *was* beautiful. Everything so beautiful and so terrible. Nothing to make sense of anymore, no reason to try. Tomorrow. He would ask Bluma tomorrow. He lay there on the ground, sky crowding with eager stars and a fine dust that resembled baking flour, sounds coming from his chest that felt so new, he almost didn't recognize them as laughter.

It is told—and generally, the teller pauses ceremonially before this part, eager to deliver a joyous ending—that the very next time Baruch went to work at a wedding, the people there laughed amply and easily, the room filling with their sweet music. And the time after that, and so on. Bluma, too, smiled easier, her smile higher on one side than the other. Baruch walked lighter, no longer so bothered by the shortness of his legs. It is told that, nights, Baruch would lie in bed looking uselessly skyward, wondering what gift or curse this visitor had left—what it was, exactly, that the weather had brought.

This is the story they tell of Ropshitz, where, several years later, the great and world-renowned badchan Naftali Tzvi Horowitz was born. Naftali Tzvi who, they say, did lovingly invoke his predecessor Baruch's name once or twice, speaking generously of his great intellect and unique sense of humor, even though not many Ropshitzers had actually heard of him.

It is told, but it's not how I tell it. Not exactly. I, of the blue jacket, of the messenger's bag, of a spirit uncommonly distractible for my kind. What you know of the messenger—everything you've read, everything you've dreamed or been told—isn't the whole story. And the whole story, it isn't hidden. It's not underneath, it's not encoded, and it's neither before nor after. It's the place we all so often forget to look. It's between.

It is told the sky over Ropshitz that night was a starlit expanse of brilliant purple. A near-impossible color, an infinitesimal point between red and blue. And that part, at least, I can tell you—it's as true as the moon.

The messenger's journey starts here. After the end of the folktale and before whatever comes next.

Between.

I could tell you the story of Ropshitz. Of Reb Naftali Tzvi, famous badchan, born in 1760, soon known the world over as the Laughing Rabbi. I could tell of a kind of wisdom made of hijinks at weddings, pranks involving sacks of onions, songs sung backward, secret doors. And that otherwise, times were stern. A pious place, for the most part. God-fearing. Benevolent windows and awestruck rooftops. Only a handful of trees, but all of them bowed and bent in the face of the diffuse divine.

I could tell you, too, about how a badchan's job is to make the bride and groom laugh on their wedding day. And the jokes? Not exactly jokes. More like intricate sacred puns, godly brainteasers, furrow-browed tom-foolery, and the occasional sober pronouncement—a necessary reminder that joy never came cheap. It barely came at all, but when it did come, the badchan brought it. Wedding dancers, uncommonly hard workers, speakers of a rare and provocative language, peddlers of exuberance.

I could tell you all about how laughter, in this place, at this time, was both a balm and a mask for the sad parts. The badchan's humor had to be relentless as the waves. Ask someone what makes a badchan, and you'll get all kinds of answers. A badchan is born, not made. Either you have it, or you don't. A badchan should be best at balancing wine on his head or squatting low for the mitsveh-tants. A badchan should be able to talk nonstop in a voice that can fill a room. A badchan must be able to make the air sing even when the air doesn't want to. A badchan's stream of wit should straddle the bawdy and the rever-ent, should fill you with something you might not recognize. Not joy, but something close; something big and breathless that doesn't leave room for much else.

But the story I want to tell you is different. Almost a century after the death of Reb Naftali Tzvi, into this tiny, complicated city of laughter, Mira Wollman—daughter of Chane and Shmiel, grand-daughter of Soreh and Yankel, great-granddaughter of my dear Baruch and his Bluma—was born. The weather would come to speak to her too, though very differently.

And today? Today, the Jewish village that was in Ropshitz is very flat. It is quiet. The air does not sing. It is razed, plains-like, a green-turned-straw, watery sky. It's still there, though, what the messenger left behind. It is flat, you know, but it wasn't always, and it won't always be.

One

The counter was a metropolis of sympathy gifts. Under the cookies, assorted chocolates, cellophane-wrapped baskets of mixed nuts, one inexplicable bottle of potato vodka, and an Edible Arrangement that the fridge couldn't accommodate but that neither Shiva nor Hannah had yet had the heart to throw away, it was difficult to see the countertop at all. All this kind, neighborly detritus had displaced the coffeemaker, which had been retired to the cabinet underneath the counter for the time being, so Shiva, too impatient to extract it, resorted to instant.

Shiva's mother was still asleep, and the house was quiet, but the house had been quiet for days. Even as the counter heaved with unsolicited snacks, the kitchen table was spotless, the dish rack on the counter neatly stacked with plates and glasses. Hannah had been methodically scrubbing the house down, purging ancient spices and old magazines and piling dented pots and pans into boxes for Goodwill. Yesterday, she'd finally thrown all the desiccated sympathy bouquets into the compost. Now the old house thrummed, oblivious to its loss, its sleepy but dedicated radiators breathing gently into the February cold. The radiators, the only sound.

Quiet had always been nice with Shiva's father. Jon Margolin—floppy and optimistic, quick to joke or forgive—had always been most content in silence, after all. The two of them could read or play a board game or drive without talking much, two solitudes alongside, such a fullness of feeling in the space between them that it felt prehistoric in scope.

But Jon was gone. Not even two weeks, and the quiet now was uneven, something missing where something should still absolutely be. And the quiet between Shiva and Hannah was something else entirely.

Shiva and her mother had never been close and had always lacked patience for one another. Jon, who had at one point very nearly pursued a career in psychotherapy, had often pointed out that his wife and his daughter's mutual resistance was a result not of their differences but of the extent to which they recognized themselves in each other. A shared stubbornness. A sometimes-indulgent moodiness, inconsistent with their shared aversion to displays of excess emotion in others. A tendency toward inertia, particularly when they felt adrift.

In the days since Jon's death, Shiva and Hannah's mutual allergy had grown more pronounced. Unmanageable sadness had frayed them both, and they were disoriented by the sudden intimate proximity of cohabitation without a buffer. Shiva couldn't remember the last time they'd been alone together for anything more prolonged than a car ride. Now, in her parents' small house, they moved as a pair, entranced by the everyday rhythms of loss, learning each other's habits and contingencies: when they slept and when they woke; what they liked for lunch if their appetites actually surfaced; how they took their coffee; how they looked right before crying, and right after.

Shiva brought her instant coffee up the creaky, narrow attic stairs. Hannah had declared the attic their project this week. They could work together to sort through the mountains of boxes, adding to the growing giveaway piles of Jon's clothing, Jon's shoes, Jon's books, and making sure to surface and sort what they wanted to keep. Nothing of Jon's was meant to languish in an attic; it would be either put to use or given away. This, at least, they could agree on. They'd needed a project too—something to do with their hands, while it was still premature for Shiva to go back to New York and leave her newly widowed mother alone. And there was no turning back from what they'd started now: the attic irrevocably dismantled, all chaotic piles and boxes whose torn-open maws might as well have been direct portals to the past.

The giant skylight in the attic cast everything in a fairy-tale glow but did nothing to keep out the cold. Shiva cranked the space heaters on either end of the room and shuttled a stack of boxes over to one side so she could work right next to a heat source. PASSOVER STUFF, said the top box. EXTRA CORDS/MISC, said the one under that. JON SCHOOL STUFF, said the next box, and Shiva slid that one out from the stack. SYL, said the bottom box, and Shiva, surprised, accidentally bit her own tongue. She slid the Syl box out, momentarily forgetting why she was in the attic to begin with. Breathing quick and shallow, she tore it open.

She tried to manage her expectations. She knew how unlikely the box would be to contain anything actually related to her grandmother. Hannah had long sworn she had nothing of Syl's in the house that Shiva didn't already know about.

And oh, when it came to Syl Zvigler, how Shiva had looked. Born not only the same night Syl died but in the exact same house—the two of them just feet apart from one another when they crossed paths in their respective transitions—Shiva had always felt almost unnaturally drawn to Syl, desperately curious about who she'd been. Unfortunately, Hannah had been no help. Worse than no help, really; the way she refused to talk about Syl had begun to seem willful. Hannah claimed forgetfulness or blurriness and changed the subject almost any time Syl came up, but Shiva was far too intimate with avoidance to mistake it for anything but what it was.

She pawed through the box, unsurprised but still dully disappointed that it had been repurposed, likely years ago. She dug through several stacks of old checkbooks with Jon's and Hannah's names on them, some bundles of business cards, and a bunch of ancient instruction manuals for hand mixers and vacuum cleaners and slow cookers long gone.

At the bottom, there was a large envelope labeled PHOTOS. She slid the contents out. Jon and Hannah and Shiva hiking in the Shenandoah Valley, the foliage around them ecstatically orange, a gleeful three-year-old Shiva on Jon's shoulders, rotund in a bundle of red parka. Shiva's high school graduation, her wavy hair puffing frizzily out the sides of her graduation cap, her closed-mouth smile hiding late-breaking braces, and Hannah smiling too eagerly, as if the photo being taken was about her and not her daughter. And then, true to the box's overselling label, a smaller envelope that contained just three photos of Syl.

In the photos, Shiva's grandmother looked to be in her twenties. She couldn't remember ever seeing pictures of Syl this young, and she felt hot in the face just looking. Her mother's descriptions of the woman always made Shiva's grandmother sound like someone stern, tight, focused—if a human person could be a locked box.

But these photos were no such thing. They were saturated with a playful charisma Shiva could almost feel buzzing in her fingertips when she touched their surfaces.

In one photo, her vixen-haired smart-bloused young grandmother wore a tight tweed skirt and a leopard-print shrug over her shoulders, playfully pursing painted lips and staring down the camera like a dare. Shiva felt the heat all over her skin morph into a kind of recognition, coating her slowly as she studied the image. She surprised herself by making an audible sound, and quickly slipped all three pictures into the pocket of her sweater, an oversize blue cardigan she'd taken from Jon's closet a few days ago and hadn't much removed since. She would spend time with them later. Not here.

But she was distracted now, too itchy to move on to the next box—a frustration she could feel growing from the roots of her teeth, which she gnashed a little against the ache. She pulled the leopard-print photo out again, staring at it as though it might tell her something, but Syl remained silent. Shiva lifted her tepid coffee to her lips, and when the smell of it made her immediately nauseous, she realized that the thing creeping up from her throat wasn't bile but anger. She was angry that her father was dead. She was angry she'd been feeling so stuck for so long. And most of all, she was angry at her mother.

Her mother, who wouldn't talk about her past. Who wouldn't talk about her own mother, or her grandmother: the women who'd preceded them both. Who, Shiva thought, had long been stuck herself, rote, beholden to some history that had less and less to do with her as the years went by, and unable to extract herself from it. Shiva wasn't the same as her mother, to be sure, but she was convinced that her mother's robotic refusals and inertia had a lot to do with Shiva's own stuckness.

The word *stuck* was the closest she could come. It was a kind of immobility even while moving; an inability to see around whatever obstructed her days and nights. She'd felt it for some time, since even before her father's diagnosis, but in these last few dreadful months, it had gotten much more pronounced. Her days increasingly meandering and driftless, and most nights bloated with existential haunting so thick she felt like she was breathing it. And haunting was how she had come to imagine it: that whatever she was experiencing had stuck around from some older place and time, and had belonged to someone else long before it had belonged to her.

She knew that her beloved father's getting sick and then dying accounted for some of this, but not all. She felt slow, late to the party. Blurry and out of focus. Thirty-one, and she'd only just begun to fully realize who she was—telling her father, just in the nick of time, and her mother, still unwilling to take the information fully in. She was still learning what the word *queer* looked like when she wore it on her body. She lacked peripheral vision, existentially; and though it embarrassed her to admit it, she wasn't really sure what she was doing with her days. She still worked at the same nonprofit where she'd started working when she first moved to Brooklyn at twenty-nine and while she liked it just fine, she felt restless and unmoved. Some mornings, she'd wake up sweaty and panicked, alive with the feeling she wasn't exactly where she was supposed to be.

It felt most distinctly like she was missing some critical piece of information—as if there were something more she needed to see or understand about herself and where she'd come from to make everything about her life snap sharply and cleanly into place. And as if her mother were the one who knew what this something was. But in the meantime, the fact that it was an absence, a nothing, only until her mother could help her understand it to be anything more than that, made her angriest of all.

Out of what had started to feel like desperation, she'd pushed Hannah harder. *Talk to me*, she'd said. *About your life. About your past. About Syl.* But her mother wouldn't. *Syl was a mystery*, Hannah would say. *A mystery who no one had ever really understood. She was incredibly superstitious*, said Hannah. *She was a storyteller*, said Hannah, *always spinning some yarn or another, but those stories were almost never about herself.* Those were the only things Hannah ever said. When Shiva asked for more details—adult details, texture-of-life details, like *How did she meet her husband? What was she like as a parent?*—Hannah's eyes clouded over like those of someone being given a catastrophic ultimatum. Hannah said *no. No.* She couldn't remember.

Shiva's great-grandmother had met largely the same fate in the Margolin household—Hannah rarely invoked her name, and when she did, the details were sparing. Mira Wollman Zvigler had emigrated from Poland to New Jersey in the early 1920s. She and her husband, Isaac, had owned a sweater store in Trenton, New Jersey; had then sold the shop and moved to an apartment in Brooklyn when Isaac went into wholesaling; and eventually, had made their way to Florida, where Isaac died shortly thereafter. Shiva had met her great-grandmother just once as a baby, told only that she'd had *an incredibly hard life.*

Shiva knew her situation wasn't particularly unique, at least in its broadest contours. Many of her friends had limited access to family histories or even living members of their family. Friends whose families had survived systemic violence, who no longer had access or connection to their countries of origin, who were cut off from family members who held these histories, or who simply came from families who'd been forgetful, bad at keeping records. Her friends—queer and trans people, Jewish people, people of color—were people whose ancestors' stories had often been hidden, erased, lost, or coded. Absent evidence of the lives and joys of their predecessors, they were left only speculation. Shiva was incredibly lucky, she knew, to have what access she did—to have some of Syl's tales, at the very least. To have the leftovers of Syl's storied vigilance too, in the temperament of her own cautious and uptight mother.

The thing was, though: her friends were finding their way. Most of them didn't seem stuck like she did. They moved through the world with self-assurance and confidence or, at the very least, bravado. They talked about how to recover or reclaim or rewrite lost and shattered histories, took classes and got degrees and worked in archives or libraries, made art and wrote books and plays. And many had company, supportive siblings or even parents who felt the pain of this kind of loss alongside them, also seeking to understand what and who it was they'd lost. And where family of origin wasn't available or supportive, they'd found queer chosen family, held each other close. They might be haunted by absence—be it collective or personal—but in community, in solidarity with others, in activism and in art and in choosing one another, the absence was overlaid by a new kind of presence, rich and abundant in scope. When her friends wanted their stories reflected

back to them, they looked for that reflection in one another, telling
and deeply listening; they gave each other generosity and kindness as
the generations couldn't or hadn't been allowed.

Shiva knew her need was disproportionate. Being in the dark about
her family's story bothered her more than it should. But something was
jammed, something slowing her machinery, and she couldn't shake the
private conviction that whatever it was, it was distinctly generational.
That there was something in the family past so shadowy and elusive,
it meant there were real ghosts here. And that if she could find and
illuminate whatever piece of her was being held hostage somewhere
in the annals of her own family, she'd come unstuck, feel more whole.
She'd see it all clearly.

The truth was, Shiva had always been looking, without exactly
knowing what she was looking for. The way her best friend, Levi, put
it, she was a *seeker*—always watching the moving horizon for some
sign of where she was supposed to be, always looking for clues. For a
time, Shiva had accepted this reframing as nearly charming, fancy-
ing herself bright-eyed and curious, open to what the universe had to
offer. But her life had started to stall under the weight of this feeling,
the one that resisted logic and language: that she didn't know what
she was looking for, and that even if she did, it might be unfindable.

With Dani, her girlfriend—her very first, whom she'd met just
months before Jon died—she'd found some respite from the stuckness
and from all the anticipatory grief. Lightness, the sparkling clarity first
queer love allows, a precision unlike anything she'd ever experienced
before. Even as the impending loss of Jon shrank her world immea-
surably, Dani's presence had expanded it. Being with Dani made her
crackle, made her want to get out of bed, unsweaty and sure-headed,
to figure out exactly what she wanted and how to say it. And in
Dani's company, she'd begun to. She knew she dearly loved stories—
telling them but also, and especially, thinking about how to understand
them—no doubt a direct inheritance from Syl, even if inherited only

through stilted half memories and smoke. *You're so good at this*, Dani had said when they first met, after Shiva told her one of her favorites, about twelve witches who lived together in a cave at the end of the earth. *You should do something with it.* Shiva hadn't known then exactly what Dani meant she was good at—the telling or the remembering or all the things she'd said about the story afterward—but she didn't care, drunk on her momentary sense that she might have the skills to do something of consequence, on the feeling of being seen. Of being someone for whom stories could be some kind of life.

But Dani had been growing distant. And Jon was gone. And Shiva, still stuck.

She went to therapy. First, several sessions with Christina, an existential therapist, who told her gently but firmly that she was spending too much time staring into what existentialists might call *the void*, and that she needed instead to show up to the present of her life and make an effort to *radically accept* the things she couldn't control. Then, a session with an energy healer, Natasha, who confirmed that, indeed, the *heat* in Shiva was all located on her mother's side of the family, that the people who came before her had been seekers too. Without much sense of what to do with this confirmation, she'd finally landed on Sharon, an Upper West Side Jew with haggard eyes, a Rosie O'Donnell contour, and a penchant for costume jewelry. Her no-nonsense attitude and strong New York accent had endeared her to Shiva, despite the fact that some of her favorite modalities included hypnosis and past-life regression.

The thing is, Sharon said at their third session together, *it's hard to keep chasing an absence. It's not sustainable. At a certain point, you have to focus on what you can see, what you can touch.* It was true. Shiva felt like the thing she was always looking for, the thing that would help her understand herself, was not a thing at all but a nothing. This made it exponentially more frustrating. If only her mother would talk to her more about the nothing, it might become a something—a something she could wrap her head around, a something she could control enough to make into a tellable story.

Hannah's feet creaked up the talkative attic stairs.

Quickly and without much additional thought, Shiva pocketed the tiny pile of Syl photos again.

Hannah was wearing a black hoodie over her crumbling Smiths T-shirt, her wavy nest of morning hair tamed by a flannel scrunchie Shiva thought she recognized from her own childhood.

"Morning," she said.

"Morning," said Shiva. She fingered the pictures in her pocket. She could feel the velocity of the words rising to her lips before she could temper them, before she knew what they would actually be. "Hey, Ma?"

"Yeah?" Hannah was surveying the attic, and Shiva could see the quick progression of overwhelm and resolve on her mother's face.

She pointed at the Syl box. "What was in here? There's a bunch of random crap in here, but it says 'Syl.' Was this Syl's stuff? Do you remember?"

Hannah stared at her, red-eyed. She looked sallow-cheeked and underslept, her mouth the shape of a cartoon frown.

"Shiva, are you seriously starting with this right now? I haven't even had coffee yet."

This was exactly the problem. The moment a conversation so much as meandered in Syl's direction, Hannah's defensiveness sizzled so hot it was the only thing in the room. She talked about Syl when she wanted to and only then. And to bring it up at a time like now, when Hannah was so aggrieved and exhausted she was unwell—well, that was just reckless fire-starter behavior.

Shiva knew what Sharon would say, and what Levi would say, but she didn't care. Right now, whether it was actually true or a wild but powerful delusion, it felt as if Hannah Margolin was the thing standing bluntly in the way of Shiva making a life that felt like her own. Her father was dead. She felt desolate and miserable standing in the middle of all his useless boxes in this freezing attic. It was enough.

"Starting with what?" Shiva's rage thumped dully in her throat. "I'm not *starting* anything. I asked you a question." Unwelcome frustration smarted behind her eyes. "We have to get good. You're standing in my way, and I need you to move so we can get good."

Hannah rubbed her forehead. "What do you mean, *get good*? And I'm standing in your way exactly how?" Her mother had always seemed marginally hipper and younger than her friends' mothers, having gotten married and pregnant by the time she was twenty-two. But this also meant she seemed somehow less mature than a mother should, prone to sullen petulance and sarcasm the way a moody teenager might be.

"It's just us." A feeling of scarcity, of something slippery she needed to hold. "He's not here anymore, Ma. I need us to try to get good somehow. You just need to talk to me. Is that so difficult?"

She could still de-escalate this, Shiva knew. She could, but she wouldn't. She didn't want to. She felt like she wanted to explode it instead. Maybe then she could finally see past whatever was blocking her.

Hannah sighed and sank down onto a stack of boxes. "I do talk to you, Shiva. All the time. I'm not sure what you want from me right now. I'm exhausted, and I just—"

"I lost him too, okay?" Shiva enjoyed the feeling of burgeoning rage, and she stoked it. "But I ask you a simple question about one box, and you're immediately furious. I can tell there's something there. Behind the way you avoid and get defensive. Call me unhinged or whatever you want, but you're one to talk. It's just like there's this giant abyss. Like you're a giant abyss, honestly. I can't do it anymore. Without him, there's nothing left. I need things to feel different. I need more from you."

Hannah's red-rimmed eyes widened. She stood, and the box stack fell over.

"Nothing left, huh?" She repeated it, her voice flat, gone quiet. "And who am I to you, again? What am I, standing over here, no more husband to speak of? I'm nothing to you? You think *you* feel unhinged? I am . . ." She shook her head, started over. "All I have ever done is protect you. All I have ever done is love you, even at times when you have been unbelievably difficult. But you need to stop with this nonsense. There is nothing to tell. Syl was nuts. I loved her; she would have loved you. I spent my life in a fortress with her, and she never told me anything about herself either, okay? Nothing except stories about demons and witches and archangels and what would happen if I dared clip my nails wrong. So that's what I've got to give. You're grasping at less than straws here, I promise you. What else do you want from me?"

Shiva's hands were shaking. Her shoulders were shaking. Everything in this moment suddenly felt like it mattered more than her mother could ever understand.

"I want you to say I'm onto something! That I'm not just imagining things, and that there is something genuinely haunted here! That I'm not just losing my mind. I didn't know my grandmother, fine. Plenty of people don't. But Ma, the way you shut down, and the way I can tell you're holding on to something deliberately, it makes me feel like I'm underwater half the time. Maybe it's not logical. But I need you to quit being so stingy, Ma. I need you to fucking admit it." Her voice shook too as it rose, its volume sharpening at an incline so intense it scared her.

Hannah's puffy face had turned a deep shade of red, which Shiva took as a kind of admission of guilt. And maybe that was an approximate win, and she should let it go. But she couldn't. A tension had finally cracked open in this attic, and she felt certain that, once she went back to New York, it would seal up again, an inert civility between them as intact as if it had never even broken.

"What on earth would I be hiding from you?" Hannah shook her head. The shaking looked sad at first and then got swifter, morphing into something more vigorous. It was the most expressive her mother had been since the day Jon died. "This is not a movie, Shiva. I get it—you're exhausted; we both are. We're grieving. And you've always had a pretty wild imagination, and I know you're hoping our family has some sexy secret hidden history. But this Syl nonsense has to stop. And you know what? Even if we did? This is real life. You're an adult. You think other people your age are at home with their mothers begging to talk about their grandmothers? I doubt it." Hannah's voice garbled as tears started to run down her face. "I know you never felt as close to me as to your dad. I'm not stupid. And I want us to be good too. But I'm not going to stand here and go on about my mother and my grandmother just because you've gotten some idea into your head. We're not special. And in fact, I think it would be better for our relationship if you just left this alone now, please." She shook her head again, one resolute single time. "And Shiva, you know what? Sometimes, when something is closed, you're not meant to open it."

Shiva pressed her lips together tightly and rolled her eyes. "That! That is the kind of shit a person says when they're hiding something, Ma. You know it, and I know it."

Hannah made a sputtering sound. "This is over. Now. I need to deal with your father's shoes. Okay? Because he can't wear them anymore." That last part spilled out of her like a terrible song, and she honked into a used tissue she pulled out of her pocket.

"Fine," Shiva barked. "Most mothers would kill to have adult daughters who were actually interested in their families' histories. I've done nothing but take care of you since I got home. You don't think I'm fucking torn up? I lost my father. My best friend."

Hannah looked at her, stricken. "Yeah," she said coolly, the quiet returned to her voice. "And now you're stuck with me."

Shiva felt herself icing over too, even as the space heater had started to burn into the side of her leg.

"No," Shiva said. "I'm not stuck with you. I'm leaving. I'll get the next train back to New York, and you won't need to worry about me bothering you anymore."

"Shiva, wait," her mother said weakly.

"And you know what? I don't need you for this. I can figure it out myself. I'll . . ." Shiva stammered, angry and unfocused. "I'll take classes, I'll go to the archives. I'll go to school if that's what it takes. I'll go to fucking Poland myself. I'll get there. I'll learn what you won't give me, whether you like it or not."

"My god," said Hannah. "I love you more than anything in the world, Shiva, but you're being ridiculous. How about figuring out what to do with your life? Your *real* life. The way you fixate on this makes me uncomfortable, and frankly, it doesn't belong to you. Not everything belongs to you, Shiva, even if you think it should."

"You think I don't know what I'm doing with my life?" Shiva was an object in motion, shooting for the door to the stairs. "Maybe you're the one who doesn't know. You're the one who's stuck," she spat. She breathed in and out, one long shaky breath. "You're so judgmental. Dad would understand." One final dagger.

She was still rattling with adrenaline when she slammed the door to the guest room, opened her laptop, and bought an Amtrak ticket home for that evening.

Alone again, Shiva tried to slow her breathing. She couldn't stop crying. She and her mother had never fought like that before. With them, it had always been the slow simmer, never the boil.

She lay on the bed listening to the shower running and to her mother clomping around the house, and then the keys jangling and the front door closing. She watched out the window, waited until her mother's Prius pulled out of the driveway, before she ran back up to the attic and rescued the small pile of Jon's things she had claimed. For good measure, she also took the compact box labeled JON SCHOOL STUFF, the one she'd been derailed from opening earlier. Hannah probably wouldn't even notice it missing. Her father was gone, and now, maybe, so was her mother. It was just her now. She had to take what she could, provisions for the journey.

She was determined now to chase what everyone so patently insisted was an absence. Even if she was wildly uncertain about everything else in her life, she was more certain now than ever that somewhere, in the great infuriating vastness of her family's void, the one threatening to flatten her in the face of her mother's defenses and denial, there might be something worth finding.

———

Permit me a story.

There was once a girl who awoke at the root of a tree from a long sleepwalk. She rubbed her eyes and walked several paces down to a small river, where she washed her face and knocked on the door of the tiny cottage she found there.

A healer answered the door. *Come in*, said the healer, whose face was kind and round as the sun. She gave the girl salve for her torn feet and hot soup and a glass of warm milk. She told the girl that, from the looks of it, she'd walked quite far from home, perhaps even a distance of days.

How long? the girl asked, eyes wide.

Long enough to be different after, said the healer.

The girl had walked in her sleep before, but nowhere too far. The last time, she'd woken up lying right in the middle of a barrel of apples in the cellar, one neatly bitten core in each of her hands.

The healer wrapped a cloak around the girl, and they set out across two nights to get her back home. The girl's parents embraced her and thanked the healer profusely, inviting her in for meat with turnips, fresh bread, and hot wine. The healer thanked them but disappeared quickly into a moonless night.

After this, the girl grew up mostly regular. She was nearly beautiful and enjoyed painting and the sound of water and cakes that had fruit hidden inside. She was still prone to sleepwalking periodically but usually found herself in the kitchen or right outside the front door, nowhere much farther than her bedroom.

But there were times when the girl did not feel regular. She felt, instead, stuck in that invisible passage of days, the story of that brief somnambulant time forever lost to her. She wanted to understand what had transpired, what had changed her when she'd so briefly abandoned her body to the elements.

Finally, one day, she packed her bags and traveled back to those woods. She looked around for clues she might have left in her wake, unsure exactly what she was looking for. She went to the river where the healer's house had stood, but there was no house. And there was no healer. And the girl found no clues.

The girl resigned herself to moving on. She returned home and took a husband and a cat. She tended a garden and built her own cellar, full of wine and apples and bushels of potatoes, a soft place for her to land if she found herself some night adrift.

Nights, she slept beside her husband, watchful cat at her feet. But her sleep was fitful. Ghostly half dreams woke her, left her panting. Sometimes, in the mirror, she hardly recognized whoever gazed back. Whatever she was now, she knew, was because of what had happened to her those lost days.

Where have I been? She whispered it quietly into the room, most nights, like a haunted prayer. *Where have I been?* Some nights the moon, like the kindest face, but still no answer.

Two

S hiva lay awake. The hour was brutal, and outside, a tropical storm seemed to have lost its way en route elsewhere and was now kicking and screaming through Brooklyn. Fevered winds banged like thieves at the windows, and trash cans scraped past on the street below, violently separated from their lids. The apartment groaned. Shiva began to feel seasick, as if her building was actually rocking back and forth in the weather.

The storm, of course, hadn't lost its way. It had only taken a detour and was paying a brief and furious visit, but Shiva wouldn't have known that.

She hadn't slept much anyway in the days since she'd been back in New York, having left her mother alone in her empty house in Maryland. She still hadn't called Hannah, and Hannah still hadn't called her, and she'd begun to feel desperately lonely.

Dani was avoiding her too and had been for a little while now. They'd texted a little—she told Dani about the fight with her mother and that she was finally home—but Shiva had started to feel Dani sliding away. She knew her own grief had ravaged not just her but the space between them, too. Theirs was a new love—they'd been together only since late October—but it was a big love already, great and wild. It seemed it should be able to withstand tragedy. Now, though, Shiva was genuinely afraid that death would take this from her too.

Levi was patient but persistent, texting and calling and stopping by. Did Shiva want to go for a cocktail? To have dinner with friends? She was unspeakably grateful to him, largely kept afloat by the nights they spent on the couch watching movies and the days they took long, ambling walks through the city. But while a rowdy tableful of people had once been her favorite place on earth, she felt oddly shy about seeing her other friends right now. She was out of practice, having all but wholly withdrawn from her social life since Jon's health had declined, especially these last few months, before and just after his death. She barely remembered herself in the company of others. And she'd begun to seem illegible to herself, even just alone in her own room.

She missed everyone. Even her mother. Even if it was complicated.

She gave up on sleep and dragged a blanket to the living room, where she finally allowed herself to open the JON SCHOOL STUFF box.

The box contained several spiral notebooks crowded with her father's messy scrawl and a couple of VHS tapes. She opened one of the notebooks and ran her finger along its first page. She could almost feel Jon's enthusiasm in the force of his pen. He'd loved being back in school, proudly calling himself a "lifelong learner," a phrase that Shiva had once thought cheesy but that now seemed to her mostly relatable.

She'd been unable to shake the thought that she should consider going back to school herself. Back in the attic with her mother, it had been an impulse, straight out of her mouth like a threat or some kind of aspirational vindication. But in the days since she'd been home, marooned in her apartment, she'd begun to feel like it might actually be a good idea.

For one, going to school was as good a way as any to come unstuck. Families, after all, could feel so constricted, all internal logic and hot breath into a paper bag. Maybe a highly depersonalized academic setting would puncture the thing. Shiva knew what a powerful experience going back to school had been for some of her friends. It gave them insight into what vexed them in much more intimate spaces. At school, she might finally be able to work through her family angst at a safe distance from the fire at home.

It would also, of course, be a way to put things on hold.

Because despite what she'd huffily proclaimed in her mother's attic, Shiva Margolin had no idea what she was doing. Now less than ever. Grad school, she knew, could, at the very least, pause time, which had grown vertiginous. Time at her uninspired nonprofit job felt like forever. Time without her father was nonsensical—had it been three weeks or three years? And queer time was brand-new, so vast as it stretched out before her that it hurt her to think about all the possibilities. Dani was an anchor in the vastness, but with Dani drifting from her now too, perhaps grief was giving her something useful after all: telling her to stop, to sit still. To make it official. To do some homework. To grow up.

She pulled one of the VHS tapes out of the box. It wore a white label that read THE DYBBUK.

Her breath caught; she remembered this tape. It was her father's final film-school project, a short interpretive take on the Russian Jewish writer S. An-sky's famous play. She'd last seen it when she was six, Jon coming home with the finished film, cracking open two beers for Hannah and him and a root beer for Shiva, and ceremoniously seating them for a viewing.

She laughed dryly to herself; years ago, Jon had given her his ancient VCR, insisting it was still one of the best and most classic ways to watch a movie. She pulled it out of the closet and plugged it in, the red wire into the red hole and the yellow wire into the yellow hole. The tape was heavy in her hands, and it noisily clacked and whirred its way into the slot.

The film's quality had deteriorated—it was fuzzy, the sound distorted—but her whole body remembered as soon as it began rolling.

The Dybbuk centers the relationship between Leah, the daughter of Sender, a wealthy man; and Khonen, a poor scholar whose father, Nisn, has recently died. As young men, Sender and Nisn had shared a kinship so profound, they'd betrothed their yet-unborn children to one another. But any possibility for legitimate romance between Leah and Khonen is obliterated when, in the wake of Nisn's death, Sender turns his back on his friend and their mutual vow and betroths Leah to a wealthy man of better standing. A devastated Khonen turns to kabbalistic means of getting back the woman he loves, but dies in the process and becomes a dybbuk—a spirit who sticks to a living body—taking residence in Leah's body on her wedding day, the possession and subsequent exorcism ultimately killing her and reuniting the two in death. The play then turns to a Jewish court as it litigates the consequences of Sender's broken vow. The entire story is narrated by a character simply called the Messenger, whose somewhat sinister presence signifies—as the presence of a messenger so often does—that something otherworldly is afoot.

Jon's short film was a brief and interpretive take on the story, minimal dialogue and strokes of moody abstraction. The dark clearing in a dark wood against a thick backdrop of mournful music. The cloaked character who strides out into the clearing and says the words "The Dybbuk" immediately before they appear in a thin font across the screen.

That's the Messenger, Jon had said. His words had mystified her at the time, but she'd been as rapt then as she felt now, watching the Messenger narrate the film's three scenes—the forest, the wedding, and the graveyard—in a trancelike voice unlike any Shiva had heard before. As the film closed and brief credits rolled, the Messenger stood in the center, head bowed.

Even as a kid, she'd somehow understood: the Messenger was at once the one who haunted the story and also the one who'd managed to catch the haunting in story form, to tame it as though with a butterfly net. A character and not a character at all, a harbinger whose presence is confirmation that everything that is about to take place straddles this world and some other. The Messenger had also seemed genderless—neither man nor woman, a voice neither low nor high but somewhere in the flat middle. Shiva had gotten a woozy feeling trying to figure out the Messenger, a feeling that scared her but also a feeling she hoped would stay awhile. She'd felt, even then, like there was more in this world than she could readily see. The Messenger, she knew instinctively, could see it.

She remembered Hannah's response clearly too. *It's great, Jon,* Hannah had said quietly, but young Shiva had turned to see her mother's face betray her: it was drawn, pale and stricken as if what she'd seen wasn't a student film but the woken dead.

Shiva had lain awake that night, too vivid with feeling to sleep. Even if she hadn't fully understood the film, it had profoundly unsettled her. But there was something more. Watching her father's film had lit something in Shiva. She'd felt it back then in her swirling stomach, her pulsing temples, her fingertips. She just hadn't yet known exactly what it was.

When she encountered *The Dybbuk* again in a Jewish studies class in college, she was shot through with the electric feeling of recognizing someone you know while traveling somewhere far away. Her body remembered it still: the sense of haunting wrought by a story physically of this world but otherwise thrumming with the transgressive otherworldly.

She'd remained captivated by the presence of the Messenger, but in her early twenties, plagued by new and wordless questions about her own desires, she had decided instead to write her paper that semester on two of the play's other characters: Sender and Nisn, the fathers of the bride and the suitor.

Foundational to the play is the intimacy these two men share—so fervent is their love that it drives them to mutual vows, betrothing their yet-unborn children. She hadn't yet been comfortable calling homoerotic longing what it was, but something about Sender and Nisn's relationship had agitated her. She'd ended up writing about the doomed union that results from the repression of untenable love. Some inextinguishable fire, she thought, traveled here. From one generation to the next.

Shiva wondered now what had drawn her father to S. An-sky. She also wondered why she hadn't revisited An-sky herself in so long. His best-known story, after all, was about a family so haunted by ancestral repression that the haunting kills love and, ultimately, the lovers themselves. And at the play's core, An-sky's twin fixations on Jewish superstition and Jewish folklore.

Shiva had spent so many adolescent Friday nights pawing through her grandmother's well-worn copy of *Jewish Folktales Through the Ages*, trying to figure out what this folklore had meant to Syl. Early on, these tales taught Shiva that the world was odder and more populous than it seemed, if only you tuned in to the right frequencies—a place inhabited by boys who laid eggs, mysterious visitors who carried enchanted cargo, fish with bellies full of gems, and shape-shifters who knew the exact route to the edge of time.

Syl, she realized now, and wondered why she hadn't thought of it before, had also seen herself as some kind of messenger. Shiva had been chasing Syl in those stories for years, immersing herself in Jewish folklore in an effort to receive whatever message Syl had spent her life trying to deliver. If stories had been the currency in which her grandmother had dealt, stories might well be the key to better understanding her, too. After all, the strongest living connection between Shiva and her grandmother was their obsession with a good folktale.

An-sky was the greatest Jewish folklorist she could imagine. An-sky, who clearly knew how to navigate not just the known and the unknown worlds but the places in between. And—the clarity dazzled her, even as she laughed at her wildly inexact spiritual math—there would be no better guide to lead her to Syl than S. An-sky himself.

Her curiosity about the playwright then was immediate, urgent. Like suddenly remembering you've been out of touch with someone important to you, someone you've been meaning to check on for a long while.

She opened her laptop. Google blinked back at her, and she was tempted to type any number of other tempestuous phrases in the search bar:

Am I haunted?

How do you know which ancestors are haunting you and why?

Why do I feel underwater?

Symptoms of demon possession, contemporary

And then,

How can you tell if someone has fallen out of love with you?

How can I get the person who has fallen out of love with me back?

She resisted the minefields and instead typed *S. An-sky*. She started scrolling through the results and reading.

Thunder, meantime, thumped at the window, trying to get inside.

In 1912, the internet told her, before he wrote *The Dybbuk*, which would premiere just after his death in 1920, S. An-sky, né Shloyme-Zanvel Rappoport, set out to create a comprehensive folk archive of Jewish life in the Pale of Settlement, a western region of the Russian Empire in which permanent residency by Jews was allowed and beyond which it was largely forbidden.

As Shiva read, a trill rose from the back of her throat, and her earlobes grew hot with recognition.

In order to create this folk archive—a reflection of the beliefs and realities of everyday shtetl life—An-sky organized a series of expeditions, during which his team painstakingly collected stories, songs, and rituals from families living throughout the Pale. Sometimes they would go to great lengths to collect these stories, traveling long distances and wearing disguises just to make sure they returned with a substantial and representative collection.

Then, using what they'd collected, An-sky and his team developed a survey questionnaire consisting of over two thousand questions about shtetl life, intended to be disseminated widely, an effort to record and capture the Jewish everyday of that time—something An-sky felt strongly about preserving.

In the end, because of the First World War, the survey was never actually conducted. But An-sky's questions themselves—informed by lovingly and tenaciously gathered family lore—were famously so leading, they might as well themselves have been answers. Questions that tell a story: *Is there a belief that during the inauguration of a new cemetery, the dead from the old one congregate near the fence and look on, and if someone sees them, he should not tell anyone?* Or, *Is there a belief that if people make a blessing over a thing in which there is a reincarnated spirit, that soul is made right again?* In the process of collecting specificities, An-sky had become master of the leading question.

Of the four children sung about at the Passover seder, Shiva had always related most to the one who doesn't know how or what to ask. One wise, one wicked, one simple, but that final child is forever wordlessly seeking, without ever knowing quite how to formulate the right question. Learning about An-sky's questionnaire only confirmed her kinship with that final child.

After all, questions themselves were such slippery commodities. So often they weren't just questions: they were up to something else, too. *Is there a custom to place a cat, pieces of cake, or something else in the crib before one lays the child in it?* asked An-sky. *Does one whisper something in the cat's ear at that time?* Shiva enjoyed imagining the cat, the cake, and the baby. She liked imagining what *something else* might refer to. But mostly, she loved the idea that a question could actually be the story itself in disguise. It was a great comfort to her that a story could exist in inference alone and also, in fact, might be a richer story that way.

It was getting close to actual morning. The light had grown subdued, and the weather mostly regular again, just a few kicks here and there from the wind. But Shiva felt fully altered. Buzzy and light-headed. Alive with something new and a little bit wild.

Her predicament, after all, was a disproportion of answerless questions; an immovable obstruction, over which she could see only shreds of light and color. And here, S. An-sky's life before her: a fiery devotion to piecing together a usable history from scraps.

There was Syl, curtained off. Somehow at once pursed and unyielding in her later years and also a starlet in a photo from another time.

There was Mira, Shiva's great-grandmother, born in the Polish shtetl of Ropshitz, a place Syl had apparently nicknamed the City of Laughter, a funny name for a place that had most certainly never been a city, only a town. The moniker was homage to the proud line of badchanim, or Jewish wedding jesters, who'd come from that place. Shiva had inherited a laugh that was more like a cackle, a loud, sharp sound that turned heads in public when something someone said was especially funny. She liked her big laugh, though. She liked to imagine it came directly from Poland.

And then there was Hannah. In some ways, there was absolutely nothing mysterious about Hannah. She was so plodding, so practical, so faithful, so careful. She wasn't without her quirks—she'd had a lifelong fixation on death and its rituals and legitimately enjoyed volunteering for her synagogue's chevra kadisha, which prepared recently dead bodies for Jewish burial. But unmysterious as Hannah seemed on paper, she was, perhaps deceptively, the greatest and most frustrating mystery of them all.

These were her scraps. And she wanted desperately to make them into something usable.

In the days that followed, she began to let the thrill of inquiry possess her. She submitted completely to the world of S. An-sky.

She read articles and interviews. She tore through *The Jewish Dark Continent*, a translation of the ethnographic questionnaire itself, and *Wandering Soul*, the An-sky biography that would become her favorite, both because it was such a layered and nuanced portrait of the man and because it explicitly posited that An-sky himself may have been queer, having left two brief and ultimately failed marriages in his wake, and possibly even having had feelings for a dear male friend from childhood.

An-sky had been a seeker, like her. Restless and voracious. Jewish writer, Russian revolutionary, intrepid ethnographer—he'd moved from identity to identity, never quite keeping still. *How appropriate that he'd visited*, she thought, because *visited* was how she'd begun to think of the appearance of her father's tape. How fitting that he'd brought with him the unflagging scrape of the wind to orient her to the rest of her life—a life that would never again contain her father and that would likely involve more seek than find.

In her reading about An-sky—the kind of person for whom inquiry without any guaranteed outcome could become an entire life; who could, in fact, relentlessly chase an absence and make it into a story—her admiration of his work continued to deepen. She felt it in her temples, in the jitter of her legs as she read, emphatically underlining. Her desire to name her own restlessness and stuckness never sharper, she desperately wanted to better understand this man and his dogged devotion to preserving Jewish families' stories.

In other words, she fell in love.

If she went to school, she could read and write about An-sky whenever she wanted, maybe even form her lumpish and inarticulate thoughts into some kind of thesis. She might be going to prove something or to stave something off or to challenge herself in a way that was completely foolhardy, but she wasn't sure she cared. There were worse reasons to go to school. It would be expensive, but she could take out loans, apply for grants. The idea that this could be the way she'd finally understand how she fit into something much bigger might be magical thinking, but she needed a little magic, or at least the prospect of it. And magic or not, her life badly needed an exoskeleton.

One tab led to another, and she found herself on the home page for New York University's Jewish studies program, which offered a specialty in Jewish folklore. The page told her that admissions were rolling through mid-March, and she still had a couple of weeks to apply.

Possessed, she applied. Possessed, she got in.

She would start in the fall.

Three

That spring and summer were an indecisive blur. Some days, Shiva felt bright with determination, immersed in the somewhat deranged self-directed An-sky studies program happening in her bedroom. Some days, she felt slumped by the stuckness, finishing out the last months of her desk job, desperately worried she was choosing wrong and that the grad program would eject her as a fraud as soon as she arrived.

With Sharon's encouragement, she'd started reaching out to her mother again, and her mother, she could tell, was trying too. They did not revisit the events of that cold, awful day in the attic, and just as Shiva had half feared and half hoped, the mood between them was one of congealed civility, an implied contract between them to never mention it again.

She went back to Maryland for a spring visit, right around her thirty-second birthday, and then again in the summer. The visits were polite—at times, even nice. Sometimes they bickered, the heat coming quicker to their faces than it used to. Hannah was an emotional flatline, and Shiva was a zigzag. The hardest thing about these visits wasn't even the threat of conflict but the twoness of it all. Just a lonely dyad in the middle of the suburbs with the aching absence of Jon, who'd once bound them together as a legible unit.

Things with Dani had felt strained at the end of winter, but come spring, their relationship began stalling out miserably. They'd chugged along past Jon's death, Shiva willfully ignoring the new and slightly shifty quality in Dani's eyes, as if Dani could see someone else she knew just past where Shiva was standing. Finally, in June, Dani had asked for *some space*. She was going home to San Francisco for the summer anyway, she'd said, like the request was something casual, and she would check in with Shiva when she got back.

Summer was tinged with a cold dread, Dani's absence shining like a threat in the distance. Not the interminable gray feeling that had come over her when she'd learned that her father was going to die, but not entirely different, either. This loss-to-be was something more immaterial, something unprovable, its emotional consequences yet unknown. She was going to lose something terribly important, though; this much, Shiva knew for sure.

She distracted herself as best she could. She and Levi went to Riis Beach and Coney Island. They drank whiskey and talked on the phone and went for long walks in the city. For one blissful week, they went together with Levi's friend Felix to a cabin in the Hudson Valley, where they drank margaritas in a hot tub with a view of the mountains. Back home, somewhat revived, she bought school clothes and new pens and drank vats of cold brew in the company of S. An-sky.

She resisted social gatherings, still. Maybe because she didn't want to account for what was happening in her relationship. Maybe because in the exponential depths of her solitude, a dead Russian Jewish playwright had become her favorite company, and she'd grown accustomed to this.

School was a welcome shift in everything. Her life transformed from a scramble of loss, failure, and dread into something purposeful, all invigorating daily rituals, the thrum of working toward some bigger goal. Stopping for coffee and a pastry with a textbook an hour before class. Navigating the library stacks with a wish list. Getting ready for school early and coming home from school hungry, the kind of appetite you'd earn after a long swim, when food tasted better because you'd worked for it.

She even walked differently, remembering herself back into sartorial pleasures and the clothing she loved most: her tweed pants, her vintage pink sweater set, her denim jumpsuit, the sweater dress covered in giant fruit, her purple blazer, her black platform boots. Structured, beautiful things that made her feel queerer, that gave her an outline.

She liked her Jewish Philosophy seminar, the tall and intimidating professor who led it always peering over a pair of tiny half-moon wire-rims like she was a wizard. She was delighted by her Special Topics in Jewish Studies seminar, a deep dive into the history and functions of Jewish humor. She even loved the thoroughness of the survey course, a gateway for any first-year who intended to pursue the discipline—how it left nothing unturned and required a relentless kind of diligence she found immediately satisfying.

She had resaved Dani's number in her phone as DO NOT TEXT. Doing it made her actually sick, but it was an important reminder. Dani was always who Shiva wanted to tell first. About anything. But it was September, and still not a word. Technically, their status was still girlfriends, was still *space*, but at some important level, Shiva knew it wasn't. They'd traded a few texts here and there when Dani had returned in August. She had all but given up, but the awful truth was that you couldn't mourn something that wasn't yet gone.

Instead, Dani was keeping them both in wretched suspension. Shiva wished she were capable of ending things herself, but embarrassed as she was to admit it, she still only wanted Dani back. If only she has enough space, she thought, she'll return to me desirous; she'll knock on my door, replenished. But there were no knocks on any doors. And DO NOT TEXT remained silent.

At the Jewish studies mixer at the end of September, Diana Berman complimented Shiva's earrings, and Shiva felt like she'd won something. She'd been taken by the flouncy-haired queer Yiddishist from the moment she'd met her their first day of classes, entranced by Diana's quotidian brand of confidence and the hot, professorly way she wore a blazer.

Diana, instantly friendly, introduced Shiva to her friends: Reuben Krauss, interested in the queerness of the rabbis of the Talmud; Arik Shem Tov, a PhD with a focus in angelology; and Mimi Garcia-Roth, doing something complicated and adjacent to the Dead Sea Scrolls that Shiva didn't quite understand.

Over room-temperature wine and cubes of waxy cheese, Shiva entertained all their polite questions and then asked if they had any advice for a newbie.

"You'll want to find a reading group," Diana said.

"Reading group?"

"It gets very tedious, all that lonely reading. The lot of us will sit around at a bar or a coffee shop and just, you know, read together," said Reuben.

"You should join ours," said Diana. "It's a good time. You can slowly get tipsy while reading a four-hundred-page tome on the postwar Hasidic revival."

"Oh, also, avoid taking any classes with Ron Felber."

"How come?"

"Well. He enjoys long walks on the beach, Israeli settlements, and Donald Trump—who, he will tell you until his face turns blue, is *good for the Jews*."

"Holy shit," said Shiva.

"Hey," Mimi asked. "Have you decided who you're going to ask to be your thesis adviser yet? I know that since the master's program is only two years, people like to get a jump on it their first semester."

"Actually, I reached out to Mel Rosen about it."

Arik and Reuben and Diana and Mimi all looked at one another as if there was something Shiva needed to know and they were trying, nonverbally, to decide who would tell her.

"Mel Rosen," Arik finally repeated. He was a bit older than the rest of them, some graying hair in his beard and temples. "He's a tough one."

This wasn't news. Shiva had already gathered that the professor was famously snobbish, a great performer of his own lore but a terrible listener. Rumor had it he was retiring next year and had all but disappeared from campus entirely, cherry-picking the parts of professorial life that interested him and abandoning the rest. He rarely worked directly with students anymore and was so elusive that Shiva didn't think he'd been on campus this semester even once.

She'd decided to reach out to him only because he was the faculty member most invested in folklore as a serious pursuit in and of itself. Shiva had noticed that not everyone felt this way—folklore was an elective, at best a semester-long class, not a whole course of study. It was often feminized, sometimes even looked down upon, and she'd decided it could only help her to work with Rosen, an older male hardscrabble folklorist who would at least take her interest in it seriously.

"I've heard this," said Shiva. "I thought it was worth a shot, just because folklore is my main interest."

"Absolutely," said Reuben. He was chipper, spearing a cheese cube and dismounting it onto a water cracker. "It's definitely worth a shot. I wouldn't get your hopes up, though. No offense, but it seems he's mostly interested in students who are really ambitious and who are going to, like, win big awards, so he can go out with a bang."

"None taken," said Shiva, trying not to think too hard about Reuben's apparent assumption that she was none of those things. Was it that obvious? She snagged three orange cheese cubes herself and ate them in quick succession.

"Hey," said Diana. "Is anyone applying for that Warsaw thing?"

"Warsaw thing?" Shiva prickled alert. Besides being a few hours' drive from where the City of Laughter had once stood, Warsaw was a significant city for An-sky: not only where he'd finished out the final months of his life, but also host of the world premiere of *The Dybbuk* in 1920, just a month after his death.

Diana shrugged. "The department emailed about it last week, I think. I almost didn't notice it; it was buried in all the publications announcements and all that. It's from the Grinberg Institute for Innovative Jewish Scholarship. I think part of the deal is that your work has to directly benefit from traveling there for research, and that you have to present about your findings at their big annual conference."

Shiva tried to seem casual, but she felt unreasonably excited about the prospect of travel she likely wouldn't be eligible for. It was barely her second week of graduate school.

"Do you think it's just for PhD students? Or . . ." She felt a little too shy to finish the sentence.

"It sounded like a master's student could apply too. But you would definitely need someone to write you a killer recommendation. I think the money is to go next semester, and you don't even have an adviser yet, so it might be tricky."

The four of them looked at her. She had a feeling that even if Mel Rosen agreed to be her adviser, she likely couldn't count on him for a *killer recommendation* any time soon. Her stomach turned a little, a disappointment that seemed extremely out of proportion.

Diana must have seen the look on her face. "But not impossible," she said. "I don't think impossible."

Mel Rosen, to her shock, responded to her email with a curt but affirmative yes, and they set a meeting for that Friday. Her first feeling was elation. She could hardly wait to show up at Diana's friends' next reading group and tell Reuben how wrong he'd been. Her second, though, was an uneasiness that quickly overtook her relief. Why had someone like Rosen said yes to someone like her? What explanation could there be except that there had been some mistake?

After all, the adrenaline she'd brought to her first few days on campus had started to wear off. She'd never shone too brightly in academic settings. She'd always been smart enough but never a standout student. Her grade school report cards had said things like "creative ideas" and "rich inner life."

Even in her compromised state of bereavement, Shiva hadn't imagined she'd prove otherwise, but she was admittedly slightly disappointed to learn that even at graduate school, energizing and challenging though it was, she was still herself. Every old *wherever you go there you are* cliché about it was true. She was no more agile or decisive, no clearer or more deeply competent when she stepped onto that campus than when she was off.

It was only September, but she was also feeling impatient. School had made her feel dimensional again, but it was still falling short of magical, as she'd perhaps ridiculously fantasized it might be. It hadn't yet begun to illuminate the contours of the great dark nothing Shiva was so fixated on. She'd started to feel like school was a way station, not the destination itself. A platform, maybe, that she could use to get higher up and farther away. A better vantage point from which to see what was so resistant to illumination.

Warsaw, of course, was farther away. And in her willful imagination, Warsaw was so high up that to stand in the city's center was to look down and see the entire world.

At home that night, she scrolled back through her Jewish studies department emails and found the application for the Warsaw research trip. It was presumptuous, but she couldn't help it. She started a Word document with bullet points for Mel Rosen. *Here's why you should immediately respect me enough to consider me a burgeoning scholar and send me to Warsaw.* Next to the first bullet point, she typed, *I've studied*

S. An-sky extensively. Then she was overcome with a sudden and disorienting nausea. Then Hannah called.

Since things between them had somewhat thawed, Shiva and her mother talked semi-regularly. She would reach out to her mother to check in, see how she was feeling, how shul was that weekend, and was she spending time with friends? Her mother would call or text to see how school was going, even though she seemed absolutely baffled by Shiva's decision to do a master's degree to study Jewish folklore when one could just study Jewish folklore at home. And how were her friends, how was Levi? She never, it was not lost on Shiva, asked about Dani. Shiva was still angry with her mother, but she was worried about her too. And she'd meant what she said: They were all they had left. They had to get good.

Shiva ignored the call at first. Like always, though, she felt guilty as soon as the buzzing stopped. It shouldn't be so difficult, she told herself. Just be there for her, say hello.

She called her mother back.

"Hi," said Hannah. "You go to school, and suddenly you're always disappearing on me?" Hannah's voice had that tone, the one that was joking and also wasn't.

"Sorry, Ma, it's been busy."

"I'm sure," said Hannah. "Well, tell me, what's new there?"

"Um," she said. "I actually just secured my thesis adviser. He's very impressive; he's this famous folklorist."

"Famous, huh," said Hannah, and Shiva could almost hear the eye roll in her voice.

"Yes." Shiva thought about elaborating but didn't.

"Well, that's great," Hannah said, and then she sighed, a particularly Hannah sigh. "I've just been worrying for you. I know Dad's being gone has been hard on you, and I know you keep saying it is, but are you sure this is what you want to do? You're so creative; you have so many talents. There's so much you could do without taking out thousands of dollars in loans to go to school for something you can study at home."

This, Shiva thought, was what Sharon meant by *projection*. Hannah was the one who'd studied business when she'd wanted to study art. The one who managed finances for a nonprofit and was always talking about how she would have loved to have become an artist, as though at a given point this was no longer possible and her path had been set forever by her early circumstances. The day they'd learned the word *agency* in Shiva's college women's studies class, she'd wanted to come home and throw it at her mother, to say, *Choose this, or choose something else! Just choose.*

"I want to be here," she said, as much to her mother as to herself. "Very much."

"Well, good. Fine. As long as you're happy." Hannah sighed again, a different, more resigned sigh. Her mother was fluent in sighs.

"How are you, Ma?" The question came out more sharply than Shiva had intended it to.

"I'm okay," said Hannah. "Hanging in there. I'm actually doing a tahara tonight."

Shiva squawked before she could stifle it. Hannah's predisposition toward the morbid was sometimes endearing to Shiva, if also completely bewildering, and endearment between them was so rare, she took it where she could.

"It really does help me, Shiv. I know you're worried about me too, but I promise I'm fine."

Shiva wasn't sure. Hannah's dour stagnation—her isolation from friends, the flatness Shiva heard in her voice every time they talked, the subtle if resolute sense of despair Shiva could see settling over her mother's widowhood—seemed like it was threatening a kind of permanence. It wasn't just concerning; it was also terribly difficult for Shiva to watch. Crawling out of her own hole was proving hard enough. Bearing obligatory witness as her mother only crawled deeper in was nearly unbearable.

God, she missed her father. The way Jon had effortlessly lit them both, bringing warmth to everything he touched. He'd been incredibly active—he biked, he ran, he did yoga—but Shiva still remembered her father most fondly at home. Jon in his ratty Hall and Oates T-shirt, vacuuming the living room, bellowing along to "The Longest Time." Jon on the phone with customer service, doodling cross-eyed monsters on discarded envelopes. Jon eating midnight cereal from a coffee mug. Quick smile and slow patience, spending entire afternoons in the front yard showing the neighbor's son how to stand on his head, demonstrating by pressing his curly head into the grass and kicking his long legs upward.

"Okay," said Shiva. "Please spend some time with some nondead people this week too."

She hung up, agitated and sad, and turned back to the application and to her growing nervousness about her first meeting with Mel Rosen. She'd need a clear and compelling justification not only for her presence in his office but also for him to believe in her immediately enough that he'd sing her praises to the people who could send her to Warsaw next semester.

Outside, it had started to drizzle, the window behind her crackling and speckling with tentative droplets.

Something sang, waiting, right outside the pane, but Shiva wouldn't have seen it.

She would be just fine with Mel Rosen, she told herself. She would need to lead with all the preparation done on her own and to make clear not only what she might contribute to the field but also what more she hoped to learn. *Try to project both confidence and deference,* suggested Diana, when Shiva told her she'd scored a meeting with the

elusive Mel Rosen. *It's gross, playing into all that, but I bet it will work.*
Shiva had to hope something would.

The drizzle outside had become an arrhythmic patter, and from
downstairs, she could hear the faint thump of whatever her neighbor
was listening to. She turned off all the lamps and crawled into bed,
where, in the darkness, the rain gave her the gift it had been waiting
to give, and she submitted fully to a deep and uninterrupted sleep.

Friday morning, not an hour before she was due at Mel Rosen's office,
Shiva got a ruinously timed text from DO NOT TEXT.

We need to talk.

Now? She reappears now?

Shiva tried to unsee the text or at least pretend it gone. She felt
scrambled and hot, channeling every ounce of concentration into
getting her legs up the Jewish studies department stairs. When she
got to the top, she willed herself into a kind of academic stoicism.
She closed her eyes and thought, *Ignore it.* Then she thought, *You
belong here.* She didn't believe it, but it seemed worth repeating, so she
thought it again. Regardless of whether she'd been right or wrong,
her decision to follow An-sky into this grad program was the first
certainty she'd had in years. The first, at least, since the unshakable
certainty—finally, finally—that she was queer, Dani serving as a
profound kind of confirmation. Certainty was sacred and rare. She
needed to hold tight to it.

She arrived at Rosen's door to find it closed, a linocut print hanging in its center that read EVERYONE HAS AN ORIGIN STORY. Arching
over the words, a jagged and meandering tree, tall but bent toward the
ground as though telling the grass a secret. There were tiny Yiddish
words curling up through its roots. The print, strange and beautiful,
endeared Rosen to her, despite his notoriety. *Please*, she thought, a word
that occurred to her any time she felt something akin to prayerful.
She wasn't sure how to finish the sentence. She closed her eyes and,

in quick succession: her father's disarming grin, her mother's flat sad voice over the phone, and the spiky tattoo around Dani's right wrist. She knocked on Rosen's door, as boldly as she could.

"Come in," he said.

Rosen was sharp-eyed and bespectacled under a mop of aggressively thinning hair that had certainly once been curly. His nose was formidable, and his eyebrows bushy as a cartoon's. "Sit," he said. She did. "Shira, welcome. Nice to finally meet you. Your semester has started off well, I trust?" He didn't wait for an answer. "So tell me more about you. About what brought you into our program."

"It's Shiva. My name. Like the mourning ritual."

Rosen gave her the look most Jews did when she told them her name. Other people born in proximity to the death of their grandparents were given names that meant things like *comfort* and *light*. Her mother, however, had chosen to mark her only daughter with a name that was also the Hebrew word for covered mirrors and sackcloth and seven days' grieving.

"Not a name I hear in this office every day. There must be a story."

"Yeah," said Shiva. She thought for a second about how it might feel to tell Rosen the actual curious story of her own birth and her grandmother's simultaneous death but thought better of it and pivoted. "My mother just liked it," she lied. "And it was sort of a nod to some family lore. Folklore runs pretty deep in my family."

"Well, yes," said Rosen. "As in most Jewish families."

"My grandmother was a storyteller, supposedly, but secretive and really selective about what she told and what she didn't," Shiva continued, understanding that Rosen had been dissatisfied with her initial response. "She didn't pass on very much about my great-grandmother's shtetl, for example, this town called Ropshitz. There was something about her relationship to the stories she told that seemed legitimately dark, and I've always wanted to better understand why. Also, I don't know—the idea that a storyteller can be so withholding, so secretive . . ." She trailed off.

"So, there are gaps in your family's story."

"Big ones," said Shiva. "Because my grandmother was the main keeper of our family's lore, I know most of it secondhand because I never met her."

"Not that you know of," said Rosen, and Shiva looked for the whimsical-old-man glint she expected to find in his eye, but he looked whimsy-free, and she realized he was serious. He tempered his grandiosity by sipping from the dented can of generic-brand ginger ale that sat on his desk.

"True," said Shiva. "Not that I know of."

Rosen looked down, picked up a stack of papers, stood them up on the desk, evened them out, and put the stack down again. His forehead shone around the forests of his eyebrows. "I appreciate family lore, of course, but what brought you to this program? You must have more specific academic interests here. Your email note mentioned An-sky?"

A hot splotchy feeling clawed at her neck. The terrible suspicion that despite the unflappable certainty she'd felt when she applied, she'd been wrong. This man would know that, she thought. This crabby man would read her immediately.

Frantic, she looked around the office. Anywhere but at Rosen. Above Rosen's head, a portrait of a group of writers from Odessa poring over a text. She immediately recognized S. An-sky, his distinctly high and distinguished forehead and his sharp and angular profile, bearded and vulpine, in quiet focus. Silently, she thanked him for being here. Of course he was.

An-sky's perspective on ethnography and on most else had been deeply populist, entrusting the work of community preservation not to experts but to the people. Zamlers, they were called, or amateur ethnographers. She didn't mind being a zamler. It was a proud tradition, and she felt she'd earned it. She'd been a student of An-sky, of the folklore he so loved, long before she'd set foot in Rosen's office. She was onto something, or at least she hoped she was. And she was here, she firmly reminded herself, in this stifling office, because she needed some guidance in figuring out what, exactly, she might be onto.

Her mind shuffled through ways to articulate this to Rosen, who sat there waiting, unbothered by her silence. Dani, who had been a poet—*was still a poet*, Shiva self-corrected; just because she'd disappeared didn't mean she was dead—had once called from a writers' conference to announce a creative breakthrough: "Someone asked me, *What does your work deal with?* And I actually knew how to answer," she'd said. "I told them my work deals with *ecological grief.*" It became their shorthand for creative certainty: *My work deals with.* When Shiva had started considering the study of story as a real pursuit, she'd imagined telling people, *My work deals with folklore and intergenerational imagination.* She hadn't exactly known what it meant. Not yet. But now, it felt like she might be closing in.

"Yes," she said. "I've been studying S. An-sky. His writings—*The Dybbuk*, of course, but more recently, his ethnographic study. His life."

"Go on," said Rosen.

"Well, my mother always called my grandmother a storyteller, but I really think her stories were more like warnings. Or clues. What she called stories were actually more like bread crumbs leading elsewhere."

Rosen looked at her, unmoved.

She coughed, mostly in the interest of giving herself a moment to compartmentalize. "The questions, of course, are also a kind of absence. They carve out a blank space, and in it, there is the implication of a lost future. Hauntology," she said. "A Jewish-folkloric kind of hauntology." She overenunciated, her tongue enjoying the feel of such an indisputably respectable word. "Something that would have been but wasn't; something that should be, but isn't. A story that exists in speculation only. Or else, a story we might already be living, that *is* present, except that we can confirm its presence only if we tune in to the right frequency. You know, when we ask the right questions."

"Hauntology," he said slowly. He sat quiet for a moment, thinking. "Chagall was from Vitebsk too, you know. Just like Mr. An-sky." Shiva thought she'd been sufficiently impressive and wondered why Rosen was suddenly talking about Marc Chagall. "Speaking of the right frequency. You know, people think Chagall's flying goats are a metaphor, or a flight of fancy, if you will. They most certainly aren't. Flying goats are among us. You just have to know where to look for them." Again, no eye twinkle. Rosen was a folklorist but not a whimsical one. Shiva wondered whether this felt like existential contradiction to him, and whether he would have gotten along with her grandmother. "Did you also know, though, that Chagall painted naked and ate half a herring a day? A stranger man than people realize." He picked up his pen again and tapped it on the desk.

"Okay," he said. "An-sky, then. Stories and questions and absence. Hauntology." He sat there for what seemed like a very long time, just staring at her. "Shiva, I'm going to be frank with you. I don't work with just anyone. You know this, right? In fact, I rarely take on advisees anymore."

Shiva nodded, afraid to say anything.

"So I'm going to need you to work hard. Really hard. Not just for me but also for you."

"Yes," said Shiva. "I know." Her whole body beat with the adrenaline it had taken to bring her into this office to begin with. She was making promises she wasn't exactly sure how she would keep.

"Good." Rosen nodded curtly.

"There's one more thing," said Shiva, spitting all the words out quick as she could, before she lost her nerve.

Rosen raised an eyebrow. He looked impatient, like he'd been ready to dismiss her.

"I didn't know if you've seen the Grinberg Conference grant, the one for research and travel in Warsaw next semester?"

"Of course I've seen it," said Rosen. "I help administer the Grinberg Jewish studies conference. I sit on the board."

She took a quick breath. "Okay, well, I know I'm brand-new here and that we've just met."

"We certainly have just met," said Rosen.

Shiva tried to ignore the skepticism she saw already coming over his face.

"I'm hoping to apply for the grant," she said quickly. "I was hoping you'd recommend me. I would, of course, need your recommendation. I can write a proposal for you. I can write up anything that would be helpful. It's just, this opportunity seems serendipitous. Um, I think it will really help me get some really good footing in my work here."

Rosen looked at her for a beat.

"Footing? Honestly, Shiva, this is quite premature. This kind of opportunity is generally meant for a student who already has footing, who has a body of work. Or at the very least, a student I've gotten to spend some time with."

"I know," Shiva said. She'd anticipated he would say this. "I recognize that what I'm asking is unorthodox. But I'm asking—what if the committee might like to see an emerging scholar get the funding? Someone to take a risk on, who would really deeply benefit from the research trip and everything that came with it. I promise I have ideas worth investing in." She hated how it sounded, but she knew she had to say it like it was a marketing pitch.

Rosen was quiet for an unbearably long time. He closed his eyes, and for a moment, Shiva worried he'd fallen asleep. But he opened them and looked at her very pointedly.

"Shiva. Look. We haven't even begun talking about your thesis yet, and I would suggest you start thinking at once about what that thesis will be. If it is a subject that you think will rely on travel to Warsaw and that could double as a truly standout paper for the Grinberg annual conference, I might consider it. But it would need to be substantial. This is a big conference and a prestigious grant. I can tell you are a lively student, but I can't be wasting my time."

Shiva could hardly believe Rosen was even considering it. It was more than she could have hoped for.

"Of course," she said.

They arranged a follow-up meeting for the next week, and Shiva walked out of Rosen's office, dazed. Against all odds, she'd completely forgotten about Dani's text, until she burst back out into the hallway, her fingers suddenly jittery, dying to text Dani about *My work deals with* and about Chagall's nudism and herring and about how she might maybe actually have the opportunity to go to Warsaw on official research. Instead, she hopped down the Jewish studies department stairs in twos and ran all the way to the subway.

Shiva knew she would have to do some serious thinking both about her application and about how she'd make an argument compelling enough to get Rosen's okay, but when she got home, all she had the presence of mind to do was to snap open her laptop and type *contemporary Jewish Warsaw* into the search field.

She scrolled past the Polin Museum and the Center for Yiddish Culture and clicked on the website for the Jewish Theater of Warsaw. Formed in 1945, the theater was now one of only two public theaters in all of Europe that regularly staged productions in Yiddish, honoring the rich cultural tradition of Jewish theater wiped out by the Holocaust.

She opened the theater's summer calendar. The fourth thumbnail down was a picture of a ghostly bride. Shiva clicked. It was a play called *Between: A Choral Production of "The Dybbuk."* Quick and fire-fingered, she found a short interview with the director—an emerging Russian Jewish playwright who'd lived in Warsaw for several years. She said in the interview that the play would be somewhat faithful to the original but that it would be *choral.* Shiva wasn't sure what *choral* meant in this context, but she didn't care. The show would open in March, so she could actually potentially see it.

She'd wanted to follow An-sky wherever he led her, and here he was, leading her directly and emphatically to Warsaw. And consistently came this feeling—against all logic or reason—that, should she follow him there, he might lead her a little bit closer to Syl and to Mira and to the murkiest corners of her own family. She knew it was far-fetched, and she didn't care. She needed it to be true.

Because she'd been a baby when Mira died and had met her only once, she remembered very little about her. From some visceral pre-verbal part of her, she remembered Mira's smile, how it scrunched up her eyes and filled her face. But she'd learned long ago that asking her mother questions about Mira had roughly the same effect as asking questions about Syl: it immediately changed the weather. *What was Mira's life like in Poland? How did she meet Isaac? Did her whole family survive the war?* No matter the question, Hannah would sigh. *We don't talk about Mira's old life,* she would say. Shiva wondered who *we* referred to. Whenever Shiva asked why, Hannah always said that Mira had never liked to talk about her past while she was alive, and so it was important to respect that in her death too.

Syl was one thing, but Mira had been born over a hundred years ago at this point. There had to be a statute of limitations on protecting a dead ancestor's privacy, right? Only once, Shiva had overheard Hannah saying something to Jon about Mira's secrets. *What secrets?* Hannah was Hannah, though, and eventually Shiva had stopped asking.

In Shiva's only photo of Mira, her great-grandmother stood in front of the sweater store she'd run with her husband, above which they'd also lived. Stocky and determined, broad nose, thick eyebrows, dark shiny eyes, and wavy hair she kept short and pinned close to her face. Smiling wide, but a smile that showed no teeth. There was clearly something in those eyes. *Hello,* Shiva would whisper, trying to speak directly into them. And when she looked long enough for

Mira's eyes to feel like they were looking back, Shiva always had the feeling that her great-grandmother had been hard to come to know for good reason.

If she somehow managed to get this grant, she would get to see *The Dybbuk* on an actual Warsaw stage. She couldn't tell whether it was excitement or nerves crawling all over her skin, inside and out, but whatever it was, it was too late to put any of it back. She would need Rosen to get this grant, and she was determined to prove to him that she'd make it worth everyone's while.

Beyond this, she supposed it might be important to periodically remind herself that she didn't exactly have anything to prove to Mel Rosen. Now that he'd agreed to be her thesis adviser, she only had to stay focused and do good work. She was getting her master's, not her PhD, and the stakes were simpler and probably less professionally bloodthirsty. But she also knew that, if she couldn't prove to Mel Rosen, the beacon of stodgy academic rigor, that she could unlock something here, a something out of all the nothing—well, then, maybe the heartbreaking truth she'd need to face was that there was nothing here actually worth the proving. And she refused to accept that this was even an option.

She stayed up late making notes for her application. She wrote about An-sky's work making meaning from scraps. And then, using the most formal language she could muster, she began to write about what it would mean to her studies to see a live production of *The Dybbuk* in the place where it was originally staged.

Academically, the truth was, she wasn't yet certain. But personally? At this point, it would mean too much to quantify.

She waited until the last possible minute—until after she'd burnt out on homework and on waffling over her application and over how she might convince Mel Rosen to be her unlikeliest champion, until after she'd finished three old episodes of *Chopped* and brushed her teeth and gotten into bed—to text DO NOT TEXT.

Okay was all she said. Period. And then she put her phone in a drawer before she could text anything else.

The following Tuesday, Shiva met Mel Rosen at a West Village coffee shop.

The place was overrun with college students, their bulky backpacks hanging off the backs of their chairs, the floor littered with napkins sealed to the tile by coffee drips and muddy sneaker prints. Someone threw a granola bar to someone at the other end of the shop, and several boys chortled. Rosen looked flustered, like he'd expected the place to be cleared entirely of customers for their chat.

He salted his avocado toast. It felt wrong to see him sitting there with any such contemporary food item in front of him.

"I was thinking of you," said Rosen, skipping the pleasantries. "A friend of mine did a talk on Esther Kreitman. I know that you're also thinking about women and folklore, and so you must read Kreitman. Isaac Bashevis Singer is one of the greats, of course, but his sister was greater. You know her work?"

"Not much." Shiva had recently read an essay that connected Kreitman to An-sky, revealing that apparently Singer had claimed his sister was hysterical and possibly even possessed. And why? Because she told a brilliant and, the essay said, wholly unsentimental story. "A little bit, though."

"It's too bad how underestimated she was," said Rosen. Shiva bit her tongue. "Anyhow, let's hear what you're thinking about your thesis and this trip you're so set on."

"Yes," Shiva said. "So. I know that war is the reason An-sky's ethnographic study remains a collection of questions, but I am very taken by the idea of a story told in implication alone, told only by its shadows. By what would have been and what wasn't, as much as what actually was. And of course, in his other work too, An-sky was a kind of collage artist. He embraced the increasingly cosmopolitan world in which he lived, but instead of abandoning ancient Jewish lore, he stitched it together with more contemporary and even transgressive sensibilities into a usable Jewish present."

"Yes," said Rosen, nodding, which she decided to take as an encouraging sign.

"An-sky's life ended in Poland, and in a way, his legacy began there, when the world saw *The Dybbuk* for the first time. Warsaw represents An-sky's final place, the culmination of his lifelong quilt. So, it feels important for me to be thinking about this there. As far as I can tell, the Jewish Historical Institute has some great An-sky resources, and the Polin Museum . . . and, of course, I'm sure you have some recommendations for scholars and archivists I might be able to connect with there." Flattery would get her at least somewhere, she hoped.

"But here's the other thing." She had saved this for last, hoping he would find it compelling. "It so happens that Warsaw's Jewish Theater is hosting a run of *The Dybbuk* that opens in March. By this young director, who got a grant for the show in advance of the centennial in 2020. As it is, you know, I'm thinking about possession. About how long we've all been possessed by the story of *The Dybbuk*. What does it mean to be collectively possessed by a story? And in fact, if you think about it, Esther Kreitman? Possessed, right? According to her brother anyway. An-sky? Of course, possessed also, in a number of ways. By revolutionary spirit, by intrepid ethnographic drive. Not only is the Jewish story made of scraps, but scraps that weave themselves into our very fabric. And sometimes, we can't know why something possesses us until we meet it at its source."

"So, I want to go. To go to Warsaw, to go to the archives, to walk the streets there, to see *The Dybbuk* where it was first staged. To meet my own possession at its source." Shiva paused for a quick breath. "And I may not even know exactly what I'm writing about until I get there. What my thesis topic will be, what the talk will be about. What my work deals with. But I know I'll find it in Warsaw. You'll have to trust me. Please."

The words had come and kept coming. She hadn't meant for them to culminate in begging, but the longer she spoke, the more she wanted this. Dani wanted to talk to her. But, thankfully, what she really wanted right now was this.

Rosen tapped his pen on his desk. He looked down for a moment or two and then looked at Shiva, eyes clear with a decision that shocked them both.

"You know," he said, suddenly speaking as though the grant and the trip had been entirely his idea to begin with. "The city where one writes one's will, where one is buried: that city is also significant to a life. And in fact, I do know a handful of scholars currently based there who would be great resources for this kind of research."

He finished off his avocado toast, washed it down with a gulp of coffee. "Warsaw is where Esther Kreitman lived too. She seems like someone you'd like to meet."

Meet was subject to interpretation here, she understood; still, Shiva liked that Rosen didn't much bother differentiating between the living and the dead. They had at least this in common.

"Oh," he said. "And, of course, the Maiden of Ludmir. You'll need to meet with Leora Magid." He scribbled something down on a piece of paper.

Shiva was quiet, crossing her fingers under the desk. She didn't know who the Maiden of Ludmir was, but she'd look into it later. Rosen making a list of contacts for her seemed promising.

"You'll have to define your work and be disciplined about your research," said Rosen. He looked at her warily but, she hoped she didn't imagine, with some amount of respect. His eyes narrowed. "This spot is usually reserved for an exceptional student, and I'd be taking an enormous chance on you, Shiva. Some of the greatest thinkers in the field will be at that conference. Please send me a formal write-up of your thoughts and research questions over email. Naturally, I'll want an update before the end of your time there about what you've landed on for your talk. And, of course, this work will need to serve as a foundation for your thesis. If you can commit to this, I'll recommend you."

Shiva nodded emphatically. She didn't speak, for fear her voice might remind Rosen he could still change his mind.

"I'm a decent judge of character," he said. "And I have good intuition. I can tell you're something of a dreamer, Shiva, a creative, which I like just fine, but which isn't enough for me. You need real drive, real purpose. Even if you're not a PhD student, I trust if you're in this program, if you're working with me, you're going to have real chops. Jewish folklore, despite its warm hearth of a reputation, is not for the faint of heart."

Shiva's tongue shot to the roof of her mouth before she could even think of a good defense, but Rosen kept talking.

"Which, thinking about it, leads me to believe this might be a really good idea for you. Look, I have a younger brother who paints. Been painting for as long as I can remember—he's quite good. He exhibits his work, he sells it. Truth is, though, my brother doesn't really paint unless there's a fire under his ass. Unless, say, he has funding to go be somewhere for a short period of time and produce work. And then, my brother produces. The Vermont Visual Arts Fund sent him to Italy last year for just a week, and you should see what he came back with. Actually, you can see it—a couple of those pieces are on exhibit at a gallery in SoHo. Point is, Shiva, I think you might be like my brother. I think that this funding—a trip like this—is the best chance you have to do solid work here." Rosen folded his napkin, done with his brief deposition. "So, good idea."

It was neither compliment nor vote of confidence; that much, Shiva knew. She resisted pushing back on Rosen's condescension or saying thanks. *The best chance you have to do solid work.* She dearly wanted to prove Rosen wrong on every front except this one.

Her father's birthday fell just a few days after Shiva submitted the application for the Warsaw grant. She was confused about what to do and how to feel, so she invited Levi over to eat piles of noodles and watch *When Harry Met Sally* in Jon's honor. Every year on his birthday, Jon had always only wanted to have movie night. And he'd loved Nora Ephron almost as much as Shiva did. He'd never been one for gifts. *Only movies and noodles and you two,* he'd always said. *What else do I need?*

Shiva had always loved gifts, but her father's aversion to them had prepared her for her time with Dani, who was allergic to gifts too. The only gift Dani had ever bought for Shiva was, oddly enough, on the occasion of their one-month anniversary. It was a tiny glass lizard, and instead of giving it to Shiva, she had buried it for her somewhere in Prospect Park.

"I think it's romantic," Dani had explained, drilling a twig into the dirt underneath her. They'd been sitting in the park on a blanket, surrounded by the dregs of a cheese-and-wine picnic. "It's like, objects keep energy, right? Like, even if you never find the lizard, but someone else finds it in ten years? That's our energy right there, in the ground."

"Where did you bury it?" Shiva hadn't been sure she wanted someone in ten years to find it. She'd wanted to find the lizard herself.

"I'm not telling," said Dani. "Someone will find it one day, someone just sitting around, bored and digging in the dirt. And they won't know it, but they'll have found something rich. They'll have found us. Even if you and I don't still know each other then—"

"Ugh, stop that."

"Seriously, even if we don't! We'll still be there, in that weird tiny glass figurine, in the ground. I think it's beautiful."

Shiva banished the thought before she could start imagining that combing Prospect Park and somehow successfully digging up the lizard would bring Dani back to her. Instead, she texted her mother.

I'm here if you want to talk.

Shiva wasn't sure her mother would, and she wasn't sure she wanted to talk either. Instead of following up with a phone call, Shiva pulled the stolen Syl photos out of her bedside drawer. She'd loved them on sight, but in the months since she'd rescued them from the attic, she'd come to feel a real kinship with them.

In all three, Syl radiated ebullience and intrigue. In one, flanked by two young men in suits, she wore a tulle party dress that showed her shoulders and fanned out at the waist, her face dewy and bright. In another, she stood in the middle of a group of handsome people raising their glasses for a toast, Syl in a tight sheath dress and high heels, her face framed by shiny pin curls and smiling like she knew something no one else in that room did. In all three, even in black and white, it was clear that Syl's lips were painted dark crimson red. They were bow-shaped, assertive. And in each, she looked directly at the camera.

Shiva wondered why Robert, her grandfather, wasn't in these photos. She knew that this was probably the mid-1950s, right around the time her grandparents had met. Hannah wasn't very close to Robert, so they visited with him rarely, but on the occasions they'd seen or spoken to him, Shiva had worked Syl into the conversation, hoping he'd be more generous than her mother. *So, my grandmother was really into birds*, she'd say. *She certainly was*, Robert would say, not usually picking up the hint, and then changing the subject, asking how Shiva's life in New York was going.

Levi arrived, and Shiva buzzed him up. In one hand, he had a bag stuffed with food from the Thai restaurant down the street. In the other, a bottle of champagne.

Shiva hugged him.

"I wore my Harry sweater in your honor," announced Levi, tugging at an ivory cable-knit sleeve.

"You make a great Harry," said Shiva. "I should have gone full Sally for the occasion. I only wish I had those pleated khaki shorts."

"Whatever, you look fantastic. You look like someone Billy Crystal would run for miles through standstill traffic for."

"And Carrie Fisher? I might prefer Carrie Fisher."

"Yes. Carrie Fisher would probably run through traffic for you too."

Levi popped the champagne cork, took out the two travel flutes he was known to bring with him almost wherever he went in case of spontaneous celebration, and poured generously into each. "Happy Jon's birthday, Shiv. I know he'd be so thrilled for you, being in school. And, you know, for everything that comes next."

Shiva's eyes glassed with the right kind of tears. She ached hard, but here was her friend, and here was the promise of somewhere farther away, somewhere new and very old all at once.

The kitchen was warm around them and Jon all around the periphery, the brightest kind of parenthetical. Out the window, the winter sky began to make promises Shiva and Levi couldn't quite hear as they kissed their glasses together and they drank.

After Levi left, finally, a text from Dani. No lizards. Only: *Thank you. Meet this Friday, if Fridays still work for you? One o'clock? You pick the place.*

Four

The rain was still only imminent on Shiva's nerve-jangled walk to the Muffin Connection. The weather collected somewhere higher than people remember to look. It was amassing, preparing itself for the kind of release that follows a great reticence and that communicates an opening—barely perceptible, but an opening still. If more humans knew to heed the weather, they would only need to glance once upon the sky to understand this. They would not miss so many slivers of opportunity.

The Muffin Connection was a place that irritated Shiva, all puffy teal couches and fluorescent lighting and a cartoon mural of dancing coffee beans exchanging punny pleasantries like *It's bean lovely!* and *Take a break from the grind!* She'd chosen the place as a kind of jab; she and Dani had talked enough trash about the place that there was no way Dani wouldn't read into the suggestion.

Their impending encounter felt surreal. She could barely conjure Dani's face anymore; even if technically still her girlfriend, she had come to feel like a vapor. Or, on the worst kinds of days, someone who had never existed to begin with.

When Shiva and Dani met the prior fall and news that Jon's cancer was terminal was still very fresh, the cataclysmic rupture in Shiva's life had brought them close, her own acute sadness rendering her ravenous. They came at each other with a fanged and glittering lust broadshouldered and husky enough to accommodate both catastrophic grief and transformative desire. But as the sadness had gradually begun to settle into the hollows underneath Shiva's eyes, slowing her, it had slowed them together too. Acute grief might be a twisted aphrodisiac, but chronic sadness, it turned out, could be a liability.

Calling Dani Shiva's first love would be underselling it; Dani was a much more elemental first: the first person alongside whom Shiva began to fully recognize herself. With Dani, everything regular about Shiva felt momentarily elevated. The spray of freckles across her nose became a decadent adornment, her own reflection like someone she'd long admired who'd finally invited her upstairs.

It was in Dani's presence, too, that Shiva first felt staggered by her own power, not having realized it was even there. On top of Dani, she found she could issue wordless commands made entirely of vertiginous desire. She quickly developed both a voracious acuity, understanding the language of Dani's clenched fists or her braided legs, and a quiet capacity for wicked benevolence, withholding pleasure until, at last, she gave it so thoroughly she thought they both might die of it.

On one such untamed night, early on, Dani had brushed Shiva's cheek with two of her fingers. *My starlet*, she'd said, worshipful, as if in response to an inaudible call, and Shiva had shuddered with the pleasure of recognition. *Starlet.* The word rearranged her and she let it. It had made her feel—swirlingly, abundantly—like the answer to her own question.

A block from the café, Shiva checked her eyeliner in the mirror of a parked Jeep. The weather was like a kind of fever on her skin, October-chilly but still heavily humid. She hated the combination of cold and damp and the fact that even in the middle of fall, she had sweat enough for her eye makeup to go full raccoon. She smudged at it, only making it grayer, and applied some lip gloss in an effort to compensate. A long jagged breath before she grabbed the muffin-shaped doorknob and walked inside.

Dani was sitting in there in a white cowboy shirt and jeans, her long legs stretched underneath her table all the way through to the other side. Seeing her in person after so much time nearly hurt Shiva's eyes, and she felt immediately self-conscious in the blue dress she'd taken all morning to select.

"Hey," she said too loudly.

"Hey." Dani's sleepy smile was an expression made for waking up on adjacent pillows to a full pot of coffee and the promise of a shared Saturday, not for this. "Thanks for meeting up. It's good to see you again."

"Of course." Shiva was formal, willing herself not to give too much away. "It's good to see you again too. It's been . . . a long time."

"I know," said Dani. She looked down, but no apology followed. When she looked up again, she was grinning. "The Muffin Connection, huh?" Dani's flirting generally transcended circumstance. Mostly, Shiva had found this charming, but right now it made her furious. Everything was fluorescent, smelled too sweet, came too close.

"Yeah," Shiva said. "Well, nobody's too attached, in case things get weird."

Dani actually laughed. Shiva had to wonder how she did it, how Dani moved through the world like she did. She slouched, smirked, laughed, easy as a spring afternoon, untouchable. Shiva, she was touchable. She felt cold and sweaty in here, her eyelashes momentarily pasting themselves to her cheekbones every time she blinked. She needed to make this quick. Irrational urges washed over her as the seconds ticked by, like the desire to scream I LOVE YOU or to shatter the muffin case, liberating rows of lemon poppy seeds and double chocolate chips.

"You want a coffee or anything?"

"Nah," said Shiva. The thought of ingesting anything made her ill.

"How are you?" The concern in Dani's eyes looked genuine. Shiva searched for the sadness in them.

"I'm—" said Shiva, letting the pause speak. "Okay. You?"

"I'm good," said Dani, the rough edge in her voice just barely enough to confirm that Dani wasn't only good but maybe she was something else too. "So."

"So, yes," said Shiva. She tried to keep her voice even. "Can you tell me what's going on?"

Dani's slouchy ease instantly stiffened into awkwardness. "Well, you know, I was in San Francisco over the summer."

"Uh-huh."

"I was staying with Dolores and Al, and it just gave me time to think." Shiva hadn't gotten to know Dani's sister and brother-in-law very well, but she'd instantly adored them and already knew she would miss them. She felt a little wave of grief in her throat, all the unquantifiable attendant parts of Dani she knew she stood to lose that weren't even Dani herself.

"Uh-huh."

"I just . . ." Dani looked at Shiva as though she hoped Shiva would finish her sentence for her. Shiva bit down so hard it hurt her teeth. "Shiv, you know how much I care about you. How important you are to me. And I know how hard the stuff with your dad has been for you, and with your mom, and everything else. But it's been hard for me, too. Like, hard to know how to be there for you, when you seem like you're somewhere else."

"I seem like I'm somewhere else?" Shiva practically squeaked. "You have been literally somewhere else for months without so much as a phone call."

"I know," Dani said. And then, finally, "I'm sorry. You didn't deserve that. I think it's been heavy."

"It sure has," said Shiva.

"And at some point, I'm not good at that. Okay? I'm kind of a lone wolf. I adore you, beauty, but I don't know if I know how to do this anymore. I don't think I can. You deserve someone who can be, you know. More present. You deserve the world. And so, I wondered if . . ." Dani looked up at her, all coy, like she had on their first date, like there was no difference between the two. ". . . we might be friends?"

"Friends?"

Dani was quiet. She hung her head down again, so that Shiva could see only the top of her curly head, the few swirls of early gray Shiva had loved the moment she first noticed them.

"Friends?" She said it again, absurdly, because she couldn't make her mouth say anything else. "That's it? You brought me to this god-forsaken place after months and months to tell me you want to be friends?" Shiva could feel her growing volume, could feel the various muffin eaters and coffee drinkers looking at her, but she didn't care.

Alarmingly, when Dani lifted her face again, her eyes were gleaming. Dani wasn't a crier. In fact, Shiva had never once seen her cry.

"That's not it," said Dani, barely audible. "There's something else."

Shiva stared.

"I'm seeing someone." Dani said it like it was all one word she couldn't even bother to separate out.

Outside the window of the Muffin Connection, on Seventh Avenue, a man with the face of a boy strode past wearing a floral baseball cap, two baguettes sticking out of his backpack. Across the street, a dirty green and white awning barely moved in the breeze. A little girl rode a fuchsia bike with training wheels, ponytailed father trailing behind. The sun, inconsistent, kept cutting from one side of the street to the other and periodically disappearing behind the looming clouds.

What had happened to time? Shiva's face felt heavy. Her insides curdled around the silly hopes she'd been quietly nurturing against her better judgment since Dani's first text.

"When," she whispered, a surrender to her fate more than any kind of question.

Outside, someone dropped an entire unopened gallon of milk into a public trash can, and Shiva was tempted to cackle.

"Shiva." She wished Dani wouldn't say her name. It was so intimate, someone saying your name directly to you. "We met in June."

All of Brooklyn fell away as the wind sucked itself from her lungs.

"I'm sorry," Dani said. Her voice sounded waterlogged. Somewhere in the blurry coffee shop outside of her aching skull, Shiva could tell that Dani actually did feel sorry.

"June," said Shiva. That was when, after months of shiftiness and scarcity, Dani had made her need for *space* official. "You know we were still technically together in June. You said you needed space. This is why? This is the space you needed?"

Shiva's stomach hurt.

Dani shook her head. A minute or ten went by. "Yeah. I mean, partially." Dani closed her eyes. "Shiva, I'm so sorry I wasn't honest. I didn't know how to tell you. You just had so much going on. After, you know. Your dad. You were so sad all the time. I loved you, but our worlds felt separate. It was hard for me to reach across. Or something. And so I guess I was more open to connection outside of you. Outside of us."

"Fuck," said Shiva. It was insufficient and ungraceful, but it was the best she could do. *Loved.* Past tense. How easily Dani had said it. Angry half breaths were tripping over themselves for the exit. "A lone wolf, huh? And here, like an idiot, I've been waiting, hoping you'll come around, and you're fucking dating someone else the entire time?"

Dani's face crumpled, and it satisfied Shiva to see it.

"Who?" The voice out of Shiva's mouth was tight and low.

Outside, the gray was giving way to something else. The sun had at last become decisive, succumbed, and disappeared, and the skyline looked saturated, even through the window. People were walking quickly, like they could see the horizon giving way.

"Um," said Dani, her voice a near whisper. "You don't know her, I don't think. We met through that living-room salon thing at Kira and Seema's in Sunset Park." A pause. "She's a poet too."

That *too* did Shiva in. The gray outside encroached, and so did the walls of the Muffin Connection. Shiva stared down the coffeeless, muffinless tabletop, afraid she might fall forward.

"I gave you so much," she muttered, as if from a kind of stupor. "I can't believe I've been walking around acting like we were still together. I should have known. I mean, I knew, I did know. I could feel it in my body, and I should have trusted myself. More than I trusted you." She couldn't believe she'd hoped something might still be possible between them.

Dani's voice was quiet. "I just needed to be honest with you. I didn't know if I should tell you, but we're serious, she and I, and we haven't been posting pictures on Instagram or anything because I didn't want to hurt you."

Shiva's dark laugh cracked on the way out of her dry mouth. "How philanthropic."

"I know," mumbled Dani.

The first few drops started to fall. The people hurrying past in search of shelter wavered in and out of focus. The sky furrowed, took aim. The trees cowered, as did the clouds.

Dani was actually pouting. Her lips—abundantly puffy, even in neutral—were no longer Shiva's concern. She was suddenly nauseated by the sound of Dani's guilty whisper. She'd spent so much energy on Dani already—on loving her and then, for these last maddening liminal months, on trying to live a life that felt possible without loving her. She wanted to be done. Maybe this ridiculous meeting was what Shiva had needed to finally let go of this love. Maybe in a twisted way, Dani was doing her a favor.

"Well," said Shiva. "Thanks a lot for telling me." She made the words bitter as she could, spat them out in an effort to convey a fraction of what she felt.

"Okay?" Dani seemed to want something more, but Shiva had no idea what she could possibly give her. "You're not mad? You don't want to know anything else?"

"Of course I'm fucking mad." Her teeth chattered uncontrollably, and she clamped them together, out of other options. "I don't know what to say. I don't know if I want to know anything else. I need to get out of here."

Dani stood. "Are you sure?"

"I'm sure," Shiva said. She staggered across the checkered floor and out into the threat of the sky.

She couldn't remember getting home. She couldn't remember walking or getting on a train, but somehow, there she was, standing in her entryway. The weather had grown into a pronouncement, the incandescent silver sky ripe for full detonation. The rain had started preliminarily, and her clothes were wet, she realized. She retreated to her bedroom, where she peeled them off and left them in a sopping pile on the floor.

And then the sky unleashed, a deft meteorological costume change. Outside, parents with strollers fled for awnings, dogs were frantically unclipped from hydrants, and people raised futile plastic bags over their heads. The rain came unevenly, water misting in through her open window, which she didn't close.

She fell onto her bed, not bothering to put on dry clothes. She could be naked with another person, easy, but it felt weirder to be naked alone. The curves where one round met another, the generosity of her skin spilling out of her clothes the moment she removed them—these felt alluring in the presence of an admirer who saw in her things she herself couldn't. But alone, she was just a body in space, jutting and rippling, not sure where to hold herself and where to let go. A red, red feeling threatened to explode her, and she closed her eyes over it.

The first time they'd been naked together, Dani had pointed a soft fingertip into the side of Shiva's rib cage, a freckled and cushioned place. "This," she'd said, her whisper wavy with admiration, tracing a part of Shiva she couldn't remember having touched before. She'd held herself still, woozy with reverence. And still, now, the cursive echo of that desire, whether she wanted it there or not.

Dani had been mostly gone since last spring, but now she was gone gone. There would be no more analyzing her Instagram for signs of maybe. No more wondering whether their story together was simply paused. Gone gone. Much like Jon. Not dead but close enough.

She moved her hands to her plush middle. She had her mother's belly; Hannah's soft, apologetic skin. Shiva didn't want apologetic skin. She remembered, as a child, coming into her parents' bathroom, catching Hannah looking at herself in the mirror. Shiva had looked in the mirror too and had seen in her mother someone pale and disproportionate, too lumpy in certain places and too thin in others. She'd worried she would become that body, even as she'd been certain she never would. She'd been lithe and small, a little muscle of energy who would never tire, would never spill out into such an expanse of skin.

And now, somehow, in the drench of Shiva's grief, it was Hannah's body she felt when she touched her own. Hannah's flatlined life, her mourning so vast and endless it had traveled all the way from Maryland to Brooklyn and was somehow here, now, in Shiva's room. It was easier to be inside her resentment of her mother than to think about Dani, so Shiva stayed there awhile.

The rain steadied, pattering at the bedroom window. She followed her pulse as it beat all across her body—thighs, calves, elbows, fingertips—and wondered if this was, in fact, a kind of traveling. And then she wondered about her mother. What had Hannah seen when she saw herself in that mirror? Had she loved her own body when she was Shiva's age? Did she now? And if she did, was it something she'd been taught or something she'd had to figure out on her own?

Five

In the wake of a dramatic autumn rain, the grass grows plump and alert, and the leaves that remain on the trees fatten, saturating with color. Everything thirsty gets to drink, and yards and alleys and walkways lean back a little, settling into the generous gloom of darker, cooler weather. Where there is a body of water, it deepens. Where there is a wood, it grows wetter and wilder. And where there sits an outdoor mikveh, it is duly fed.

Outside of the folklore she so wholly loved, the Judaism of Shiva's childhood had the trappings of strict observance. It had been kosher off-brand cheese and kosher fake Oreos, because most of the good real cheese and the real Oreos were treyf. It had been dancing in circles with the Torah, and morning schnapps at shul for the adults when someone got engaged. It had been foil-wrapped kosher sandwiches on vacation when everyone else was eating burgers, and no food whatsoever at Chuck E. Cheese, a place Shiva hated anyway. It had been the sukkah she helped Jon build every year, the one they'd adorned with beads and paper chains and dried flowers; heaping trays of latkes and brisket at their annual Chanukah dinner; and guaranteed lox and bagels every time her parents got invited to a bris. It had been long, drawn-out feasts and tables full of guests, strict rules but a warm and candlelit room in which to follow them.

In other words, a squarely mixed bag.

We're Modern Orthodox, she'd learned to tell her friends who weren't. She was proud of the attendant implications of diligence, though by the light of her father, she'd only ever known a wide berth of flexibility around that diligence. She'd always equally loved the rambunctiousness of the holidays and the intricate thoughtfulness of the laws and traditions. She'd been taught from an early age that questions and curiosity were sacred but that unquestioning adherence was evidence of inner strength. She'd also always resented the laws that made her feel small. The ones that said women couldn't sing in front of men, that they had to cover their knees and elbows. The ones that seemed so strict and inflexible, they eventually made it impossible for Shiva to imagine sacrificing joy for them.

While Shiva no longer considered herself observant, Hannah still observed Jewish law in exactly the same way Syl had: obedient to a fault and unwilling to reconsider what she'd been taught. Shiva could respect the rhythmic zeal of such piety from someone who seemed truly moved by it, but Hannah seemed to treat her Jewish practice like drudgery or condemnation, like something that no longer belonged to her. Like she only practiced under the thrall of her mother and in the name of some vague promise to keep alive a flame long ago snuffed.

And then, there was the mikveh.

Nights Hannah went to the mikveh when Shiva was young were cloaked in euphemism. Hannah would slip out the door, mumbling something generic, like *We need something from the store* or *I have a meeting*, and leave quickly, as though she'd be found culpable otherwise. Two hours later she'd return, damp-haired, to find Shiva and Jon reading quietly in the living room. She always seemed a little shifty on these nights, avoiding eye contact. Not sad, exactly, just unavailable. *Where did you go?* Shiva wondered, but she had at some point inferred that the question shouldn't be asked. Hannah would kiss Jon's head, and the two of them would make a notably quiet exit upstairs.

They hadn't gotten to the mikveh unit at school yet, so Shiva's read on this monthly phenomenon was unclear at best. She mostly understood that whatever this was—the secret trips to the store, the meetings that even twelve-year-old Shiva knew her mother would never have at night—it was neither for nor about her.

Later, when Shiva went back over all those evenings and applied her somewhat horrified feminist adult lens to them—the one that understood that immersing in the ritual bath was a cleansing ritual for women, who, after their periods, had to purify in order to resume having marital sex—she wondered how her mother had felt about it. Complicated, she hoped. But then again, her mother was a traditionalist to a fault.

Jon wasn't. Hannah's traditionalism had always been balanced by Jon's crooked insinuations, his compulsion to laugh even when things were bleak. Without him, the world was a string of obligations. Something fairly leveled. And Hannah had always been level. Shiva thought her mother might be a mixed alchemical reaction to Syl: she'd inherited none of Syl's witchiness but all of her dutiful caution.

Jon and Hannah, so cartoonishly opposite they may as well have been archetypes: Jon, the mischief and impulsivity, and Hannah, the practical that brought everyone back to earth with a thud. When Jon got a long-awaited promotion at the Discovery Channel, he'd proposed an impromptu road trip.

"Get in the car," he said. "We're going to Scoop City." Her father's favorite Baltimore ice cream shop, the one he swore made the world's finest kosher boozy milkshakes.

Hannah did not get in the car. "It's almost nine on a Wednesday night, my dear," she'd admonished. Everyone had to go to bed, and Wednesdays were not for road trips, and boozy milkshakes were not for twelve-year-olds. "I can go pick us up some Entenmann's at the grocery store?" Hannah's idea of a party had always been grocery-store donuts, no matter what time of day or night it was.

The momentary nonverbal exchange Shiva saw transpire between her parents right afterward had always stuck with her: Jon, generally unshakable, regarded Hannah with an expression that read as something like disappointment but also like the loving edge of laughter. And Hannah had looked at Jon wearing an expression that resembled annoyance, but that Shiva later understood to be the expression a person wore when they loved another person so much it hurt.

———

In the mikveh, you must immerse entirely. Free yourself of any barriers that might separate you from the water—nail polish, lotions, jewelry. Once you are rid of everything but your skin, walk past the mikveh attendant, the one wearing the same stern kerchief she's been wearing for centuries, and find the ancient kind of privacy you can reach only by opening the door behind a door. Move into the small room that contains nothing but a body of rainwater, tiled and narrow and deep. Move toward the water.

To truly immerse, you must at some level understand the word *immerse* as onomatopoeic. Make it so that the line between you and the water doesn't exist. Make yourself porous. Keep going, small steps, soft bottoms of your feet. Repeat the word *immerse* under your breath until the word changes shape on your tongue. Can you feel the cloaked quiet? Can you turn toward what the water carries? Can these depths really take you elsewhere? You have time to figure this out. Not much time but enough, and the hush will make everything clearer.

Some bring a witness. In the event you emerge from the water changed, a witness might remind you of who you were before the immersion. A friend or a guide, a lover or an acquaintance. As you become the water, your witness can offer prayers, blessings, afterthoughts, or, if you prefer, nothing at all.

Some, though, prefer to plumb their depths in solitude, leaving their secrets and prior selves to the water and to no one else. Of course, those people have witnesses too. It's just that their witnesses are not in that room. They're not of this earth or even of this time. They just happen to have access to our most secret places, and they know a thing or two about the power of water.

On the night before her wedding—the night before Sylvia Zvigler became Sylvia Diamond, at least for a time—she went to the mikveh. She had asked her mother to accompany her, but Mira had been a proponent of solitude. So Syl went alone.

The room was small, rectangular, a shape most rooms aren't. It wasn't wide, but it was deep, and Syl walked naked toward the water. She squared her shoulders so she would appear frightening.

Should getting married feel like preparing for war?

She took the first step down into the water. The water wasn't cold and it wasn't hot. It felt just like an extension of her body. This surprised Syl, and she liked it. She took the next step. She felt like she was giving her life to this tiny patch of deep water. *Take it*, she said, and she meant *everything*. They were the only words she spoke between the moment she walked in and the moment she left.

She already felt so different than she had before, but not in the way the nosy synagogue ladies promised she would at the edge of marriage. Her face pinched tight. She felt herself sinking, the impending heaviness of a life devoted to caution and only rarely tempered by the pleasure of breathless, reckless love.

The mikveh had no windows, and Syl had always loathed a windowless room. Windows were a way to see out, even a means of escape. She relied on constantly being able to see the winged things in arches and eights across the sky. To remember what came before the husband.

To see past him, above him, through him, to what she could remember. To where she really wanted to be.

Husband: a foreign word, already enemy territory. She understood she should be different about this. She should be warm and wide, soft-breasted and open-armed. She should go swimmy-eyed at the sight of someone who wanted to share meals with her until the end of time. And how Robert did.

But she already knew. She would avoid her husband's eyes. And in the rare moments she looked directly into them, she would see everything she'd given up. She would see someone else's eyes. Someone else's wings. Hundreds of them.

———

Shiva shuddered awake from an accidental afternoon nap. The rain was over, everything bright again. It was only three thirty, still the same draggy and accursed Friday it had been, even though it seemed like days since her miserable non-coffee with Dani. Her phone was making sounds. She looked at it.

Levi: *I know you've had a rough day, but are you still up for coming with me to Rebekah's Sunday night dinner thing?*

He had mentioned this invite weeks ago, the dinner far off enough for Shiva to give him a tentative yes. She missed her friends. The social circles she'd once adored—that had once made her feel legible and elegant and queer, where she could perform bejeweled lesbian socialite, always asking things like *Who wants a nightcap?*—had started to feel like a gauzy impression from a past life.

It didn't matter that she'd had a feeling this ending with Dani was coming; she was still a mess. No instincts, no matter how spot-on, could have prepared her to absorb both heartbreak and the revelation that her first great love had been cheating on her, all in the wake of her father's premature death. But here she was. The great loss she'd suspected would befall her had now at last befallen. She could, at least, move forward. No more waiting.

She needed to remember the things outside of Dani that made her feel alive. A dinner party was exactly what she needed. Also, it was terrifying.

Particularly because the dinner was being hosted by Rebekah.

Rebekah was a queer femme who intimidated Shiva, mostly because of her height, the pack of other femmes in which she'd moved—Shiva had once overheard her referring to them as her *girls*—her fantastic collection of cropped jackets, and the surety with which she made eye contact. The first time they'd met, Shiva had felt something akin to awe—*my first femme*, she joked to Levi, after making him promise he would never tell. Levi and Rebekah were actual friends, whereas Shiva and Rebekah were just New York touchpoints who only ever saw each other refilling at the bar between songs.

She was loath to admit how much she wished to be included in even one gathering of Rebekah's *girls*—to improve her winged-eyeliner skills or to better understand how to pick out actually sexy underwear instead of underwear that advertised itself as sexy but wound up being bunchy or scratchy or both.

And then there were those pictures of Syl. Thinking about Rebekah now reminded Shiva of her grandmother. Maybe it was Rebekah's big red hair, but more likely it was because at some tentative intuitive level, ever since she'd gotten her hands on those photos, Shiva had come to consider Syl her truer first femme. Absent anything living, those glimmering photos of her grandmother had become a kind of reminder, a talisman against the hollow ache she'd developed right underneath her skin, like the conspicuous absence of a binding agent.

Syl's lips, a perfect tiny heart. Her hair, burnished waves perfectly pinned. Those clothes, the way they hugged her form, made her look like the most elegant kind of sculpture, squinting long-lashed into the sun. Like some kind of celebrity. Like a *starlet*.

Starlet, a word in which Shiva herself had only recently found home. In the wash of light cast by Dani's favorite term of endearment for her, Shiva had grown larger and more luminescent. She could steer the bedsheets, could hard-press her palm into the warmth of Dani's sternum, could pin Dani's arms to the bed, dizzied by the syrup-low sound of her own voice saying *no* and *no* and *not yet*, her power in her stature, her skilled and silken prowess, her musical and gracious modes of denial and permission. In the phosphorescent glow of *starlet*, there was no ache beneath her skin, only certainty of her own body and the spoken languages of her own bent desire. Her appetite capacious, gentlemanly, bottomless.

Starlet was bedroom, in their lamplit world, for *femme*. Dani had said it aloud for the first time, but Syl, Syl was the one who'd given her the generational permission. Shiva hadn't known Syl, but when she looked at her across all those decades, she couldn't help but see saturated color, gossamer mischief. In these photos, Shiva couldn't help but shyly recognize herself in Syl; she saw a queer femme. Whether it was projection or she was picking up on something true, she didn't know.

Femme, when she first put it on, became a name for the lush excesses with which Shiva had always brimmed. She had always laughed loud and talked loud, and even when she wasn't feeling particularly bold, she could call boldness to the surface by wearing a bright lip or hanging faux gemstones from her ears. Every new month of queer, she'd brimmed a little fuller. She'd stretched vaster, more expansive, ever more accommodating of that fullness.

For years, she had been so quiet, keeping herself and her desire contained. Her inheritance was the kind of withholding that came from stinginess, not erotic lavishment. Femme meant more. Ever more. Femme in the face of scarcity. It meant sartorial power and aesthetic largesse; it meant volume and texture. It meant hyperbole and gossip and bighearted intimate friendship and steamy low-lidded backroom flirtation. It meant accessories and never saving anything for a special occasion. It meant abundance.

There was a cliquishness, though, to Rebekah's *girls*. Even Shiva's mostly very uncool Jewish high school had had its cliques—its well-adjusted popular girls, whose Herbal Essences you could smell from all the way down the hallway, and who swished their hips in their denim skirts like they were famous. She'd never quite made their ranks, and now she felt on the outskirts of the femme-famous, too. They had secret online groups and exclusive brunches. They were the ones who threw all the queer New York dance parties, and while pre-breakup Shiva had religiously attended, she had often also felt a little out of place: never quite glossy enough or impeccably painted as the other femmes. She hated when it felt like a contest. What was the point of making all that joyous queer space when there was a whispering and bangled elite hiding out in the hallway.

For dinner at Rebekah's, she would need to pull herself together, aggressively de-puff her face. But she should go. She shouldn't need Dani to remember herself into *starlet*, and she certainly wouldn't let Dani destroy her weekend. This would be good practice.

Levi came over early. Shiva had begged him, said she needed a buffer before her first fatherless, girlfriendless dinner party, and *could he come and have a whiskey with her first?*

He brought over a bottle of Bulleit that they opened on the fire escape.

Shiva's second-floor fire escape was the perfect height from which to eavesdrop on passersby without being noticed, and the perfect height at which to feel on top of the world. In the summer, it was a no-brainer; now, though, in autumn, Shiva wrapped her jacket tighter around her.

"You're cold?" Levi looked incredulous. He was a human furnace, even in the dead of February. Their bodies had been well paired during the winter they had dated, Shiva's skin running snake-frigid, and Levi's fever-hot. Over the summer, Levi had sent temporary and highly conditional thanks to the gods of capitalism and hid out in the aggressively air-conditioned Macy's near his midtown office. Now he was wearing just a T-shirt, and the oak-tree tattoo on his left shoulder glistened in the chilly white sun.

"We are different men," said Shiva, "I know." She took a swig from her glass, which warmed her instantly. "Thank you so much for being here. It helps."

"Of course," Levi said. "I'm just so sorry about Dani. Do you want to talk about it? Or too soon?"

Shiva swallowed hard. She had barely begun to internalize what Dani had told her just earlier that day. In the meantime, the truth of it had hardened, so irrevocably blunt it was nearly physical, impossible to think her way out of.

"God, I don't know. Like, how . . ." *Say it*, she thought. "How could she just disappear? How could she ask for *space* when what she meant was that she was cheating on me? How could she blame my grief, my dad's death, for her absolute cowardice? To just abandon the great thing we had like it was, I don't know, some old filthy tote bag? To walk out on that great a love? It just feels actually not possible." She shook her head hard, her throat thick with a frustrated accumulation of tears. "And this whole time she's been casually in love with this fucking poet she lied to me about?" *Fucking* felt nice coming out of her mouth. She washed it down with a sip of bourbon.

"My god, she didn't say *love*, did she?"

When Dani first told Shiva she loved her, she'd had to lie down and close her eyes to do it. *Lie with me in the grass here*, she'd said. They were in Prospect Park, after apple-cider donuts at the farmers' market. *Because you were nervous?* Shiva asked in the thrill of recounting the first profession over and over in the weeks that followed. *No, not nervous*, Dani said. *Not nervous at all. Just extremely focused.*

It felt good to be talking about it now. Levi had a kind face, but he had great emotional range, reliably bringing forth righteous fury in defense of the people he loved most.

"Nah, she didn't say it. But I can tell." Those generous hands around someone else's hungry fingers. How did anyone move on from anything? How did anyone imagine desire in any other shape except the first?

Levi shook his head. "I can't even imagine. After Dav broke up with me, it took me two years to feel like going on another date was even a possibility. And there wasn't even any lying or betrayal involved."

Levi was extremely selective about dating, but when he did fall, he fell absolutely and without hesitation. They'd had that in common, and both had fallen hard for one another those years ago, but only for a short time before realizing that they were meant for greater things—meant to drink together on fire escapes and to give each other perspective when they were so awash in feelings for some other person it became temporarily difficult to have any themselves.

Below them, two women pushed strollers, chatting loudly about a Molly Ringwald lookalike they'd met at a party and debating whether she was or was not the actual Molly Ringwald. A bike swooped in and out between the parked cars jutting into the bike lane, a boom box attached to the handlebars blaring "No Scrubs." Across the street, two very tall, broadly smiling people held hands as they strode past the laundromat, looking not at one another but straight up at the sky.

Maybe the moving was not *on* but *through*.

"I know," said Shiva. "Will it go away?" She meant the feeling, the skin ache, the constant inability to see around the perimeter.

"I mean, sort of," said Levi. "But somewhere, in some parallel life, it feels exactly like I'm still in Greenpoint at Dav's apartment, them making me Turkish coffee, showing me their drawings, calling me *little bird*. Like we never ended. I guess everything everyone says about grief and time, it's all true. Some losses are so hard that only the passage of time will soften them. I hate that. Stupid time."

"Stupid time," echoed Shiva.

They were quiet for a minute, both swinging their legs.

"None of it ever actually goes away," said Levi quietly. "It's just that you have to start layering over it eventually, I guess."

"I guess," Shiva said. Underneath them, an entire family passed by eating matching unseasonal pink ice cream cones.

"For what it's worth, I got home from that hellish coffee and immediately revenge-downloaded a dating app. And then started to think, *Hey, maybe if I get this Warsaw thing, I'll have a fling in Eastern Europe. Is that bad? Am I supposed to feel more somber and celibate about a trip to Poland?*"

Levi laughed. "I doubt everyone in Warsaw is somber and celibate."

It was ridiculous to admit how badly she wanted all the poetry to be right and her ancestral homeland to be the place she found something vast and transformative. She ached for Dani all over again, but she also resented Dani hard, and, right here in this brisk autumn-possible moment, she felt ready to start something else. To start everything else.

She was no longer hiding behind anything, after all. She was queer and single and semi-armed with academic credentials. She could think only of Warsaw now, of the City of Laughter, enthralled with the potential of the encounter.

"Maybe this is where everything starts for me," she said.

"Well," Levi said. "This could definitely be a new start. Like, you're all raw and busted open from loss and now this from Dani, and you get to go on this trip that might be important to you in ways you can't even understand yet. But this is definitely not where *everything* starts for you. You've already started. You're not new at any of this, you know? Not as new as you think."

"Yeah," said Shiva, not sure how she felt about the burden of knowing more than she thought she did.

"Come on," Levi said. "Let me swipe for you. I have great taste."

Shiva rolled her eyes and handed Levi her phone. Below them, a dog howled and it sounded like singing.

Rebekah's Fort Greene apartment was impeccably decorated. Aesthetically located at the precise intersection of minimalist and opulent, it was the kind of place someone had clearly put a lot of thought into, replete with adornments that hadn't been rushed. The hallway leading to the living room was painted a dark emerald green, a floor-to-ceiling art deco painting hanging at its center. It opened into a bright white living room, brown leather couch and shag rug, a leggy coffee table in the middle.

Rebekah was all warmth at the door, ushering them brightly inside, and Shiva shook off the memory of their last encounter—a queer Valentine's Day party Rebekah and her friends had thrown at a rock venue in Williamsburg, to which Shiva had worn a vintage pink party dress she'd thought would be just the right balance of cute and camp, but that actually made her feel dowdy and childish when she saw the other femmes wearing variations on leopard print and lingerie, particularly when Rebekah, who'd met her countless times, hadn't even seemed to recognize her at the door. She followed Levi into the apartment.

Inside, a small crowd was assembled around a large glass pitcher brimming with batched Manhattans alongside a bowl full of brandied cherries. While everyone attended to their cocktails, Shiva peeked into the dining room. It was cozy, just fitting a long, dark wood table at its center, and was painted the same shade of green as the entryway. On one wall, a large, gilt-edged mirror, and on the other, three gold-framed vintage botanical illustrations. At the center of the table, a tall and modern pair of candlesticks reached upward, their two white tapers looking very eager to be lit.

Back in the living room, everyone sipped, lavishing praise on the apartment, the decor, and Rebekah's getup, a short mustard-colored smock dress, glossy white earrings, black tights, and white platform shoes. Rebekah flitted from guest to guest, making pleasantries elegant as only some people truly could.

"Aria!" Shiva was thrilled to see someone she knew well enough to throw her arms around. A theater-maker with a bottomless capacity for mischief, Aria had grown up in New York, and even though she and Shiva had known each other for only a couple years, Shiva felt like it had been forever. They'd briefly been co-workers and had adored each other instantly. Aria quit soon after to found her now critically acclaimed experimental theater troupe, Blue Place, known for its neighborhood-specific performances all over the city. "Is Marv here too?"

Marv poked his head out from the kitchen. "I thought I heard my name." Aria and Marv had met and fallen in love after working together on a big benefit show for the Brooklyn organization for BIPOC queer and trans youth Marv had helped found years prior, where he still worked as a community organizer. Shiva had also been volunteering at the benefit, working the door, and had spent the entire after-party hanging out with Aria and Marv until the two of them peeled off at last, slinking ecstatically into the night. She hadn't seen or spent time with either one of them in months, and seeing them now made her realize how much she'd missed them, two of her favorite people in all New York.

"Hi Marv," she said as he wrapped her in a hug. "Oh my god, you guys, it has been so long."

"We've been thinking of you a lot," said Marv. "I can't imagine how the last few months have been for you."

"Yeah," said Shiva. "And hey, I'm in grad school now. And as of . . ." she looked at a fictional watch on her left wrist, ". . . Friday, I'm officially single." She was testing her capacity to say the words aloud, and it felt masochistic. She grimaced as she said them.

"Oh my god," said Aria. "Oh no. Dani? I can't believe it. Can't a queer catch a break? Here, do you have a cocktail? Can I refill you? Do you need three more?"

"I know," Shiva said. She paused, searched for something encouraging to say. "But school has been good. And being here. Being here is already precisely what I needed."

"Ugh, we missed you," said Aria.

Shiva looked around. This reunion felt like emerging from the dark into someplace crowded and bright. It was disorienting, to feel so forgetful about who she'd been socially before, uncertain whether she'd recognize herself here now. But it felt good, too. She was so relieved to see Aria and Marv and to remember their friendship. And meta-relieved, too, to remember what that kind of relief felt like.

Felix was here, and Shiva waved at him across the room. She also recognized Olga and Gwen, two of the other towering femmes in Rebekah's crew, and Kyle, who Shiva barely knew but found disastrously handsome. It was a social whirlwind of the perfect size, she decided, with the perfect amount of attendant social adrenaline. She hadn't banked on a good time but already felt the shimmer returning, feeling more herself than she had in forever.

"I hope it's not *too* hot in here," said Rebekah, seating everyone snugly around the dining room table. "The second summer ends, these radiators just start cranking." Deftly maneuvering like she threw dinner parties all the time (Shiva was certain she did), she edged past Levi, Felix, and Aria, touching each pair of shoulders as she passed back into the kitchen.

"Can I help?" Kyle, the gracious first to offer, started to get up as they asked and was shooed by Rebekah.

"Uh-uh," she said, popping back into the dining room with two bottles of white wine. "Sit, drink, enjoy!"

Levi glanced at Shiva as if to say, *Is this okay so far?* Shiva felt the corners of her mouth turn up at the fashionable company, the plentitude of wine, and Rebekah coming back into the room carrying a large salad bowl and a tray of homemade rolls. Levi must have read her face. He poured her a tall glass, and they clinked.

As Rebekah returned again, this time carrying a mess of rice and chicken and grilled vegetables on a large platter, Shiva sipped at her wine and warmed to the company. It was nice to be in a roomful of people who didn't all know each other intimately but, constellated by queer New York's munificence, could sip wine in one another's company and grow only happier.

"I love your necklace," said Olga.

It took Shiva a moment to realize Olga was talking to her. The compliment swam upstream, going straight to her head along with the wine, and she let it.

"Thank you. And your top is gorgeous," she reciprocated. Sleeveless high-necked lace, it truly was.

Hands crossed over hands, passing salt and wine and butter and rolls and more wine. The room was small and excitable, spicy with food and sweat and periodic yelps of recognition or scandalized excitement. Shiva watched Levi and Felix across the table, their faces close together as Felix whispered something that made Levi dissolve into sloppy laughter. She'd missed the particular joy of watching someone you love in delighted cahoots with someone they love.

The conversation snaked around the table, meandered from books to movies to who had hooked up and who had broken up (though most present company was in the dark about Dani, which Shiva appreciated) to speculation about the open relationships of several celebrities, to some more intricate gossip about the Brooklyn queer party circuit, and then over to the question of whether He-Man and She-Ra were queer canon.

Shiva let it all wash over her, periodically jumping in with a bit or a pun or an impassioned addition. It was under these conditions, a cocktail and two glasses of wine in, confident she'd accessorized well, and sandwiched between Rebekah and Olga, who were far friendlier than she'd ever remembered, that Shiva began to shine. Physically.

She felt the rare hot glow of being amid and among people to whom she dared feel she might belong, even just for the evening.

Other times she'd felt like this, she'd been known to own a party. She could stand on a pair of heels and toss her hair, and was famous among those who knew her best for telling a story so inviting it could open up a whole room.

"Shiva," Levi said from across the table, looking up from a side conversation he was having with Marv and Felix. "You have to tell the story about the wrong mandolin."

Shiva cackled. "How did *that* come up?"

"I decided to start mandolin lessons," said Aria. "I think since I last saw you; it's been forever. Just, I've been working my ass off on this recent run of shows, and so much in the world feels so shit right now, that I felt like, what's a sweet instrument I could learn? Mandolin, that's the one. Even Kermit the Frog can do it, right?"

"She's good, too," said Marv, raising his glass. "And as a musician, I can say that officially."

"You are too kind, good sir," said Aria. She looked at Shiva. "I'm god-awful. But it's fun. And Levi says you have a weird mandolin story?"

"Yes," said Shiva, leaning forward. "So, fun fact, I very briefly played the mandolin."

Aria squawked. "What? Shiv, you've been holding out on me."

"It was brief! And Marv, I was not good either. I just did it for a little bit so I could accompany my singer-songwriter friend." She let the story be a fun little detail, swallowing the part where the friend had actually been Dani's best friend, Olive. Only a week after Shiva and Dani had met, Dani took Shiva to a house show Olive was playing in a Ditmas Park living room. At one point, several drinks in, Shiva had found herself standing at the front of the room with Olive, singing harmony, unsure exactly how she'd wound up there, watching the awe spread across Dani's face as she sang. *You're good*, Olive had said after. *Do you play an instrument? Maybe you could accompany me sometime. I've been thinking a mandolin would sound nice.* Shiva shook her head but decided she'd learn, and quickly.

"But, so when I started playing, I didn't have a mandolin of my own. I didn't want to buy one, because I had no idea if I'd be bad at it, so, why invest, you know?"

Marv gave Aria a look. "You cocky bastard." He winked at her. "She bought one, obviously," he told the table. Aria grinned.

"I would just call that . . . healthy aspirational confidence," said Shiva. It wasn't that funny, but it got a chorus of tipsy giggles. Kyle punched Marv in the shoulder. "Anyway, so, I asked around, could I borrow someone's mandolin?"

"I love that you thought multiple people in your life would just happen to have a mandolin," Rebekah said. She looked amused, not judgmental, and Shiva was relieved.

"Well, as it just so happens, I did find several people who had mandolins, but all of them were weirdly hard to access. One friend of a friend's father had one he wasn't using, but he was in Georgia."

"State or country?"

"State."

"Okay, so, doable."

"Doable but not ideal. Another friend had one, but it was back at their childhood home in Massachusetts. And finally, I find this person—through Blue Place, actually, Aria—who had one not outrageously far away. But still, it was in Beacon." Everyone groaned, good-natured participants in the slapstick. "She was like—Aria, do you know Mari? That's whose mandolin it was. Well, her uncle's actually. Mari was like, *You can borrow it long-term, he'll be fine with it, you just have to go and pick it up.* And I said, okay, great."

"Right, she said *okay, great* knowing that I would be the one to drive her," said Levi. He had a car he mostly used when he was playing gigs, but it was very handy for large grocery hauls, evenings in north Brooklyn, and jaunts upstate.

"And I am forever grateful, my dear," she said. "Because, you know, it's suddenly so extremely urgent that I have this mandolin, like, yesterday. So Levi agrees to drive me that weekend, and I'm texting with the uncle, and he prefers that I come first thing Saturday morning. We leave the city at, I don't know, seven that morning?"

"Definitely six," said Levi.

"Fine, six. And Levi's a sport, and he drives, and of course she said Beacon, but it's a bit *past* Beacon, so we're circling around, and the GPS is glitching, and we're trying to find it, and finally we think we find it, so we pull over. And I'm, of course, highly anxious, because at this point, we're late, and it's this huge favor from a stranger, and also I'm doing all of this for a mandolin? Why again?"

Kyle looked glint-eyed, wine-flushed, and fully entranced by her silly little story.

"So we roll up and park, and it's this gargantuan house, like the kind that would be seven hundred dollars a night on Airbnb, and I tentatively walk up to the door—"

"We felt like cartoon crooks, sneaking in our weekend schmattes around this gigantic estate," Levi interjected.

Rebekah lifted a bottle of pinot grigio. "Yes?" A chorus of *hell yeah*s and emphatic nods. "Okay then." She opened the bottle and started pouring around the table.

"So I knock on the door, real quiet, and no one answers, so I knock again. Finally, we hear footsteps, and someone opens the door. A woman. We assume she's not the uncle."

"She wasn't the uncle," Levi offered.

"And the woman was ungodly gorgeous. Like, tall and slinky and the longest eyelashes I have ever seen, and in my imagination, she's wearing a gown. I think it might have just been like a very expensive muumuu, but it had a gown-like quality.

"And I'm assuming she's maybe somehow connected to the uncle, like his wife or girlfriend or daughter even. But she looks startled and says, *Hi, who are you?* And I say, Mari sent me. I'm here to pick up Ed's mandolin. She still looks pretty confused, but then she's like, *Oh, okay, right, hold on a second.* And so she leaves us in the entryway, this surreal little anteroom that's mostly glass and looks like it's been lifted directly out of a magazine, and we're there for a while before she comes back and hands me a mandolin."

"Thank goodness," said Felix. "I was worried this was going to get murdery or something."

"Well, wait," said Levi.

"No one gets murdered, but we leave with the mandolin feeling like, okay, that was a little weird, but mission accomplished, should we stop for bagels? We're halfway back to Brooklyn, when my phone rings, and it's a number I don't recognize. I answer it, and it's the woman from the mansion. *You have to come back right now*, she says. *I gave you the wrong mandolin.* You guys have to understand, she sounds utterly panicked."

"And I'm thinking, the wrong mandolin? How many mandolins could there be? Was the uncle not specific enough? But of course I don't say any of that. I just say, okay, we'll bring it back. And the woman says, *hurry, we don't have much time.*"

"Wait, what?" Olga looked impressed that the story had taken such a dramatic turn.

"So, obviously we hurry, because we've been told to hurry—Levi even speeds, which he never does. And it takes us a full hour, and we're starving by that point, but we get back and we knock on the door again. The woman opens it, completely beside herself. *Oh, thank god*, she says, *thank god.* She snatches the mandolin out of my hand and says, *thank you*, like she's about to close the door on us. Thankfully, Levi felt bold enough to say, *wait, what about the right mandolin? The one we were supposed to borrow?* The woman looked at us disdainfully and was like, *Stay here.* So we did, and she brought back this other mandolin that, at least from the outside, looked practically identical to that first mandolin, and we got the hell out of there."

"I fully ate two bagels out of sheer anxiety afterward," said Levi.

"Later, I talked to Mari, who is lovely, and I asked what the deal was. And it turns out, her uncle Ed plays with—and I kid you not—Bruce fucking Springsteen. He's been a part of his band on this folky acoustic project, and he's one of the go-to mandolin guys." Gasps and shouts from around the table. "I know, and I have one of Uncle Ed's janky mandolins, but that day, apparently, his much younger girlfriend had accidentally given us his favorite mandolin, not having known the difference—I mean, who could blame her? The day we borrowed the mandolin, the uncle actually had a gig with the Boss, and he caught wind of the mix-up. We had taken his *prized mandolin*, the one he plays at shows. I came this close to low-key sabotaging a Bruce Springsteen show—which feels to this day like one of my biggest accomplishments," she finished with a flourish.

"Both the evasion and the potential sabotage bring me immense pride," added Levi, a lifelong Springsteen fanatic.

"Jesus," said Rebekah. "Fucking l'chayim."

Shiva beamed, clinking glasses with everyone else at the table. She loved how she felt here, in her beloved city, in a room full of people who saw her and loved her and in whom she could see herself. Maybe there *was* no bangled elite. Maybe there had never been to begin with, or maybe they'd all by now outgrown it. She'd managed to fend off any feelings of lostness or sadness for the entire evening, and mostly felt precious, glittering, funny, found.

She hugged both Aria and Marv for longer than she ever had, promising them both she'd see them sooner than many months this time. And as she and Levi left, Shiva and Rebekah traded numbers. "You have to swear to come again next time," said Rebekah. "Bring her," she said to Levi. "She's a good one."

Shiva tried to play it cool, but she felt positively exultant. It was always queers and story, she thought. Queers were where she felt most at home. And story was where she shone.

The energy from the dinner party reverberated with her into Monday, where she sat through Special Topics feeling sharply alert.

They were finishing a unit on Jewish dark humor—how the sinister or ironic twists in so many Jewish tales were no accident, how the iconic fools of Chelm became fools, and how Jewish storytellers had known for a very long time how to slyly wield a clever joke against the oppressor. They'd learned a Yiddish term for *laughter through tears*, a feeling that characterized so much of the Jewish folkloric tradition. *Like hot water so hot it's cold, or cold water so cold it's hot—by the time you get to the end of a Jewish folktale*, the professor had finished, *you're often in that nebulous place that is neither laughing nor crying but is also both. Your heart*, he said, *feels something like remembering.*

Post-breakup, the learning came in even sharper, early winter light through an uncurtained window. Those hours she spent in class, she was able to extinguish every other feeling, getting ever more intimate with the folkloric tropes she knew so well—the archetypes of the king and his three sons, for example. The preponderance of wild birds and chickens and goats. The binary of wisdom and foolishness, as if there were nothing in between.

The demons, of course, and the superstitions. Possessions like the one in *The Dybbuk* were all over Jewish folklore. Nothing was immune to being magical: the presence of a fire, the significance of the rain. The weather was never an accident; this, Shiva knew well. The sale of an enchanted song for a pittance. The way archangels shifted shape.

Folktales, too, could shift shape. They were less formula and more alchemy. This, perhaps, was why some of her grandmother's folktales had full arcs, and some were barely stories at all. A folktale had to bring a message. It had to travel. It had to make you see something in something else.

But when class ended, when she arrived or when she left, or when her mind got tired of paying such focused attention, she fell back into her weary default state. She hungered for clarity, maybe even more than she had when school had started. *Please*, she said, in the general direction of Poland, knowing full well she was being ridiculous. Still, it couldn't hurt.

She got off the train at Seventh Avenue; stopped at the grocery store (bread, kale, half a rotisserie chicken because she was too tired for cooking), the drugstore (paper towels, more new pens, one king-size Reese's peanut butter cup), and the library (her holds: two hefty novels, two folklore collections, and, wishful thinking, one Lonely Planet guide to Warsaw from 2014); and made her way home.

She got home and checked her email, and there it was: a short, official-looking note from the department, saying she'd secured the funding for the Warsaw trip and had been chosen to speak at the Grinberg Conference. *Your research ideas sound very promising*, it said. *We are excited to fund emerging Jewish scholarship.* Tired just moments before, the buzz of an institutional *yes* woke her right back up. She scanned the rest of her inbox and saw a curt email from Rosen, extending congratulations and reminding her that he needed to see a proposal, too.

She opened her laptop, her tabs already a parade of Warsaw-related websites—several An-sky-related research tabs, the Jewish cemetery, the Jewish Historical Institute.

She should buy tickets, she thought, or none of this would be real. And it should be ceremonial, so she went to pour a drink for the occasion. The section of her counter she affectionately called her bar was dreadfully spare. Just some brandy, an ancient bottle of limoncello whose provenance was a mystery, and the end of a bottle of Maker's. She used to keep vermouth on hand for when she had Dani over, along with Dani's two favorite simple syrups, saffron and cardamom—*fancy-ass sugar water*, she'd called them—but Shiva had torn through those once Dani's visits had diminished and then entirely ceased. She put an ice cube in a former olive jar and poured the bourbon over it. Then she sat down on the couch again with her laptop.

Warsaw. She knew the ghetto, of course. The uprising, of course. But now? She imagined squat, square buildings and Holocaust tour groups, gray weather and faces saturated with despair. Pierogi, maybe. Stone, memorials, monuments. Stern sky. What else did they eat in Poland? Who lived there now?

She image-searched *Warsaw*. Shiva had seen mostly old pictures of the city and was surprised every time she looked at a contemporary one, the touristy Old Town with its Disney-colorful turrets and cobblestone. The Warsaw in her mind was grayscale. She tried to imagine Mira against one of these fantastical landscapes.

She searched *Ropshitz*, which brought up a handful of images of Naftali Tzvi Horowitz, the famous badchan they called the Laughing Rabbi, the one Hannah would invoke every time Shiva burst out with her signature cackle in public. Then she searched *Ropczyce*, using the contemporary Polish spelling of the town, and there, more hypercolor images, nothing like the warm and moonlit Eastern European village-scapes she'd always imagined.

She entered the March dates she hoped to travel and winced at the prices. She should buy the ticket before they got even higher. She was starting to feel wiggly from the whiskey and hadn't even begun to think about dinner.

Drunker than she should be on a Wednesday, she let her cursor hover dangerously over *purchase ticket*. In some past life, she would have texted Dani about this. But there was nothing to say to Dani anymore. Nothing left to talk about.

Their third date had been a breakfast date. Very little talking at all, just the bright chill of a late autumn morning shot through with the mutual adrenaline of early courtship. Mimosas and generous stacks of pancakes at a little brunch place, passing the maple syrup back and forth under stripes of sun through the restaurant's great glass windows. Afterward, they'd walked to Green-Wood Cemetery, one of Shiva's favorite places in Brooklyn.

"I would never have thought to take a date to a cemetery," said Dani.

"Verdict?" Shiva asked. Her eyes were shining so hard she could feel the shine from the inside.

"The verdict is very promising," said Dani. They walked behind a mausoleum, and Dani stood on her toes trying to see inside. Shiva came up behind her. Dani turned abruptly, pulled Shiva close, their bodies sealed against the cold stone, foreheads pressed hard together inside the stillness. Occasionally a reverent breeze, and under the slight swish of the crown of branches above the graveyard they didn't quite kiss. Instead, something galloped drum-furious through the tight space between their chests. Shiva bright and aloft, her vision woozy, and the sun, champagne fuzz. Dani's skin a warm new texture.

The way the official loss of Dani compounded the ever-deepening ache of missing her father was so particular. The two losses were sort of inextricable. Along with everything else Dani had been, she had also been the person into whose arms she'd fallen into just hours after Jon's funeral; the person who'd patiently sat with her as she wept, who'd listened to her fragmented stories about Jon, and who told Shiva she wished she'd been able to meet him and really meant it. *Here was what he used to cook*, or *he always beat everyone at Monopoly*, or *he put maple syrup in his coffee*, the stories went. They were barely stories; just moments, really. Scraps. Dani had been her first anchor in grief, and in light of this excruciating and sacred fact, it sometimes felt like the parts of herself she'd given to Dani were irrevocable.

Shiva's face ached now from the back-and-forth choreography of crying and trying not to cry. She turned to her glass, but it was empty. She felt lonely and sorry for herself. In her old apartment, she might have been distracted by the din of roommates cooking, gossiping around the clink of wineglasses—on a night like tonight, she might even have confided in one. But here, in her one-bedroom, it was just her and the weather.

She picked up her phone again. She considered Instagram, started to type Dani's name, and then heard Levi saying, *unfollow her, already.* She couldn't quite, not just yet, but in homage to her best friend's wisdom, she closed Instagram, instead letting her drunken thumb scroll over to the dating app.

No, she thought. *Why?* But it was a hazy, easy way to pass the time. She swiped left a dozen times out of habit, rejecting the same Brooklyn profiles she'd seen before, none of whom were Dani. Then, suddenly remembering her conversation with Levi, she updated her settings to *within 25 miles of Warsaw, Poland,* the idea of romance in Eastern Europe still dazzling, like it could be just the right kind of distraction.

As it had before, the instinct boomeranged into shame. Not even a plane ticket yet, fresh out of a relationship, and already trying to scheme intrigue in the place where her people's collective trauma still hung in the air. What would Mira say? she wondered. The shame, though, was fleeting. She was tipsy and giggled at the thought, because who knew what Mira would say? Not Hannah, that's for sure. Cruising in Poland felt wrong and thus thrilling.

She swiped left. And left again. Magda, with the rainbow scarf. Zofia, whose face was partially obstructed by a tree. Alma, who looked bored and had a dog. Christine, on a Fulbright from Cleveland, touristy photo and overeager grin. PhD student, barista, music teacher, veterinarian's assistant. Left, left, left. Shiva picked up her empty glass, willing someone to top her off, but she knew she'd killed the Maker's and that she should be responsible and eat instead. Left, left, left. The universe telling her that her fantasy had been tasteless and off base. Her thumb kept swiping, as though she could swipe

Dani out of her phone and her consciousness by swiping her way through all of Poland. *Just ten more*, she thought. *Just until 8:05. No, 8:07.* Left, left, left.

And wait, this one. Shiva's thumb stopped. No full name, just the initial *G*. A face made of severe angles and a swatch of black lash over bright green eyes. Shiva tightened at the throat. *G*. What did it stand for? She scrolled down to the profile part. There wasn't much. *Self-summary: Motorcycles, old films, theater.* Next to *I value*, just a little rainbow flag icon and a moon. There was only one other photo: G, next to a motorcycle, helmet under her right arm. *I'll never find someone with Dani's kind of swagger*, she'd told Levi, crying, one whiskeyed recent night. This, though, was someone else's kind of swagger. And she could feel her temples getting hotter, her tired thumbprint beating as she swiped right. She felt like she should hear bells or be congratulated on some abstract mission accomplished, or at least like someone should bring her another drink. But it was fairly anticlimactic: swipe right and wait.

She switched back to the travel tab she still had open, the round-trip ticket she'd selected but not yet paid for still staring back at her from the screen. The department money wouldn't come through for another couple of weeks, but she had just enough in savings to buy the ticket. *Don't overthink it*, she thought. *One simple click, and suddenly I'm a person who's going to Poland.* She felt momentarily existential, re-forgot and re-remembered dinner, realized she had to get off the couch before she disappeared into a lightweight whiskey-fueled vortex, and clicked *purchase*.

She texted Levi: *Holy shit I bought a ticket. I'm going to Warsaw.* Then, wobbly and flimsy-headed, she walked to the kitchen, ecstatic to remember the chicken still sitting on her counter.

She didn't know yet that the coming days would bring a near-constant exchange of text messages with a stranger called G, the unfettered note-passing between them as giddy as a slumber party.

Is your laugh as loud as mine?
Do you have family ghost stories?
My brother is the one who taught me to fish, on the Vistula river.
Cake is important.
Do you cry easily?
My mother was too indecisive.
When did you get your first motorcycle?
How did you come to love the theater?
When did you know you loved stories?
I know.
I know.
Tell me more?
My mother raised me on punctuality.
Will you teach me how to fish?
I know.
I know.
I forgot to tell you about the catastrophe of my twenty-first birthday.
Is there more?
Do you want there to be more?
What happened to all the potato salad?
Was it the kind of dream you want to return to?
Is it too soon to tell you I am imagining your skin?
She didn't know yet.

For now, it was very late in Brooklyn, and Shiva was already fast asleep, when her phone dinged to announce that she had a match somewhere across the ocean and a message that simply said, *Hello.*

———

The messenger's journey starts here. At the top of the origin story. Or the bottom, or the left- or right-hand side, depending on where you're currently standing or how you're looking at it. Sometimes it starts right in the middle. I could tell you that the rhythms of my travel are predictable by now, that each journey is an echo of the last, but that would be lying. This particular journey is different. They just are sometimes.

Desire is a propeller. In ancient Greece, Pheidippides is said to have sprinted twenty-six miles to Athens to bring news of the Greek victory in the Battle of Marathon. Couriers run. They carry things by camel, by horse, by dog, by wagon, by wheel. And what kind of desire fuels the courier's speed? The desire to bring? To be first? To be necessary? Maybe the courier just needs a job and was blessed with runner's legs or a keen sense of direction or a calling.

A calling.

I usually work by foot.

This is a matter of preference.

In some cases, a fire on a faraway mountain tells you everything you need to know. But in others, the messenger is the only way to get the answer you need or to have what is to be had. Imagine, if you will, the courier's hand—greased with effort, dry with travel, cramped with grip. Imagine the courier's bag—rebounding against a quick hip or strapped to a thick back, bulging with bounty or flapping loose, threatening to release its meager contents at the slightest trip or fall. Imagine the vitality of the mission. Imagine you carry the thing that will change the shape of the story. Imagine the drudgery of a three-day-long walk. Imagine you wake up somewhere with no memory of your arrival. Imagine you leave before you've seen the cycle of a full day unfold and before anyone's learned your name. It's kinetic work. It's not for everyone.

I mean cement alleyways and smoky doorways, fat leather office sofas whose pores are saturated with businessmen's cologne, bumpy sidewalks and potholed streets, brown-paper envelopes through smudgy windows and thin sheaves of bills over countertops. I mean first names without last ones and last names without first ones. I mean groaning backpacks of heavy goods and tiny, fragile artifacts you'll break if you move too fast. I mean legal documents, proclamations, predictions, potions. I mean boxes of letters, unopened or returned or ravaged or, in the most tragic cases, never found at all.

I mean that desire is a propeller, but it is also sometimes the cargo. I mean that we are all subject to the force of what wants us to stay put longer than we should, even if we are meant to keep moving. I mean that sometimes I want to stay longer than I should, and this is uncommon for my kind. I mean that sometimes, I am light-headed with my own hunger. I am subject, that is, to love.

Some lifetimes are smooth and steady, but some are craggy and turbulent and parched. Some, like this one, are mutinous with want. Every so often, once in a great while, I bring a message all my own, one that no one has asked me to send. Never mind the consequences. Sometimes, I stay to see what happens. Sometimes, I am looking endlessly for a yes. Or at the very least, a hello. But what you are looking for isn't always what you think you are looking for.

I want to tell you a story about a family looking for itself.

I want to tell you a story about something I wasn't certain how far to carry.

I want to tell you a story about a box of letters.

I want to tell you a story about the City of Laughter.

I want to tell you a story about love.

Six

*E*veryone *has an origin story.*

Hannah Margolin was born Hannah Elana Diamond on February 24, 1964. She was born to Syl and Robert Diamond in Silver Spring, Maryland, in the yellow house on Gibson Street, under close watch of a midwife whose other salient skills included divination, agricultural medicine, amateur women's wrestling, and pastoral care. *Make sure she comes out facedown so it won't recognize her,* Syl said to the midwife mid-grunt, and the midwife, praise God, knew exactly what she meant, so Syl knew they'd been well matched. Upon her triumphant emergence, Hannah was rinsed, patted, and immediately placed in a green woolen pod, a swaddle cut from a sweater that had once sat on the shelves of her grandparents' sweater shop. The midwife had said that a garment from an ancestor would be the best initial protection from the evil eye. Syl, undomestic as she was, repurposed the old sweater—*why not pair demon protection with warmth*, she thought. The woolen pod enveloped Hannah, who was born especially small, and whose face was less a face, more an angry golden raisin. Inside her green sheath, she looked positively goblin-like.

Syl was known across town for hurling insults at newborns. *My,* she'd say, *your child is hideous.* Followed by a three-spit salute to the befuddled new parents. When Hannah was barely old enough to ask her mother about this, Syl introduced Hannah to the evil eye, so oft discussed it may as well have been a family member itself. "You are *never* to say *anything* nice to *anybody* without assuming that the evil eye could be around the bend. It's always better to say the opposite of what you mean and to confuse him than to say what you actually mean and to entice him to bring harm." Hannah, growing, learned to be cautious with her compliments, to speak in a kind of code, an effort to evade the wrath of someone whose name she couldn't know.

And every single Saturday morning would find Syl at the synagogue, primly dressed, somber-faced, ready for prayer. Couples and families bounded up to the synagogue, chatting brightly, eager to sing as the Torah came out of the ark and to gossip wickedly over gefilte-fish balls. Not Syl. Syl sailed in and out, quick and quiet. Her kind of religion wasn't joyous or communal, nor were her prayers ecstatic. They were private and devotional, a cosmic commitment she never wavered in keeping. While she prayed, she held her father's battered prayer book, the one he'd brought with him from Poland, and while the rabbi gave his sermon, she rubbed its softened cover like an amulet.

Syl's piety came with caveats because, while every member of her synagogue knew her to be an upstanding woman, she was no fool or romantic when it came to notions of God. She was reverent, yes, but less of God, specifically, and more of the wilder elements she knew the universe to contain. People were too careless with those. Trained by her own mother, she'd learned to see the world as part sacred magic but mostly catastrophic danger, from which she'd need to protect herself and her family. Her prayers were maintenance, negotiations with God to make sure he upheld his side of the deal.

Everything that had brought Syl to this point in her life had keened her edges, made her a weapon. Against what, Hannah wasn't sure anyone knew. She was embattled, a well-oiled secret. Syl had two modes: stories and silence.

Stories first: when Syl decided Hannah was ready to receive them, she started to tell them.

Syl's stories had often felt to Hannah like fragmented clues all building to some much larger story to which Hannah didn't have the key. But one story stood out as Hannah's favorite, mostly because of the way it seemed to light her mother; it was one of the few stories she ever told that had felt to Hannah more like an open invitation than a warning. The curlew story.

One season, a group of curlews lost its way. Curlews move in clusters, and the weather had been wily, confusing this particular flock. The birds found themselves on the edge of a small, dark town where, hook-beaked and impossible to sex on the basis of proportion or plumage, the curlews stood out. This didn't seem ideal, so they argued about whether to stay or to leave for the season.

It is warm here, said one. *The soil is rich and there is ample shelter in this grass from the storm. Also, the woman in the small house across the road sings those beautiful songs. It is dark here,* said another. *The water is loud and rough, and the windows shuttered. The tree branches are so sharp they look like claws. And besides, the woman's songs are only beautiful because they are so laden with sorrow, and the man who passes by in the throes of woeful longing can't possibly know she longs for someone too. Let's stay,* said a third, breaking the tie. *Nobody will bother us. If the woman's desire makes her sing, and the man is heart-hurt and pining, perhaps we can help the sad man and the sad woman find one another.* When the other curlews looked skeptical, the tiebreaker reminded them, *This is what we are best at.*

Curlews make excellent messengers, after all. They sometimes see our desires more clearly than we do.

All that summer, the curlews presided over the man and the woman. When the man passed their nest, the curlews accompanied him, led him toward the woman's house. When the woman sang, they sang back, one haunting, collective cry, as if to say, *He is out here, your love is out here, come look outside.*

That was the whole story. When Shiva was a child, Hannah told the curlew story as best she could, but when it came to a close, Shiva would look up at her wide-eyed and ask, *So, what happened?* Hannah had never quite known how to explain to Shiva that Syl hadn't really *done* endings. It had baffled Hannah too, and one night, when she'd asked her mother, Syl had told her the ending to this story lived in some other one. That stories lived in a great circle, they neither ended nor began, and people could be so foolish about this sometimes.

Sometimes Syl spouted superstitious advice, neither solicited nor couched in a story. *Do you know why you should never clip your nails over the ground?* she would ask Hannah, horizontal and under the covers, a captive audience. *You know you should never tempt a mirror,* she would say. *The mirror is a window to parts of the world we shouldn't touch.* Hannah brushing her teeth, Syl would appear in the bathroom doorway. *You should never leave the water on, Hannahleh. Just ask the man who left the faucet on so long, it brought forth the demons of the sea.* Hannah only nodded, filing these *nevers* away. Mostly, she understood to sleep with the windows shut, to not investigate anything too deeply, and to listen for the kinds of warnings she knew to heed. Beyond that, nothing was certain.

And then the silence. Most afternoons, Hannah would find Syl alone in the backyard with her ever-present notebooks. She was an avid birdwatcher, not by any technical training but by her own obsessive study. She looked up and wrote things down, even when the sky above their suburban backyard was empty. Hannah wondered what her mother could possibly be writing. She spent more time poring over her notebooks than she did talking with Hannah's father or with Hannah herself. At a certain point, the notebooks began to plague Hannah. She didn't understand what could be so much more important than anything or anyone else.

Hannah was seven when her curiosity first got the best of her. Syl left the table where she'd been writing and went upstairs, and Hannah gathered her courage, counted to three, and walked over to the notebook on the table. Gingerly, she touched its soft, worn cover and peeled it back, cringing as if afraid something might jump out. The first page brimmed with Syl's loopy handwriting. Notes crawled up and down the page. At the sound of footfalls on the steps, Hannah recoiled like she'd been bitten, hurrying back to her chair. She stared hot-faced into the book she'd been reading, trying to ignore the hammering in her ribs. Syl would know, she thought. Even though she hadn't quite been caught, Syl somehow always knew.

Syl walked back toward the table, eyes directly on Hannah. She put a hand on her notebook like it was a small injured animal. "You know," she said to Hannah. "Not all stories are meant for everyone." Hannah could feel her mother's wrath from across the room. "If something is closed, it is meant to stay that way." Syl grabbed her notebook and walked out the back door like a bitter teenager.

Nothing, it seemed, could be hidden from Syl. And nothing went unpunished.

That night, after a particularly quiet dinner, a storm grew. Hannah lay in bed feeling young and lonely and afraid, rolls of thunder pounding at her window. She was convinced that the violent weather was a punishment entirely her own. Maybe she imagined it, but the fingertips on her right hand—the hand that had hurried open those pages—still smarted, like they'd touched a hot pan. Hannah had been desperate to understand what Syl did with her hours, but now, more than that, she was afraid. She had crossed one of Syl's invisible lines, she thought, a stab of sorrow in her rib cage between thunderclaps, and now she'd never get to know. *One day*, she thought, and the thought burned bright behind her eyes. *One day I'll be old enough, and she'll let me see.*

Hannah's father, Robert, well-intentioned, had also always competed for Syl's attention. He was a kind man with a gentle face, but he was no match for Syl's commanding presence and her impossible particularities. He'd tried to love Syl well but could never quite solve the puzzle, and a love held by only one, a love in two separate rooms? That was no kind of love. He left when Hannah was five.

Just hours before Robert Diamond departed the house on Gibson Street for good, he lined up his suitcases on the black-and-white-checkered floor of the foyer. While her father was preparing his car, Hannah visited his tidy pile of bags. She knelt, face pressed to his green duffel, and sniffed. The bag smelled like hay. *Horses*, she thought, and wondered where her father would go.

Syl remained dry-eyed all through that last Robert afternoon. Immediately after he left, she resumed use of her maiden name, Zvigler. *Did you even love him?* Hannah thought, in her mother's direction. *Did you even love me?* she thought, in her father's.

She'd loved her father in an early intuitive way but was too young when he left to have known him well. She knew he was long-legged and could scoop her up easy as a handful of peanuts. She knew he taught history at the college and that sometimes he was in his office late reading. She knew, most of all, how dearly Robert loved her mother. The day after Robert and his bags had gone, Hannah sat on her bed, pounding her pillow, wondering whether there was a proper name for an anger made entirely of sadness.

Under her mother's watch and fierce protection, Hannah continued to grow. Sometimes quiet, mostly for worry of saying the wrong thing. Grown and more grown, into a serious countenance, an unexpected knack for numbers, a forgetfulness she cursed with every season, and a permanent ambivalence about both her past and her present, one she often confused with sadness or, perhaps even more often, fear.

———

Everyone has an origin story.

It was an unusually beautiful art print, and Professor Mel Rosen couldn't help but fall in love with it the moment he saw it. It was embarrassing, really; he wasn't normally the sort to fall in love with Judaica-shop kitsch. But he'd been shopping for a new menorah to replace the one he and Millie had lost at some point shuttling between their city apartment and their home in Kingston, and there it was.

It made him feel immediately emotional, like he was remembering something. The words, somehow at once precise and slightly undulating, like flames. That tree leaning over at an angle, a formidable protector, all those intricate letters in its roots. The print didn't seem to belong in this shop, where all the artwork looked downright Hallmarkian, Jewish mass-market God propaganda, airbrushed and worthless. This, though. This had life.

Whose artwork was this, he had asked the young ultra-Orthodox man who stood behind the register. The man mumbled something inaudible, and Professor Mel Rosen didn't have the patience, so he paid for it and took it home.

Before he was Professor Mel Rosen, he had just been Melvin, a young scholar obsessed with a couple of stories he'd read in an old book of his father's, the ones that ultimately led him to search for the most obscure Jewish tales he could find, the weirdest, the darkest, from the farthest-reaching corners of the earth.

He and his two brothers had had a fine but humorless youth—stern parents who had rarely modeled anything adjacent to enjoyment or, God forbid, laughter—so they'd barely ever learned to laugh or joke themselves. Melvin came to understand, after a time, that he'd been duped: while his tradition was often dark and even bleak, it was also extremely funny. Even in adulthood, when he studied Jewish humor, he never got very good at it, and it embarrassed him to miss a joke, which he often did.

He may not have been funny, but Melvin Rosen was so studious and hardworking that he intimidated others, and he grew so accustomed to this that he learned to thrive even when he was largely disliked. This, he often said to Millie, had built character. It was good to learn how to survive without, he always said. Then you were only ever pleasantly surprised.

He'd been teaching a class at NYU when the Jewish studies department was being founded, and, always one to keep busy, he'd come on as one of the faculty's earliest members, helping to establish the department's reputation. As the years crept on, the school hired funnier, brighter, wittier, cleverer faculty members. Younger, more diverse, as they liked to say so often in faculty meetings these days. But Mel had seniority. There was something important about that too, wasn't there?

And he liked his reputation. He certainly wasn't adored by the young coeds; far from it. Most of his work was of no interest to them— too obscure, too niche, too dense. But the thing Mel Rosen cared about most was hard work. To his mind, it was the only way to make meaning in this earthly life.

Funny enough, it was the day he'd brought home that print that, out of the blue, he'd received the email from the young woman who'd asked if he'd serve as her thesis adviser. It was rare these days for a student to be bold enough to ask. He hadn't planned to take on anyone that semester, unless he found a PhD whose combined intellect and ambition particularly excited him. He'd earned the right to be discerning, after all.

But he'd been all caught up in the romance of the linocut, and she'd seemed interesting enough and impassioned—her ideas were underdeveloped, and she seemed to lack focus, but he liked her fire, he said to Millie, who laughed because she couldn't remember the last time her husband had given a hoot about fire of that kind, or really any kind at all.

Upon further reflection, though, he wished he'd said no. Not for the sake of cruelty, and certainly not because he was some old-fashioned sexist. It was just that he was nearing the end of his career, and if he was going to work with a young woman, he wanted her to be a serious woman, someone who knew exactly what she was doing and why she was doing it, someone so driven as to be unstoppable. *I mentored her back when*, he could say then, and it sounded silly, but it mattered. Some of that honor would belong to him, then, too. And shouldn't it?

His elder brother, a rabbi, liked to talk about how important it was to say no to a person who wanted to convert to Judaism. You tell them no, he'd say, and then you tell them no again. If, after the third time you say no, they still want to go through with it, you know they're serious.

If he'd said no, and this young woman, Shiva, had said *but yes*, he'd admire the chutzpah, at least. But he'd been too easy, Mel Rosen had. This is what happened when you let nostalgia get the better of you. He loved a good tale, a well-placed romantic trope, but in life, you couldn't get swept up by things like fictional trees.

Millie always said he needed to lighten up, to laugh a little. She was the only one he would hear it from. *Let's go to the movies*, she'd say. *Let's have a picnic, let's take a walk without a destination.* Without the light of Millie in his life, Mel Rosen would have atrophied, frowning, somewhere around the mid-1990s.

He couldn't well say no to the girl now, but at the very least, he could push her. He would push her like his father had pushed him, and if she couldn't rise to the occasion, well, there was her answer, and there was his. But on the outside chance she could, well then, there was that beautiful potential. It was the best he could hope for.

———

Every origin story starts somewhere.

For Shiva Margolin, that somewhere was the cul-de-sac at the end of Pinegrove Lane, Silver Spring, Maryland, eleventh grade. A Shabbos she'd spent at her classmate Miriam's. Miriam had a couple of friends visiting her from New York, and she'd told Shiva she might enjoy them.

"They're a little weird," she said. "In a good way."

Shiva wasn't sure what that meant, but she was curious.

They were two girls: One, a raspy voice and a strong Brooklyn accent, shaved undercut beneath a more modest ponytail. The other, curly hair that framed her face like a mane, a small nose with a tiny rhinestone stud on one side, big expectant eyes that looked unshy. Amy and Shosh. She felt something like awe as she watched Shosh lace her fingers through Amy's when she thought no one was looking, and watched Amy get extra cake for Shosh at dessert.

Shiva didn't know exactly what she was seeing. Most Friday nights found her quiet, reading in the living room alongside her father, her mother asleep on the couch. She was in the middle of a novel about a woman on a long solo road trip, and last night had finished a chapter where the woman pulls over, checks into a seaside inn, and sits topless on a balcony overlooking the ocean, eating a pouch of salty hot french fries and drinking scotch. Shiva felt something like desire reading this, some string tightening in the middle of her rib cage. She was used to feeling abstract desire—longing without any real target—but not to the specifics of want. Now, though, Shosh and Amy made her feel something distinctly less abstract.

"Let's do tarot," said Shosh, after Friday-night dinner, everyone stuffed and in pajamas. Shiva didn't know what tarot was, but she didn't want to tear herself away from Miriam's guests, so she kept quiet about it. They sat around the coffee table after Miriam's parents and little brother had gone to bed.

"My dad would think this was like idolatry," Miriam said, giggling nervously, as though she might not be so sure herself. "So we should be quiet, in case he comes down."

"Shosh says it's a way of getting at Hashem sideways," said Amy. "So there's nothing wrong with it at all. It's not like a séance or anything."

Hashem sideways. Yes, and besides, Shosh didn't seem too worried about the degree to which it was or wasn't like anything. She shuffled the deck, clacked it a few times on the table, and set it down. She looked at Shiva first. "Think of a question you want to ask the deck," Shosh said. "Any question. About any part of your life."

Shiva sat quietly, her panic rising. In her head, that song about the four children from the Passover seder. She was that last child. She wished she were wise or even wicked, but she was always the one who didn't know how to ask. The constant feeling that she was searching, but when pressed, she wouldn't have been able to tell you what for.

"Do I have to tell you the question?" Shiva spoke quietly and pointedly, wanting to seem like she had a handle on tarot and on girls who held each other's hands.

"No. It's better if you don't. Just think about the question, shuffle the deck yourself, and then, when you're ready, draw a card."

Shiva thought the word *please*, sending it out to no one in particular. She thought, for some reason, about an infinite vertical line, all the way up and down through the world, through the generations, through layers of earth and of time. Plum cake came to her mind, a revelry of small black birds in a delicate loop, blue light in the snow, and then, for some reason, laughter. She drew her card then, and placed it faceup on the coffee table.

"The ancestor," said Shosh, reverent. "This is an amazing card." On the card, a picture of a figure with a reindeer's head, striding through the woods and pounding a drum.

"What does it mean?" Shiva felt a little scared. In her head, she rifled through the long vocabulary of intricate superstitions she'd grown up hearing about, wondering whether, according to Syl or her mother, the card would be some kind of bad sign.

Shosh flipped studiously through the tarot booklet to the corresponding page. "She's a traveler," she read. "She's one with both the land and also the spiritual world, and can anchor you on a journey, or if you're searching for the answer to a big question. Because she has been everywhere already, and she has also been here for a very long time." Shosh looked directly at Shiva. "Is there something big you're looking for? Something an old-timer might be able to help you with?"

Much later, Shiva would mostly remember the warm orange quality of the light, how it made Shosh's curls a straw-colored cloud around her face, Amy nestled in next to her. She would remember the vertical line she'd imagined earlier, but this time, it ran up and down through her body like a bolt, crosscutting her very center. She would remember the walk they took the next day, Shosh and Amy walking ahead, she and Miriam walking behind, and the feeling she had looking at the two of them, almost like nostalgia, but they were nowhere she had ever been before.

She has been everywhere already, and she has also been here for a very long time.

Shiva would repeat this like a prayer before she slept for many nights that year, until, finally, the right question began to emerge. She saw it in dreams and in waking, peeking quietly out from behind trees and signposts. And when the question finally sounded, she held it like something delicate. She took it with her to college, where she had queer friends but didn't date. She took it with her to her first job at a music-education nonprofit, where she met Levi, a musician she learned was queer and trans, and silently rolled the words *queer* and *trans* around on her tongue until she could finally say them aloud. Was there such a thing as a slow bloomer?

Everything sped up when she moved to New York at twenty-nine. Levi moved too, and they rented apartments just blocks from each other, eventually falling into a brief and consuming love that ultimately dissolved into a rapturous friendship. Her question still wordless and private, she didn't tell her parents, though she gave them clues. She gave herself clues too, holding the question up to lights and mirrors. She experimented with jewel tones on her face, jade eye shadows and hot red lipsticks, borrowed her new friend Yvette's FEMME AS FUCK tank top and never returned it. Signed up for a workshop on Yiddish and the queer erotic, embraced smoked fish as aphrodisiac, and on her way to Russ and Daughters for the first time, finally came to understand the meaning of the phrase *making eyes*, thanks to the character across from her on the train who wore one long earring and a floral blazer and stared softly at Shiva through gold-rimmed glasses. She wore her body prouder, her jeans softer and tighter, and her bras cuter, and walking anywhere at all required an accompanying coffee and felt like a mission. She bought lacy underwear just in case. The first time she rode her bike over the Brooklyn Bridge she wept, but not because she was sad. When she got to the other side, she leaned the bike against a park bench in Tompkins Square Park and sat there for hours, nursing an iced latte and a raspberry hamantaschen from Moishe's. It was here she came to love the vantage point of a park bench; here where she learned the families and the cyclists and the artists and the husky theater dykes of the Lower East Side, already impatient to learn all of this city's textures by heart.

She learned to cook. She wasn't a superb cook, but she baked great cakes, learned her way around a kugel, and had a killer meatball recipe, so she got by. She auditioned for a bit role in an amateur burlesque show and got it. She bought a donut and a dildo in quick succession. She was smitten with possibility, with the everyday act of walking out her front door. She had crushes: drag king in priestly garb at the Slipper Room, German skater dyke at Metropolitan, hairdresser she met at her friend Laura's loft party, undercut and mesh person on the F train, person sketching tomatoes in Tompkins Square Park, person working the bar at Ginger's, person hogging the pool table at Ginger's, person on the sidewalk screaming *that doesn't make it a rainbow* into their flip phone, person wearing homemade wings on the street, person through a frosty window in the Meatpacking District in winter. She got a new job at an organization that gave grants to filmmakers and moved to Smith and Ninth Streets in Brooklyn, a little apartment whose front windows kissed the Brooklyn–Queens Expressway so they rattled when cars passed. She shared the apartment with three roommates she'd never met, depositing her toothbrush into a cup that already bore theirs.

She rounded the corner to thirty, the year Jon got his cancer diagnosis. In her memory, that day lived in the exact kind of bleak permanent slow motion in which it had originally unfolded, but from that day on out, everything sped up: Hannah, already spinning deep into a vortex of mourning and denial, and Shiva, reliant on queer New York's ungodly speeds to keep her from falling into the depths of sadness she knew the occasion required. She'd surrendered wholeheartedly to the rush of it, and somewhere in that rush, in October 2017, she'd tagged along with her roommate Selma to the party where she met Dani.

It was Dani's housemate's birthday party, and Dani was the one mixing the drinks. "We're doing Boulevardiers and French 75s," she said, not looking up from her shaker. She was tall, focused. "There's also beer in the fridge. Can I make you something?" She finished shaking and poured, then looked up. She looked like early-party adrenaline, light sheen and brown eyes under a shag of dark hair and eyebrows that seemed permanently raised.

"I've never had a Boulevardier," said Shiva, aware of the low cut of her tank top.

"Well, allow me to make you your first," said Dani. "You won't regret it." Dani could say things like this, somehow; this was already clear. Her smile, wide and elastic, filled her face.

Later, Shiva came back for a second Boulevardier.

"I told you," said Dani.

Later, Dani stopped bartending, slouched onto the antique couch, unbuttoned the top two buttons of her shirt, cracked open a beer can.

"Tough day at the office, huh?" Shiva's two Boulevardiers had made her bold.

Later, Shiva and Dani were still on the couch, talking about snow. Dani had grown up in California. Snow was still novel to her.

"We should probably trade numbers," said Dani. "If we get a good snow this winter, you can take me sledding. Show me how it's done."

Later, Shiva would finally curb the subtle trembling in her wrists and knees.

Later, she would realize she was the last person at the party.

Three days later, they were pinball-speed texting and making plans for Thursday night hot toddies. And three days after that, they were planning a Friday-night dinner date that turned into a euphoric thirty-six-hour retreat in Shiva's bedroom, drinking coffee and then champagne and then coffee again, oblivious to the changing of the light.

November and December and January felt at once like three years and three days. A whole ecstatic life compressed into weeks, the world opening up into a gorgeous starry chasm Shiva kept stepping into and stepping into, not believing it could possibly have been there her entire life.

At the end of January, her mother called and said it might be a good idea to come home for a visit. A great sadness washed over her. And she knew she would tell them. It had been a long time coming, the telling, but before there had been no Dani. Now there was a Dani, and the time had come. Jon's cancer had progressed, and his prognosis wasn't good. Maybe two months, said the hospice doctors. Maybe less.

She was consumed by thoughts of Dani. She'd fall asleep wriggling her toes in anticipation and wake with the sun, too excited to stay sleeping. Rest and appetite on hold as they only were in the name of desire this big. And, of course, in the name of grief.

The Saturday-night bus to Maryland took an eternity. Everything felt heightened, urgent; the stakes near impossible: it felt like she had the narrowest window in which to fully reveal herself. In the last hour of her trip, the sky turned violet-gray as they catapulted down I-95. Hypnotic speed gave way to magical thinking, and Shiva became increasingly convinced that her humble shred of radical honesty might actually save her father's life.

Hannah was standing in front of her car in the bus-station parking lot when Shiva arrived. Her mother wore dark layers, as usual—black leggings, a black tunic top under an unzipped black coat, a loose dark burgundy scarf. The straight line of Hannah's mouth made her face look haggard, but right underneath the haggard was a kind of fortitude that transformed it into something nearly beautiful. Her dark eyes wet and clear, her hair wispy around her face. She looked shorter, hunched by the suspended state in which she'd been necessarily living, and while Hannah had always been soft through her middle, she was crystal-cut in the cheeks, which, due to either worry or weather, shone pink in the waning light.

When they got to the house in Takoma Park, it felt different than it had before. A readying feeling.

Hannah went to brush her teeth, and Shiva stood in the doorway of her parents' room, just watching her father breathe. Jon's face just looked like his face, if a little bit thinner. She stood there until Hannah returned, and then went downstairs to her old bedroom, where she fell into a sleep so deep it felt as though someone had turned the lights out in her.

Sunday visits home during the later months of Jon's illness went like this:

Jon woke up buzzing with breakfast energy. Even Hannah usually seemed rested, her weekend skin looking more resilient and her face less overturned.

Sometimes Shiva would take a short walk around the neighborhood with Jon. But then, back home, her father would retreat, either back upstairs to lie down or to the recliner, now piled high with blankets. Between meals, he mostly read or slept or watched movies.

Sometimes Shiva sat with him, and when he was up for it, they'd play Scrabble or talk a little.

Hannah, though, would putter around, compelled to fill the absence Jon's customary good-natured clatter had left behind. She'd bake (she wasn't a baker) or craft (she wasn't a crafter), keeping her hands busy before and after work, shopping and online shopping, clacking away at the kitchen table at odd hours.

Shiva and Hannah often didn't much know what to do with each other across the great yawn of a Sunday. On Saturdays, they had synagogue, which helped. But Sundays were harder. No holiday rituals or boisterous guests as buffer; just the blank of an afternoon at the edge of collapse.

That particular morning, Shiva found Jon making blueberry pancakes.

"Dad," she said, her face prickling with an undifferentiated rush of worry and affection.

He turned from the burner to face her. Shiva was surprised at how remarkably alive her father looked in his faded blue Champion sweatshirt, glassy sun coming in through the window behind him.

"Shiv!" He put down the spatula and wrapped her in his arms. She kept her face in the skin-soft fabric of his sweatshirt as long as it would have her.

Then, succinctly and between bites of pancake, she told them.

The telling itself was uneventful at its surface, though internally, for Shiva, *eventful* didn't even begin to touch it. She answered their questions (*no, she's not my first; no, I haven't always known, not exactly; yes, it's complicated; I know, but I couldn't tell you until I was ready*), and Hannah cried a little, but Hannah could cry at the creak of a closing door those days, so Shiva couldn't be sure what the tears signified. Jon beamed at her, his face filled with something nearly hopeful.

"Wow," he said, nodding vigorously. "Wow. Thank you for telling us." Followed by a coughing fit. "I want to hear more, kid," he rasped. "But the pancakes took it out of me. I'm going to lie down for a little bit."

Her parents dispersed, and for the rest of the day, the house was exceptionally quiet, even for the late-cancer era. Shiva sat at the table finishing her coffee, listening for signs of affirmation or otherwise, but she couldn't even hear any shuffling or puttering. Only stillness, and Shiva, magical thinking governing her entire weekend, felt like she'd temporarily shut off the universe.

Finally, the stillness drove her outside. She went for a walk, past the colorful houses along her parents' block with their wind chimes and their little gardens. Instead of feeling relieved or revealed in the wake of telling her parents, Shiva felt restless. She walked circles around the neighborhood, avoiding the shops on Laurel Avenue, where she'd certainly run into people who knew who she was and would ask her how she was doing.

It wasn't that telling her parents had gone badly. It was just that time was the thing she most wanted. The luxury of getting ahead of herself, of reaching the point where calling Dani her *girlfriend* felt less awkward and more natural, some easy gorgeous cashmere thing wrapping around the both of them. Of bringing Dani home and introducing her to her parents so that she could geek out with Jon over long-distance running, or with Hannah about their shared affection for 1980s pop, lingering over after-dinner coffee. Maybe Dani would mix everyone a cocktail. She wanted time for them all to grow into the selves they would become. She wanted her sweet father as witness.

They reconvened at dinner, Hannah looking uncomfortable and distracted. Time, Shiva could tell, was something Hannah would need too. Not the pure kind of time Shiva longed for with her father. Hannah needed the unquantifiable kind of time required for someone to start thinking in a new way. Her mother made small talk for the first while, chewing her food in the manner of someone who might have a lot of things to say but isn't saying any of them.

Jon grinned into his salad. He was winded these days—eating, sitting upright, doing most anything—but Jon was still Jon. "So," he finally said. "Will you tell us more about this girl?"

"Dani?" It felt good to say her name out loud and for Jon to know it. "She's so great."

"What does this Dani do?" Such a Hannah question. She asked it pointedly, as she topped off her own wineglass, and then Shiva's, with the bottle's remaining cabernet.

Shiva took a dutiful glug of wine and then carefully put her glass down on the table. "She's a poet. She's really accomplished at it, too. She's already working on her second book. She's also really funny. Tall."

Hannah didn't reply for a moment. She pushed her fettucine around. "She sounds nice."

But I haven't told you anything about her, Shiva wanted to scream. *I've barely learned anything about her myself! Wait, just slow down, let it all unfold.* Instead, she wound her remaining pasta around her fork and took a bite.

"I'm going to go lie down for a little while," said Jon, softly, pushing his plate away. "Shiv, if you're still up for it later, maybe another round of Scrabble?"

"Definitely Scrabble." Shiva picked up her plate and her father's. Her mother sat quietly, finishing her food. Jon kissed Hannah on the head and then shuffled up the stairs, and Shiva sat down again at the table, sloshing the last of the wine around in her glass.

Hannah didn't look up from her plate. "The next time you come home, Shiv, you might need to stay a little while."

Shiva, in the suburban silence, outside the rush of her big, hot, loving city, wanted to lie down and make it all disappear.

Jon, her humor, her friend. The quiet permission by her side. The laughter in their house. She squeezed her eyes shut, trying to will away the imminent end.

December 6, 1920

I know this is silly, but I found a piece of paper on Papa's desk before anyone was awake, and I'm writing this before I get to my chores. Silly because I am writing to no one. And anyway, Papa says, a girl shouldn't be writing. Papa would be angry, and I know that just by sitting here these few minutes, I risk his rage.

But I feel I have no choice. I need to put what is in my heart into words. I am not in the mood to pray, not in the regular way. So my prayer is this piece of paper instead, and I direct it not to God but to the friend I wish I had. Still, a small part of me hopes that maybe if I write, that friend will come to be.

For my friend, in case you find this: My name is Mira Wollman. I live on the Jewish street in Ropshitz, Poland, the northern end, closest to the woods. I am sixteen years old. I love foods that taste of garlic and cakes made of walnut, and I love big trees and the earth from which they grow. Things are scarce in Ropshitz, but I have had joy in my life. Now, though, I am afflicted, and also in danger. In danger at the hands of people I don't know, but also in danger at the hands of my own family. People who think I am a stain, or worse, a threat. None of what is happening to me is simple to understand, not for anyone else and not even for me. And I need help.

Not a great rabbi's help, nor a scholar's. Not someone who couldn't possibly understand how it feels to be living on the outskirts like this—outside of joy and laughter and kindness.

It is your help I need. I need you.

In this small house in this small village, there is no hope that these words will find their way to anyone else's hands, not outside of my imagination.

Still, it feels like a little bit of hope to write them down.

Mira Wollman

Seven

Syl had been dead thirty-two years before she first visited Hannah in a dream. Maybe because at fifty-four, Hannah had finally reached the age Syl had been when she died. The knowledge she was about to outlive her mother was a dull trepidation that had lived under Hannah's skin since her birthday that year.

The dream woke her abruptly with the jarring feeling she'd fallen from very high up. But when her eyes opened, lids pulsing with relief, it was only her bedroom: its clean whites and grays, the familiar lavender smell of her sheets, milky sun seeping in through half-open linen curtains. She breathed, waiting for her body to unclench. She knew, had Jon been here, he would have made her take some deep breaths, and she would have grumbled about it, but also, he would have been right. She moved her right palm in circles around her stomach, a self-soothing habit she'd picked up when she'd been pregnant with Shiva and never quite kicked.

Hannah rarely remembered her dreams. She had a terrible memory generally, and her dream memory was no exception. She was fretting lately about feeling like a human sieve. She liked to have control, and forgetting was a sure way to feel like you were losing control altogether.

And control, of late, had been scarce. Things between her and Shiva were not good. She was grateful they'd been back in touch, little by little, but it all still felt wrong. Wrong for the obvious reason that Jon wasn't there anymore to bind them into the little family they'd once been. But wrong, too, because she'd never imagined that this was what having a daughter would feel like. That she'd feel at once overcome with love and pride; and also backed into a corner by this daughter, defensive and unsure how to account for herself: a grown woman, a mother. What would that account be? What could she say?

Shiva had visited last month, and instead of fighting about dead ancestors, they'd fought about religious practice, a topic that had only grown more heated and divisive in recent months.

It was Shabbos, and Shiva had suggested walking to the park.

"Sounds lovely," said Hannah.

"I'm going to bring a book. Want to bring a book? We can lay out a blanket, bring some snacks, read the afternoon away."

"We can't."

"What? Why not?"

"We can't carry books or a blanket. You know that. The eruv is down."

"Ma." Shiva looked at her sharply. "That's not real. You know that's not real."

"Of course it's real." Hannah could feel her mouth flattening, the way it did when she didn't want to reckon with her daughter but knew she needed to. It wasn't Shiva's place.

"What do you think will happen to you if you carry a book to the park? Ma, it's ridiculous. This isn't who you are."

"What do you mean, who I am? Of course it is. Who else would I be?"

"Ma." Shiva said it loudly. "It's just, you never seem like you're doing any of this for you anymore. Like you're doing it out of obligation, and like you're not happy. What do you think Dad would say?"

"Don't bring Dad into this. It's not fair."

"Well, you leave him out every day by acting like some downtrodden pious villager instead of a single woman who can do whatever you feel. And honestly, it's hard to watch."

"You don't understand anything about what I'm doing." In the face of her frustrated daughter, Hannah felt petulant, and she hated it. The particular way Shiva both read her and misunderstood her made her feel small. But also, her daughter could see things. Her daughter was right. It frustrated her to the point of seizing.

"But you don't let me understand. I'm trying. And I need my energy for other things right now. My own grief. Don't you see me trying?" Shiva paused. "Just because I eat bacon now, doesn't mean I'm not close to God." A pause. "Or something like God."

"You eat *bacon*?"

Shiva's cheeks flushed. "Yes. And it's delicious. So, you can bring your novel to the park. Okay?"

They walked. Her own daughter? Bacon? A small part of her wanted to giggle, to lean in, to ask, *What does it taste like?* Why couldn't she? What was she so afraid of? Her fears too vast to name, so unbelievably old they exhausted her.

Hannah did bring a book but made sure to hold it differently than she usually would—under her arm, instead of in her hand—as though this loophole rendered the carrying something entirely else. They walked straight to the park, their old route, Saturday afternoons, except no Jon here. Just the two of them.

They were quiet for a long time. Hannah crushed a dried-out acorn with the sole of her flat. Why didn't anything feel like it was getting better?

"I joined a new synagogue," said Hannah.

"That's great, Ma."

"It's more liberal than the other one. I thought you'd appreciate that."

"Also great," said Shiva. They walked. "I'm sorry, Ma. I didn't mean it."

"You meant it," said Hannah. "It's fine."

Quietly, Hannah often wondered how her relationship with her mother might have changed had Syl stuck around a little bit longer.

She'd died when Hannah was still young enough to be attached to the resentments of young-adult daughterhood, but she wondered whether they'd have moved closer to one another with time. Would Hannah have come to appreciate the harsh enigma of her mother? Would her mother have learned to give an inch once in a while? Would they argue as freely as she did now with her own daughter? Would she have eventually come to understand her mother's relationship—or non-relationship—with her father?

Robert lived in Seattle now. She had never been particularly close to him, but the series of funerals over the past few decades had allowed them to get closer than Hannah had ever been to her father as a kid. Their conversations never went too deep, but it didn't matter—they would always be linked by having spent time living in Syl's reality—a reality that hadn't ever completely included them but that had formed them both all the same. Hannah could have used Robert as a memory aid, but, at this point, she felt too silly to ask her father for stories when they spoke. They were now just a grown woman and a father who hadn't stuck around to storytell when it might have been more appropriate.

After Jon's funeral, though, Robert had told her a Syl story. He'd found Hannah in the kitchen, crying into a half-unwrapped lox platter.

"You loved each other so much." Her father's somehow knowing this without having witnessed it moved Hannah. He cleared his throat. Hannah remembered this from when she was a girl—always clearing his throat when he seemed nervous. His brown eyes a little watery, and his hair much whiter now.

"We did," she said. "Weirdly, this also makes me miss Mom." Robert was the only other person on earth who might understand.

"You wouldn't think it possible a whole lifetime later, but I still miss her too." Robert poured some seltzer for himself and then some for Hannah. "I didn't know what I was going to do without her then, either, and even though it would be years before she actually died, I do know what it's like to have to grieve someone you truly can't be with."

Robert had come to Syl's funeral but only for the ceremony. He hadn't lingered. He'd been happily remarried for years now, with a new family.

"You know I had to work for it," he continued. "I had to work in cahoots with your grandparents for Syl to even consider seeing me, and then, once she did, I had to work to keep her attention." He chuckled a little. "But there were a few rare times when it really felt like we belonged to each other. You're lucky, Hannah." Robert's voice got a little sorrowful. "It seems like you got to have that with Jon all the time."

Hannah nodded. Something like whiskey moved through her throat.

"This one time, I took Syl to a bird sanctuary. I was desperate to impress her, and you know, she never went for fancy dinners or anything like that." Hannah knew. Her mother's three favorite foods had been rotisserie chicken, moo shu pancakes, and coffee ice cream. "I asked if I could blindfold her in the car—told her I had a surprise for her, and she was skeptical, thought I was taking her to dinner or an art film. It was hard work surprising your mother."

"Did she let you?"

"Begrudgingly." He let out a short laugh. "I played her favorite Tchaikovsky on the car stereo the whole way over, and when we got there, and I pulled off the blindfold, her eyes actually glowed. 'Robert,' she said out loud, and it honestly felt like the first time I had ever heard her say my name."

"Birds were her Achilles."

"Birds were her everything," said Robert. "It sometimes felt like birds were her real family—didn't it?" Hannah almost nodded but was stopped by a pang of protective loyalty. "She was so excited. I remember her pointing and telling me their names. 'That's a warbler,' she said. 'And that's a kestrel. And oh, that green beauty over there? That's a monk parakeet.' Then she looked at me, her face all flushed, and right in that moment, I got to have some of the leftovers of the enthusiasm she always reserved for those birds. I almost suggested we go get our things and our bed and move into that bird sanctuary right then and there. I would have done that for Syl."

And Hannah knew this to be true too. Robert had been devoted to her mother, but Syl had never had room for Robert. She had married him, Hannah always knew, because it was the right thing to do. When Hannah thought about it now, a grown woman herself, Syl seemed like a woman who'd been meant for solitude. Or, at the very least, meant to be something other than married.

The dream. The memory of it came rushing back into her face, the way memories rarely did. She'd been standing in the Jewish cemetery where both her mother and her husband were buried, but right in front of her was a huge gash in the earth, surrounded by piles of dirt and strips of grass that had been ripped from the ground wholesale. The gash was full of water. Across from her, on the other side of this unsettling moat, Syl had been sitting upright in a small, wooden chair, her red hair wild around her face. And maybe she'd been conscious, but those eyes were not the eyes of a living person. In the dream, Syl's wild dead eyes had stared at her, burning into her from all the way across the water.

Hannah's room felt full. Even though there was something pure horror film about the visitation she had just experienced, she could feel clearly that Syl had been watching her, and it didn't feel like when Syl had monitored her in life, either. As grotesque as the dream had been, it felt less like a threat and more like a looking-after. And Hannah needed a looking-after. She was lonelier than she ever had been, missing Jon only more as time went on and floating further away from the people and things she loved, her daughter very much included.

She lay on the pillow for another minute, letting the dream wash away, even though she knew she wouldn't soon forget it. *Ma, I hope you're well*. It felt formal, but she was still learning how to talk to her dead, even after so much practice, and at the very least, she really meant it.

There was a story, Hannah remembered, a Syl story. Water. A girl. Something about the rain? She suspected the tone of it had grown less dire under her watch. A girl who loved the rain, for some reasons she could explain and for some reasons she could not, and who had never felt fully immersed, though she lived in a rainy city. It wasn't enough. The girl longed to bathe in it. So she set out to capture the rain.

She started by sitting outside with a large clay bowl, waiting for the drops to find their way inside. At an hour's end, she had a wet bowl but no collection. She tried next with towels. When those grew saturated, she wrung them into the bowl. Some rainwater, but not enough to fill any tub. She then lay teacups all around the garden one night, but when she awoke, only a scant few had collected muddied rainwater in their bottoms.

The girl was frustrated. She'd dreamed of bathing in rainwater for so long, she felt silly for failing to figure out how to collect it. That night, she took a new approach, laying her own body down in her garden as the rain began. Slow patters at first, and then the torrent. She closed her eyes to the drops on her face, grinding her frigid fingers into the dirt. Water pooled in her nostrils and eyes, made her clothing heavy, and rolled down her temples to the sopping ground. Did she sleep? Sort of. The water took her elsewhere. She lay, collecting. She the vessel. She returned to her body in the morning, exhausted and aching, skin wrinkly and cold to the touch.

Rising from the ground, the girl walked into her house and stepped into the bathtub. She wanted only warmth now. She finally understood that the rain simply wasn't meant to be caught. For this, the girl cried. But then, she couldn't stop crying. Water poured and poured from her eyes, water neither warm nor salty, and filled the tub where she sat.

It was the rain, she knew then. She *had* collected the rain. It came forth from the girl until the tub was full, and in it, she shivered. The rain continued to come forth from the girl, night after night. In time, the girl grew red-eyed, having become the dispenser of something that was never meant to be gathered in the first place.

This wasn't the clear moral it seemed, Syl had said. The girl, schooled, was also something close to content. The girl had become the rain. The rain had become the girl. The girl had defied her form. The girl had eliminated the vessel. The girl, in her very eyes, contained an element that had been previously uncontainable. And for the rest of her strange and saturated life, she did her best to be worthy of uncontaining it.

On her drive home from the mikveh, Hannah got a text from Shiva asking how she was doing. She panicked momentarily, as if she'd gotten caught doing something she wasn't supposed to do. This was ridiculous, of course; she didn't need to answer to Shiva, and she had every right to go to the mikveh, even though it was true that, now no longer married, Hannah wasn't ritually obligated to immerse, even by the strictest law.

The truth was, she still went because she'd come to rely on the ritual and hadn't yet quite been able to figure out how to let it go. And also, if she was being honest with herself, she kept on going just in case. Just to be safe.

Hannah was no fool. She knew the reason she and Shiva had fought about the eruv, and she knew why she was afraid to tell her own daughter she still went to the mikveh. Shiva was suspicious of her adherence to tradition. Hannah could tell Shiva thought it fear-based, a cultish compulsion to live out someone else's wishes. This wasn't the whole truth of it, but it wasn't entirely false.

The true part was that she was stuck. *Look,* she said to herself, *this is tradition. Look, Syl would have wanted . . . Look, Jon would have wanted* . . . But what would Jon actually have wanted? Shiva was right—he'd always tried to get Hannah to open her mind, to expand her capacity for adaptation and interpretation.

Hannah's observance had always been steadfast as an engine. For Syl. For God. For the evil eye. For Mira. For someone. She didn't know. She'd never really known. She knew only that one of her mother's few wishes was that she neither stop practicing nor let her guard down. So she did her part.

For Syl, this had meant not only making sure fingernails were properly disposed of and that the fish was facing the right direction on the platter when you served it but also keeping a humble profile, covering one's knees, showing up at synagogue on time, and maintaining a godly diet. For herself, too, Hannah thought, it must mean something akin to this. The way that fending off dark forces and paying daily homage to the God who kept you safely lit were two sides of the same coin. But somehow, as a result, Hannah had lived a whole life at the nagging in-between. Neither in the shadows nor in the sun but hovering right in the middle, unmoving, for fear of toppling in either direction.

And what about that God, anyway? She'd always oscillated between a foggy God and a non-God. The fear of what might be, or what mightn't. What if everything she feared was true? After the loss of her love, it felt like it actually might be. What if nothing she hoped was? She never felt like she had the capacity to figure it out, so she defaulted to the most conservative possible estimate. Everything was true, and she was probably skirting the edge of trouble. She wasn't married anymore, unless you got medieval or Mormon about ideas of eternity, but she still wore her wedding ring, still immersed monthly even in her stark celibacy, and even still sometimes wore a kerchief to cover her head when she went to services. Putting it on, she always thought, *just in case.* She wore it half-heartedly, itching and resenting the cloth that covered her hair for no reason she could ever articulate.

She was just afraid of stopping. Faith, as she'd learned from her mother, was a duty. She was no longer sure, but she was stuck with the feeling that to stop attending to the God in her life might bring everything crashing down. To be alive, to stay safe, she'd concluded, a kind of relentlessness was necessary. To maybe not fully believe in a God but to insist on one.

If she stopped, who would she be? If she replaced the word for God, what would she replace it with?

Hannah was never not hungry when she left the mikveh. Sometimes, afterward, she would drive past the kosher burger place, pick up a burger with extra pickles, and eat it in her car on the way home. It was a private ritual, a hunger that was hers alone.

Underneath all her fears and her dogged commitments was the most honest thing. Hannah's monthly visits to the mikveh weren't just the fulfillment of some obscure promise. They were for her. For how the mikveh made her feel.

The first time she'd ever immersed, she'd been shocked to learn she felt more like a whole body in that water than almost anywhere else. Jon had always touched her with reverent curiosity, like she was not the treasure, but the x-marked path along the way. But sometimes she needed a reminder of her solidity, and when she walked naked into that sacred water, ate her private burger, and came home to the only person on earth who wondered at what shone in her, she was reminded.

Her days, now far lonelier, were hungry days. And her body, even when fed, was ever more forgetful.

Eight

Maryland, April 1986, and death hung from the sky and everywhere. It was dank, threaded inextricably through the heat and the humid fog, and it meant to stay awhile. It was in the wet smell that rose up from the concrete, on the rare and languorous wind, and in the ripe growth of dark petals and sagging honeysuckle, a saturated suburban green.

Hannah and Jon kept the doors open on both sides of their little Takoma Park house in the interest of cross ventilation. The windows fogged around their edges as if they knew something, and the windows in that house were everywhere. It was a house made for watching. The small guest room at the end of the upstairs hall had the most windows of all. Looking out from that room you could see the small yard behind the house and beyond, to the woods. You could see trees in their various states of dress and undress, nervous raccoons, squirrels of both the lazy and brazen varieties, and the occasional orange fox. In anticipation of Syl's arrival, Hannah and Jon had replaced the guest futon with a queen-size bed that took up most of the room. It didn't matter that the room was now all bed; Syl had always loved sleeping in there—waking to too much sun, falling asleep soaked in moonlight. It was Syl's favorite room, and if one must die in some room, it may as well be her favorite.

Hannah was also more pregnant than she thought it possible for a human to be. April. She was due in early May and still deeply uneasy about the whole thing. How did skin do this? Stretch to accommodate? She woke daily into stilted swollen choreography, trying—slow motion through her mundane morning rituals, hand to toothbrush, toothbrush to faucet—to process the expanse of her flesh, how taut it pulled without tearing.

The other, more alarming, thing was that she was burning. She had taken every precaution her mother had taught her to thwart the evil eye. Her dresser housed a makeshift altar featuring a pile of preserved esrogs she'd bought at a bargain rate from the outgoing rabbi of Etz Chayim, who'd been dutifully collecting them from his congregants for years. Syl had always sworn by the potency of an esrog, said it was uniquely powerful and that the evil eye couldn't stand the smell. There were ancient tekhines about childbirth hanging on the refrigerator, for good measure, and she was extra careful about not dropping fingernail clippings on the floor. She felt she had done her due diligence. But something was wrong. Nothing was supposed to be this hot. No body.

At first it had been a subtler kind of heat—a stuffy, sharing-your-body-with-another-body feeling. Hannah kicked off the covers, her pants, started taking lukewarm showers and, eventually, downright cold ones. Maybe this was normal, a pregnancy thing, and Hannah half-heartedly thumbed through the pregnancy books, assuming that a nine-month hot flash was something she had unknowingly signed up for. Her belly felt like a thing she wanted to remove, as though whatever was in there was the source of the heat. *Get it off me*, she would murmur to Jon in the night, as though the movement was *off* instead of *out*.

She got hotter. April, weather temperate, in the low sixties, but Jon came home to find Hannah prone in front of the portable air-conditioning unit, bags of frozen corn placed in strategic locations on her body. Jon said things like *Is it hot in here, or is it just you?* But instead of laughing like she normally would, Hannah threw a sagging bag of corn at him and wept.

•

By the time Syl arrived to die with them, Hannah's heat state bordered on the otherworldly. She had begun hallucinating—the clouds frothed, and the couch cushions wobbled like jello. She'd seen fangs on the postman and lips on the faucet, and more than once, she swore she'd seen a squirrel beckoning her closer.

Back in February, when she was not yet so hot and news of Syl's impending death was still only minutes old, Jon and Hannah drove Syl home from the doctor in Jon's Volvo. Syl sat up front with Jon, and Hannah sat in the back. It was quiet until Syl turned on the radio, and "50 Ways to Leave Your Lover" came on, and all Hannah could think about was how irritating a song it was, who cared about Jack and his impending heartless, sexist betrayal, and who got away with rhyming *back* and *Jack* like that. You shouldn't do that, not even if you're Paul Simon—*especially* if you're Paul Simon; the world should expect better of you. *Get yourself free*, indeed. It's all she remembered from that ride home now, still, how impossibly hot she had started to feel, how incredibly angry she was at Paul Simon.

Syl's doctor was a thick man with a thick mustache and the shoulders of a sea captain, and he had tried to be poetic about it when he delivered the news. "Life is like a glass of wine," he'd said. "You've been drinking heartily for some time now, but your glass is nearly empty. You're going to have to savor the last little bit." Syl's chuckle was stiff. "I don't drink," she said, ignoring the metaphor. Everything in Hannah turned to metal. Her palm fluttered to her round midriff, moving absently in circles, searching for reassurance. "So that's it?" Syl's eyes were sharp, her movements precise, wasting no time, snapping her compact leather purse as if they were closing out a business meeting. "Maybe it's time to take up drinking," she said. She laughed again, more like a bark this time, edge of violence to it. No one else laughed back, not even the sea captain.

They got back to Syl's house, the house on Gibson Street where Hannah had once been a child, and no one knew what to do but eat, so there was rotisserie chicken from the kosher market with rice and the garlicky green beans Syl loved. They tore through the chicken, first polite, with forks, and then, soon, with fingers. When there were mostly bones left, and Jon was chasing the last few slippery green beans through the orange grease at the bottom of the takeout container, Hannah found herself staring at her mother's hair, knotted messily at the back of her neck. She could think of nothing more living than that hair, big and red and semi-kempt for as long as she could remember.

Syl broke the desperate quiet with aggressive nonchalance. "I mean, I'll get news like this every day if it means I get to eat as much rotisserie chicken as I want." She looked around for reactions. "Did we get dessert? Should we?"

Hannah's eyes sharpened and watered. "Ma." She stared at Syl, angry, slow to make the shapes of words. "How can you joke?" In response, Jon elbowed Hannah, and she glared at him. "She's *my* mother," Hannah hissed.

"I'm right here," said Syl. "Don't talk about me in the third person yet. Look," she said, giving Hannah the eyes she gave her when she was about to deliver an edict or an ultimatum disguised as a story. "Look at Sarah. She's ninety-seven years old when this strange man comes to her four-door tent and tells her she's going to have a baby. Can you imagine?" Syl returned to the chicken and began gnawing on a hopelessly meatless bone. "She's ninety-seven, practically dead already, and suddenly she's going to have a baby?" She spat a piece of bone onto her paper plate. Hannah rubbed her belly again. It wasn't exactly an instinct so much as free association and something to do with her hands. "Sometimes things don't go as we expect, is the point," Syl said, with an implied flourish. "So I'll die. I've lived, haven't I?"

Had Syl lived? In that moment, Hannah couldn't be sure.

Syl dropped the bone into the bottom of the empty container and carried it to the garbage can. Then, she knelt down to one of her kitchen cabinets and extracted a dusty bottle of slivovitz. She brought it back to the table, looking from Hannah to Jon and back to Hannah again.

"Okay. I'll come stay with you," she said, as though she'd been invited, as though they'd discussed it thoroughly, as though it was already decided.

Hannah refilled the salt bowls. You had to change them with the moon, and Syl had never let her forget it. For Syl, Hannah had bought pink Himalayan salt from the food co-op, the kind that she and Jon couldn't quite afford. She brought a small glass bowl of the large pink flakes into Syl's room and placed it on the windowsill.

Standing in the crook between the bed and one of the windows, Hannah took a closer look at her mother, Syl's face almost frightening in its unguarded softness. Even with the telltale night circles around her eyes, Syl looked alarmingly ageless.

"I do hope I get to meet the baby." Syl's voice was odd, stripped of its signature sting. "But I also think we stand a chance to cross paths in transition, which would be something to write home about. Hopefully, they have postcards there." She laughed at her own feeble attempt, and her laugh, once sharp and punctual, came out dusty.

"I hope you do, too." Sometimes, Hannah hardly knew what to believe. If there was a chance her mother and her kid could meet, she would do almost anything to make it so. "Do you need anything, Ma?"

Syl, who had always loomed so large, reduced to a horizontal sliver. Syl, who was fifty-four. This wasn't how any of this was supposed to go. *Complicated* didn't even touch the knotty dynamics between her and her mother, but Hannah swore they just needed time. If they had time—more time, enough time, any time—maybe they could still figure each other out. Maybe even learn how to love each other well.

"Yes," said Syl. She sat up, and her voice came back sharp. "There is something."

"Of course. What is it?"

"I need you to burn my notebooks."

"What?"

The notebooks. The ones Hannah had been resentfully fixated on since the childhood moment she'd tried to look at their contents, still fervently wishing she'd be allowed a peek now, at age twenty-two.

Some people's parents hoarded old issues of *Newsweek*. Syl hoarded herself. Hannah could still picture it clearly—that entire closet shelf stacked with steno pads. Hannah had considered trying to peek at the notebooks again, but the fear of Syl had long lodged in her, and she never quite could. Syl would know somehow, and the act would come back to haunt her. *If something is closed, it's meant to stay closed.* The only comfort she'd taken, small and twisted though it was, was in the thought that one day, when Syl died, Hannah would pour herself a glass of wine, pull out a stack of those notebooks, and finally begin to get to know her mother.

"No," said Hannah. Even if they'd been vigilantly kept from her, she needed those notebooks, and they were also her mother's life's work.

Syl looked back at her, cheeks pulled tight. "This is not a negotiation, Hannah." Hannah felt seven again, in the shadow of her mother's stern stature, being told *no*. "You've never been able to understand this. A person's writings, their communion—it's the material of their soul. And that's not a figure of speech. The contents of these notebooks, they're not for anyone else. They're not meant to outlive me. They belong to me. With me. So, with me they'll go."

"But Ma." There would be no fighting with Syl—not now, not ever again, she thought. "I'm an adult now. Couldn't I just see them? Wouldn't that be okay?"

Syl sighed, raggedly. She extended a hand. Hannah put out her own, and for a brief moment, fingers held fingers, palm rested in palm. "Hannah," she said. "Everything you need to know about me, you already know. Please do me this kindness."

"Okay," Hannah whispered. She couldn't even begin to touch her own anger, surrounded as it was by a thick shell of grief.

"Now," said Syl. "Do it now."

"What," said Hannah. "You don't trust me?"

"I trust you. I just want to see them go." Syl pointed to a large suitcase in the corner of the room. "They're in there."

Hannah's eyes widened. "You brought them?"

Syl coughed up a short, breathless laugh. "Of course I did. This is a priority."

The things that Syl considered *priorities* had always baffled Hannah. Unexpectedly dying in middle age, and the first thing she does is pack an entire suitcase full of her own precious journals for kindling.

"Fine," Hannah said. She looked out the ample windows onto the yard where, just a couple of weeks ago, she and Jon had sat with icy glasses of ginger beer, talking about music and watching the sun sink without any sense of foreboding. "I can do it in the yard. You can watch from up here." Her mind shuffled through all the ways she could get away with not burning the notebooks or, at least, not burning all of them. What could she manage to keep? But the answer, she knew, was nothing. Her mother might have been dying, but her mother would know.

"As soon as Jon gets home," said Syl, her voice at the edge of crisis. "Please. He can help you carry them. We don't know how much time we have."

Hannah went downstairs and sat at the table with her hands in her lap, unable to think about or do anything else until Jon got home. When he finally arrived, she felt breathless, though she hadn't moved.

"I need you to do something for me," she said.

The suitcase was heavy to maneuver down the stairs, but Jon was strong and a good sport. By the time he'd dragged it out into the yard, Hannah had prepared the firepit. She knew that she was being reckless, swinging her weight around like this. People as drastically pregnant as she was should hardly be walking around, let alone setting up pyres. But if this was actually going to happen, Hannah needed to be the one to do the burning. Jon brought her the suitcase. He looked at her, the question plain on his face without his needing to ask it.

"I'll explain later," she said. Jon nodded, stood in the doorway, just in case.

Sweat poured down the sides of Hannah's face and back, and she was quickly drenched in the heat of the sun and the fire. The flames grew quickly, and she hoped that, over the fence, the neighbors couldn't see it. A backyard fire in the middle of a spring afternoon would seem suspicious.

She unzipped the enormous suitcase and began throwing the notebooks in, one at a time.

Each was a small violence. In between, Hannah's hands shook. She felt sick from the smell as they burned.

She didn't have to look up to know that Syl was there, in the window, looking down on her, watching her years turn to ash.

Sunday, end of April just around the bend. The hospice nurse went out to get some air, and Hannah waddled in to check on her mother.

"Hi, Ma," Hannah said.

"Promise me," Syl said.

"Promise you what? I'm not burning anything else, Ma." Dying people could say cryptic things, Hannah knew, but her mother had been speaking in frustrating code for decades.

"I know you don't always understand me, Hannah. But I swear to you, my mother suffered, and I don't want that to have been for nothing. We can't take our safety here for granted. We can't let our guard down." *Our guard.* Hannah's childhood home, a desolate island.

And Mira, of course, still very much alive, had long been treated by Syl like someone already dead.

Mira and her husband, Isaac, had relocated to Florida when Hannah was young, and Syl had rarely taken Hannah to visit. *Your grandmother is a person who needs solitude,* Syl would say. *The chaos of visitors might be too much for her.* The few times they had visited, though, Mira seemed neither weak nor overwhelmed, as Hannah had imagined she'd be.

Their last visit was just a couple of years before Isaac died. Hannah was fourteen, surprised and a little bit scared when Mira came to the door, her face fully lit by its smile. She hugged them quickly and then held Hannah's face in her palms for a moment, just looking at her. Isaac came up behind her then, patted Hannah on the head, and showed her and her mother to their rooms. That night, around the Shabbos table, Mira served honeyed challah with golden raisins, roast chicken with silky carrots and turnips, and a bright pink beet soup, of a color Hannah had never seen before.

"Your grandmother doesn't talk too much," said Isaac over dinner, "but it's not because she isn't listening." And it was true. Mira listened emphatically—her brown eyes bright and open—as Hannah talked about school, about her friends, about drama club. After dinner, they retired to the living room, and while Isaac chatted with Hannah, she noticed her mother and grandmother looking at one another in a way that made her worry. Some silent conversation between the two of them hummed with warning, something she didn't want to touch or interrupt.

On the plane home, Hannah felt like she would explode if she didn't ask the thing she knew she wasn't supposed to. "Ma, is there something wrong with Grandma?"

"No," Syl had snapped, with the defensive tenor Hannah only now understood to belong to liars. Then she calmed a little. "There is nothing wrong with your grandmother. She's incredibly special.

You saw her beautiful meals? Those intricately braided challahs she baked from scratch? Your grandmother speaks a different language. The language of the hands."

The last time Hannah had seen Mira at all was at Isaac's funeral, two years later. Mira had gazed somberly at her husband's casket without crying. Afterward, Syl had helped move Mira into an assisted-living facility. She wasn't quite that old yet, but Mira needed this, Syl insisted. She needed support to do some of the everyday things the rest of us take for granted. She needed protection.

"Promise me," said Syl now, insistent, demanding an answer. "Promise you'll be faithful to the things I taught you. They are important. More important than you know."

"Ma," Hannah started to protest but wasn't sure how, or on what grounds. *What are you so afraid of? What was Mira so afraid of? What made her so strange and quiet? Will I be able to speak freely when you're gone?* "Okay," she said, unsure of what she was agreeing to.

"And don't tell," Syl said, her voice cracking. She looked so small and unmoored that Hannah worried she might fall off the bed or perhaps disappear altogether. "Please."

"Don't tell what, Ma?"

"Just keep our secrets. They're for us. No one else."

Hannah was quiet. Which secrets? From whom? *Can I tell my daughter?* Hannah wanted to ask. *The one you'll never meet, not in a way we can understand, anyway?* With Syl, everything felt a little bit like a secret, and every telling, a bit like betrayal. Syl had succeeded in making the secrets almost indistinguishable from the non.

"Okay," said Hannah again. *What else do you say to the dying?*

And no sooner than she'd made a promise she didn't understand and likely couldn't fully keep, the room, once electric with fear and alarm, went still. Fire extinguished.

Syl lay back, bare eyelids lowered to sallow cheeks. She looked quiet then; not quite contented but almost.

"There was once a season," Syl said, as if it were suddenly story hour. "Such a happy season." Her face lit, remembering. "Sometimes we only get one season. Sometimes that's all we need."

"Wait," Hannah said. "Please tell me."

But Syl's eyes were closed again, and she was silent. Hannah reached out, held her mother's thin, cool wrist in her hand. Something scalding shot through her, leaving in its wake an ache so big it filled her. *A happy season.* Nothing more came, so Hannah sat until she was certain Syl was asleep, and then left.

That night, Hannah couldn't sleep. She was too sweaty to be sharing a bed with another person. She got up as quietly as she could manage, trying not to wake Jon, and paced the hallway naked. She'd given up wearing anything. She could barely stand wearing her own skin. She went to run the shower again, but she'd already showered twice that night, so she walked to the front door and out through it. It was late and dark, and she didn't go far, just stood there naked under the monochromatic sky. She was no free spirit, no nudist. But here she was. She squeezed her eyes shut, trying to forget she was a body, trying to extinguish something she couldn't see, to will something wet, some new kind of rain.

That whole week it did rain, nonstop, a thing for which Hannah felt partially responsible. Monday, Syl watched *I Love Lucy* reruns, her sharp cackle cutting through the laugh track. Tuesday, Hannah at the guest-room door to find Jon sitting with Syl. They hadn't had long to get to know one another, so they weren't close, but there they were, her husband and her mother, together. Jon was looking at Syl, and Syl was looking out the window, elsewhere. Hannah lingered in the cracked doorway breathing smoke, bewitched. Wednesday, Syl's speech slowed, and she called Hannah in with some urgency several times throughout the afternoon. She told beginning after beginning, letting each story trail off into something like sleep. Hannah left rings

of sweat at the edge of Syl's bed, but Syl didn't notice. Thursday, the
rain got reckless and showy, thunder and lightning and heavy winds
that made you feel like you were hearing things. Hannah, loopy, was
tired of sitting so she stood, elbows on the kitchen sink and head in
her hands. It was so quiet, even the faucet stayed lipless.

Friday.

And Hannah between two rooms, skin growing skin, writhing
music spinning deeper into her suffocating core, a pillowed unbreath-
ing, no more room for bones, sweet blown-open, a scream turned
hollow. Someone or something said *push*, and so she did. Tear at this,
tear desperate at that, nothing wet enough, nothing dry. Smoke-darked
vision, and lips no match for ice chips. *Push*, something said. *Push*.
Middle wide. Try. Who was here? The burning like praying, the
burning like singing. Was someone laughing? There must be a more
precise word than *burning*. There must be.

And Syl died, quick and nimble, her face so thin and smooth it was
no longer her face at all.

And Shiva was born. And they called her Shiva before they'd
even begun knowing how to mourn, because she was their mourning.

It was Friday around seven a.m. that some of the neighbors
reported seeing the flames. No one on the park side of the house could
say—not the birds nor the raccoons nor the deer nor the occasional
foxes—but the young man two houses down reported seeing smoke on
his morning run, which, he was sorry to say, he mistook for weather.
The couple across the street, the one with the triplets, noted that the
gray had climbed higher than seemed natural, and that they'd been
concerned. They'd almost called the fire department, but then, quick
as it had risen, the pillar of smoke had fallen, nowhere to be detected
thereafter. And the elderly couple four houses down thought they saw
the actual flames—red, orange, hungry, licking the sky. But flames
don't dance like that, don't fly like that, they told themselves. And it

was so brief. We are old, they said to each other, laughing, convinced they'd been imagining things.

And so Syl died.

And so Shiva was born.

And so the kind of fire no one can catch in time to name.

———

It is told that at Syl's funeral, once the smoke had died down—Hannah no longer burning, Shiva safely on the other side, the passage between two worlds sealed again, at least for the time being—a strange man turned up. A man who offered neither name nor pleasantry, just stood up during the burial and asked whether he might say a few words.

When people tell the story, they tell of a man.

I, of course, know different.

"Once," he began, "there was a woman who lived in a small town and went looking for a bird she'd never met before. *I lost my bird*, she kept saying, though in her language, the phrase she was using meant, *There is a bird I think I am supposed to meet, but we don't know one another yet*. There is no such word in our language, in yours or in mine. Trust me, I've looked.

"The people in the woman's town did not understand her methods, nor what she could possibly be looking for. She was the kind of woman townspeople tended to wonder about, largely because they were projecting their own needs and desires onto her and envied the liberty with which she made controversial decisions. Anyway, these townspeople asked, *What do you mean, a bird*, as the town square filled with an embarrassment of pigeons. *Everywhere there are birds. This town may as well be made of birds.* She ignored them, shimmying under benches and ducking into gray alleys. One day the townspeople would find her rifling through each and every book in the mystery section of the town's small library. The next, they'd see her scuttling up neighbors' walls and peeking down their chimneys, emerging sooty and flushed.

"Finally, one day, the townspeople saw the woman sitting in the town square, staring up at the sky. *What are you doing?* one of them finally got up the courage to ask her. *Why aren't you looking for the bird you're supposed to know?* They had grown used to seeing the woman overturning their trash cans and running her fingers through the tall grasses of their weedy gardens. The woman looked her neighbor straight in the eye. *The bird is dead,* she said. *I'm grieving today.* When the man asked the woman how she knew this, she said simply that the sky had changed color. And this is usually the reason for an altered sky. If you notice, you notice.

"Two beings who were supposed to meet do not meet. And you'd better believe the sky feels it. The man nodded gravely and went immediately home to kiss his wife, though he couldn't name the urgency that drove him there. The woman, meantime, did not resume searching. She spent seven days in the park then, gazing upward in mourning. She was quiet, even though the neighbors drew closer to her now, and they could only assume she was thinking about the bird she was supposed to know but never did."

After the man finished his story, he put a stone on the grave and bowed his head there in quiet for longer than a stranger should. Then he unbowed it, looking around with those curious green eyes. "I, too, hoped she'd find the bird," he said. "The precise bird she'd been looking for. Even after it became clear that she wouldn't. Like someone in love, I hoped even when I knew there was no hope at all."

And then, a nod to those gathered to mourn the loss of Syl Zvigler, he walked away.

Nine

"I'm a widow," said Hannah, when Marla Garfinkel asked within the first two minutes of their conversation in the Beth Emeth lobby whether she "had anyone." Marla was not only a member of the synagogue board but also the director of Garfinkel's Funeral Home, and introduced herself to Hannah one Saturday after services.

"Oh," said Marla. She seemed unfazed. "Do you want to come out to Gertz's with me for lunch tomorrow? It's new, but they have a very convincing pastrami Reuben." Without being sure of what the sandwich had convinced Marla, Hannah agreed.

At Gertz's, they were presented with two fat stacks of meat between slices of rye bread, and Marla wasted no time, applying mustard and lifting one enormous sandwich half to her mouth. As her bright magenta lipstick slowly transferred from her lips to the bread, Marla skipped pleasantries and launched into the harrowing tale of that week's funeral for the matriarch of the warring factions of the Milstein-Singer family.

None of the adults had spoken to one another in years, and the generally recalcitrant college-aged children had shoddily facilitated all the burial details. At the funeral, smack in the middle of the eulogy, Perry Milstein had a heart attack and collapsed. Amid existential panic and emergency logistics, several of his siblings reconciled on the spot, collectively embracing in the hospital parking lot. After Perry survived, they all stopped for sushi on the way home, catching up after a decade of estrangement, and sent Marla a very generous fruit basket in gratitude. "I would have preferred fancy chocolate," said Marla, embarking on sandwich half number two. "But you take what you can get. You wouldn't believe, though, what can happen at funerals. In my line of work, you have a constant backache, but you always come home with a good story."

"I don't know," Hannah said, thinking of the strangeness of her mother's funeral, the horde of birds that had gathered over Syl's grave in the wake of the rabbi's daughter's Cheerio spill, and the mysterious eulogist. "I've seen some weird things at funerals too. I sometimes think I should go into death professionally myself." She knew she could share this inclination with Marla, for whom death was passion, hobby, and profession. "I *am* a widow," Hannah reiterated, assuming it was at least sort of a credential in this department.

Usually, you tell people you're a widow and something washes over their faces. *Widow* implies a secondary tragedy, a tarnish almost worse than your spouse's death itself. You're now a listless and undesirable ghost. But Marla, Hannah could tell, had other things in mind for her widowhood. For Marla, sadness was kin. But it could also be a door to elsewhere.

And, of course, sadness had also been Hannah's kin since long before widowhood, since long before she'd grown this worried about her relationship with her daughter, as if some toxicity from the past could creep all the way into her future. Syl, of course, had the sadness. Mira, it was clear, had the sadness. It was simply an inheritance, the way some families passed down money or heirlooms. Sometimes it was a sadness Hannah could touch. Sometimes it was vast and enveloping as snow. The sadness felt arcane and ancient, calling for reverence and grief all at once. Hannah was always trying to find the balance between the two. She would be in the shower or in a spot of late morning sun or holding a mug of tea or sitting in traffic at four in the afternoon, and suddenly be overcome with it: the feeling that something had shattered, and there she was in the slow, unbearable after-spill. The sadness was unquantifiable. But maybe most important, it was quiet. The family sadness had no sound.

———

In the seven days after the death of a close family member, all the mirrors in your home must be covered. Use your thickest bedsheets, else you be tempted to peek. The mirrors will look like they themselves are ailing, which may or may not be a comfort. The absence of luminance will shrink your home in a way you didn't expect, and the walls will move inward, hungry. After seven days, removing the sheets will feel like an unburdening that might give way to flight. Later, when you are ready, you will look back into the mirror and begin to see things you weren't looking for.

———

Syl Zvigler was physically and spiritually tight-lipped. When she spoke, even the kinder words came out sharp. Syl never laughed in vain, but when she did laugh, just for a moment, her face blew open and lit up so you could see all the sky in it. Mostly, though, a ventriloquist's lips. She wasn't afraid to speak her mind, but she didn't waste her time with pleasantries or with people she didn't think had anything worthwhile to say. In the watchful and cautious thick of her parents'—Mira and Isaac Zvigler's—home, Syl had learned that words weren't meant to be squandered.

The quiet of Syl's childhood was rhythmic and daily. Monday morning in Trenton, New Jersey, in the 1930s: Whistle of the water boiling, snaking hiss and crack of the fire. Steady mechanical whir of Mira's sewing machine, hum of car motors, distant shuffle of the train, clack of sharp heels along the sidewalks. The musical clang of the bell that hung from the door to Mira and Isaac's sweater shop, which sat right below their apartment, and the dull daily thump of yarn parcels falling to the shop floor. Come evening, sounds of homecoming: Doors creaking open, windows opening or closing depending on the weather, people flopping onto chairs or sofas. Crinkle of newspaper, drip of bathtub faucet, sobering news from Europe on a bed of radio static through one neighbor's open window, scratchy spin of a phonograph through another, oil sizzle and garlic pop on the stovetop.

There was not much in the way of words in the Zviglers' little apartment. Love, to be sure, but only occasional conversation. Mira moving from room to room, a notebook in the pocket of her apron. Her impeccable penmanship did the work a voice otherwise might, her hand making such quick work of a story that she could spin a yarn quicker than Isaac could. Mira's notes confettied their table, littered their floors: shopping lists, questions, half tales, whole tales, warnings, reminders. Sometimes, when she got tired of paper, she pantomimed. Isaac, who had known her for so long he understood her quiet like it was a language all its own, spoke sometimes for her or with her. They tag-teamed. Mira needed no one, but for Mira really to tell a story, to transmit the fullness of what she wanted to transmit, at least for a time, she needed Isaac.

And finally, when Syl was twelve, and Isaac sold the shop, trading their soft Trenton existence for a modern New York wholesaling businessman's life, the large Brooklyn brownstone where they landed was no less hushed. In Mira's capable hands, it was an impossible kind of haven: a pocket of quiet swaddled by all that city noise.

Mira Zvigler ran a home buttressed by beliefs and protections that, while bone quiet, were powerful enough to fill every single room. And Syl carried them faithfully, memorized them, tied her fates to them, passed them on to her own daughter.

Some children were afraid of the dark. Syl Zvigler was afraid of the sound. She kept her lips tight because she had grown into someone who often wanted to scream but had never learned how.

It is told that mirrors were once just the stillest darkest water, receptacles for the moon and the occasional curious traveler or wayward fox. Then they were obsidian and more deeply considered. Then copper, bronze, silver, gold, lead. Modern mirrors appeared during the Renaissance, when the Venetians figured out how to make mirror glass clearer and more dazzling than it already was. Back then, mirrors were for the wealthy, so it was a lucrative trade, and rogue Venetian mirror merchants would sell the secrets of the mirror in black markets and back alleys. Those who spent their days bending light and making glass refract in new ways were furious about this betrayal, and the traitors rarely escaped punishment.

The secrets the mirror holds are sacred. Approach any mirror with respect, and it may show you something true.

———

Hannah began seeing Marla for lunch at Gertz's once a week. She was by now certain that if anyone could understand her strange morbid sensibilities and her widow's plight, it was the funeral home lady. Marla was better at talking than she was at listening, but Hannah had started to rely on the ritual of their Wednesday pastrami lunches. She told Marla about the pitying comments she'd gotten at synagogue that week, not to mention the condescending matchmaking efforts of the Metzgers. They'd tried to set her up with a twice-divorced dentist who was imminently retiring to Asheville and loved Jimmy Buffett. She didn't look *that* old or boring, did she? Marla frequented church rummage sales and brought Hannah bags of patterned leggings, Swarovski earrings, and shoulder-padded blazers she hadn't asked for. Once, exceptionally self-satisfied, Marla walked in with a Chanukah sweater, tags still on—a blue menorah embroidered underneath the words JOY VEY, which Hannah could only assume was meant to be some kind of complex holiday pun.

"The Metzgers have nothing on the Ben Davids," said Marla, gleefully leaning in, elbows on the table. The Ben Davids had apparently gone to absurd lengths to try to convince the Flickmans—who were uncommonly strict with their adult children—to allow their daughter Shira to go on a blind date with the Flickmans' handsome and eligible son, Noah, leaving artisanal cheese-and-cracker baskets on their porch and dropping by with extra baked goods and subtle hints every Sunday afternoon. Eventually, and only after the desperate Ben Davids left a particularly expensive bottle of merlot, Sherri Flickman poured herself a glass, called up Judy Ben David, and begrudgingly authorized the date. Shira—and here, Marla smiled wickedly—went out with Noah exactly once before she decided he was way too conservative for her liking and called it off. Marla, unsubtle, delighted in the mundane folly of others. She made death jokes at the wrong times. But she was also becoming a friend. Hannah needed those. There was nowhere in her body her loneliness wasn't. And not just normal widow-lonely, but a cellular lonely that Marla Garfinkel, of all people, seemed to know something about. Marla was someone she knew she could trust with her sadness, inherited or otherwise.

Marla Garfinkel née Horowitz had once imagined she would become something fancy. A film mogul? An art collector? A lady who lunched? For much of her Brooklyn youth—a life lived largely around a rickety table in a dim-lit Bay Ridge kitchen—she couldn't imagine a lunch that didn't consist of egg salad or cottage cheese, but she was convinced she had potential.

Marla went to a local college, held down four part-time jobs, saved some money, moved out on her own, got a perm, joined a synagogue, worked her way up in its baubled ranks, and appointed herself chair of its annual black-tie gala. Yanky Garfinkel ran the local printing operation. Marla called on him to print the programs for the evening. He had good business sense and a decent reputation, not to mention a formidable beard. When he arrived with the boxes of glossy programs, Marla said, "Take those to the sanctuary, please." Yanky nodded, and Marla blushed uncharacteristically as she watched him stride obediently into the sanctuary in his navy suit. After a lightning-speed courtship, she married him. But the marriage didn't last. Yanky, as it happened, was neither a kind nor an industrious man. He was handsome, and he made a mean potato kugel, but he was also unkind, and when he wasn't at the print shop, he didn't like to do much else. Yanky the Schnorrer, as she called him now, emphasis on every syllable. That was it, decided Marla. In this world, you needed to be self-reliant, to have something you could call your own, even when the people around you disappointed you over and over again. Marla already had a car and a set of crystal goblets. So she sold most of her assets, took out loans from the few banks that gave her the time of day, and bought a funeral home.

"Doll," said Marla, biting into her half-sour. Marla favored overly familiar pet names. "My funeral home is the best thing that ever happened to me. It wasn't easy, none of it, but it was worth every bead of sweat and every cent." She wasn't too much older than Hannah, but in a particular light, sagacious Marla Garfinkel appeared to have been alive forever. "You'll have that too," she said, though Hannah hadn't asked. "You'll have that again too."

There are several antiques dealers in the greater New York area who, at this very moment, have notable mirrors in their collections. The retired history professor who works out of a warehouse space in Queens and is known to only his most irreverent and familiar as "The Antiques Jew" has a mirror rumored to have been owned by Albert Einstein. The precocious young couple who recently moved their growing collection to a family property in Rhinebeck procured an ornate and very likely cursed mirror, owned at one time by bootlegger and high-rolling giant of organized crime Arnold "The Brain" Rothstein. And in Borough Park, Nachum Alterman, whose vision is blurred from years of reading the too-small print on very old things, too proud to admit he desperately needs glasses, has, perhaps, the biggest mystery of all in his collection. It is a mirror with a delicate frame of real gold, the crest at the top bearing the intricate likeness of a violin. On the back of the mirror, at the bottom left of the frame, is tiny print that appears to be Aramaic but that Nachum hasn't been able to make out, even with a magnifying glass. And when you look in the mirror, you see yourself clear as day—Nachum has, of course, lovingly given it a beautiful shine. Except for one spot in the bottom right of the mirror's surface. There, when you look into it, you see no reflection. You see only light.

When Jon was dying, Hannah joked that she was going to make a crummy widow, that she'd wear red lipstick and tight dresses to synagogue events way too soon after Jon was gone and alarm all the old ladies. She said it for Jon's sake, and he laughed, like he always did.

For all their differences, Hannah and Jon laughed together with symphonic gusto and alarming frequency. Hannah could be pretty funny when she tried, and with her husband, she'd tried. When she ran out of morbid humor, she lay clinging to him quietly, wondering whether, if she held tight enough, she might outwit death. *I was raised with the tools to do exactly that*, she thought. If Syl had taught her zero other skills, she'd be damned if she wasn't now an expert in at least making a strong spiritual effort to evade catastrophe.

When Jon finally did die, long before Hannah had a Marla, she and Shiva flew solo, and Hannah was thorough. She'd made spreadsheets and phone calls and checklists. With Shiva's help, she'd planned a beautiful memorial service that featured a handsome bagel-and-lox spread and even an interactive funerary trust-building activity, at Jon's request. Afterward, they'd spent days boxing and donating his belongings. Before the fight. Before Shiva left, tearing open their long-held default silence, leaving it gaping there, Hannah inside it now alone.

The one thing Hannah had known she wouldn't be able to handle alone was covering the mirrors. She could barely imagine approaching the hallway mirror, let alone flinging a bedsheet over it. She feared the act of covering it might unlock something terrible in her, something she might not be able to lock back away. She also genuinely wondered—not without some embarrassment—whether covering her mirrors might be seen as a snub by whoever lived on the other side of the glass, and might bring her family further misfortune. Not worth the risk. She asked Shiva to please handle that part. Shiva asked no questions. *Of course*, she said. Her daughter couldn't possibly know or understand what kept Hannah from getting too close to the mirror.

The day the hearse came to take Jon's body from his transitional bed, Shiva had already removed her mother's best bedsheets from the linen closet, stacked and tidily folded. Hannah watched her daughter unfold each as if unwrapping a delicate gift, spreading one over every mirror, smoothing rogue creases with the kind of careful attention that made it look like the most important job on earth.

———

Under the decree of the pharaoh, the ancient Israelites were commanded to stop having babies. So, no sex, said the men. No way, said the women. They were not interested in abstinence. They may have been enslaved, but they had no interest in relinquishing their intimate lives. It was what little they had. It is said that, in order to entice their men to collaborate with them on this erotic resistance, the women used mirrors. They held up their mirrors to their men, teasing, *I'm prettier than you.* The men were surprised to learn they had an investment in competing for prettiest, and surprised to be shown their soft and rounded masculinities. It was only a matter of time before they followed their wives into their bedrooms, despite what the pharaoh had commanded. It was in this way that the ancient Israelites did not stop having sex just because the pharaoh decreed it so. It is also said that the ancient Israelites were redeemed from slavery because of righteous women. This is no coincidence.

Later, when the Temple was being built, these righteous women offered forth the very same copper mirrors to build the laver, the sink where the ancient priests would cleanse their hands before the service. Moses rejected the offering. *These mirrors are vanity and frivolity*, he said. *Not befitting one of the purest sites in our holy sanctuary-in-progress.* He grumbled about it a lot. But God was not pleased with this grumbling. In fact, in God's opinion, the copper mirrors were the most precious contribution to the Temple's construction. In the end, the laver was built from these erotic mirrors. It was built for the priests, but it shone with undeniable invitation.

———

One Thursday, over matzoh ball soup, Marla asked Hannah to join the chevra kadisha. "You said you have experience, right?"

Hannah did. She had not been a regular member of her old synagogue's chevra kadisha but had filled in now and again. It had always felt like a kind of therapy to her, learning how to clean the bodies of the dead, prepare them for burial, and escort them out. Being with the dead somehow made her feel more alive. In their presence, she remembered her own body as something urgent.

"It's not a huge commitment," continued Marla. "But I want trustworthy people. People who aren't freaked out by the prospect of spending time with a dead body."

"It doesn't freak me out at all," said Hannah.

"Well," said Marla, looking Hannah up and down as if this was suddenly a legitimate audition. "I could really use someone like you in the mix, Hannah. I know we haven't known each other long, but I have a good feeling about you."

The words *known* and *good* lingered on the tip of Hannah's tongue before they slid down her throat. She swallowed. She hadn't made a new friend in she couldn't remember how long.

"Well, thank you, Marla." She slurped up a spoonful of soup. "I'll consider it."

Marla looked delighted. "Really?" She wiped at her fading pink lips with her napkin. "You're going to be such a big help to me, doll. I already know I'm going to want to keep you around."

The server came to take their bowls, and Hannah hurried to scoop up her last bite of matzoh ball, thinking about what it might mean to be kept.

———

If a mirror is broken, you will have seven years of poverty. If you place a mirror in front of a sleeping man, he will follow you wherever you go. One may not pray before a mirror. One may not break a mirror. One may break a mirror, but what ensues may be an explosion of grief. One may not dishonor a mirror, as the mirror contains one's soul. One must guard one's soul, so one may not break a mirror. One may not tempt a mirror after someone dies, as the person's spirit is contained in the mirror. One must keep out the restless spirits, so one may not break a mirror. One imagines that breaking a mirror is the worst violation. But sometimes, the easiest thing to do—simply looking into the mirror—is far more consequential.

———

Hannah celebrated her sixteenth birthday with Lydia, Rachel, and Devorah at the house on Gibson Street. Syl made macaroni and cheese and bought an ice cream cake for dessert. Nurturing though she wasn't, birthdays always seemed to bring out her most aggressively affectionate side.

"Ma, I'm sixteen, it doesn't need to be such a thing," Hannah said, but Syl still insisted, lining the table with small bowls of jelly beans.

"Birthdays are important rituals," said Syl, her stern tone out of place for the occasion. "Help me fold these napkins."

Hannah folded. She did not tell Syl, but she was happy to have a small dinner, because the real birthday ritual would come later that night. She'd known for months, and she couldn't believe the day had finally arrived.

Here was the thing: she had it on good authority from something she'd once overheard her mother say and from Rivka, the rabbi's daughter, that if, on your sixteenth birthday, you went to sleep with your window ajar and a piece of that week's challah under your pillow, and if you then woke up a few minutes before midnight, took that piece of challah, burned it by flame of candle, carried that same candle to your mirror, and looked into the mirror at the stroke of midnight to see your face there in the firelight, you would also see the face of your future husband reflected behind you.

The catch—because there is always a catch—is that this magic trick would take two years off the future husband's life. This seemed, to Hannah, at fifteen and in the scheme of things, a small price for so critical an investigation. She was taken by the mirror's mythology and its promise. Her mother had raised her with instructions about what was to be warded off but not very much about what might be invited in. Syl's convictions, cold and slender, passed as empirical, so Hannah rarely questioned them and almost never actively challenged them.

But one Friday night, shortly after Hannah's fifteenth birthday, she'd felt frustrated enough with her mother to think more rashly.

"It's a full moon tonight," Syl said. "Don't forget to close your curtains before you go to sleep."

Hannah's mother had been lecturing her all evening, about everything from why she couldn't skip Thursday-evening services to go to the movies, to why she had to be more careful about the words she used and the tones in which she spoke them, and while fourteen-year-old Hannah would have been mostly docile, fifteen-year-old Hannah was tired of it. She rolled her eyes, letting her pent-up frustration with Syl propel them in a full circle around their sockets before glaring back. "I think I'll keep them open, Ma."

It felt good to talk back. Hannah didn't even flinch at her mother's momentary glare. She was tired of living according to rules she couldn't understand.

"Don't be smart," said Syl. "Unless you'd like to issue an open invitation tonight to be sought after, you will please close your curtains."

Sought after. What did it mean? Maybe she didn't mind being sought after. Daniel Mendelson from student council had left a hand-drawn comic in her locker last week and had finally asked her to go see a movie sometime. He was tall and had very straight teeth. Was this what it meant to be sought after? Maybe she would marry a high school sweetheart. Maybe it would be him.

That was it then. Damn her mother. She was going to try the mirror trick. She would count down to sixteen, and then, finally, she would sit at her mirror and see what a piece of challah and a candle could conjure.

After Hannah's friends left and Syl went to bed, Hannah opened the freezer and took out the slice of challah she'd hidden there, wrapped in a paper towel. She took it upstairs, slid it under her pillow, and lay uselessly awake, eyes burning with anticipation. One of her windows was open, and the bedroom was warm. As she lay, time arched its back. The night stretched out and expanded, shining with the promise of forever, and then shrank into one marble-size minute, everything in the velvety galaxy condensed into the thick seconds that turned 11:54 into 11:55, when Hannah's alarm finally sounded.

Her body crystallized with fear at the sound. One by one, lining up in her chest: anticipation, preliminary regret, edge of anger, and that sadness. Whatever it was that made her mother sad and that had made her mother's mother sad before her. The sadness was the temperature of glass, the size of an eternity of stretched-out nights. She steeled herself, embarrassed by the childlike urge she had to run to her mother's room, to confess and beg for absolution. She needed to do things differently this time. She sat at the vanity, lit the candle, held the bread to the flame, prayed her mother wouldn't smell the burning from down the hall. Then, she waited.

In the mirror, she saw herself. Her freckles lit by the blue-dark, eyes spooked wide. Her moon-shaped face cut by worry, eyelashes long in the flamelight. It was a simple face, a good face. Nothing to be afraid of. The flame licked the last of the bread, and she shook the ashes off her hand into the wastebasket.

Was it ridiculous to believe that she would meet her future husband tonight? If she did, would she tell Lydia or Rachel or Devorah about it? If the husband was someone she didn't yet know, she hoped for bright black eyes, kind and curious. Nice cheekbones, and curly hair to complement her waves. A nightgown strap slipped down one of her shoulders and she adjusted it, realizing she wasn't sure if, when she saw the husband-to-be, the husband-to-be would also be able to see her. This suddenly felt like important information to have had before starting the ritual. Quickly, candle still in her right hand, she leaned from her chair and reached for the pink blouse draped over the chest at the foot of her bed. Passing the candle from hand to hand, eyes steady on the mirror, she put an arm in each sleeve and buttoned two of the buttons. She smoothed her hair, dipped her pinky into the pot of tinted lip gloss on her vanity, and applied some. If there was a chance he would see her, she needed to look ready.

11:59. Hannah blinked. A creak from the hallway, and she held still. She could hear Syl's litany of *nevers* as though her mother was speaking them directly in her ear. *Never walk barefoot on wet grass or eat cake warm from the oven; never pour someone a drink backhanded or clip fingernails over the floor; never wear socks in bed or walk shoeless in the home; never miss a day of prayer; never throw bread; never spill the honey or the salt. Never bargain with a mirror.* Hannah knew it was on the list somewhere, probably toward the top. *Never do anything that might invite an unwelcome spirit.* When Hannah asked what *unwelcome* meant, Syl always said, *You'll know what's unwelcome when it feels like something you shouldn't touch.*

Midnight. Emboldened by her own follow-through, Hannah touched the mirror with her right hand. It was cool against her fingertips, and the pleasure she felt when she touched it surprised her. She pressed her fingers firmly into the glass and sucked in her breath. A little bit of hot wax dripped onto her finger. She adjusted the candle. If Hannah was powerful enough to invite what she shouldn't—if it might actually come inside—what other power might she uncover? Her mother, she thought, was a coward. And she felt angry at all the cowardice. What was the point of not touching? Touch—and now she stroked the mirror a little bit, coaxing—felt so good. *I can touch this,* thought Hannah, though she knew she was still unpracticed. *I am not my mother. I could be powerful.* It was the first time she'd thought the words and actually begun to believe them.

Hannah shifted in her seat, the skin around her wrists and thighs beginning to prickle and sing. She began to feel large, the vanity chair underneath her less consequential. Time opened its maw, yawning, and the dark room grew ocean-wild around her, pouring her into midnight.

And then, behind her in the mirror, something rose. Just an indigo blur at first. Hannah squeezed her eyes shut and opened them again. The blur came into focus. It was a face. A woman's face.

Hannah's stomach folded. The details of the woman's features swam in and out of focus in the dark, but the woman was a fact. Her eyes, the clearest part of her, were uncommonly green. Her skin, like sand, seemed of no particular age, and her lips were parted like a question. Hannah hadn't thought about what she would do if a face came into view, so she just held the woman's gaze. Who was this woman? A future Hannah? Hannah's eyes weren't green. Maybe she was related to the husband, the one she had staked her bets on encountering? Had she done the ritual wrong? The woman's shape quivered, and Hannah felt a sharp stab of fear. The candle quivered too.

It didn't occur to Hannah, of course, that the woman in the mirror was the one whose life might be cut short by her looking, the one whose green eyes Hannah would only see again decades later.

Hannah also didn't notice how dense the dark had grown. The room had filled with wind, even though the hot night was still. She watched for many minutes as the woman's face flickered, eventually fading, nearly gone. Not completely, though. Still, the green eyes, distant and blinking softly in the dark. Hannah's ears rang, and she was struck by the desire to sing. She felt the eyes on her, even as the green finally dissolved into black, and a warm feeling from the center of her stomach down to her thighs.

And then the wind stilled, and the dark blew out.

Syl stood in the doorway in her black silk robe. Her red hair was matted, but her gray eyes were clear with rage. She had never looked so tall.

"Hannah," Syl roared, as if giving her daughter a new name.

Syl didn't say anything else, just stood in the doorway, looking at Hannah in her pink blouse with her cold mirror and her cold candle. Hannah knew. She had invited in what she shouldn't have, exactly the thing her mother and her mother's mother before her had been trying to ward off all these years. It was the worst kind of betrayal. And—candle out, crosswinds gone—Hannah felt small and scared and full of regret.

"What did you do?"

Hannah had a hard time finding the words over the pounding in her chest. "I just wanted to try the mirror trick. I just wanted to see." She crossed her arms over her thin blouse and nightgown. "You won't let me touch anything, Ma. You won't let me see for myself. I don't care anymore." She realized she was crying.

"This is no trick. Do you know how dangerous this is? Do you understand what you're playing with?" Syl's voice was hoarse. "When you leave this household, I can't stop you from being as careless as you choose to be. But in my house, what I have taught you is to be taken seriously. Do you hear me?"

Hannah nodded. All her hunger for what the mirror held dissipated into a melt of grief. She felt young and very old all at once. Syl stood for another moment, her face opaque. Then she pulled Hannah's door shut and walked back down the hall.

Hannah got into bed without taking off her blouse. She was shivering, though it wasn't cold. She had been close to something. Someone. She could feel it here, even still. Now the clock read 12:22, and time was regular again. Hannah felt like throwing something hard directly into that mirror and smashing it. She clenched her teeth and mashed her face into the pillow, muffling tears she didn't understand, all the while telling herself to pull it together and go to sleep. That it hadn't been a big deal.

As early light and birdsong seeped in through her window, so did a dull new resignation. Hannah would keep clipping her nails over the toilet and refilling the salt bowls with every new moon, because it was her duty. A daughter effectively made afraid, she would heed her mother. She knew that she had stepped too close to the edge. All her questions spat back in her face, unanswered, and somewhere, the woman from the mirror floated farther and farther away. Enough with the asking. There were never any answers, much less anything she could touch.

It felt like a clean break, quick and without further ceremony. First morning of sixteen, sleepless and woozy, Hannah went downstairs to eat breakfast. The grief she'd felt the night before was still heavy in her, but over it, a layer of resolve. Hannah would stay focused on what she could touch. What she could see in the light of day. Nothing more.

———

To understand the law of reflection, it is important to understand that light is not beholden to time, and that time is not beholden to any law at all. That mirrors were destined for greatness, and if pushed, they'll remind you. That the angle of incidence creates a shape that mimics the mouth when it's surprised. That the angle of reflection is negotiable if you offer the mirror something in return. It is difficult for us to hold two things in our minds at once: For example, we remember that the law of reflection is fixed. We forget, however, that we are not.

———

The nearly two years that stretched between the night of the mirror trick and the morning Hannah left for college were characterized by a sustained and quiet tension. Syl hunched at the dining room table, face in her notebooks. Hannah, scarce as she could make herself, sat in the corner of the living room with her homework or holed up in her room on the phone, door shut to her mother's dour puttering. *What are you always in a fight about anyway?* friends would ask. *It's complicated,* Hannah would say. *We're not in a fight. My mother is just a problem.* Dinner was perfunctory, rituals and festivals kept brief.

It was a nocturnal period too. Sometimes Hannah woke in the night and padded downstairs for no real reason, thinning brown carpet between her toes all the way to the living room, where the furniture appeared ominous and animate in the dark. Sometimes she found herself standing in the foyer—the glossy black and white tiles she loved cool under her feet—as though she'd meant to go somewhere.

She could still clearly see her father's bags lined up against the wall there from the day he left, ghost luggage. The smell of her father's duffel bag and the anger that rang in her ears long after he'd gone were the only things she remembered clearly from that day, but Robert always felt like a fixture in the purgatory of that foyer. This was the exit. The place you stood and took one last look before you left.

And even though she wasn't actually going anywhere, it was good to remember it was there, just in case.

Sometimes late at night, even in her bedroom with the door closed, Hannah could hear her mother traveling around the house too. Shuffling around or compulsively rearranging the furniture. And just once, springtime, there was that late-night visitor.

She'd heard someone knock and then heard Syl hurry to the door. 11:14, said her bedside clock. *Thank you.* A woman's voice. Then the kettle boiling. Her mother didn't typically have guests, not even during normal hosting hours. She had a few friends, but she usually went out with them instead of inviting them home. Hannah rarely had guests to Gibson Street either. It wasn't that she couldn't; it was just that the house—her mother—lacked a warmth. It wasn't *comfortable.* Nobody grinning or hugging or offering bowls of popcorn or asking how anybody was.

Hannah sat on the floor of her room, straining to hear what was happening downstairs. Mugs on the table, spoons. Hushing, her mother hushing, and a long, whispery conversation, whose slight peaks in volume Hannah caught in bits. *How have you . . . She didn't know . . . I'm not seeing it . . . I know . . . my mother.* Stirring, someone stirring honey into tea. A sigh—long, dramatic. *She's going to college . . . Alone . . . I can't tell . . . tell . . . Feel anything?* And then, unmistakably, a change in tone, a pronouncement at speaking volume: *It's still here.*

After that mystery visit, Syl had thawed a bit. Mostly only technically, as if she were a robot who'd read a textbook on how to parent a high school student. *How was school?* she would ask. *Any weekend plans? What do you want for dinner?* Hannah knew her mother loved her. But there was something else there. Something about Hannah—or, more likely, she now understood, about Syl herself—that scared Syl too much to get very close at all.

She told no one about the mirror—what it held, and what it had taken back. More nights than she liked to admit, she'd wake up, splayed and wanting, missing the softness of those green eyes and the generosity of night's cover. She'd remember then, and close her mouth over it, embarrassed to realize that, once again, she'd been crying.

When Hannah emerged from the dim strangeness of her final years of high school and arrived at college, she felt like someone seeing daylight for the first time. The bright, well-peopled campus of the state school she'd been so excited to attend could not have been more different from the shadowy internal world she'd shared with her mother. At first, she skulked timidly around, overwhelmed and supposing herself uninteresting to these light-dappled students. Eventually, though, she began to realize the simple appeal of being at college: out of the context of home, you could be anyone you wanted.

She'd half wanted to put on a sweater set and pretend to be as well-adjusted as the next Jewish coed. But Hannah had always been a little shadowy; she'd been made that way, and there was no running from that. At least now, outside of her mother's house, she could be her own kind of shadow.

Death fascinated her, but not in the threatening and supernatural ways it had always captivated Syl. For Hannah, death was inevitable, a practical consideration rather than an otherworldly one. Death was worldly. But it allured her no less. She spent nights alone with popcorn and documentaries on the end of life. She read a book on the history of embalming and a fat philosophical tome on the death rituals of world religions. She read Nietzsche and Maimonides, and when she liked a boy, she tried to talk with him about mortality. If it worked, she considered it a win and decided he liked her back.

Her unconventional interests were balanced by her highly conventional major—business, which she'd ultimately chosen for its practical potential after yearningly studying the art department's course catalogue. And egged on by her new business-school friends and the girls from the Jewish student union, she began to attend mixers and met people who had blissfully little to do with the tenebrous world from which she'd come. She bought festive dresses and tight mock turtlenecks. She occasionally went dancing. Invested in her first lipstick. Listened to the songs she loved on repeat. She joined clubs: Jews in the Woods for Sunday hikes; Art Appreciation Club for going downtown to see the galleries; and Cinema Club, because Hannah loved movies and admittedly had developed a weakness for boys who were also cinephiles.

She went to Saturday services at the campus Jewish center, but some Friday nights, she'd sneak into a movie the Cinema Club kids were watching, telling herself that, even though turning on a movie on Shabbos was forbidden, she was only a bystander. Only just watching. Those nights, she'd head directly to bed afterward, where she'd send messages to the cosmos in defense of her reckless behavior. Those nights, she avoided the mirror. Days, though, she felt fully awake. Nothing and no one looking over her shoulder. It was maybe the happiest she'd ever been.

And then she met Jon Margolin.

Jon was a transfer student who started sophomore year and joined Cinema Club just in time for animal week. The co-chairs changed their minds at the last minute, deciding to screen *National Velvet* instead of *Jaws*. One of the co-chairs responded to the groans of each attendee patiently. *It's animal week. Murderous shark story or heartwarming movie about a horse?* In the end, the other co-chair brought extra buttered popcorn and several flasks of bourbon, so the complaining presently subsided, and by the end of the movie, even the few frat boys in the Cinema Club ranks had to pretend they weren't crying. After, standing around some cans of contraband beer, Hannah noticed Jon. Tall and the only redhead in the room; there was a certainty to the way he looked around, taking everything in. He was eating a chocolate bar, still half wrapped.

"Want some?" He extended the bar, his eyebrows zigzagging. She smiled and shook her head. "I'm Jon," he said, offering his hand.

"I'm Hannah," she said, taking his hand and not shaking it, but standing there and holding it as long as she dared. He didn't let go.

Hours later, Hannah and Jon were still sitting on the floor of the dark rec room, his jacket around her shoulders. Jon, as it turned out, loved horses. Loved all animals. Loved movies. He was studying psychology, but he wanted to make movies one day.

"What about you?" he said. By this time, one of his freckled hands was on her arm—nonchalant but not accidental.

Hannah thought about what she could tell Jon. That she was still afraid of her mother. That she was haunted by a woman she'd seen in a mirror. That she was more religious than she thought she would be, and that she had wanted to learn about art but instead was here learning about business, just because it had seemed safer. Something about this boy's crooked eyebrows, though, brought her back. Reminded her that she was something weirder than a business major and that she didn't entirely mind.

"Well," she said. "Have you read much Nietzsche?"

Jon laughed. He had a great laugh. "Nope," he said.

Hannah's smile was involuntary. He didn't seem remotely freaked out by her oddball answer, which, to her, was answer enough.

"I'm a business major," she said. "But I've been reading a lot of existentialist philosophy. I'm very interested in death."

"Well," said Jon. "I'm very interested in life myself, so maybe we'll have something to talk about." He winked at her like a cartoon character, the way only Jon Margolin ever could.

A year later, Jon took her to a screening of *Jaws*. At the ice cream store afterward, he proposed.

The wedding was humble, fairly traditional. They were two kids right out of college after all, so it needn't have been a major splash. There were yellow tulips, though, and there was a beautiful pink cake, made by the most whimsical kosher caterer they could find—a hippie baker named Yael who ran a small home-kitchen operation.

And Hannah, joyous as she felt, wanted to do a little something for her shadows, the ones she'd never quite left behind. So Jon wore a white tuxedo, and Hannah stood under the chuppah wearing all black.

The waiter came with the check. Marla put up her bejeweled left hand, as if to say, *don't worry, I got this.* She liked to feel like a big macher, Marla Garfinkel did, even if Hannah knew her funeral home was truly all she had.

"I'll do it," said Hannah.

"What's that, dear?" Marla was absently signing the check.

"I'll join the chevra kadisha."

"Oh, doll, that's wonderful." Marla beamed at Hannah as if she'd just agreed to her hand in marriage. "Welcome to the best funeral club in town." She put the check down with a flourish. "We're all dying to have you."

"I bet you say that to all your recruits." Hannah looked down, suddenly shy. She imagined being of use. And that this group of people who occupied the most secret corners of the night, frequently peering behind the veil that separates us from everything we can't see, might be the people to whom she actually belonged. Exactly two disastrous and begrudging internet dates since Jon died, and somehow, a platonic pastrami with Marla Garfinkel and the prospect of a lifetime of burial rituals and death puns was what made Hannah feel quivery.

Marla waved away the dessert menu, and the server took their empty plates, and in the quick lift of the pile of mustard-dotted and lipstick-smeared napkins, there it was: the sadness. The spill of it, bright and wide. Into the bottom of Hannah's glass of ginger ale, into her lap, across the red tabletop, and onto the checkered floor. Lazy light flooded in through the windows, and afternoon announced itself like some combination of warning and promise. Hannah closed her eyes and basked, letting the spill slow. In this moment, it felt familiar, like someone she recognized but couldn't place. *Are you still here?* The question flashed behind her eyelids as it sometimes did, and she never knew whether she meant to address it to her husband, her mother, or the echo of someone she may have imagined in the dark nearly forty years ago. *Hello.* She breathed in, squared the sadness like a pair of shoulders until they felt more like wings.

"Hello." She said it out loud this time, in case anyone was listening.

"Hello," said Marla, not missing a beat. She just brushed the crumbs off her lap, picked up her oversize purse, and like a gentleman, offered Hannah her arm.

March 4, 1921

Dear L,

I have to admit it is strange to be writing to someone I've just met. But I also must admit how dearly I have been longing for someone to write to, especially now. It is uncommon for sixteen-year-old girls here to spend time writing, and I am self-conscious to be sitting at the table while Mama does the laundry. But the truth is, I have always loved writing things down, much as it is discouraged for girls my age, and for women at all. And of course, no one is to write for frivolous reasons. Men can write great literature or God's word. Women, they can write shopping lists, letters to cousins or friends. But I've written hopeful letters in secret, and the truth is, I'm grateful to know someone real is reading this on the other side. Jacob got me the paper scraps from Reb Itzhak the soyfer, and we both saw Mama's eyebrows go up when he brought them home to me. But you told her this was important for my healing. I heard you tell her myself when you were leaving yesterday. I hope she understands. It is an unusual assignment, but I am glad for it. I am nervous to write my heart on the page to a stranger. But something compels me to trust you, to do what you think best. Something in your face encourages me.

Mama says you are from a neighboring village, one so much smaller than our modest Ropshitz that I probably wouldn't know its name. Is it true? Does your village have a name? I am not sure I am allowed to ask questions of you, but perhaps, if I am lucky, next time you come, you'll tell me a little bit more about yourself. It seems only fair, no? Maybe you have been to Ropshitz before for one of our famous fairs? People from neighboring towns do attend sometimes, with their families and in their finest dress. I love to see the men and women adorned in velvet, in hats and silk head coverings, wearing pearls and crystals, lambswool and embroidery. Rich, poor, everyone dresses opulently for the fair, much as we do for the major Jewish festivals. If you have been here before, I will be curious to hear about it. I have a keen eye. I believe I have encountered everyone in Ropshitz at the fair, or at the butcher when Mama sends me, or at the synagogue. And I have never seen you before.

In the event this was your first time visiting, I will tell you that we are like a small island in a sea of surrounding Polish villages. Papa says this is a danger, but I feel protected by the greenery that envelops us and the Wielopolka River, which encircles us like a tight embrace. A small handful of yidn hidden among the hills. I wonder which bridge you crossed to get here, and if you noticed the rabbi's house on the corner or our beautiful synagogue. If my charge were to show you the town, I would first take you inside the synagogue, where the walls are painted by our own artisans, pictures of foxes and wolves, birds and fish, lush trees and flowers. I would never dare tell Papa, but when everyone else at synagogue is praying, I am looking at the walls, imagining traveling elsewhere.

If my charge were to show you the town, I would also take you past the flour mill, where Papa works, and past the church (we are told to hold our breath when we pass, so that we do not catch a curse), and all the way to the outskirts of town, to my favorite place: the forest. It is thick, and, especially in spring and summer, the trees are crowned with glossy leaves, shiny as emeralds, yellow at the parts that catch the sun. Sadly, Mama cautions me not to go there. She says it is dangerous to leave the confines of where we are. I have never been allowed to wander to the forest and had only been there twice until three weeks ago.

But that's a story for next time. And my charge is not to show you the town.

I know you are here to help me. I don't know if you have heard the rumors about me, the ones that make people stay far away. To be near me may mean to be close to what none of us should touch. I used to deny this with all my heart, but I'm no longer so sure it bears denying.

I will see you the next time you come. May it be soon. I don't know you well, but your company already brings me comfort that nothing has in quite some time.

Yours,
Mira

Ten

M el Rosen had clearly been at the café for a while by the time Shiva arrived. "You're late," he said. He had the tail end of a frothy mug in front of him, and his plate bore two neatly discarded pumpernickel crusts.

"I'm sorry," said Shiva. "I lost track of time."

Winter break had been brief and busy and whiskey-sodden. She'd spent a week volunteering with Aria's company at a community show they'd staged in a former church in Queens; a few days hibernating with a fat novel and the first season of *Fleabag*; and two days in Beacon with Levi for luxury, not for anyone's mandolin. She'd forgotten the clip at which life moved when school was in session, and the clip at which her adviser moved, making him slightly early one hundred percent of the time.

"In any event," said Rosen. "Did you know that Isaac Bashevis Singer was notoriously late?"

"I didn't," said Shiva.

"Singer was a real character." He sipped at the foam at the bottom of his mug. "I got to meet his son, you know."

Shiva uselessly glanced at the menu. Once Rosen started talking, there was no coffee to be had.

"I met him at a gala once in LA. We were seated next to one another. We both hated the soup and then hated the lamb. I never liked lamb; it's a controversial position, but I can't help it. And then?

We hated the dessert. Some kind of sweet cheese thing. What kind of a dessert is cheese? We went out for a proper dinner afterward, steak and scotch. Great guy. Prolific writer in his own right."

"Wow," said Shiva. "I didn't even realize he had a son."

"He died," said Rosen. "The son." He wiped his mouth. "Anyway, let's discuss your research. Your proposal."

"Oh, yes," said Shiva. It was time. She'd sent Rosen several paragraphs, written and then rewritten, about what it might mean—outside of the literal demon world—to be individually, collectively, or culturally possessed. She'd posed questions: *Where do we see examples of this? Of what significance were questions to An-sky? What were the sources of his own possession, and how do we see them manifest in his life's work?*

She'd worked hard on her application and on this Warsaw proposal—perhaps harder than she needed to—but she'd still kept it necessarily vague and indeterminate. She reminded herself that she'd stated her own conditions: she wouldn't fully know exactly what she was doing until she got where she was going. Her questions—the same ones she'd submitted with her application, the ones that had, at the very least, been compelling enough to convince the committee she'd been worth betting on—were still loose and open-ended enough to leave her some room to improvise. She didn't need to commit to anything just yet. She needed only to get Rosen's research contacts, and his blessing, and she hoped to walk away with both without much struggle.

"It's certainly interesting," he said. "But it's still fairly vague. Of course, you've read a lot yourself, so you know that much work already exists about An-sky's questionnaire and about the role of ethnography in creating a usable folklore. I think you're asking good questions here, but I wonder what your unique take on it would be. How would you apply An-sky's ethnographic logic to storytelling in the contemporary world, for example? How will you put these ideas in conversation with the ample existing scholarship on this subject?"

She started to speak, but he didn't let her get a word in.

"Look, what's done is done," he said. "Just show me. When you go there, show me I'm not making a mistake here with you."

He pulled a folded piece of paper out of his pocket and handed it to her.

"I have a good nose for these things, and there's a part of me that still wants to tell you that you should go off and pursue creative writing." Shiva's chest contracted. She opened the piece of paper, which had several names and emails written on it in a crooked scrawl that sloped down the right side of the ripped page. "But you're off to Warsaw in just a couple of weeks, and I'm ready to be proven wrong. It wouldn't be the first time." He looked her in the eyes, and she willed herself to look back. "I think these contacts will be solid places to start, given your interests."

Shiva scrambled for a redeeming thing to say. "I can do this," she said, but she said it so quietly that even she wasn't convinced by her pronouncement.

Rosen didn't respond. He simply extended his hand, which Shiva dutifully shook. "So," he said stiffly. "Have a great trip. I'll expect you to be in touch."

Shiva felt frayed, unsure whether she should walk out or wait for Rosen to walk out, or just hide in the bathroom until it was all over.

"You should get a maple latte," he said, solving the problem for her, and putting on his jacket. "You know, I run into Gwyneth Paltrow here sometimes when she's in town. Very nice. I knew her father. Jewish guy. She swears by these lattes."

A maple latte did sound called for. She got in line, her brain making frantic emotional calculations.

On the one hand, academia had never really been the point. In part, Shiva simply needed access. She'd zealously maintained her unfounded conviction that S. An-sky and this trip would lead her somewhere crucial; had even fantasized that she'd be led all the way through the thicket of past lives to some nonexistent archival room that contained the key to all the mysteries that had shaped her.

On the other hand, though, academia *was* the point. Before she'd finally emerged into the queer and expansive life she was finally beginning to live, so many of her unformed questions had been about how to inhabit identities she didn't quite yet understand. How to want. These questions had never required articulation. They took the form of fashion experiments, like walking out the front door in high-heeled boots and trying to strut. They took the form of experiments in desire, buying a cock at an inappropriate hour of the morning—brilliant silicone magenta, currently gathering dust in her nightstand drawer—after a night spent in lace, trading queer erotica readings with Dani, eager to feel the cock's malleable heft hang from her like nothing ever had. They took the form of experiments in femme excess, trying to move fully into herself—her body, her voice, her laugh, a bold color, a low cut—without worrying she'd expand past her own capacity.

But now, for the first time, she wanted to ask questions with more precision. To put them into words. And perhaps even to begin to answer them. And this was something she dearly hoped to find here, at school, in her research. After all, she felt like she'd looked everywhere else.

Whether or not it was the point, academia was how she was getting to Warsaw, and she would need to deliver. Somehow, she would need to use Rosen's doubt as fuel.

Blessedly, by the time she got back to the table, he was gone. The initial fluttery excitement she'd felt about her trip had stilled into apprehension. Her ideas and her instincts were truer than anything she'd been able to put on a grant application, she reminded herself. They would animate her, and she would prove him wrong. Or, maybe, she would prove herself right. That had always been the plan. She would go seeking, and she would find something sharp and true, something that would cut away all the rest.

Her phone dinged. It was G. *I just made chocolate mousse for the first time. Want some?*

Shiva grinned, the shadow of the terrible meeting momentarily lifting. *Please*, she texted.

Their texting, rhythmic, had burgeoned into something humbly symphonic these last weeks. The notes between them at intervals, like little constant offers, and Shiva, falling into the new shape glee had taken, kept saying yes. Shivery every time she got a message from across the world. G, whose given name, it turned out, was Gabriela. G, who felt like someone Shiva had known for a long, long time, even though that was silly; they hadn't even really met yet.

She sipped. Admittedly, the latte was delicious. Her phone dinged again. *You still want to get on the back of my bike?* Imagining herself on the back of a Polish stranger's motorcycle sent her coffee down wobbly. She would need a green dress. She couldn't explain why, but she felt clear it would be necessary. A green dress and a new matte red and a fresh haircut and a stack of blank notebooks. And a scheme, of course, for how she was going to get herself approximately 223 miles away from Warsaw, all the way to Ropshitz.

Absolutely, she texted. She had quickly reached the bottom of her coffee, which made her bold, and she texted G again. *I'm thinking about the first thing I'll say when I meet you.* Send. *I start shy, but I get bold. Takes me just a minute. And maybe an engine.*

She left the coffee shop and went off in search of a green dress. Several vintage shops later, she had one in hand. *Check*, she thought. She looked at her phone. No dings. G usually replied quickly or at least let Shiva know when she'd be going offline. Maybe she was busy with the chocolate mousse. Shiva pushed her luck, texted G one more time. *Maybe you'll kiss me first, stranger?* Stranger—a fact and, now, a term of endearment.

She took the train home, making mental lists of things she wanted to get done by the weekend. She should call her mother. Even though Poland seemed to fall squarely in the category of things she could no longer talk to her mother about, she'd begun to feel guilty about all these Warsaw machinations, like she was going behind Hannah's back to investigate their shared ancestry all on her own. Maybe she was, and maybe that was okay, but it still felt wrong. Maybe she just needed to accept that her relationship with her mother had largely come undone. They were sad little satellites now, spinning farther away from one another, headed toward distinct galaxies. That was natural, wasn't it? Some of her friends didn't speak to their mothers or had mothers who didn't speak to them. Those friends were making their motherless way. It certainly wasn't the end of the world.

Someone got on the train and briefly lip-synched to Boyz II Men. A platinum-blond woman with a businesslike chin wearing pants that could only be described as slacks stared in annoyance at her phone. A kid dropped a fruit snack, and her mother tried to convince her not to pick it up and eat it.

No, that wasn't true. It might be the end of the world. Or at least the end of something. That vertical line through history, through her body. It ran through her mother too. She needed Hannah. Hannah was a part of the question, the one that would gesture toward the story. She was also a part of the answer. Maybe that was why things felt so complicated. Hannah should have been both. And lately, she'd been neither. She would call her mother later, she decided. After she tried on the green dress.

The first thing Shiva did when she got home, after hanging up the dress—perfect, structured, sleeveless, emerald—was check her phone. Nothing. Just her own *Maybe you'll kiss me first, stranger?* sitting there, unread. Or no, wait. Read. The checkmark, the one that meant it had been read. Her stranger must just be out or sleeping. It was hard for her to keep the time zones straight, anyway. G would text back soon, Shiva told herself.

She got a seltzer out of the fridge and called her mother.

"Hey," she said. "I'm just getting ready for this trip, and I was thinking of you."

"Hi," said Hannah. "Good to hear your voice." She sounded tired but not sad, which was unusual.

"You sound good, Ma," said Shiva. "What are you up to?"

"Well," said Hannah. "I'm joining the chevra kadisha at my new synagogue. I've actually become friendly with the funeral home director who's on the synagogue board, and she really wants me to get involved. Which is nice!"

"Classic," Shiva said, and Hannah laughed.

"I know, I know. I just . . . It's just a way of being there. Being closer."

"I get it."

"You do?"

Shiva did get it. It was nice to remember that, sometimes, Hannah made a kind of sense to her. "That's why I'm going to Warsaw, kind of. To get closer."

Hannah was quiet for a beat. "Yeah. Warsaw will be pretty close."

That guilt again, then. She knew her mother hadn't ever traveled to Warsaw. Maybe Hannah should be the one taking this trip.

She weighed the question only for a second before asking.

"Have you ever wanted to go to Poland yourself?"

"It's a good question. I've always been curious about it, of course, all that history." Hannah's voice tightened. "Your great-grandmother never really talked about it much. Anything I ever knew about the City of Laughter came from my mother, you know? And it wasn't much. Those Jewish wedding jesters. All these ideas about laughter and humor being really holy and important. It was a very religious shtetl; not all of them were, but this one was. You know, but the point is, Mira's time there was hard."

"I do," said Shiva. "But wasn't everyone's? I mean, if you were Jewish and living where and when Mira did, isn't it likely your life was hard too?"

Hannah sighed. "Yes, Shiva. But Mira's time was its own kind of hard."

"Yeah, I just—" said Shiva. She shouldn't. Not again, not now.

"What?" Something uncommonly spiky in Hannah's voice.

"Look, I'm not going to try to talk to you about this right now, not in any real way. I don't even exactly know what I'm looking for on this trip. So I guess just . . . If there's more you remember about our family's stories, or more you decide you're comfortable telling me? Now would be the time, Ma. Dad is still gone. Still just us here. And if you want to tell me there are no ghosts between us, then fine, tell me that. But tell me something." Her breath came fast, like she was panting. And then, sharply, as quickly as she felt certain it was true: "I'm going on this trip, and I'm not going to ask you again."

A crinkle on the other end. A silence that stretched out to forever.

"I'll think about it," Hannah finally said.

Shiva's eyes burned at even this hint of yes. She pressed her lips together and felt them silently form into something *please*-shaped.

"How else are you?" Hannah surprised her by changing the subject, continuing the conversation instead of hanging up the phone.

She felt panicky, like she didn't want to talk to her mother about anything real. It felt momentarily impossible. She knew that if Jon were on the other end of the line, she'd want to tell him everything, to regale him with her triumphs and flirtations and foibles, the Brooklyn tales that had always made him laugh.

In recent conversations with her therapist about her mother, Sharon had suggested experimenting with *opposite action*. In moments when she wanted to recoil from her mother, she should try moving *toward*. What you are recoiling from in those moments, Sharon said, is not just your mother. It's also yourself. Shiva didn't fully understand this, but she trusted Sharon, so she tried.

"Well, here's something. I've been texting a lot with that girl."

"What girl?"

"That Polish girl I mentioned when we last talked, who I met online. We've been texting, and it's been . . . Well, it's honestly been incredible."

"Wow," said Hannah. Shiva could hear her mother formulating on the other end. "I hate to sound as old as this is going to make me sound, but I can't believe you can just get on the internet now and find yourself a Polish lesbian."

Shiva laughed. "I just really like her. I can't explain it. I've never even heard her voice. But I message her, and I feel like I'm messaging someone I've known forever." She glanced down at her phone, the read message. No reply.

"That's really something," said Hannah, who at the very least sounded like she meant it.

"It is," said Shiva. It really was. Something. "You're okay, though?"

"Day by day," said her mother.

"Okay," said Shiva.

"Okay," said Hannah. "Exactly."

After she hung up with her mother, she looked back at the app. Nothing. Hours had gone by, and no text from G. Something felt wrong.

She couldn't stop herself, then, masochist that she was, from going to Instagram and typing in Dani's name. Dani had posted a poolside photo just a few days prior from somewhere warm. She was wearing a tank top and trunks covered in tiny palm trees, and standing next to a femme with long dark hair and sulky eyes in a pink vintage two-piece. The *poet*. Twin grins, the kind you can't contain when the connection, Shiva's teeth clenched at the memory, is *so intense*. How many photo opportunities had Dani and the poet forgone over the summer, when they'd begun dating behind Shiva's back? How many cemeteries had they kissed in? The poet didn't look the cemetery type, but then again, she was a poet.

Shiva squeezed her eyes, as if trying to make a headache go away, and then opened them again. Maybe she could win this night back. She pulled out the perfect green dress, ready to be romanced by its contours again and by the possibilities it promised, but she no longer felt like it. She texted Levi, *I'm scared the Polish stranger is ghosting me.* She stood at the counter and finished off her seltzer, wishing it were something stiffer. Mostly, she was hot and dehydrated. Sad. She put the green dress back on the rack. Nobody texted, and nobody called. Inside of all this fitful waiting, she fell asleep.

March 17, 1921

Dear L,

Thank you for coming back yesterday. It was good to see your face again. The herbs you give me taste bitter, but I enjoy the time you spend sitting with me. I hope you aren't bothered by my saying so, but you have a face for telling stories. Your eyebrows are so dark and thick, for a woman.

Thank you, also, for telling me more about where you live, over the hills, at the edge of the woods. I can't stop thinking about it—a woman, living alone, closer to animals than to people. Not married or attached to family. Who are your friends? The wolves? I can only imagine. I know it is not my place to worry, but I hope you have a neighbor or two, otherwise I might wonder how you survive. I wish I could bring you some soup, but I am not allowed on the outskirts, and besides, I am sure you have long figured out the ways to sustenance where you are.

I know that, in order to make progress on my healing, I am supposed to tell you what happened, why Mama first sent for you, why I write instead of speaking now.

I write instead of speaking now.

It is already difficult for me to remember my voice.

You must promise to keep these letters to yourself, to never show them to anyone. And under these conditions, I will tell you.

It starts with my father. Papa works for the miller, but I think he wishes he were a talmid chochem. Try though he might to study holy texts with the rabbi, studiousness and wisdom were never his calling. Instead, his shoulders and legs ache from hard labor every day, and he comes home angry. After we eat supper, he has his vodka, snorting like a bull when anyone gets too close. I think that if he could speak with God, if God could grant him some respite or kindness, he would be less angry with us. With me.

Put plainly, my father is a giant. A big, strong man, blackest beard in town and a chest like two barrels. He wears rough-hewn tunics the tailor makes special for him, since it is difficult for him to find shirts that are his size. He gets called on to carry everything an animal can't—the aron koydesh, when it needs to be moved, or the coffin, when somebody formidable has died, and they need someone to bear the pall. His size and strength intimidate small children and visitors. And nobody is quite sure where it comes from—my father's father was a tailor, meek, by all accounts, and tiny. But my father is a tower. Commanding as he looks and hard as he works, I think my father is afraid. This fear, I think, is part of what makes him angry, but I can't exactly explain this. I know he is afraid of God and afraid of whatever else this world holds, and most of all, he is afraid of me.

I was born on the night of a hailstorm, and they say the weather that night was unlike anything the people of Ropshitz had ever seen. Usually, our sky is kind, a dark velvet blue. That night though? The sky was cold, the color of ice. The weather itself was angry. It was a warning, of course, and everybody should have seen it as such.

The story goes that the sky, stone gray, unleashed itself that night. Mean-looking dark streaks chased the hail all the way down to the ground. *Stay inside*, shouted the neighbors. *Pray to God*, shouted the rabbis. *Shut your windows*, shouted the crones and soothsayers. The midwife couldn't get to us in time, so I was born right here in our home, in the room where you sit with me and administer the herbs. Freyde, the blacksmith's wife, came from next door to help Mama the best she could. She boiled water and gave Mama whiskey from a flask, applied warm washcloths to her face, and squeezed her hands as I began to emerge.

I was a short baby but a wide one, so my birth was hard on Mama's body. She is the opposite of Papa—slight and delicate, with shoulders you can feel the knobs of. She crouched on the floor, sweating me out, one raggedy breath at a time. *It's so hot*, Mama cried, *it's so hot*, and so the blacksmith's wife opened all the windows. Little shards of ice shot in when she did, angry bits of universe confirming that God did not want my arrival to be peaceful. The blacksmith's wife rubbed Mama's back, murmuring the tekhines she knew by heart, a vain effort to keep the harmful spirits out, but the night was unrelenting, and the darkness had already entered my room.

Papa, meantime, was gone. The moment Mama started to feel pains, he'd shot out the door to find the doctor, even though we were cautioned not to go outside that night at all. When I finally arrived, Mama was so weak and in such pain she fell unconscious, and the blacksmith's wife hurried to tend to her, leaving me wrapped in a bundle of towels on the floor. Pellets of hail pelted the walls and swarmed in through the windows, gathering in icy heaps in the corners as the wind sang its shrill song, the backward lullaby that was my welcome to the world.

The door swung open then, and Papa and his companion stomped up the stairs, still wearing their boots. Papa hadn't been able to find the doctor, so instead, he'd returned with the first man he could find— Kalman Hirsch, the rabbi's assistant, a gruff, stocky man who spoke in short sentences at synagogue and always looked upset. And there I lay, alone and unguarded, in the middle of a room embattled by the night's weather. A bundle on the floor. No one had blessed me or ushered me in. My eyes, I am told, were already wide open. The storm had cast the room in a ghostly gray-yellow glow that still lit the room, even after all the windows were closed and the curtains drawn. The light, it is said, also pooled in my eyes so that they gleamed.

All this and all that is to come I know from Freyde, the blacksmith's wife, whose walls are paper-thin, whose house is right next door, and whose kitchen window looks into ours. Freyde is thrilled to tell anyone everything she knows about anything going on in our town. One only need ask. She knows, by now, to tell me. She feels I deserve to know.

The next morning, Mama rested, weak from giving birth, and I beside her, ragged from coming in with the storm. Papa went to see the rabbi.

He blazed back in through the door in a panic. "She's cursed!" he announced dramatically, his face aflame with passion and with the cold. Mama's eyes fluttered open.

"Shmiel?"

"Cursed," my father repeated, kicking off his muddy boots.

My mother's eyes opened, alert. She had long learned not to challenge my father in the conventional ways, but this she would not have. "Shmiel, what nonsense is this? From the rabbi? He couldn't have said such a thing. Our Mira has been in this world for one day." Nonetheless, I am told, my mother looked worried. She waited a moment and sighed. "How would she be cursed?"

My father now seemed hesitant to worry my mother, but it was too late.

"She was brought into the world unaccompanied, subjected to the elements. That neighbor, she let in the darkness and the ice and the filthy weather. And with it, those accursed laughing demons, that see the birth of a new baby girl as their favorite kind of pleasure: an opportunity to roost and feast as they cackle. They feast, you know, on the most vulnerable. And last night, that was Mira." My father's words landed like lightning. My mother shuddered, and I started crying. "We don't know for sure, Chane. But I saw that room, the windows open like that, no protection. I saw what came into our house. You must rest now, wife. We will just need to watch her carefully. We won't know what she is capable of until she is older."

I am starting to believe that I am capable of much more than my father will ever realize.

Somehow, though, the person who fears me is the very reason I have been so afraid.

Can you understand this? I hope so.

Yours,
Mira

Eleven

At this point in the telling, it bears explaining that laughter is a cosmically moderate element, wispy as lace. But when enough of it amasses, it becomes substantial. Palpable, too, a shift in the weather you feel but can't quite place.

One season, though, the laughter accumulated well past moderation. It gathered, quietly collecting in one corner of the universe, until there was, frankly, way too much of it.

I'm not sure what you'd call it in your languages. A clot? A mass? I think these words may connote something dangerous. An ingathering? A disproportion? Maybe there is nothing you would call it. This isn't the kind of naming you are generally expected to do.

At the end of the day, be it a threat or a glut, an excess of laughter needs to be dealt with.

And this was the most dramatic excess of it any of us had ever seen. While laughter is, of course, thought to be a joyful thing, a surfeit means a disturbance. A rare and unexpected spike in the stratosphere. An imbalance; an overwhelm.

No one was quite sure what to do about it. Given that the challenge we were facing was the redistribution of something at once mysterious and effulgent, I was tapped for the job. Everybody knows I possess uncommon depth of feeling. So this would be either the most perfect task for me or the most difficult. What do I know, after all? That I love more easily than my kind. That I love easily. That I love at all. That I would love so wildly, even once.

I promised I would deal with the excess of laughter. I would find the right thing, the right place, the right way to make things even again.

I watched closely, collecting stories. This is what I do. I wanted to be strategic.

There was the middle-aged neurosurgeon who began to complain about the tedium of his work, prestigious as it was, until one day, a man around his own age came into his office for a consultation. The neurosurgeon began reviewing the man's chart, clucking politely to let the patient know that he was paying close attention and stopping to ask things like *So, you drink plenty of water?* And *So, your grandfather suffered from gout?* At the word *gout*, the man doubled over, and for a moment, the neurosurgeon wondered if the man was weeping or in fact vomiting on his office floor. But when the man lifted his face, it was stretched into a mouth-gaping grin, eyes squeezed shut, tears, the pained guffaw of someone who is being mercilessly tickled. The neurosurgeon, confounded, let the man laugh for the three minutes and twenty-four seconds it took for him to compose himself; and then compose himself he did, graying, slightly exhausted, wiping a tear streak from his left cheek.

"You see my problem," said the man, wheezing a little bit as he spoke. "I can't control it. It just happens."

The neurosurgeon's cheeks went hot then. He was moved by what he had just witnessed and made shy by the knowledge that he could still be surprised. The wonder in him felt like the point in an old movie when the black-and-white has just gone Technicolor. He was self-conscious about this big, wide, childlike feeling, so he cleared his throat, blinked back the sting in his eyes, and moved on to talking with the man about his sleeping and exercise habits.

I am not exactly known for being strategic. I did try, though. No one can say I didn't try.

Why does anyone decide to put anything anywhere, after all? The tulips go in the middle of the table because they are more pleasing there than, say, in the corner. The children are raised somewhere the sun rises high, rendering the grass a glimmering yellow-green, because this is a color you'd like the children to come to know. The bed goes against the wall, the stake goes into the ground, the rocking chair goes on the porch, the stars get scattered across space, the roofs atop the houses, the clouds above like a cover, the lust a sheen over back seats in late-night cities, the cars straight down the road except when they swerve, the sparkles in the tar, the letters in envelopes, the dust in corners and on forgotten surfaces, the piano at the level of the fingers, the ocean wide at the far edges. And laughter goes. The extra laughter goes.

But what if the tree cover hung low from the moon, a lush world-wide hammock? What if the stars were kept in wells and the ground glowed golden hot at night? What if the windows went on the floor so you could see the ground underneath, what if the eggplant went in the freezer, what if the children went to big corner offices with desks every day and the train conductors went swimming? What if the frosting went on the inside like a surprise, what if the heart and lungs lived outside the skin, pulsating, warm to the touch? What if the mermaids beached themselves and the empty eggshells went under pillows at night? Where would laughter go then? Would it matter?

Some call me mercurial.

It may be so, but I put the excess where it seemed to want to go. My instincts are older than some of your planets, after all.

•

There was the jogging man who followed the sound of another man's laugh down twenty minutes of alleys in the pouring rain without an umbrella. A laugh so like musical theater and bells in winter that he thought the man sounded like Judy Garland and needed to know if he was, in fact, a distant relative. He caught up to the laughing man, finally, following him into a pharmacy without a second thought, wondering why he had been laughing and with whom.

The laughing man was buying crackers and rubbing alcohol, and the jogging man shook out his wet hair in the deodorant aisle. He wiped his wet hands on his wet shorts and straightened out his wet hoodie. There wasn't much to be done. He considered stealing a spray of cheap cologne but thought better of it. The laughing man turned to the window from the counter, and the jogging man could see his face plainly for a moment, long nose and long eyelashes, jags of rain across thick blue glasses. The jogging man didn't need to see the laughing man to know he was beautiful. He knew it from the sound of him. He didn't spend twenty sopping minutes following just anyone.

After the laughing man paid for his items, the jogging man approached him, nervous, hair still dripping. *Hello*, said the jogging man. The laughing man asked, *Do I know you?* He took off his glasses as if to see more clearly. *No*, admitted the jogging man, clearing his throat. The laughing man didn't look like Judy Garland. *I see*, said the laughing man. The jogging man drew a breath. *I think I heard you outside. Were you laughing? Outside? Just then?* The laughing man looked the jogging man directly in the eyes. *Always*, said the laughing man, breaking into music as if on cue. *Pretty much always.*

The point is, my cargo called for a measure of recklessness, and I took that seriously. You understand. There was no rational calculus here.

Laughter is no controlled substance. It goes where it wants to go. It led me. I let it.

Should I admit that I lost sleep over this? That I wondered whether I could have found my way into precision, could have made things better by being attentive, slow, cautious? I don't need sleep, actually, not much anyway, but I do relish dreaming. I dream about her sometimes—her scribbles of red hair, her sharp gray eyes, how she, like King Solomon, spoke the language of the birds—and I wake up saturated. But before the day's journey, I do my best to shake off the dream. My kind are meant to remain unencumbered by want.

But, oh, in this life, how I want.

I want nothing complicated. Quite the opposite. I want strawberries on a soft picnic sheet in the sun. Washed glass, saltwater-smooth. Assemblies of birds or leaves or stars or snow, whichever season. Round-sounding words whispered directly into the ear. A kiss and the half kiss that comes before that one. I want sweet small things. Things to make me feel close to the ground once in a while.

Would you call it a spill? An overflow? A rejection? An accident? It is true that I was looking for a sad place, a place that might desperately need what had elsewhere seemed excessive. I went searching for gaps, thirsty cities, islands threatened by the sea, beleaguered families, valleys of forgotten things. But there was no such clarity. There were so many towns weighted by their histories and sagging toward their futures. There was no one proper place.

I could tell you the laughter escaped me, the way *escape* can refer to something inside of you that, in a rare unguarded moment, flees. A forgetting. I could tell you I lost the laughter, but that would be a lie, and I don't lie, not even like this, not even now, not even to you.

In the end, the truth is tiny. The truth is that one moment I had it, and the next I didn't. The truth is that it fell, that I fell, that it wasn't quite accidental, that it wasn't quite meant to be, that no one is perfect, not even me. Hardly me.

There's a reason I'm collecting all this here: this repository of family secrets, this embarrassment of story. It's not quite a defense, but I hope it can serve as something close.

The place the laughter led me was dark and quiet. It had been a place once. It was still a kind of place, the kind that would be destroyed and remade again, irrevocably different on the other side of time. Held tight only by the Wielopolka River.

Time is never the point. The point is that watching it land in that place was one of the most beautiful things I've ever seen. I knew then, at first sight, as you might say: things would never be even again, but still, there was no doubt I had come to the right place. The laughter slid from the sack in my arms to the dry red dirt and rose like a clap of flour, warm and light, almost fragrant.

I wouldn't just leave it here, I thought to myself. I would show someone, I would tell someone. I had a feeling that somewhere in this place the laughter had led me, I might find a worthy guardian for my cargo. Someone else who would revere it as I did. Someone who might look up and notice the starry velvet gray that lingered there, a luxuriant hue whose extravagance seemed meant for kingdoms and oceans, fireworks and burlesque. Some may have thought it foreboding, but I watched rapt as it swirled and danced, beastly, like smoke into something living. Someone who would want to see with his own eyes how everything shone under that shadow, and how my empty hands shone too, palms still wide open from letting go.

Twelve

Marla called every Tuesday at four in the afternoon. When she decided she liked you, Marla got good and old-fashioned about it and started calling weekly. And especially since she'd agreed to join the chevra kadisha, Hannah had learned to be ready by the phone. This particular Tuesday, Hannah was sitting in her parked car, early for a four-thirty yoga class. She mostly did yoga because Jon no longer could, squeezing into her Lycra leggings in homage to her husband's fanatical relationship to stretching. She watched the phone light up, let it ring twice. Then she picked it up.

"Marla, how are you?"

"Hi, Hannah. I'm so glad you picked up." This was a part of Marla's phone ritual. Hannah never didn't pick up. "Listen, I have a bag of clothes I think you'll love. Size twelve or so, silk blouses, pencil skirts, nice stuff. That woman who died a few weeks ago, Rabinowitz, remember I told you? Very well-off, very fashionable. Really tragic; those kids are still in middle school. Anyway, she would have wanted someone as good-looking as you wearing this stuff, Hannah. You want me to hold it for you?"

"Sure, they sound classy," said Hannah. Marla was difficult to say no to.

"Oh, good. When can you come by? Tomorrow, maybe afternoon?"

"Tomorrow works." Hannah paused long enough to hear Marla sigh dramatically, an invitation. "How are you doing, Marla?"

"Oh, you know, I'm all over the place right now. We have a funeral for a four-year-old tonight—just breaks my heart, cancer, never gets easier. And then I need a crew for Dottie Golding's tahara tomorrow. She finally died last night, which is the other reason I'm calling. Did you hear she died? Long time coming."

"Oh, no, I hadn't heard."

"Just in her sleep, and the neighbors, they really showed up. Sometimes the elderly, when they go, they're so lonely, but people loved Dottie. Such a doll. Always a smile on her."

Hannah hadn't known Dottie well, had only seen her at synagogue once or twice, but on matters of basic human goodness, Marla could generally be trusted. Tomorrow was Hannah's birthday. And two days later, her husband's first yahrzeit. It would be a strange way to spend a birthday, but she had a feeling birthdays would be a little strange for the rest of her life, given their proximity to what she'd lost.

"So, listen, Hannah, you want to get in on this one? You could just stay after you come to pick up those Rabinowitz clothes tomorrow. There are at least two designer pieces in that bag, Armani, did I say?"

"Sure, Marla. I'll do the tahara tomorrow. If you need me."

"I always need you. Thanks so much, doll."

Hannah hung up the phone at 4:07, still remarkably early for yoga.

Hannah was late to Dottie Golding's tahara. She'd already done a couple of taharas with the Beth Emeth group and was just starting to get to know the other members, so was mortified, making a flaky impression so early on. She hated being late, especially when it came to preparing the dead, though walking into Garfinkel's, she had to stifle a laugh, as the Jon who survived exclusively in the outer corners of her lips whispered, *late, you know, as in dead.* She adjusted her face, wondering why people were called *late* once they'd died. She knew some now-dead people who had been incredibly punctual in life—Jon very much included—who would resent that.

Slipping in with a whispered apology, Hannah took her place easily. By now she had done enough of these that the choreography was intuitive. Slide in between two of the seven women, feel just the right amount of space between her shoulders and the shoulders of the women on either side of her—not close enough to touch but close enough to feel unalone. Take the jug from the speckled and doughy hands of the older woman on her right, pour the water slowly over the form lying on the table, the form that used to belong to Dottie Golding. Pass the jug to the younger, slimmer set of hands laced with delicate gem-studded rings on her left. Wet, slowly and carefully, and then dry. Lift one leg, lift another. Scoop under and arch over the body. Move around the body, a slow carousel. Move arms across arms across the body, a somber shadow Twister.

When Jon was first diagnosed, he'd proceeded straight to a silent meditation retreat. It was the sort of thing Jon did: instead of fleeing, her husband had gone to face his bleak prognosis, stone silently, amid droves of hippies. The first thing he reported, via rogue text message from his monastic dorm room, was that at the retreat center, even when they ate together, they were encouraged not to look too closely at one another's faces. Something about not fixating on the facial responses of others because they were there to be alone. Alone, but alone together. Hannah thought about a tahara this way. She always registered the other women there, but it seemed strange to actually look at them. She felt that all attention should be reserved for the body. At a tahara, the living were just accomplices. The dead were the main event.

For whatever reason, though, this time, Hannah felt the overwhelming urge to look. Maybe it was her curiosity peaking. Maybe it was the fact that during one of Shiva's recent check-in phone calls—the ones where she could continually hear her own daughter running out of patience with her and wanted to say, *wait, let's slow down, let's be sad, let's not let him go yet*—Hannah had finally conceded that she felt lonely, a humbling confession to make to a daughter, even a fully grown one, especially one to whom she felt like she had something to prove.

Maybe something was cosmically awry. That possibility could never be discounted. She could actually hear Syl's voice warning her that if Hannah felt this compelled to do something, it was probably because she shouldn't. She ignored imaginary Syl and looked up anyway, cautious at first and then open-eyed, egged on by the absence of any lightning striking down.

She was immediately taken by the focus on the women's faces as they tended to the body. The room thrummed with a no-nonsense tenderness she thought rare between the living, though, to be honest, she couldn't quite remember. She missed human touch.

It was the nose on the woman directly across from her that snagged her. The way it beaked sharply from her face and then zagged dramatically, a proper triangle, back into her pointed lips, small and circular in their concentration. Long and delicate silver-fringed earrings. The woman was slight but worked from her broad shoulders with unmistakable strength, a wave of peppery bangs hanging over her eyes as she worked to clean one of Dottie's feet.

It was too late now; Hannah couldn't look away from the woman. She was certain she'd met everyone in the Beth Emeth chevra kadisha by now, but she had never seen this person before. Even so, the woman looked uncannily familiar, like a character from a dream who wants to stay forgotten. She didn't realize how long she'd been staring until the woman looked directly back at her, probably finally sensing she was being watched.

Her eyes, a dazzling green.

Something small but definite erupted in Hannah's chest. She kept her hands moving, but her mind spun into an expanse of midnights past, some ancient birthday, the green eyes keeping her awake some nights until early morning. The feeling she had long lived with, that someone was supposed to find her, and that said someone never had. She felt like she might fall over.

Hannah worked to steady her shaking hands, terrified she might drop the ceramic jug onto poor Dottie. In any other situation, she would have swiftly and graciously averted her gaze, and, God help her, it wasn't that she didn't desperately want to. It was simply that she couldn't.

Eye-locked, they lifted and washed and blessed and let go. The strong-shouldered woman blinked rarely and seemed unashamed to keep looking at Hannah. She worked no less swiftly, as though this kind of staring contest was commonplace. Hannah had no idea how to feel. Possessed? Her cheeks burned, which embarrassed her, so they burned harder. The corporeal communion of a tahara was already so devastatingly intimate, but coupled with the intimacy of being locked in a stranger's eyes, it was brutal. They stayed looking until the tahara was over, Dottie's body wheeled out, now cleaned, shrouded, and ready for burial.

Hannah stumbled out of the room, disoriented. Usually, the after was a bit like the surgeons scrubbing out on hospital dramas—clear-eyed, rhythmic reverence dissipating into sleepiness—but tonight, Hannah felt scrambled and wrung. She looked around the lobby for the green-eyed stranger, but no stranger. The last two women were exiting through the glass doors into the parking lot, and Hannah felt unreasonable disappointment rising in her throat.

Shiva had just told her the kids had a thing called ghosting. People leaving a substantial mutual encounter suddenly and without explanation. It wasn't like a breakup, explained Shiva. It was worse because it meant the person had disappeared without a trace or an accounting. Shiva herself had just been ghosted. In the weeks leading up to her Warsaw trip, her Polish crush had vanished. Shiva had told Hannah about their exchanges, which had sounded vigorous and thrilling, even though it was hard for Hannah to imagine that real romance could unfold without faces or voices and across such distance.

When this woman—and *woman*, too, felt new in Hannah's mouth, even still—had disappeared, Shiva was upended. There was something, Shiva had tried to explain, about never even having had the chance to try. *She had such heart*, Shiva had wept to her last week, after she was certain her suitor was gone. Hannah, sheepishly greedy for her daughter's rare tears and her secrets, feeling, even just briefly, like a good mother. *I just wanted to see what was possible.*

Despondent, Hannah walked to Marla's office door and found the garbage bag of clothing, her name written in Marla's bubbly handwriting on a piece of paper taped to the plastic. She heaved it over her shoulder, overcome with the feeling she'd seen proof of something she'd wanted to believe all her life, something long closed that had just creaked slightly open. She felt ridiculous swaying out into the dark winter parking lot, desperate to bring herself back to earth. *I just wanted to see what was possible*, she thought.

But the thing hottest in her was the thing she'd barely allowed herself to admit, even in the safe recesses of her own brain. Those eyes. Those glass-green eyes, like something from a hungry memory. Something she'd almost seen once, in a mirror, in the middle of the night.

The following Tuesday, Hannah found herself waiting by the phone. It was silly that she didn't just call Marla herself, but she'd grown oddly fond of their tradition, of being reached out to. After Dottie's tahara, though, she could barely wait to talk to Marla. Marla would be eager to gossip. Hannah drew circles on the countertop with her finger. 3:57. She imagined Jon teasing her for waiting to hear from the world's most persistent funeral home director like a high school girl waiting for a boy to call and ask her to prom. *But Jon*, Hannah said defensively to no one. *Marla is my friend*. When her phone finally buzzed, true to teenage form, she let it ring twice before picking up.

"Hannah, hi, it's Marla."

"Hi Marla, how are you doing?"

"Oh, Hannah." A long Marla sigh. "It's a hard week."

"What's going on?"

"Just so busy, dear. Feeling my age. My right knee, have I told you about that? No good for hauling coffins, but I worry about the young guys—sometimes I just want to pitch in."

"Aw, Marla, you should just let them do the heavy lifting. It's what they're paid for."

"How was the tahara last week, hon? I didn't get to catch you afterward."

Hannah paused, suddenly unsure about how to answer. "Well, Marla, it was a little weird. Have you talked to anyone else who was there?"

"I haven't, dear. Like I said, a very busy week. Right outside my office right now—you know who's here?" A dramatic pause. "The whole Schimmel family, all the kids and both parents. The whole family comes here! They can't just send one. They're all so worried about the grandmother's funeral. I understand, but when whole families come, it's exhausting. And you know the Schimmels. Not a quiet bunch."

"It sounds really overwhelming, Marla."

"Listen, I'm glad you called actually." Marla sometimes rewrote the story so that Hannah had called her, not the other way around. "There's something I've been meaning to ask you."

"Oh?"

"I mentioned my office manager quit, right? She's going to graduate school—great for her, lousy for me. And also, the chevra lost a member when Naomi Bar Lev got married last week to that military guy and shipped off to Phoenix. I'm feeling so worn thin now, doll. It's hard to keep things afloat."

"That sounds like a lot, Marla."

"It is a lot," she agreed. "So I want you."

"Me?"

"Yes, dear. You. I know you have a job already. But I think you're a natural at this stuff. Funeral home stuff." This was high praise from Marla Garfinkel. "So maybe you'd want to take on more of a leadership role? We could start with just a few hours a week. It wouldn't be office management, either. I'd want you to be my right-hand person. I have a feeling you'd enjoy it. Plus, I pay pretty well."

"You're recruiting me?" Hannah wasn't sure whether she should laugh. "What do you mean by *leadership role*, Marla?"

"You know, coordinating the chevra kadisha, helping with some things around the house, learning the funeral home ropes, if you know what I mean." Marla put on her big macher voice then. "And then, if you want, doll, I can groom you for this business. I'm not going to want to run this place forever. You never know."

They were on the phone, but Hannah could imagine Marla's exaggerated wink. She could almost hear the *lookin' at you, kid* at the end of that sentence. Hannah was not a kid. She was fifty-five now. And yet, how gratifying to be recognized as a natural.

"Wow," Hannah said. Spending the rest of her life at the helm of a funeral home didn't actually sound terrible. She was aware her days were flat and low, her joys rare, and her sense of possibility almost fully quashed. Maybe the dramatic change she needed was to go into death professionally. She imagined it would feel something like reuniting with a dear old friend. "Thanks, Marla. This is . . . intriguing. I'll think about it."

"That's all I ask," said Marla. "Now, I've got to go talk to the Schimmels."

Hannah felt silly as her chest tightened with disappointment. Next week. She'd ask Marla about the green-eyed woman next week.

Shiva called that night to check in.

"I'm fine," said Hannah, tired of answering the question.

Shiva's attention was elsewhere, though; Hannah could tell. She wanted to tell her daughter how lucky she was, that the kind of loss she'd described as *ghosting* wasn't true loss. She still got to go to Warsaw, after all, to investigate their history, unencumbered by fear or hesitation. Emboldened with professional and academic purpose. What abundant luxury. But Hannah knew she had to be kind. Shiva was right; they needed each other. They were all they had.

"You'll have enough to do in Warsaw," said Hannah. "You don't need to be chasing a Polish lesbian ghost."

"Ma." Shiva gave her a weak laugh. "When somebody ghosts you, it doesn't make them a ghost. It's just the verb, *ghosting.* The noun is still *human.* I like to hang out with the living. Unlike some people."

Hannah took the dig in stride. She had, of course, asked for a lifetime of this, having named Shiva after a Jewish mourning ritual long before she'd been widowed, long before she washed bodies more often than she went out to dinner. She'd been raised to do everything she could to distract the evil eye from spoiling a good thing, and naming her daughter after death itself was the ultimate ruse. She knew, at the time, that had her mother been watching, she would have been proud.

"Okay. Polish lesbian ghoster, then."

"I actually kind of like *Ghost.*" Shiva paused. "I think I'm still going to try to find her. Maybe that's nuts, but it just felt like I knew her. Or, I know it sounds stupid, but like I was supposed to."

Hannah bit her lip. She wanted to be sure to say the right thing here. "Are you sure you're not just still heartbroken about—"

"Dani?" Shiva's response was quick.

"Yes," said Hannah. Her teeth clenched involuntarily, and she pushed the name out. "Dani."

"I'm a mess about Dani. I still can't believe I lost her. But this is someone else. It's different."

"She's the one who lost you, Shiv. She lost a good one," said Hannah, meaning it. On her brighter days, Hannah felt like she still had time to correct for how she'd been mothered by Syl. To support her daughter's venture into some unknown or other, much as it scared her. And to correct, too, for how slow she'd been to adjust to the idea of a Dani in her daughter's life.

She didn't know how to equip Shiva for a trip like this, especially when even the mention of it brought up in Hannah equal shares vicarious envy and vertiginous anxiety. She missed Jon most in moments like these. He'd always known exactly what to say, how to reach across distance and make their daughter laugh. But Jon wasn't here, and Hannah didn't know what she was capable of giving.

"I'm excited for what you'll find in Warsaw," she pushed herself to say. "Even if it's not your Ghost."

"Thanks, Ma," said Shiva. And then she was quiet. "I want to be where Mira was. I'm not pretending I'll understand anything better, but I think I'll feel closer to her. Or to something."

Hannah breathed. "I understand."

Something like relief, then, suspended just out of reach, on both ends of the line.

The following Tuesday, it was four thirty already, and Marla still hadn't called. Hannah felt restless. She should make plans with a friend for once or go to yoga. Finally, at four forty, she caved and called Marla.

"Hello?" Marla seemed surprised, as though she and Hannah didn't have an unspoken standing date for this weekly time. "Garfinkel's." An afterthought.

"Marla, it's Hannah."

"Oh, Hannah, hi honey, did you love the clothes? Are we on for Gertz's tomorrow?"

"They're great, Marla," Hannah lied. "A whole wardrobe upgrade in one garbage bag. And yes, definitely. Gertz's tomorrow." She took a breath. "Marla, a question for you."

"What is it?"

"There was someone at Dottie's tahara I didn't recognize." She waited for Marla to know exactly who she was talking about.

"Really?" She could hear paper on the other end. "I think you know the whole gang by now. Libby was there, and Lana Kreitzler, you've met her, and . . . let me see, who else . . ."

"No, there was someone I had never met. Short hair. Bangs. Green eyes."

"Hmm," said Marla. "I'm not sure. I didn't train anybody new. Are you sure you're not misremembering things?"

Hannah wasn't sure at all. "But you would have to know who she was, right? She was at Dottie's tahara."

"I would, yes. Hannah, are you doing okay? Are you sleeping, eating, seeing people?"

"Marla. You sound like a grandmother." It did feel good to be asked after.

"I don't mind sounding like a grandmother." Marla had never had children, and Hannah often wondered whether she regretted it. "But I'm used to this. People think, *her husband died a year ago already, she's fine.* They leave you alone, stop checking in. But grief is a funny beast, isn't it? One year and you might be fine, five years and you might be a wreck."

"I'm fine," said Hannah, quick as a reflex. Yes, she had maybe just hallucinated an entire other human. Yes, she still seized up when she thought about the secret phantom she'd seen in a mirror at sixteen. Yes, all right, she was achingly lonely. She missed everyone she'd lost. She missed her husband unspeakably. She missed her own daughter, even. She could tear her hair out with all the missing.

"I mean, of course I miss him." Marla was a friend. It was okay to admit this. "But I'm okay. And there was this woman. She looked a lot like someone I met once."

For a full beat, Marla was remarkably quiet for Marla. "Well, we'll go to Gertz's tomorrow. We can talk more there. And if you're truly okay, doll, let me know if you've had the chance to do any more thinking about my little funeral home proposal. I should probably be pushing you to get out more, not pushing you closer to the morgue, but I also really do need you."

"Okay," said Hannah. "We'll talk more tomorrow."

Marla excused herself, saying she actually had dinner plans with a gentleman caller. While she was thinking of it, Hannah stuffed the unworn clothing back into the garbage bag, destined for Goodwill. It was early, but she was eager for sleep, just so she could wake up again. In the light, the unlikely always seemed at once clearer and infinitely farther away.

March 30, 1921

Dear L,

I have been writing down the incantations exactly as you told me, and trying, as I do so, to clear my mind of anything else. It helps to start by picturing the forest, as you suggested, which makes me feel like I am in the safest place to pray.

I have so many questions for you, L. I hope they do not make me seem ungrateful, but you make me so curious. How did my mother find you? And how come you are not old and craggy, like the other healers I have met? And why are you known only as L?

I could see your eyes full of pity the last time you were here, and I think it is because you know now about Papa and the unfortunate circumstances under which I was brought into this world. I am glad you come to see me when Papa is at the mill, because I am certain he would not approve of an unmarried young woman with such an unconventional vocation coming into our home. I hope this does not offend you—my father is a temperamental man. But I don't want you to pity me too much. I am grateful for your herbs and your help, and I am getting stronger every day. Writing these letters, strange as it may sound, is helping me find my way back to myself. At least to remember a bit better who I have been. Maybe, in your wisdom, you knew this would happen well before I did.

I can tell you what happened after. Between then and now. Maybe that will help.

Papa watched me carefully indeed.

I grew into a curious child. I always wanted to touch everything I could. I loved the slip of the fish when I combed my fingers across the surface of the river, and the pungent smell of the oniongrass that sprouted up around our home. I loved the immensity of the trees and the way the birds sounded, and I often came home from cheder with dirty hands, having dug up a strange mushroom or a shiny rock I mistook for buried treasure. Jacob sometimes came home dirty-handed too, but that is okay for a boy. Especially a boy no one suspects of possession.

Vilde chaye, Papa called me, his voice barren of any affection. Wild beast. *Like a wolf, this girl, playing in the dirt*, he would say. *Go clean up and be useful. The world doesn't need your dreaming. It needs the laundry cleaned and the fires kindled.* And Mama, she tried to protect me from him the best she could. *Shmiel*, she said. *She's only a child.* My father didn't listen. He is strong and capable, but he is not a good listener.

I tried to tame my curiosities, in the event this might convince my father to love me. I began coming directly home after cheder and started on my chores immediately. As the years passed, Jacob and I grew closer. He knew I needed his protection from Papa, and he tried to provide it the best he knew how. And my brother, he is funny. You wouldn't know it from the thin line of his mouth and the serious furrow of his brow, but Jacob? He could make me laugh at a funeral. How we would laugh. My life at home has been hard, but my walks home from cheder and to the synagogue with my brother made everything better.

And this, dear L, is important: My laugh is no regular laugh. It is a piercing thing, a screaming witch's cackle straight from my gut. If I laugh in public, people turn and stare. Once, a lady pulled Mama aside and told her I sounded like a barking seal.

Not only is my laughter loud, but it takes over my whole body. My eyes squeeze shut, my fists clench, and I convulse, rocking and shaking as the sounds come. I have never been able to help it, not from the moment I was born. I believe that the first time my father heard me really, truly laugh, he decided that all his suspicions about me were confirmed.

You must also understand something about laughter in Ropshitz, if you do not already. Laughter is fundamental to this place, and so the laughter here is governed by certain laws. Here, laughter can be sacred or it can be evil, but it is not usually possible for it to be both. Ropshitz, for example, used to be overrun by demons the townspeople called "clowns." They took residence in this place long ago, playing elaborate pranks that exhausted the townspeople who preceded us, dancing on their roofs and sucking the soup from their dinners up through their chimneys and throwing bricks at passersby.

And the "clowns" would laugh. Their laughter, nothing joyous, came out in the form of profane screams you could hear, shrill in the night, long after everyone was sleeping. They meant to ruin the Ropshitzers' lives, to take much more from them than their soup. Our famous Hasid Reb Naftali, our beloved badchan, known for the sanctity of his sense of humor, was able to match their wit and rid the town of these demons. But demons never fully leave a place they have once called home. Ropshitzers now, we are trained in two ways: to immerse ourselves in sacred laughter, and to suspect the laughter that is profane or worse. Only the discerning pupil of the teachings of Reb Naftali truly knows the difference.

My laughter, it was the wrong kind.

One day, just a few years ago, Jacob was walking me home from cheder, pretending to be one of the beavers from behind our house. He had one hand behind his back like a tail, and his front teeth outside of his mouth, running circles around me making high-pitched sounds. We were nearly home when the laughter flung forth from the back of my throat. I laughed so hard my stomach muscles hurt, and I had to stop walking, bending over as I howled.

Suddenly, a giant hand clamped over my mouth. Papa. He was home early and had come outside to get some wood for the fire. His voice, then, in my ear, quiet, so no one else could hear him: *You make unnatural sounds, daughter. You make sounds like you are a monster beckoning the devil himself.* He tightened his grip on my mouth, and I felt my lips drain of their blood under the rough heat of his enormous palm. *I won't have it in my household. It's a disgrace to God.*

But Papa, Jacob said, all the joy stricken from his face, too. We were still close then. *It was my fault.*

He tried, my brother, but my father brought me to my room and locked the door. The very room I was born into, the one whose door my father liked to keep shut when my behavior disturbed him. I stood on the other side, heart pounding, all the sound gone from my lungs. When my breathing slowed, I walked to the center of the room, the place the blacksmith's wife had left me. Cursed or not cursed, it was the place I'd come from and so the place I felt most at home. I rocked back and forth there for so long that, by the time Mama came up to fetch me to help with dinner, the room was fogged with dark.

I ate quietly. I was always quiet for a long while after Papa stopped my laughter. Sometimes for hours or, when he approached me with great violence, days. I could always see him, eating his stew, sizing me up, waiting for the demons to emerge from my mouth again when I stopped chewing. I was his family, but I was also the thing from which he was trying to protect his family.

Papa wasn't the only one afraid of me. Kalman Hirsch, the rabbi's assistant, had been afraid of me since the moment he'd seen me come into the world, unguarded and, by all accounts, possibly possessed. Rumor had it he was always trying to convince people that the town needed to take more drastic measures—exorcism, he insisted. It hadn't happened yet, but people kept their distance. I had to be cautious in the public square. I had to spend less time in public with Jacob, for example, because I couldn't laugh in front of others. I wanted to keep the few friends I had.

It was a desire to belong, but it was also something else. I felt stilled by people's fear. Tongueless with sadness. And in the silence that started to fill my days, I began to understand why people thought I might be possessed. Possession—such thorough displacement—doesn't sound so different from feeling so alone, or feeling so much without the sounds to say it.

I am tired, but I will write more next time.

Yours,
Mira

Thirteen

S hiva landed at Warsaw's Chopin Airport on a balmy Tuesday afternoon in March.

She'd never traveled internationally before, and even with the directions she'd printed out to get to the apartment she'd rented, she was overwhelmed by the zigzag of transit options, not to mention how to use the money she'd gotten at the airport exchange and where she'd find dinner. *Take the bus to the Centrum stop*, said her notes, *and then take the tram to Muranów.*

At the Centrum, she walked through the chaotic crisscross of people into the first noodle shop she saw, where she ordered by pointing to the item on the menu with the longest name, hoping it would be the most filling. She dragged her suitcase to a little orange table in the corner, and when her noodles came out, she slurped them down, grateful for the savory fact of them.

Dazed, she moved through the crowds, edging around businessmen walking purposefully in one direction or another, families ambling past in inefficient blob formation, and groups of teenage girls who leaned laughing on one another, sharing sodas and skipping in and out of clothing stores. She bought gum at a magazine stand, where a kindly English-speaking cashier directed her to the tram.

It was dusk by the time she got to Muranów. She'd looked at dozens of pictures of the former Jewish neighborhood online—the place where the Warsaw Ghetto had once stood—but everything felt alien now: the ground under her feet, the quality of the air, the way the trees bent and the streetlights shone. When she reached her rental apartment, Shiva opened the lockbox and let herself into a windowy studio furnished with a white couch, two white armchairs, and a bed clothed in white linens so inviting that she took off her shoes and clothes, not bothering to shower or unpack, and crawled directly into it.

The sun announced itself through the windows early the next morning. From the couch, Shiva could see people walking and jogging and commuting, an everyday texture with which she wasn't yet familiar. She could see memorials, stone and bronze, even from where she stood at the apartment window. She looked farther out, scanning the severe buildings. She'd read that Polish authorities had ultimately enforced a socialist-realist style in postwar rebuilding, but that Bohdan Lachert, the architect charged with designing a new residential district in Muranów, had insisted on using the actual physical rubble from the razed Jewish ghetto in the new buildings. Muranów itself, he believed, should physically be a memorial to what had happened there, even though the place in its modern contours was barely recognizable as what it had once been.

On Anielewicz Street, she found a coffee shop. Dawid, gregarious and amply bearded, made her latte. *Cześć*, he said, and she said it back, proud of the humble first Polish word she'd gotten to utter. He taught her a few more beginner Polish words. *Do zobaczenia jutro*, she practiced. *See you tomorrow.*

Coffee in hand, she walked. It was what her body always wanted her to do first, and she needed to get this place under her feet in the light of day, so that Warsaw would begin to reveal itself. To tell her the stories she needed it to tell.

The thing was, when she really thought about it—thought with her whole body, to the rhythm of her breathing as she walked—her crisis was one of indeterminacy. On paper, she knew exactly what she was doing here. Emotionally, intellectually even, she mostly knew what she was doing here. But at her core, what she was really reaching for, past the vortex of her family and the dullness of her grief, was a kind of existential precision. She craved a spiritual articulacy she'd never had, something sharp and clear she could hold up and look at. An-sky, she knew, had craved this, too. His life had unfolded in the realm of questions and chameleonic gray areas, but he'd remained relentless in his search for the things that might confirm his presence in the world as having been something definite. Something people could touch, could name, could remember.

She wanted out of the murk—she walked, she walked—and into something more lucid. Something she could find the words for. She'd followed the indeterminacy here, hoping that a combination of intentional alienation and homecoming would bring her into some kind of clearing.

She felt her way down side streets, past apartment buildings and the independent movie theater. Past the Warsaw Ghetto Uprising monument, where she stood for a moment staring up at the statue, at once mammoth and also wildly inadequate. Something in her throat thickened as she looked at it in three dimensions for the first time, unable to fully process what it stirred in her. How was a person supposed to interact with such a monument in an everyday way, on a commute to work or on the way out to a bar some Saturday night? She walked past bright street murals and small, boxy shops with brightly colored doors. Down black alleyways that could well be empty or teeming, past plaques and tram tracks and cigarette trash, past ice cream shops and tall brutalist buildings and small squares lousy with birds.

As she walked, expecting to encounter mostly grief in the layers of what used to be here, she realized that her feeling being here was less spectral and more kinetic. It was as if Warsaw past and Warsaw present just coexisted, facing one another; past Warsaw was still so present in these streets, it was as though it had insisted on staying.

And in a way, Shiva knew, it had. The daylight here stung yellow, and the city, preternaturally crowded, was uneasy, even inside its urban everyday. Even on her walk to the coffee shop, she'd had to step over the boundary marker of the edge of the former Warsaw Ghetto. A walk in the park was never just that, when the monuments—be they towering homages or faded engravings in the concrete—wouldn't let her forget where she was. She went to the newspaper stand, and suddenly she felt the sky looking at her funny, like she'd been there before.

As she walked back to her rental, she stopped in the square across the street from her apartment and did what she always did when she wanted to make her way among strangers somewhere new: she found herself a park bench.

Her bench was at the perimeter of the square looking outward and facing the tram stop, a small grocery store, and the coffee shop that turned bar come evening, when everyone ignored the outdoor tables and instead sat with their beers on the concrete steps, half an eye on whatever sporting event was on the multiple screens.

She ran her hand along one of the bench's planks. From here, she would see the city. Perhaps, after a time, it would notice her too.

Immediately, she found herself wondering about the Ghost. She could be anywhere here. They had been at the edge of something, she swore. *How silly*, she confessed to the bench. Preoccupied by the fantasy of a grandiose reunion with a lost internet crush when she should be only reveling in this place. But as uncertain as she was about so much else, Shiva felt certain that the acute desire her first encounter with the Ghost would generate might crystallize things in a way little else could.

People poured across the crosswalk with dogs and grocery bags. Shiva closed her eyes, trying to assume an open-ended pose. The kind of asking only the body can do. The sun shone on her strong as a wish, and in that light, it was difficult to imagine ever finding anything so critically disorienting as love.

———

The thing you are waiting for isn't the thing you think you are wait-ing for. It is eye level, visible directly from your perch on some park bench. It is ordinary: root or turnip, dirt or lock, palm or slat or barrel or grass or mud. Let it be surprising anyway. The way a minute turns into a different minute, the way the sun turns its cheek, the way the trees bow to no one at dawn.

Park benches are invisible until you see them. Then, suddenly, they're everywhere. The park bench can be a place to encounter or a place to withdraw. Benches are designed to invite or to fend off, and either is deliberate. Friendly or sinister, aluminum or concrete, steel or wood. Park benches are the best places for waiting. The waiting makes park benches heavy. And the benches, they feel the weight.

There are fifteen park benches in the memorial square at the center of Muranów. They are simple and unadorned, a light birch. Nine of them line the thick-treed path that winds around the inner center of the square; six are set along the perimeter facing outward. The ones inside the square are for waiting. The ones along the out-side of the square—the ones that face the street and the bigger park across the way—those are for keeping watch.

———

The next day, standing in the entryway of the Jewish Historical Insti-tute, Shiva was nervous, even more nervous than she'd been for her first meeting with Rosen. She stood there long enough that she was approached by a bespectacled young researcher, who introduced him-self as Oren and asked in stilted English whether she needed help. She must have looked as misplaced as she felt. She told him she'd made a reading-room appointment. Did he know where she should start in terms of English-language archives and materials pertaining to S. An-sky, or was there someone she should ask?

Oren escorted her over to a hunched elderly woman in a red sweater. He said something in Polish, and the woman creaked into a standing position, leading Shiva to a table in the reading room. Oren followed close behind. The room—its stacks of prewar periodicals and blue- and brown-bound books—looked like it was from another time, except for the computers that allowed researchers to access the digital catalog.

The woman looked at her expectantly. *An-sky*, Shiva said. Oren elaborated. The woman raised her eyebrows but shuffled off. Minutes later, she returned to the table with a box that looked heavier than she was.

"Zacznij od tego," the woman said, warily, and shuffled off.

Shiva started pulling things out of the fatly packed box. Most of the institute's resources focused on life in the ghetto during World War II, after An-sky's death and after Mira was already living in the United States.

But in these files, she found newspapers published during the time An-sky had been living in Warsaw, journals and books teeming with accounts of prewar Jewish life, and newspaper reviews of the premiere of *The Dybbuk* itself, shortly after An-sky's death.

Oren, still standing behind her, cleared his throat. "Do you read Polish or Yiddish?"

Shiva shook her head, feeling embarrassment rise from her neck.

"You know," he said. "I finished my work here a bit early today. And honestly, you might need a little help, unless you have a lot of patience and a few good dictionaries. Is there anything I can help translate for you for a few minutes, just to get you started?"

Shiva's gratitude for this stranger's unnecessary kindness almost canceled out the humiliation she felt about being so wildly underprepared.

"That's so nice of you," she said. "I promise I won't take up too much of your time, but yes, that would be really helpful."

As Shiva took diligent notes, Oren translated two of the shorter reviews aloud.

In the weeks following the premiere, both papers said, Warsaw itself seemed possessed by the sensation *The Dybbuk* had so swiftly become. No one could shake it, a whole city seized. There was truly, actually, a public frenzy over this piece of theater, the streets and tram cars mobbed. She couldn't imagine such collective thrall around a performance. What would it have looked like?

She thanked Oren again for his time and turned her attention toward the books and papers in the box that were in English. Before she knew it, three hours had passed, and she had barely made a dent in the materials on the table in front of her, even just the materials in translation.

Shiva felt saturated. It was an overwhelming feeling, sitting with such riches. To have everything you've wanted at your fingertips and to be too staggered by its breadth to find focus. The feeling made her want to burst out of the room full of books and files and into the sun, where the city waited.

She thanked the old woman on her way out. *I'll be back*, she wanted to say, but she hadn't learned enough Polish yet and didn't want to pull out her phone. And without any further detours, she retired to her bench, where she watched Muranów's afternoon become its evening.

The day after that, at the Polin Museum, she met with an older archivist, Yigal, who was Israeli and spoke to Shiva in a mix of English and Hebrew. *What are you looking for?* She told him about her interests in An-sky's ethnographic study and in Jewish folklore more broadly. Yigal nodded. He set her up at a table with a computer and showed her how to search the various databases most relevant to her research.

She clicked past An-sky's ethnographic study to An-sky's death. She read a long history of the Vilna Troupe, the group that had first performed *The Dybbuk* in Warsaw in December of 1920. Before An-sky died, the play had been rejected by a number of theaters for being too heavily folkloric, but the Vilna Troupe had seen something in it. At An-sky's funeral, the manager of the troupe stood up, vowing not only to stage the play but to premiere it exactly thirty days later in remembrance.

She read the history of the Mausoleum of the Three Writers in Warsaw's Jewish cemetery, where An-sky was buried alongside Isaac Leib Peretz and Yankev Dinezon. She read all about "Di Shvue," the labor anthem An-sky wrote when he became active in the Yiddish socialist movement the Bund.

Two hours later, she'd forgotten herself, having gone from reading about *The Dybbuk* to reading about the idea of the dybbuk more broadly. The word *dybbuk* came from the root *to cling*. Dybbuks were often restless male spirits that entered the bodies of women. They'd existed in Jewish communities for centuries but flourished and dominated the cultural imagination most prominently in the nineteenth century.

In many cases, a dybbuk was a spirit with unfinished business. Often, though, it was also the soul of someone who was seen to have transgressed; a manifestation of something a community simply did not want to see, coming back to haunt it. A dybbuk could become a scapegoat then, the community members blaming the possessed for whatever it was they were so afraid of. And the possessed often bucked tradition, refusing community participation or resisting gendered rules.

The possession itself often featured fainting or dramatic collapse, constant crying, or body spasms. Afterward, the possessed might speak in a strange or unrecognizable voice, or suddenly have access to impossible knowledge of people's sins or secrets, or news from afar.

In many cases, possession allowed a woman to do what she needed to do or say what she needed to say. Perhaps she needed desperately to escape from an arranged marriage. Perhaps she didn't want to be with a man at all, but the alternative seemed simply impossible outside of the most cataclysmic of means.

Shiva brimmed with thoughts she couldn't keep up with. She felt the dybbuk was important for her to understand, to come to know better, unknowable though she knew it to be. She took notes, as fast as she could. If she was this full with wondering, she thought, wouldn't her body run out of room for it sooner or later? Wouldn't the wondering need to expel itself from her eventually, in the form of something so definite as language?

Outside, her bench awaited her, empty, but on the bench next to hers sat the three old men who'd also been sitting there the afternoon before and maybe, she thought, the one before that. She wondered whether these three men came every single day. It seemed like the opening to a dad joke—three old men on a bench. But these three seemed more dynamic than that.

One, short and rotund, wore a red track jacket. He was pink in the cheeks and looked distressed even when he was laughing, which was often, even when the other two didn't think anything was funny. The second, tall with broad shoulders and a distinguished mustache, wore a green windbreaker that hung large. His facial hair more groomed than the rest of him, dingy white tufts poking out around his flat tweed cap, he seemed scattered, easily distracted by a passing dog or baby. The third, petite with a trim gray beard, wore a brown tweed jacket. He was the most effusive of the three, often looking delighted and emphatically gesticulating.

The old men moved around one another with a choreography so natural it seemed as if they'd been sitting on this bench since the dawn of time. Their volume ran the gamut, a spectrum of mumbling to vigorous shouting. They drank tea or coffee, or shared nuts from a paper bag. She wished she could eavesdrop, but lacking much Polish, she was left to tonal interpretation. Every so often, a snippet of their conversation would waft her way, the sound of it so familiar, she felt she could nearly understand it. *How long had they lived here in Muranów?*

How often had they assembled? Shiva listened until she didn't know how to listen in another language anymore, and then even a little bit longer.

———

The thing you are waiting for isn't the thing you think you are waiting for.

When Piotr met Jakub, Piotr was waiting for a friend on a park bench at the northeast corner of Pole Mokotowskie, the biggest park in Mokotów. They were going to catch up and feed the pigeons, and he'd worn a new sweater for the occasion, enjoying the sunshine as he waited. This was neither his usual bench nor his usual park, but he loved it just the same.

He looked up to see a tall and thick-jawed man in black glasses and a long gray jacket shuffle past with the aid of a silver cane, his scruffy brown terrier galloping ahead of him on a pink leash. Piotr noticed the man noticing him and felt shy. Being noticed these days was uncommon. He followed the substantial man with his eyes as he felt his own weight press hard into the bench, hoping—suddenly, absurdly—that his friend wouldn't show. Suddenly warm, he wiggled out of his jacket.

Ada was due home from visiting her niece the following evening. She'd been gone for two weeks, the longest trip she'd taken apart from Piotr in years, and he'd missed her but was loath to admit how lovely it had felt to be alone. Alone, thoughts of Ada and her soft brown eyes and her tomato rice soup turned to thoughts of Józef before he could stop them. What kind of happily married seventy-six-year-old man sat on park benches thinking about the sharp-witted clear-eyed gentleman he had worked with at a restaurant back when he was in his twenties?

Józef, who'd been a friend to Piotr at his job in a new place, just once, on a break in the back lot from frying onions and baking trays of rolls, had put his arm around Piotr's waist and left it there longer than he should have, moving it back and forth as if to say, *this is no accident*, and then looking him square in the eyes to confirm. Piotr and Józef had gotten close, but there was something about that afternoon, laughing and being foolish together, that still gave Piotr a crackly feeling every time he remembered it. That spot on his waist still tingled sometimes, a thing he would never admit to anyone. He wondered about Józef still, even considered asking his granddaughter how he might find someone on the computer, but thought better of it.

A few minutes later, the man in the glasses returned, heading straight for Piotr's bench. He asked if he could sit, and Piotr nodded, wondering why, in a park with so many benches, a man would want to sit next to him on this one. The man introduced himself as Jakub. Jakub liked his sweater, said it was a lovely blue. Piotr couldn't remember the last time he had heard a man describe something as *lovely. It goes nice with the grass*, Jakub said.

Jakub continued to make small talk, and Piotr responded in kind, feeling more reserved than usual. He looked down at the grass and noticed it was getting greener, particularly at its tips. It reached for the sky. Jakub asked Piotr a question then, and Piotr finally turned to face him. Jakub's eyes were warm and wide. The grass got even greener then, a rush of green, everywhere green. The ground, Piotr noticed, trying to resist vertigo, was rising fast, too fast, and the trees were vibrating, and when he looked up, he didn't see the other park benches anymore, as if they were now invisible or maybe gone. Disappeared, every last one of them.

On Dawid's advice, Shiva decided to break out the green dress and check out a bar in Mokotów known mostly for its expansive craft beer selection. It wasn't a queer bar, but he had heard from a reliable source—his sister's best friend's girlfriend—that the performers in Warsaw's feminist burlesque scene and their friends and lovers hung out there sometimes post-show. It was the best lead Shiva had gotten so far on a place she might run into the Ghost.

Out the window as the tram sped toward Mokotów, a blur of brightly colored doorways, an endless propagation of vibrant street art that memorialized Jewish Warsaw, little shops with signs that said this *sklep* and that *sklep*, museums and squat stone memorials and ice cream stands. As the tram got closer, the Warsaw dark lit up with hip bars, trendy restaurants, boutique shops. Here, there were fewer older people and many younger, as the streets populated, illuminated, and shed their trees. Two Warsaws. Many more than two. She pushed the button and stepped down gingerly onto the sidewalk, proud of herself for not getting lost.

The bar was crowded and a little garish, lit by strings of multicolor lights and plastered floor to ceiling with black-and-white photos. From the speakers, something that sounded like Pearl Jam but wasn't. She walked up to the bar and pointed at the IPA on tap that featured a picture of an orange. The mustachioed bartender, who wore a shirt covered in pineapples buttoned all the way up to his chin, poured her drink without paying much heed to her fumbling with Polish currency. Once the beer had been ordered and successfully paid for, she had nothing to do but sit and drink it.

Shiva gazed out the bar's front window, watching people amble past at an early evening pace, headlights turning starburst as they caught in the dark glass. She'd had some fantasy that people *really did this*. They searched faraway places for mystery people who had zero interest in being found. They then, of course, found them. Just barely, but they found them. They found them in absurd places against impossible odds—lying on the floors of planetariums, in trolley cars, on abandoned ice rinks, or on densely populated seashores. And then they kissed them, dipped them, married them, brought them home to ecstatic sets of well-adjusted parents, set sail with them, penned epics about beating the odds. It was inflated and cinematic. She didn't even speak Polish.

She missed Levi acutely suddenly. She missed Aria and Marv, missed the tipsy diligent rhythms of her grad school reading group, missed the queer starshine of Rebekah's dining room. She imagined coming home at the end of this strange day to a late-night living-room-floor debrief or a boozy luxurious brunch where she would tell her friends everything. But what was everything, exactly? Being in Warsaw did feel closer. But not knowing how close yet felt disorienting.

She saw a flash of green reflected in the window, and it took her a second to realize it was the green of her own dress. She'd sat at bars in Brooklyn before, alone with a book and a cocktail, but this felt different, this looking at herself.

Who was she here? She must be someone. Someone outside of Dani's love, outside of Rosen's preemptive predictions of her failure, far away and also incredibly close to her family of dead ends. What was the story of her in this place? When she retold it with gusto to a group of her most beloved, would it have a start or an end? *Could there be a story*, she wondered, *that was entirely middle?*

Central Park has 9,485 benches. Some people make a project of attempting to sit on every last one of them. At least a thousand of the benches have experienced marriage proposals. If you have ten thousand dollars sitting around, you can adopt a bench and name it what you'd like. Some of the benches are engraved in memoriam, in love, in dedication, in cryptic code. In the mid-1950s, a sea captain slept for three nights on a concrete and green-wood bench at Miners' Gate because he wasn't accustomed to dry land or the plush softness of his bed. In the mid-1970s, a marginally famous romance novelist wrote three of his seven books on the same bench by Artisans' Gate. In 2002, a girl left her journal on one of the benches near Woodman's Gate, only for it to be found by another girl, who read it greedily and then, transformed, returned it to the bench with a note of gratitude on the inside cover. And all the millions of secrets, overheard and kept—the benches in Central Park are itchy with them.

Park benches watch. They sense when you're coming and perch at the ready. Take a look. There's a stance. Each is a shape-shifter. A guard. A place to sleep or think or pretend to think. A place to lose or be lost or forget. A place to watch or be watched; to hide in plain sight.

In Pole Mokotowskie, unlike in any park in New York City, some of the benches are designed to lean back so that you can sit almost horizontally, facing upward. For those who keep company with the sky. For those who know where to look for the company they won't find anywhere lower down.

———

Halfway through her pint, two handsome Polish queers came into the bar, and Shiva tried to guess if they were a pair of friends or a couple. They burst in talking loudly, like regulars, one of them dressed for a night out in platform heels and a blue scoop-neck dress, and the other, just as tall as their high-heeled companion, dressed simply in a pair of brown work boots, jeans, and a white T-shirt. The one in the dress laughed musically at some yarn the bartender was spinning, as the white T-shirt walked in Shiva's direction with two tall glasses, beer sloshing over their edges. They nodded at Shiva, put the beers down next to where Shiva sat, and said something in very speedy Polish. Shiva's hand flew to her heart, her embarrassing and now-habitual way of saying, *I'm sorry, I don't speak Polish.*

"Ah, English, okay." They had a toothy smile that turned on all the lights in their face. "That's all right. I thought I knew you from somewhere, but maybe you aren't from here?"

"I'm not from here. Unless you count three generations back." She laughed nervously, unsure whether she'd just made a joke. "But now, from New York." Shiva wondered how legibly queer she looked to this person whose eyes were searching her now for traces of shared social history. She hoped the dress spoke for itself.

"Were you at Krzysztof's party last night?" They squinted at her.

"I wasn't," said Shiva. She had, in fact, been whiling away the end of daylight with her old men.

"Ah, it was a blast. He does it every year for his birthday, him and his partner, a big dance party. They make these delicious cocktails and rainbow-colored cupcakes. Oh well, cheers." They lifted their beer.

"Cheers," said Shiva, raising hers to meet it. "I wish I had been; it sounds very fun." She ran a fingertip around the edge of her glass. "Hey, now that you mention it. Do you know someone named Gabriela? Maybe she was at Krzysztof's party." She felt ridiculous as soon as she asked, so kept talking to try to make it better. "I think that's her name. I mean, I don't know her last name. I don't really know her. She's just someone I'm looking for."

"Gabriela. She lives here?"

Shiva nodded. Could this be her chance encounter? Her abandoned ice rink?

"She rides a motorcycle." The extra detail felt desperate as it came out of her mouth.

"Emi!" The woman in the heels turned. "Do we know someone named Gabriela, maybe in the burlesque? Who's that one with the motorcycle?"

"I think her name is Magda, the one who rides. She has such good hair, it's disgusting." She said something else in Polish, then laughed. "Who is Gabriela?"

"I don't know." The T-shirt pointed at Shiva. "She's from New York, and she's looking for someone with this name."

"My name is Shiva." She extended her hand, immediately feeling awkwardly overformal.

"Shiva. I have never heard that name. It's pretty." The T-shirt took Shiva's hand in theirs but didn't shake it.

"Thank you," said Shiva, deciding, for the moment, against explaining its origins to this stranger.

"My name is Elzbieta, but everyone calls me El," they said. "How long are you in Warsaw for?"

"Just another few days," said Shiva.

"Well. You should definitely come to the queer porn screening at the burlesque on Saturday. I bet your Gabriela will be there."

Shiva had momentarily forgotten about the Ghost. She was focused on El's slight overbite and the tiny stud in their right ear. Something about them reminded her of Dani, who had always looked simultaneously prepared for a stand-up comedy set and a bar brawl. She blinked the thought away.

"Will you be there?"

"Of course." El grinned. "My friends are organizing it."

"Fun," she said, hoping she sounded like she meant it. She wasn't about to admit that she had never been to anything like a public porn screening before. Talking to this queer who didn't know her but thought they had, it was a home feeling. "And cool that your friends organize that. Have you lived in Warsaw a long time?"

"My whole life," said El. "My family goes back five generations here."

Shiva couldn't imagine. Mira had left Poland relatively young, between the wars, but the families of most of the Eastern European Jewish people she knew from Poland had been either driven out or killed. All those family stories marked and changed irrevocably by their violent interruptions. The prospect of having been in Poland for five generations felt impossible. If El's ancestors were Polish gentiles, she wondered what their relationship would have been like with the Polish Jews who would have been hers.

"That's a long time," she said.

"Yeah, for a strange place with a lot of hard history. I'm sure you are more than familiar." They sipped at the froth on their beer. "So, what brings you to Warsaw?"

"I'm here on a research trip," she said.

It wasn't untrue, of course, but it sounded thin.

She tried again. "I'm studying Jewish folklore, specifically S. Ansky, the Jewish playwright who wrote that play *The Dybbuk*, and also trying to learn more about my family. My great-grandmother is from nearby here. Nearish."

El raised an eyebrow.

"Also," she said, almost apologetically, "I'm trying to get in touch with this . . . motorcyclist." She immediately regretted bringing up Gabriela again, not only because it was humiliating but also because, at least in this moment, she felt much more curious about El.

"Right." Between them, the motorcyclist hung and dissipated in the air. "You said your great-grandmother is from nearby. Can I ask where?"

Before Shiva could reply, Emi trampled back over in her mega-heels. Shiva didn't want to be a droop, standing around at bars talking about great-grandmothers.

"Do you ride a motorcycle too?" Emi asked, seamlessly joining them.

Shiva let out a monosyllabic cackle. "No way. I can barely make my way down a crowded street without injuring myself." El smiled at the self-deprecation, which gratified Shiva.

"Elli, Kaśka and Doro are here." Emi gestured to a booth toward the back of the bar where two other attractive queers were waving enthusiastically. "Come on." She looked at Shiva. "You want to join us?"

"No, that's okay," Shiva said, though nothing would have made her gladder that night than to keep talking to this queer who reminded her of something of which she felt she needed reminding. She didn't want to insert herself where she wasn't welcome. "Thank you, though."

Had they been back in Brooklyn, she might have been able to
stay, to have another drink, to charm, even. But tonight, even in her
green dress, she felt displaced and socially flabby, and could think only
about how she might most smoothly exit. She downed the remaining
eighth of her beer.

"Hey, it was nice to meet you," she said to El and, to her own
horror, stuck out her right hand again.

El ignored the hand this time, leaned in and kissed Shiva's right
cheek. "We don't really shake hands here. Or at least I don't."

Shiva could feel her cheeks purple. She turned to Emi. "Nice to
meet you too," she said, even though they hadn't. Emi smiled politely.
Shiva picked up her bag and walked toward the door as the sounds of
laughing behind her meant that someone's night was just beginning.

There is, for example, the story about the line cook and the librarian.
They were set up by a friend and decided to meet in a park between
their apartment buildings, right in the middle of Żoliborz. The line
cook said she would wear white; the librarian, bright pink. The day
they met threatened rain, and while the line cook was early, the librarian was late. Above them, even the horizon wobbled with anticipation.
They sat together on a wrought-iron bench tucked underneath a tree.
They sat talking past their dinner reservation.

The line cook liked to travel, chasing adventure and spicy food, and
felt suspicious of the provincial nature of blind dating. She liked the
librarian, though, who wore bold patterns and asked detailed questions.
They took to meeting often at their bench in the park in Żoliborz.
The librarian felt tipsy whenever she saw the line cook approaching,
those long and practiced limbs, wolf jaw, and the confidence of a
prince. The air hummed around them. The bench held them there
as long as it could.

When the line cook grew afraid and left one day, not showing up the first warm night in May; when the librarian arrived to an empty bench—no messages, no explanations; when the librarian stopped eating with worry; when the librarian berated herself for skipping meals over someone she'd barely known; when the line cook cried tearlessly in a way that embarrassed her; when the line cook went off with a bartender who asked fewer questions, the bench left too.

The librarian avoided the park for two weeks, walking the long route to her tram stop. Finally, she returned to the park in Żoliborz to grieve a woman she'd almost come to know. She stopped where their bench had been. There, tucked under that tree, there was no longer any bench—no ceremony, no ghosts, no notice, no GONE FISHING. Just an unclean exit, a rush job, two small metal nubs where the front legs had been, grass mostly intact.

———

Shiva walked out of the bar. She felt too amped up to go home yet, so she picked a direction and walked in it.

She was only three blocks from the bar when she saw him: the man from the park bench in Muranów. Even beer-tipsy, she recognized him, the petite gesticulating tweed who always looked delighted. Her favorite. He was walking at a clip, faster than Shiva might have imagined he would walk. Without thinking, Shiva followed him. Though they didn't know it, the three men had become her kin, but she hadn't even considered that their lives extended past the time they spent on that bench. She wanted badly to know what he was doing in this neighborhood, speed-walking after dark.

The man moved so quickly that it was hard for Shiva to keep up in her kitten heels. She walked toe-first, trying not to clack. He zigzagged through the neighborhood, the busy thoroughfare giving way to blocks less populated with retail and more pocked with alleys, and then directly through one of these alleys, down a darker and quieter street, across an intersection, and right into Pole Mokotowskie.

Shiva followed, relieved to be walking noiselessly on grass and only a little afraid to be trailing a stranger into an unlit park. He followed the path that curled around the central green. At this hour, the park was mostly empty, save for a few shadowy figures. Except for the crickets and the rustle of the wind, it was quiet.

The man finally slowed. Shiva stopped behind a fat tree, watching as he approached a particular bench. He did not sit but stood very still. Presently, another man arrived. He was tall, and Shiva could see the broad silhouette of a long jacket and a pair of thick glasses. He was walking a scruffy dog who was quiet too. She watched as the two men stood and faced one another, nobody speaking, not the watcher nor the watched. A solitary black bird flew past as the tall man leaned down and whispered in the ear of the shorter man, who stood on his toes to listen. A light wind softly rustled the leaves. Did she imagine their smiles? She hugged herself, shivering. She watched as they did not sit down, did not dip, only took one another's hands and stood facing one another in the dark for a long while. And then, as briskly as they had approached, they embraced briefly and parted ways, the tall gentleman and his dog one way, and Shiva's petite neighbor the other. The only person who didn't move then was Shiva, whose chest was in her mouth, whose feet were heavy on the ground, who'd found something that made her want to stay much longer than she'd planned.

The thing you are waiting for isn't the thing you think you are waiting for. It's not a revelation. It's not a stack of evidentiary documents, nor is it the obvious thing you've forgotten. It's neither long-lost love nor mysterious stranger. It's backshadow, skeletal, something peripheral, nothing head-on. The end streak of a fox; a sudden stillness, an echo.

Everything has been here for longer than you can imagine.

Piotr won't find Józef, of course. Piotr with the tweed jacket and the nervous fingers and the things he can't find names for. He won't find that hand on his waist again. But in Jakub, a kind of echo. In everything, a kind of echo. Finding a surprising pair of arms in the dark. Someone you had no idea you were allowed to look for.

They skillfully catch what echoes fall, the park benches. They remember who came before you, who gave you your laugh, who gave you your stories. They remember who barely escaped, who buried strange desires in parcels and envelopes. Remembering is part of their job.

They are here even when you can't see them. You, baffled traveler. You know why you're here even if you can't fit your mouth around it yet. They are ready to show you if you are ready to notice. They'll be here for you when you grow weary, when you grow curious, when you need a place to stay awhile. They'll be here when you come back, and even when you don't.

April 12, 1921

Dear L,

I know that people are afraid of me. But I have been afraid too. Every time I laugh or move or make a sound, I risk the wrath of people who wish me to disappear forever. And I don't want to disappear.

Last summer, Jacob put his hat on the table by accident, bad luck for a year. Mama jumped to flip it over, fast enough you would have thought she was trying to tamp out a kitchen fire. She threw a potato and an onion into it, like Jacob's hat had always been a bowl. *No hats on my table*, she growled, spitting on the floor for good measure. I saw the way she looked at him, like we couldn't afford any more reasons to be visited. When I was small, we kept bowls of salt in every corner of the house. This helped keep them away, Mama said, but some winter nights, all the fires went out, and the rooms went dark, and the wind swept through our windows all night long. I shivered under my thin blankets, training my lips on someone else's name so that whatever whispered through our entryways would not recognize me for the vessel I was.

We already have so much to be afraid of. Our people, we are not beloved. We must protect each other.

You were sterner with me today than usual, L, which I know means I have to talk about what happened those weeks ago, what silenced me this way. I will tell you. But I pray again, please tell no one else. I am shunned as it is, and I couldn't bear a single enemy more.

One afternoon, I overheard Mama and Papa talking in hushed tones about what is to be done with me. I heard Mama insist that I am capable of being married, of making a home, even though something has so clearly broken in me. *She's still a young woman, Shmiel*, she said. *Doesn't that count for something?* I couldn't hear Papa's response, but shortly after their conversation ended, he left the house. Jacob was not home—he had already started spending days studying with the rabbi. This, I think, is for the best. When he is here, things are more joyous, which in turn puts me in danger. It is also sad, because when Jacob is gone, I miss my friend. And in the bright glare of all this fear, our friendship is thinning.

The very next afternoon, I made myself useful, sweeping ash from around the fire and dust from the corners, and I heard a knock on the door. *Hello, Isaac,* I heard Mama say. *Thank you for coming. Can I boil you some tea while I go and fetch Mira?* I had seen Isaac, the innkeeper's son, several times at the fair. He seemed nice, though not handsome. A soft chin, almost no chin at all. Eyes that looked watery, if kind. Like someone who has been sad before and could be sad again.

I heard Mama pull out a chair for Isaac and fill the kettle. I sat right here, in my room—the room where you visit me, L. And for some reason, right then, I felt more afraid than I ever have. I didn't want to have tea with Isaac, the innkeeper's son.

It is hard even for me to believe what I did next.

Everything comes back to the forest.

I want you to know that the moment I heard Isaac's voice, its slow and hesitant lilt, saying, *yes, I'll have some tea,* I became a bouquet of wings. I do not know how else to explain it. Something within me—call it an evil spirit if you will, I don't much care anymore—took flight, and I had no choice but to fly along with it. I put on my coat and scarf and opened my window, throwing one leg over the window ledge. The wind grabbed at my skirt, and the wooden sill was rough against my legs, even through my stockings. I was wearing my house shoes, and I looked up and down the street, assessing who might see me if I leapt down. I wobbled there, trying to figure out a way down, and finally swung my second leg over the sill, ducking my head under the window, and lowering myself until my foot touched the top of the next window. Holding tight to the window frame, I cautiously climbed down to the first-floor sill—the window was curtained, thank God—and then to the ground.

On the ground. In my house shoes. At the edge of evening.

And I ran.

I rarely run, so my legs were baffled by the effort, but I ran as fast as I could. Past the houses and the synagogue and Papa's mill, without daring to look. Past the cheder and the women in line at the evening market. Along the river and across the bridge to the very edge of the woods, the blue-green place where the air gets colder and the sky gets darker sooner than anywhere else.

I kept running.

I ran into the woods, feeling stones and twigs through the thin bottoms of my slippers. Out of breath, I finally stopped when I reached a small, rounded clearing, a majestic tree in its center.

There, I was alone. I couldn't remember the last time I had been alone. Not locked in my lonely room, but alone by my own choosing. It was cold, but I didn't mind. My eyes stung with the chill, and my feet sank a little in the soft dirt. The weather swirled around me, and I shivered. A fat bird flew over my head, and I felt so absurdly free, so disbelieving of what I'd just done, that I started laughing.

I hadn't laughed for so long that, once I started, I couldn't stop.

For me, laughing is one of the wildest things about being inside a body. Smiling is calm. I have seen brides smile on their wedding days, men beaming down at their children, children smiling when they receive a rare piece of cake instead of a handful of prunes, but it is another matter, entirely, to be seized and lifted by laughter. I rarely laugh anymore, but when I do, it feels like being broken open, and that is when I am most afraid someone will see me. That everyone might truly see me. And at this point, to be seen would be the most terrifying thing of all.

I stood there in the clearing, screaming peals of laughter as if everything inside me was sprouting. My nerves prickled, skin singing like the trembling bow of a fiddle. I felt awake.

It might sound strange to say, but this felt more like praying than anything I've ever done at synagogue. I closed my eyes and felt the fluttering of the dry winter leaves, heard the brush of the trees' long branches.

Something was in the clearing with me, listening as I let my laughter become a kind of asking. *Let this place be mine. Only mine.*

I didn't even think about stopping until I heard the sounds. At first, I thought they were wild animals. But they were voices. Men's voices. Angry. My father. Kalman Hirsch. Getting closer. Something happened then, at the very back of my throat: two tiny doors slid shut. My ecstatic roars were swallowed back into silence. I shuddered—it felt a little bit like choking, and I gulped once or twice to make sure my body was still working. It worked well enough for me to run back out of my secret clearing, rasping breath from my looted lungs, toward the very voices that threatened to contain me. I would sooner turn myself in for fleeing than have Papa and his accomplice discover my newfound sanctuary.

I met them at the edge of the woods, right at the bank of the Wielopolka River. I made my eyes meet Papa's. For a moment, he looked sad, almost like I was someone he loved, or at least wanted to. But then, something in his face switched.

"Enough," he hissed.

Kalman Hirsch stood back, the weakest kind of man: hiding behind a giant from a girl. Papa had brought a schmatte with him, which he tied around my mouth like a gag. He was angry, and his voice was loud, drowning out the beauty at the woods' edge. "Keep the sheydim where they belong, daughter. Your screams are the screams of hell." When tears began to fall silently down my cheeks, he looked at me a little bit like a father might, even as he finished knotting the dirty rag around my mouth. "Laughter is no gift you get to keep, daughter. Your job is to protect us all from what lives inside you. And you can do that by being quiet."

How do I explain this, L? In that moment, another door inside my throat slid shut. And another. Layers of doors closed and locked over the thing that had once been my voice. I swallowed the darkness I felt in my lungs, my ribs, my chest. My father in all his brute strength dragged me back home, where my mother told me in a voice quiet with worry how disgraceful it was what I'd done and how dangerous. Where had I gone? What had I been thinking?

"I am going to try to find someone who can help you better than we can," she said, untying the gag around my mouth. "Your father is too harsh, I think," she whispered, so he wouldn't hear. "But you need help from someone who knows the spirit world, and who can protect you and all of us from whatever feeds on you."

As punishment for running from Isaac, I would agree to have tea with him again in a few weeks' time, when he returned from some travels. We would sit under my mother's watchful eye. No rash escapes.

I opened my mouth to speak, to protest, to ask, even just to cry a little bit, a relief from the violence of the gag.

And nothing came out. No sound, no words, nothing.

Those doors upon doors in my throat and my chest, they were shut now.

And you know this part, of course, dear L, but I haven't heard my own voice since.

Thank you for listening. It is more helpful than I expected, writing this heaviness into a story.

Yours,
Mira

Fourteen

The second Tuesday in March, Hannah stopped at the Kosher Counter on her way to the funeral home. She was going to meet Marla so that they could discuss her prospects, but she'd left early enough so she'd have time for the stop. She didn't make a habit of it, but a Kosher Counter knish in her car was one of the few remaining sentimental rites she had for her long-gone mother. She made a point of getting one when she needed to feel a little bit closer to Syl, and rare as this was, right now she thought it might help.

She walked back to her car with the knish and an Orange Crush to wash it down, slid into the driver's seat, lay a futile napkin across her lap, and ate, oily flakes snowing onto the floor mat. When she was done, she crumpled the grease-spotted napkin in her right hand and chugged half the soda. Soda was occasional but matchless when it was the thing you really wanted. *Thank you*, she said, to no one.

Afterward, Hannah checked her face in the rearview mirror and drove to Garfinkel's. She was nervous, like she was about to walk into something significant. Maybe it was just that it was notable she was leaving the house and walking into anything at all. The thought made her feel pitiful, and Neil Diamond on the easy-listening station didn't help.

Early as she always was, Hannah let herself in with the spare keys Marla had given her and locked the door again. She moved slowly through the empty funeral home. It was strange to be here during the day and strange to be here fully alone.

She looked at her phone. Marla, who was often late, wasn't due for at least another forty-five minutes. *I'll give you the lay of the land*, she'd promised, even though the land wasn't that big, and Hannah felt like she already had the lay of most of it. In the time since they'd last spoken, Hannah had started to warm to the idea that the funeral home might become partially her domain. She had always been drawn to death, even in its catastrophic aftermath, even as it also made her profoundly uncomfortable. She'd known this about herself for a long time, but maybe she was finally beginning to fully accept it.

Hannah had also been thinking more than she wanted to admit about the green-eyed woman. She didn't want to get carried away, but it had been odd, hadn't it? Over and over she replayed the surreal staring contest in her head. Why had it happened? How in the world, those same green eyes? Her memory, ordinarily disastrous, was crystalline when it came to those eyes. She couldn't ever forget the curve of the lashes, so real and delicate through the mirror glass, she'd felt like she could touch them.

Even just the memory of that desire was an animal uncurling in her gut.

Syl, Hannah remembered, had a story about potatoes. They were beautiful, she'd always insisted, in a way most people refused to notice. Syl hadn't been much of a cook, but she could peel a potato in one deft swirl, never once lifting the peeler. *I learned from my mother*, she'd say, her mouth hinting at a smile, as Hannah watched, mesmerized, her mouth wide around an unspoken *how*.

In a town whose name very few people remember, Syl would tell, there was a shopkeeper who had an unusual tradition. Every Friday, he sorted the good potatoes from the bad. He discarded the rotten potatoes but often ended up with at least one strange potato—misshapen, slightly too green, doubled, or in one case, bright purple. Of these strange potatoes, he would pick his favorite and bring it to the foot of the humble bridge for which, at one time, this town was marginally renowned. There, using a stick to dig, he would plant the potato in the ground. Then he would kiss the ground, blow a kiss to the sky, and say, *gut Shabbos*, in a voice so choked with joy, it was as though he'd won the lottery.

Townspeople began to wonder whether this man was fit to keep a shop. *Why do you do this?* they asked. A small crowd had begun to gather to watch the weekly plantings, a ritual no one admitted they'd come to rely on. *I believe that one day, from one of these blessed potatoes, something will grow from the ground that will allow me never to work again.* The townspeople laughed. Townspeople should learn to suspend judgment sometimes, but that is for another story.

One Sunday, a young woman and her suitor were strolling past the river, and they stopped short at the foot of the bridge, where by now, the shopkeeper had planted dozens of misfit potatoes. There, before their eyes, stood a plant, the likes of which no one had ever seen before. It twisted skyward, its enormous leaves shiny and intricately patterned. Its tiny flower buds were multicolor, purple and yellow, pink and orange. The young couple ran to the shop to tell the shopkeeper, who dropped the bushel of apples he'd been holding and ran to the bridge, trailed by stray apples. He approached his plant. He touched it. It was thick and strong, like it had been there for generations.

The mysterious potato plant grew until its curled tentacles had overtaken the bridge. People began to come from neighboring towns to see this miracle, and the shopkeeper set up a small stand at the edge of the woods, charging two pennies per family to come and witness the handiwork of God. (God, he was certain, would understand.)

Eventually, the plant grew so large and strong it consumed the bridge entirely, and having done so, the plant itself eroded, leaving in its wake only a sizable pile of potato starch. But by the time that happened, the shopkeeper and his children were already dead and had been amply fed for the entirety of their lives.

In all her fifty-five years, there was exactly one July that Hannah remembered clearly: July 1985. She only retained fragments of all those other Julys, most of which had fallen victim to a lazy, hazy forgetfulness.

There was the long, dull burn of the steel slide under her sticky thighs at the playground, and the buggy little suburban creeks walking home. There were the peanut-butter-and-jelly sandwiches her mother would pack in sweaty plastic baggies and produce from her purse wherever they went. There was her small blue bedroom at the end of the hallway in the house on Gibson Street, the curly blue telephone cord the summer Syl finally agreed to let Hannah have a phone in her bedroom. For a long while, the phone had hung in the hallway, but inevitably, when Lydia or Rachel called or, every so often, a boy Hannah liked, she would pull the cord as far as she could and close her bedroom door over it, creating a tightrope as she lay on the carpet talking for hours. There was ninth-grade summer, when Rachel's family moved to a house around the corner from Hannah—they couldn't believe their luck, *around the corner.* All those evenings they walked together to the drugstore and read each other the names on the bottoms of nail-polish bottles and ogled pop stars in the magazine aisle. They'd split a candy bar on the walk home, promising to call one another as soon as they got back to their rooms. There was the summer after freshman year, which she only remembered being so hot, they all sought respite in the movie theater. It was that summer she went on a couple of movie dates with Alan Rabinowitz, a lanky and bumbling statistics major with crooked teeth whose hair was so coiffed he got away with seeming handsome, if by a narrow margin. She still thought fondly of Alan; he'd been so unreasonably confident that the first time he told her she was beautiful—outside, after a particularly funny double feature—she felt, despite herself, like she truly was.

The July Hannah so clearly remembered was the July right after her junior year of college. It was the year Tears for Fears released *Songs from the Big Chair*, and Hannah had been entirely possessed by the song "Shout." She had a debilitating crush on Roland Orzabal, having developed a taste for moody and effeminate men, but even more, the song felt trancelike, transporting. Something came loose in her when she listened, the pounding insistence of the refrain a fervent desire she felt in her entire face. And most of all, his voice. A voice at once unlatched from masculinity and saturated in it, shiny with wet longing. A shimmer of unshed tears, a wanting so kinetic she could taste it just listening. It broke her heart.

July was always slow, but this July felt mud-slow. Hannah was working as a barista at Daisy's near campus, and all summer long, the boom box in the kitchen played Prince and Tears for Fears and the Cure. Jon had gone home to North Carolina for the summer, and it felt good to miss him while he was gone. It was so unlike missing her father, who had left without consulting her. Jon's absence was temporary, and its reasons clear. Not the eviction of pleasure but its long delay.

The days ambled at a summer pace toward whatever might come after she graduated. The little house Jon already had his eye on in Takoma Park. *For when we get married*, he said. She blushed every time she thought about these plans they were making. She felt pretty that season. The short black skirt and crisp white top she wore to work didn't look awful on her, and she had taken to berry-colored lip gloss. She had learned to inhabit her curves—the thick of her thighs, her broad hips and wide freckled back—and wore her wavy hair in a high ponytail that made her look more fun than she actually was.

She remembered it was July because of the fireworks. The chaos engendered by recreational explosions had always stressed her out, but Syl, for whatever reason, had always adored them. On July 4, 1985, Syl stopped Hannah before she ran out of the house for her shift. Syl was

writing in her notebook at the kitchen table, as she was most mornings
before she left for her part-time job at the library.

"You're coming with me tonight," she said.

"Ma, you know I can't stand fireworks. Do I have to? Can't you
ask Marisa?" Marisa was one of Syl's few friends, another birder who
worked part-time at the library checkout counter, like Syl had back
then.

Syl pursed her lips. "I'd rather go with you. We can get pastrami
sandwiches after."

You couldn't say no to Syl. She so rarely asked you to say yes. And
things had never gone fully back to normal—even Syl-normal—after the
sixteenth-birthday incident. Long since thawed, the specter of mutual
betrayal had petrified into a cold and permanent distance between them.
Hannah knew that what she'd done that night had been an irrevocable
slap in her mother's face. But Hannah was also beginning to understand the extent to which Syl's outsize response—the hurt, the anger,
the disproportionate fear—had damaged her right back. Syl was the
mother. The one who was supposed to forgive, to support, to keep
things in perspective. Instead, this grudge-holding world record, and
no one ever quite bouncing back.

Being asked to go on a fireworks and sandwiches date, then, was
the promise of more familial intimacy than Hannah had experienced
in forever. Plus, it was always novel to see her mother doing normal
people stuff—shoes kicked off, lying on a summer blanket, eating ice
cream. Watching the sky for nothing more arcane than spectacle and
pure entertainment.

The fireworks display was blessedly brief. Hannah kept her ears
plugged and her eyes open and lay next to her mother. The sky, streaks
of pink and periwinkle, orange and gold, electric threads of green and
white-hot dust pouring toward the earth. Even Hannah had to admit
it was a visual feast. Syl right next to her, taking it in, her light blue

men's dress shirt tucked into black slacks, her only opulence her rings
and bracelets, red hair in an unruly bouquet around her head.

Afterward, they drove home in Syl's '76 Chevy, the air conditioner
broken and the windows uselessly rolled down. The heat murmured,
city noise coming in from all sides. They stopped for gas. And then,
at last, they stopped for pastrami sandwiches and a potato knish to
share from the Kosher Counter. They were too hungry to wait until
they got home, so they sat in the parking lot to eat, windows rolled
all the way down.

Could you get drunk on soda? Hannah remembered wondering. At
some point—*Songs from the Big Chair* playing on her mother's cassette
player, Syl gabbing like a best friend after a football game—Hannah
decided there must be something in the Orange Crush. Things hadn't
been this easy between them in a very long time. Maybe ever. *Why
was this night so different?* she wondered.

"This is so good," said Syl between bites. "Does Jon like pastrami?"

Her mother so rarely asked about her fiancé that the question
made Hannah blush.

"He loves it."

"Thank God," said Syl.

"I mean, could we date if he didn't like pastrami? I don't think so."

"Of course not," said Syl. "I was worried you would tell me he was
a vegetarian. Can you pass the knish?"

Hannah handed the heavy foil-wrapped parcel to her mother, still
steaming hot. She watched the joy on Syl's face as she peeled back the
wrapping, a savory potato fragrance filling the car.

"Is that smell not heavenly?" She blew on it a little and then took a
small bite. Syl closed her eyes. "Hannah, you must try this." She took
another bite and handed it to Hannah.

Hannah closed her eyes too. It was just instinct, when that smell
got close enough to you. She bit through the soft oily dough into the

onion-laced potato mash in the center. "This might be the absolute best thing I have ever eaten."

Syl took the knish back. "This is holy food. Miriam's Well should have supplied the Jews in the desert with pastrami and potato knishes."

Hannah laughed. "Mother, give me back the knish."

"I think as long as they had accompanying soda, it would have been the perfect snack for exile."

"Okay, whatever you say," said Hannah. "You're the expert on ancient Hebrews around here."

Syl took one more big bite of the knish, and then passed the end of it back to her daughter. "That was damn near perfect," she said. Pleasure words sounded foreign out of her mother's mouth.

They crumpled up the paper bags and finished their sodas. Then Syl revved up the groaning Chevy and drove them home.

The next morning, Hannah came downstairs to find Syl, nose in her notebook and cross-eyed with focus. Remarkably, she looked up when Hannah came into the room. Her lips curled into a slight smile, and she murmured, *good morning.*

Hannah made the coffee then, feeling giddy. Like her life might be possible again.

———

Scrub and rinse four red potatoes. Leave the peel on each. A potato likes a container. Bring a pot of salted water to a boil. When the water is bubbling, drop the potatoes in. Pause between each for the splash. Let the potatoes fully cook, and then lift them out by slotted spoon. Don't discard the potato water right away—you'll find it milky and distasteful, but your face will benefit from its steam, which will bring you closer to the earth. Return to the potatoes once cooled. Bring nothing with you. Slice them, when you're ready, with a sharp knife. Don't forget the steam. More salt. Always more than you think. To serve, one whole potato per person. Each a slip of oil, a melt on the tongue. Every private bite. The next time you want something—anything—remember the feel of the potato in your hand.

———

Marla's office door was wide open. *Marla*, Hannah thought, internally rolling her eyes as if at an incorrigible family member, even though Marla was the only other person with a key to this place, and even though if someone did break in, they wouldn't walk away with much. A bagful of free yahrzeit candles, maybe, or if they were lucky, one of the limited-run and dubiously conceived lollipops imprinted with the Garfinkel's logo that had gone both in and out of rotation in 2016. She turned on the overhead light, which commenced buzzing as it cast the room in sleepy yellow. On Marla's desk, a stained white coffee mug, half an inch of old coffee in it, wearing the cartoon image of the grim reaper, scythe in hand, saying, THIS JOB MAKES ME FEEL SO ALIVE. An assortment of seemingly unrelated knickknacks, including a little bobblehead of a pudgy bearded rabbi with a tie-dyed prayer shawl, a plastic skeleton wearing a T-shirt that said, YOU ONLY DIE ONCE, and a crystal paperweight engraved with Marla's name. Hannah sat down in Marla's desk chair, leaning into the rumpled blazer slung over the back. The desk was covered in file folders, and Hannah made a mental note that she should encourage Marla to hire an intern.

Hannah leaned back in the chair and spun around to face a bookshelf that held a series of clinical-looking funeral home books, several lavender-bound poetry collections, a giant tome called *The American Way of Death Revisited*, and a multifaith afterlife anthology called *Where We Go, No One Knows*. Mounted on the wall above the bookshelf, right at eye level, a mirror. Hannah imagined Marla reapplying her lipstick after lunch, checking to make sure there weren't caraway seeds stuck in her teeth.

Now, Hannah looked at herself. Her hair, grown longer and wavier these days, a little frizzy. Her eyes, as she got older, got proportionally browner. Not darker brown; just more of it. Less sclera, more iris. Shiva often told her it made her eyes pretty but that Hannah also sometimes looked kind of high as a result. She knew what Shiva meant. Jon had loved her eyes, even stood up at their wedding to serenade her with an off-key version of "Brown-Eyed Girl," telling her time and again that they were beautiful, even though she knew they were plain, if exceptionally whiteless. She felt thirsty and noticed her lips were chapped. She applied clear lip balm and then rubbed at her cheeks, as she sometimes did when she felt sallow, trying to bring the life back into them.

She had the flicker of an idea she tried to shake off but couldn't quite. She looked at her phone. Forty minutes until Marla arrived. She got up, closed Marla's door and her mini-blinds, and turned off the overhead light. She reassured herself no one could see her. Inexplicably apprehensive, she returned to Marla's chair and looked directly into the mirror. She wasn't sixteen, and it wasn't midnight, and she didn't have a candle or any challah, but it was time, she guessed. It was decidedly unceremonious, which she didn't actually mind. There was the mirror, and there she was, in front of it.

The green-eyed woman at the tahara. The prospect that she'd actually encountered something spectral, that her mother had been not only remarkably wrong but also remarkably right. She needed proof. She could almost hear Syl's sharp laugh. *If you need proof that this world is full of things we can't see, you're not looking closely enough.* She looked into the mirror now, against the brutality of her own skepticism. She knew, rationally, that nothing would *happen*, but she made herself look anyway. It had been years since she'd simply looked into the mirror in a black room. Thirty-nine years, to be precise.

Still, only herself, glass-darked and blurry. Her face, square with rounded edges, a stubborn chin. Marla's cluttered office, a dim soup of monochromatic shapes, swimming behind her in the glass. She wondered if she should say something. A prayer? An incantation? Should she reason with her childhood ghost? What was she doing here, a middle-aged woman in somebody else's dark office looking for the nonexistent? *You're a widow,* she explained to herself, as though that excused everything. Still, she stared, willing herself not to turn from herself. Still, the dark quiet.

The noise at the front door of the funeral home startled her out of her uneventful reverie. She glanced again at her phone. Three thirty. A half hour before Marla's scheduled arrival, but someone was jiggling the handle of the front door, trying to get in. Hannah abruptly got up from her private experiment, flipped on Marla's light, and walked across the lobby to the front door.

On the other side of the glass, a woman.

Her.

There was no doubt. Hannah stared, feet nailed to the floor. She made no moves to open the door. The green-eyed woman stopped jiggling the handle. She stared back at Hannah. She was wearing a black T-shirt and black jeans. A brown leather bag hung over one of her shoulders, and one silver fringe dangled from her left ear. She was still slight but decidedly not spectral.

Hannah commanded her hands to unbolt the door, and the green-eyed woman walked through it. She brought an unnatural charge with her, and the March air felt like a breath.

"Hello," Hannah said.

"It's you," said the woman.

"It's you," said Hannah. Their stilted conversation echoed into the empty afternoon light of the Garfinkel's lobby.

It turned out her name was Riva, and she strode through like she owned the place, heading for the cubbies at the back of the room.

"Are you looking for something?" Hannah's voice liquefied as it touched the air.

"Yeah," said Riva. "I seem to have dropped an earring." She paused. "At that tahara." Hannah knew the one. Riva didn't need to say. She flicked at her single fringe. "I wore its mate in hopes of finding it. I've managed to keep this pair intact for almost a decade, so it seems a shame to lose one now."

Hannah managed a *hmm* that came from someplace so high in her throat she could taste it. "I'll help."

Hannah and Riva combed the lobby. There wasn't much to comb. Hannah uselessly rifled through the stacks of brochures on the entry-way table and tried not to watch as Riva dipped her hand into each pocket of each of the four stray coats on the coat rack.

"Nothing," said Riva. "I guess it was time to let it go, huh?"

"Huh," said Hannah.

Riva made no move to leave, so Hannah screwed up her courage.

"Are you new in town?" she asked, as if they were making small talk in line at the grocery store.

"No," said Riva. "I don't live here."

"Where do you live?"

"I'm just here for a few days," said Riva. "For work."

Hannah tried to ignore the desperate disappointment she felt hearing this.

"What is work?"

"I don't want to bore you," said Riva. "It keeps me on the road a lot."

"So, wait," Hannah said. "You're just passing through, but you showed up to our little funeral home to prepare Dottie Golding for burial?"

Riva laughed. Her laugh had a severity to it and reminded Hannah a little bit of her mother's.

"Well," she said. "I just like to do them."

"Taharas?"

"Yes," said Riva. "Some people like meditation. I like preparing the dead for transition. I know it sounds strange, but it's something that always helps me feel grounded, particularly when I'm visiting somewhere unfamiliar."

I get it, Hannah wanted to scream. "So, you're like a funeral crasher?"

"No," said Riva. "They're not funerals. That would be different."

"Oh, sure," said Hannah, attempting playful sarcasm.

Riva turned to face her. Her shoulders still square, her skin a little flushed, and her eyes still startling. That green. Nothing about her betrayed her age except a few salty streaks in her otherwise dark hair and a few smile lines that reassured Hannah she was certainly over forty. But beyond that, it was impossible to tell.

"Okay," said Riva. "Not entirely different." She rooted around in her bag, the gesture of someone who is trying to leave a place. Hannah scrambled for ways to keep Riva from walking out the door again.

"Here," said Riva. She'd pulled out a business card. RIVA HIRSCH, it read. CONSULTANT.

"Oh," said Hannah. "Thank you." She paused, unsure how to follow up. "Is this just in case I need any consulting?"

Riva bark-laughed again. "Yeah," she said. "Or."

"Or?"

"Or," said Riva, "in case you need to find me."

"You mean if your earring turns up?" Hannah asked weakly.

"Sure," Riva said. "If my earring turns up." She looked at Hannah head-on, then shrugged, rushing out the glass doors almost as though she were being dragged by forces beyond her control.

Hannah stood there tingling.

She turned Riva's card over in her hand, as though the motion would reveal any additional information. *Consultant.* Infuriatingly vague. Syl had peddled in secrecy her entire life, so Hannah rarely trusted anyone who made a business of being mysterious. But this was different.

The jangle of Marla's keys announced her arrival, black leather purse sagging with the weight of its contents, leopard-print sunglasses sliding partially down her forehead. She dropped everything she was carrying with a dramatic flourish right in the entryway.

"God, the traffic was awful," announced Marla. "Where are people going, anyway? It's the middle of a Tuesday!" She pulled a water bottle with the synagogue logo on it from her bag and took a dramatically long glug from its spout. "Sorry, doll, have you been waiting long?"

"Nah," lied Hannah. "I just got here." She didn't ask Marla about Riva again. Whoever she was, Hannah wanted to keep Riva for herself for now.

"Good. Great. So nu, let's get started? I want to show you the whole works. How I keep track of our clients, the workflow for planning a funeral, all that good stuff." She started leading Hannah back toward her office. "This is a family business. My office is a mess, and I'm sort of a mess." She went to unlock the door and then opened it, realizing it was unlocked. "I tell you this because I consider you family."

Hannah felt a little like crying as Marla ushered her into a room that now, despite all proof to the contrary, felt like the portal to the elsewhere she'd been looking for her entire life.

———◆———

There was a girl once who found a potato plant so luxuriant against the plain and dirty ground, she thought it was the most beautiful thing she'd ever seen. It must be something precious, like treasure. Potato plants, you see, grow like fireworks. Little stars, surprises up from between the grasses. For the blossom of such a plain thing, they are oddly resplendent. Put a potato plant next to an orchid, for example, and there's not a clear winner.

She brought the plant home to her mother. Her mother, in whose impoverished youth potatoes had been nothing more than survival.

Take that thing away, said the girl's mother, who knew better than to trust a thing just because it was pretty. So, the girl hid the potato plant under her bed.

Underneath the girl's bed then, things began to grow. First gradually but then with more alarming speed. A thin grassy layer grew first, and then a series of very dainty white flowers. But the fireworks were the last to come—potato plants every few inches, little surprises, delicacies so bright and opulent, it was hard to imagine they'd ever become anything so homely and pragmatic as potatoes. The girl, upon learning that she now had a proper garden underneath her bed, watered and tended to it as best she could. She had never had a way with plants before, but now was as good a time as ever, and besides, she had no choice.

One night, as she carried a jug of water up the stairs to her semi-subterranean garden, she heard the sound of someone crying. Nervous, the girl walked into her bedroom, where she found her mother lying underneath her bed, in the middle of all of those fireworks, holding one small potato bud to her chest with both of her hands. There, on the floor, her mother, whose life had been hard, and who had no more husband to speak of, looked extraordinarily beautiful.

"I told you to get rid of it," her mother sobbed, but she clutched the bud even harder. The girl set down her jug and lay down next to her mother, and together they lay, surrounded by the smell of something new and green and just born.

———

Hannah drove home from Garfinkel's powered by adrenaline, flicking off the pesky phantom desire to call her mother. *My mother is dead,* she said out loud, to the inside of her car. What would she tell Syl, anyway? *You were right? You were wrong?* Both?

She owed her father a call. He'd called several days earlier, and Hannah hadn't felt like navigating the small talk that calling Robert sometimes entailed, but she figured calling him would be as close to calling Syl as she could get at this point.

He picked up after the third ring.

"Hannah?" He sounded a little nervous, as he did whenever Hannah called.

"Hi, Dad. How are you?"

"I'm well, just getting some work done. Emily is at a training in Atlanta this week." Robert's wife was in higher-education administration.

"Yeah? And how is Essie?" Robert's daughter was about to start her junior year of college. Emily was significantly younger than Robert was, and he'd waited a long time before having another child, so Essie, while younger than Shiva, was technically Shiva's aunt. Robert lived in Seattle now, so Hannah had met her half sister only a couple of times. Sometimes she thought about Robert and Essie's relationship with a mild envy that embarrassed her, but more often, she thought about the fact that Robert was getting older, and Essie would surely spend most of her adult life dadless too.

Robert chuckled. "She's doing great at school. She has two majors, and I think she's also directing a play of some kind. I'm not sure if she ever sleeps."

"I bet," said Hannah. She paused, struck by the clarity of the realization in real time: she needed to say something. Not later, but right now. It was long past time.

"Dad, I have to talk to you about something." Her nervousness about bringing up the subject with her own father surprised her, and she felt a sliver of shame about how she'd responded to her daughter, who only ever wanted to know more about where she'd come from.

"I think Shiva should know more about Mom." She cleared her throat. "She's curious. She's asking real questions about Mom, and about me, adult questions, and . . ." She was humiliated to feel her throat tightening. She cleared it. "It's embarrassing, but it's starting to scare me. It's hard to talk about. You know, to talk about her, to talk about what it was like, or even know what's right to say and what's right not to say, you know?" She wasn't sure Robert did know, but he was the only other person she knew in the world who'd managed some worldly proximity to her mother. "I also don't think she's going to take no from me anymore. And to be honest, I don't feel right saying no like I used to."

"What kinds of questions?" Robert rarely brought up Syl himself. Hannah had often wondered if it was respect, his own kind of secret reticence, or even just self-preservation.

"Every kind," said Hannah. She wasn't exactly sure what to say to her father. Shiva's questions blended in with her own, and her own questions about her mother always felt too big to speak out loud. *Was my mother hiding something? Why did she keep me from my grandmother? And what of all the cautionary tales? How many of them were really meaningful to her, and how many were smoke and mirrors?* "Mom was so private."

"*Extremely* private," agreed Robert.

Just saying the words and hearing them back from the man who'd been married to Syl felt like puncturing a small hole in a powerful force field.

"I wish we had more recordings of her," said Hannah. "What she talked about, what was important to her. It always kills me—we had no idea she would die so young, and once she got her diagnosis, we had other priorities. We didn't have time to document her ending." She swallowed these last words, her gut remembering, as it often did, how angry she was about the waste of those notebooks, and how she'd been single-handedly responsible for the destruction of the archive her mother would otherwise have left behind. It wasn't the first time it had taken hearing her father's voice to feel that, at some basic level, she'd betrayed not only him but also herself.

"I know," said Robert. "Look, it's funny. I had actually wanted to call you for a related reason. I found something of your mother's."

"What?" Syl's minimalism had been brutal, and Hannah couldn't imagine what he could have found.

He hesitated. "Two of her bird-watching journals. Earlier ones."

"But." Hannah's skin prickled. She breathed in, the smell of burning paper a sense memory. "She didn't want any of them to survive her. She . . . she made sure of it."

Thankfully, Robert didn't ask any follow-up questions. An intelligent man who'd lived a lot of life, he knew Syl had been a complicated woman. Hannah wondered whether he felt guilty for missing out on not only most of Syl's life but also her illness and death. The day after they'd received Syl's diagnosis, Hannah had called him, and he'd asked whether there was any way he could be of use. He'd never offered to fly in, nor did Hannah ask. It wouldn't have made sense—they weren't part of one another's lives in that way anymore. But when Robert arrived at the funeral, slipping into the back of the chapel quiet as a ghost, she saw on his face that he felt remiss in not coming sooner.

"I know," he said. "She was adamant that no one ever see them. But it seems like the ones I have were from when we first married. I think they got mixed up in my teaching files. Emily and I cleaned out the attic a few weeks ago, and there they were, between some ancient class rosters."

A few weeks ago? She couldn't believe Robert hadn't called her immediately. Then again, maybe this omission made them even. They were both in search of Syl, now and forever, like it or not. Syl had not been coy; she had just genuinely wanted never to be found. And yet, here, she'd accidentally left two crumbs.

"Unbelievable. Do I get to see them?"

"Of course. I'll mail them to you immediately."

"Dad, what's in the notebooks?"

"Well."

"Dad, what?"

"Hannah, I didn't ever know this, but it seems like Syl was seeing someone else when I met her."

"What?" That didn't make sense. Of course, Hannah had always assumed Syl had dated. The few photos Hannah had of her mother in her twenties made Syl seem like a woman with a brimming closet, an easy twinkle in her eye, and a rich social life, even if she'd never been able to reconcile the hardened Syl she'd known with the effusive young belle in those photos.

"Yes," said Robert. "There are a couple of hints in here that she was dating someone that same winter she starting dating me."

Hannah felt her mouth physically drop open. "What does it say?"

"Just little things," said Robert. He was quiet for a moment, and Hannah could hear him flipping pages. "But here, top of the page says, *Winter 1955*, and she's writing about hummingbirds, and in one corner, she's drawn a picture of something like a bird and written, *When I came to you after dinner with Robert and my parents, and we danced underneath two hummingbirds who looked like they were dancing too.*"

"Anything else?"

"Well," Robert said. "Let me see. Oh yes. Right here it says, *I miss you when I see lamplight. I miss you when I see the birds and their wings, which is always. I miss you after dinner, and when I look out the window. I miss you at night. I wonder where you are.* Next to it, she's drawn a picture of a carrot."

"And that's not about you?"

"It can't be." Robert's voice sounded far away. "Syl never wanted to watch the birds with me. And I'm not a night person. Your mother was, of course. And I saw her so frequently that winter, she couldn't have missed me. I was right there."

Hannah's mind raced, looking for possibilities, but she found none.

"You'll send me the notebooks, Dad?"

"Right away," said Robert. "And Hannah?"

"Yeah?"

"I'm glad you called."

The day she got the USPS email notifying her that Robert's package had arrived, Hannah left work early. She knelt slowly to pick up the box from her front stoop, as if it actually contained her mother's ashes. She used a box cutter to slice it open. Inside, under a lot of newspaper, were the notebooks, their yellow covers slightly browned with age. Hannah laid them out on her table and then opened the first.

She couldn't believe that, after the exhaustion of a haunted childhood lived alongside her mother's stingy solitudes, she was sitting here with one of the precious notebooks splayed open on her kitchen table. There was a hint of that old fear, as if she were doing something she shouldn't. She probably was, but that didn't matter now.

Female finch with broken leg, her mother had written on the first page, alongside a tentative drawing of the bird in question. *Is that a male finch, too? Do they know one another?* A quiet conversation conducted by one, entirely on paper. Hannah flipped the brittle page to reveal more drawings—these in fuller color, less tentative. *An entire congregation of mourning doves. Hummingbird, goldfinch, osprey, woodpecker.* In some of the drawings, Hannah recognized the house on Gibson Street—a corner of the foundation or the large maple tree out back, the one whose branches Syl had always called arms. Syl in the backyard, her pouch full of colored pencils, eyes on the sky. The renderings weren't beautiful, exactly, but they were attentive, delicate. *Loving,* Hannah wanted to say, but the adjective felt dishonest when it came to her mother.

After her first foiled notebook break-in attempt at age seven, Hannah had repressed her curiosity for a long time. But then, one late summer afternoon when she was eleven, Hannah sat reading under the maple in the backyard while her mother sketched in the lawn chair. Hannah had a clear memory of the feeling—perennial, but particularly acute that afternoon—that she was deeply, truly alone, and that her mother, even mere feet away, was entirely elsewhere. She'd watched Syl's eyes flit upward and then back down, flyaway wisps of red around her face. She had wanted, fairly desperately, to show her mother something. Was it a passage in her book? An interesting leaf? She couldn't remember.

"Ma," she said.

Her mother looked up from the notebook, surprised. "Yes?"

She was only eleven, but it didn't feel right to Hannah to have to beg for her mother's attention. She was tired of feeling less important than her mother's inner life. It wasn't fair. Hannah was rarely defiant as a child, but when the instinct did surface, it came in hot.

She'd walked toward her mother, crossing the never-spoken boundary that existed between them. In their house of two, when Syl was somewhere, Hannah was expected to be somewhere else. And when they were in the same space, Hannah was meant to keep herself occupied. Syl needed space. She could guide and discipline, she could love even—but all this from afar. Hannah moved across the yard, tightrope-like, as if she veered too far in one direction or another she would lose momentum. She got very close to Syl, almost close enough to touch.

"Ma," she said, through determined teeth. "I want to see your notebook."

Syl flipped the steno pad's cover shut. "No," she said, without hesitation. "You know this by now, Hannah. These are not for you. Not even when you ask nicely, which, might I remind you, you haven't." Syl's voice sizzled, a pan of oil getting hotter as she spoke. "My notebooks are not for you. I'll always respect your privacy, but I need you to respect mine."

But I don't want privacy, Hannah wanted to say. *And what's so private about a bird-watching notebook? And why can't you be a normal mother? Why does our house feel like a graveyard all the time? Neither one of us is dead.*

Syl's lips were tight, and her slate eyes dark, and Hannah understood right then very clearly that she would never be able to make this request of her mother again. The realization made her unbelievably sad, as if she'd lost something, even though it was nothing she'd ever been allowed to hold to begin with.

"Okay." Even her voice sagged as she said it.

"Look," said Syl, cooling. "Have I ever told you about King Solomon, how he could understand the language of the birds?" Syl was harsh, but she wasn't cruel, and Hannah could tell her mother felt bad, even if she had no intention of changing her mind. Her stories, opaque as they could be, were as close as she ever got to tenderness.

Hannah had learned to sit back quietly and let her mother's words wash over her, a rare and occasional balm. "No," she lied.

Syl got up from her chair and sat on the ground next to Hannah. "He could. His wisdom was so profound that he knew many nonhuman languages. He would stroll in his garden and listen to the birds speaking with one another, chattering away, having all kinds of conversations. Birds arguing, birds talking about the weather, birds in love."

"Birds in love?" Hannah gawked.

Syl laughed. "Oh, yes. Birds fall in love." She was quiet for a long moment. "If I could tell you anything true about what I do in my notebooks, it's that I'd like to better understand that language too."

"Ma." Hannah measured her words as they came out of her mouth. "Do you understand the language of the birds?"

Syl looked at Hannah sharply, something flickering across her face. "No," she said. The silence hummed between them as Hannah wondered what her mother wasn't saying.

Together, they sat in the grass under a stretched sky. Grasshoppers chirping, birds chatting, the *shhhh* of the wind through the maple tree, when rarely it came. The earlier tension had fully dissolved into the melt of late afternoon, and everything got sleepy. Stillness was rare for Syl, who, herself birdlike, was always pecking restlessly in some far-off direction or another. Hannah fought her heavy eyelids. The wind rested in the bushes, drawing out the honey from the flowers there. There was no water nearby, but Hannah, overtaken by a sweet slowness, thought she heard something trickling.

From somewhere, her mother's voice.

"I do," said Syl.

"You do what?"

"I do," she said, "understand the language of the birds."

Hannah's fists tightened. She didn't know what to say or what to believe. She untightened them, then lay back against her mother—a woman who might or might not understand the language of the birds—and fell asleep.

Hannah turned the pages of the first notebook with far less caution than she'd used to open the package. *Syl can handle it*, she thought. There would be time to inspect dates and try to decode. But for now, she turned page after page—scribbles of pencil; a bird looking directly off the page, alarmed or alert; the sweet edge of a willow tree; a dreamlike marginal note: *wonder if the sky knows*, or *crowds of hummingbirds by the park today*, or *the tree I could almost hear crying*.

Hannah was hot. Having unbridled access to Syl so late in life made her feel childish and angry. She was overcome by the desire to throw the notebook across the room. In the depths of Hannah's lonely childhood, she'd played a private game, imagining what magical or important thing her mother might be doing, and it had comforted her. But her mother had not been concocting spells or studying some mad avian science that would change the world. Nothing of the sort.

She didn't throw the notebook, but she banged it down on the table so it made a sound. She picked it up and banged it down again, grunting as she pounded her mother's selfish musings into the tabletop, and wondering, as always, whether Syl could hear. Then, looking around and out the windows to make sure no one was in the vicinity, she threw back her head and screamed so loud she could feel it in the lining of her stomach. It was an ugly, guttural sound, and it shot forth from Hannah so forcefully her throat hurt afterward. For what felt like a long time she sat, palms on her mother's two forgotten notebooks, ears ringing with the unfamiliar sound of her own animal voice.

Once she calmed down, the day felt easier. Hannah walked to the hallway mirror. She looked into it. Outside, the ebbing light softened through the kitchen windows, and she was no longer afraid. Here were Syl's notebooks, and they were just notebooks. Here was the mirror, and it was just a mirror. There, the sky; only the sky.

Hannah poured herself a glass of water. Something lifted from right in front of her eyes, clarifying; something heavy and off-balance inside of her shifted, landed, and settled into place. Shiva was right. Hannah had not communicated honestly enough to her daughter about her own strange and myopic childhood. She had probably even unknowingly replicated some of the bizarre dynamics of her own upbringing in raising Shiva. Hannah was exhausted by the acrobatics of secrecy. She knew she needed to share with Shiva what little she could. Shiva was onto something: much of what Hannah did, at some level, was still for Syl. To protect Syl. To honor Syl. But no more. Syl was no longer in charge. She wasn't here, and she hadn't been for a very long time.

She pulled the index-card box where she kept addresses out from the cabinet under the counter. *You can keep all your contacts in your phone now, Ma*, Shiva always said. She flipped over to "L" and pulled out the card she was looking for. *Chani Lieber*, it said. Underneath the name, a phone number. Hannah took a sip of water. Then she dialed.

April 23, 1921

Dear L,

Thank you for being kind to me again and again, even after what I've shown you about myself. This is the thing I have feared most—telling you about me, about what happened, about what I want and what I am afraid of. And now I have begun to tell you. There is safety in your eyes. They are not kind eyes in the sleepy way Isaac's are; I like how green they are, how they remind me of the sea. Your eyes do not fear me. They see me, I believe, as someone in a world that doesn't always want me in it.

You said something when you were last here that made me curious. You mentioned that you used to travel from place to place, but now, for the time being, you are here. I am wondering what it is that would drive a woman to travel from place to place instead of marrying. How is it that the world allows you to be alone? Your family? I know you might not answer my questions—that these letters are supposed to be about my healing—but as I spend more time with you, dear L, I must ask.

Today, I have two things I need to tell you.

The first is that Isaac finally came back, after weeks away. This time, Mama did not let me out of her sight. She explained to Isaac that I have had a laryngitic throat and have not been able to speak. She brought down some paper for writing, and the three of us sat and had tea. Mama asked questions, Isaac answered them dutifully, and I nodded often and as enthusiastically as I could muster. I looked into his eyes, finally, and the smile he gave me was weak but genuine. Right then, for one moment, I thought I could have a life that would be recognizable. Even if my mouth doesn't know how to open anymore, I could peel potatoes and chop carrots and arrange kindling for the fire. I could draw a bath, and I could have a husband. We could have a bed and a home of our own and maybe even a child. Is this what makes nights less lonely? Is this the kind of home joy considers returning to?

The truth is, Mama has been frantic over my permanent silence. Even Papa, who has never seemed to want anything more than my muteness, seems concerned that I now make no sounds at all. He still keeps his distance, but now regards me as a curiosity, and doesn't seem to know how to address me without a reason to lock me up or shut me up. Jacob is sad, I can tell, and trying to protect me from his sadness too. Jacob, in one way or another, is always trying to protect me from something. When Mama talked to the rabbi, who said this was a matter for a woman healer, she asked around in the market and found her way to you. I don't understand how or why she found you, and not someone local, but I'm afraid if I ask her, you will disappear, and that is the last thing I want.

After Isaac left comes the second thing I need to tell you.

Mama sent me to the market to get some things for Shabbos tomorrow. She sent me with a list. She doesn't want anyone to know that I can't speak any longer, because there is already too much attention on our family, so she asks that I hold up the list and instructs me that, if anyone asks, I should put a hand to my throat to indicate that I have lost my voice.

It is true, really. I have lost my voice.

I left for the market and walked quickly, because I knew I needed some extra time. I wanted to return to my clearing in the forest. The place where my voice filled the air and nobody was afraid of me. Where I asked for protection, maybe from God or maybe from someone else. Whoever was listening. I needed to get back to that place, to continue that conversation. I wondered if my voice would return to me there. I walked, kerchief over my head and shoulders hunched, past the river, past the edge of the woods. It was easy to find the place I had been, the clearing with the big tree. As easy as the place I was born. It was a place that wanted me, and I felt its invitation as soon as I entered the first grove that led me there.

When I arrived, I had a feeling I barely recognized as comfort. I only had a few moments before I needed to head to the market lest my absence be noticed, but I stood in the hushed dance of my clearing, basking in a calm that doesn't exist elsewhere.

I opened my mouth to see if anything would emerge and surprise me. And it did.

The unguarded sound that came from me wasn't a sound I recognized. It was piercing. It was purely an animal sound. It scared me at first, my own changed voice. But it felt good, powerful. It felt loud and unleashed, like laughing. And the funny thing was that I wanted it, L. I wanted this animal sound I harbored, the thing born of my stifled laughter. I realized I have been starved for it. I would give up my sanity for this. For my body to stop sleeping, for the world to erupt inside me. To bray, scream, convulse under the lit moon. To be alone and not alone, wild as a wolf, and for no one to touch me ever again.

I had felt defeated, like my father had closed the tiny doors in the back of my throat, had taken my voice from me.

But here, in my clearing, the truth revealed itself. He had not taken my voice from me; *I had taken my voice from him.* I had hidden it away, in a place where it couldn't be heard by those to whom it had never belonged. Could never belong. In a place where even I could barely reach it. But I could reach it. Here, in this wood, in my sanctuary, I could reach it.

And, truthfully, L, I thought of you. How you might encourage me to find a place where I feel calm. How I have a feeling that you don't want what everyone else wants for me, but that you see something else is possible. You, who have chosen to be alone and know the freedom of being unguarded.

My face burned with these realizations. I am not weak, L. It is the opposite of what I have always thought. I am the monster here. I tower over the townspeople. I am capable of great and glorious volume.

I opened my eyes, wrapped my scarf around me again, steeled myself to start walking toward the market. I don't know how I hadn't seen it sooner. There, right before me, in the nook of the great tree, was a small esrog. I had to move closer to it. Closer and closer. I knew not to easily trust something that could be evil in the disguise of temptation. But when I got close enough, the sensuous citrus fragrance was unmistakable.

L, someone left this for me.

There is no other explanation.

I don't know who or what it is, but I am seen.

In this secret place, I am seen, and I am safe, and I am becoming something I didn't know possible.

Ever yours,
Mira

Fifteen

No one Shiva met with in the days that followed had any kind of casual attachment to the people whose histories they studied. Their fixations were enduring and deeply personal, and Shiva, an audience of one, basked in their rhapsodizing.

"I've been taken with the study of S. An-sky for decades," said Alicja, a friend of Mel Rosen's, whose tiny home office was stacked with piles of books that towered so high they nearly blocked a large window overlooking Pole Mokotowskie.

So it wasn't just her. She felt a kind of glee then, and the desire to throw her arms around Alicja, but she refrained. It had long been obvious to Shiva that An-sky's work wasn't made for casual interest. The pursuit of it was for his spiritual and intellectual descendants: people whose hunger and thirst manifest as a bottomless seeking. People for whom story might be an obsession and for whom a question, if pointed and attentive enough, might be something holy.

"He had such a complicated relationship with the community," said Alicja. Shiva had read some of Alicja's writings on An-sky, but listening to her talk was different, almost like chatting with one of An-sky's close personal friends. "As you must know. It was never as simple for him as being in and falling out. Our relationship to where we come from is rarely so simple. He left, yes, and he came back, but he came back different and left again different. And every time, for slightly different reasons. He was fundamentally restless."

"Restless," said Shiva. "I think that's what excites me about him. He's so elusive, you can't pin him down. And I've been wondering, is that why he spent so much of his time asking questions? With the ethnographic survey, especially?"

"For sure," said Alicja. "I think the restlessness was complex. Maybe at some level he wanted to be rooted, but rootlessness was his most organic state. In a way, he wanted both. He was eclectic and always evolving. He collected selves, not ever to discard them but to incorporate them into a greater whole. He understood that people are made of many stories, and not just one, and that the story of his people was necessarily partial. He was doing his best to reflect that story wholly, even if that whole ended up being fragmented. And so his ethnographic work is both love story and elegy. He was an everyday collector, asking these thoughtful and deeply researched questions, and as you know, they didn't even need to be answered for us to now vividly infer what life in the Pale of Settlement was like."

"He never stayed married." It wasn't a question, but Shiva had to know what Alicja thought about the possibility that his aversion to marriage wasn't only about a resistance to domesticity but about a kind of queer desire.

"He didn't," said Alicja. "And of course, many possible reasons why. He was not particularly cut out for the home life, but as you know, the things he wanted were generally uncommon for that time. There was a wildness to him. He was passionate and seemed fairly unafraid to follow that passion where it led him. I'm sure you've read Gabriella Safran's work on the matter, but I sort of love that we'll never fully know. It seems fitting that his sexuality was an open question, and now one we can never really answer."

An open question. Shiva sat quiet for a moment, as Alicja's words dissipated all around her. She'd come all this way in hot pursuit of some kind of proof, but she also understood that some things resisted proof, and for good reason. *Proof* could be so reductive. Some part of her wanted to face S. An-sky himself more than anything, to take him by the shoulders, to ask, *Well, were you?* But queerness laughed in the face of proof. Queerness was not about a body of evidence but about layers of presence; a cumulative kind of hereness, insistent and glittering. A vertical line, even, lives and lives stacked on top of lives. Renegade desire that left no evidence behind; only a kind of residue that flickered in its wake. *S. An-sky was here.*

"I sort of love that too," said Shiva, breathing slowly out.

"Since you are in Warsaw," Alicja continued, shifting gears, "you should start with *The Dybbuk*." She gave Shiva a litany of recent productions of the nearly hundred-year-old play, and the scope and variety were even greater than Shiva had imagined. There were old retellings, new retellings, ultra-contemporary adaptations that were only refractions of the original. There were performances in countless languages, dance performances, horror and comedy adaptations, even operas. In An-sky's story, the dybbuk clung to the bride, but in a number of these productions, the dybbuk had a further reach too: it clung to the soul of a Jewish woman who, in one way or another, defied convention. A woman who was a threat to her community.

They talked about An-sky for what felt like hours, in the manner of two people catching up and talking about a very old and beloved friend, to the point that Shiva wanted to ask, *So, how do you know him, anyway?* Then she realized she could.

"It's actually very personal," said Alicja. "How I know S. An-sky. I didn't used to be an academic at all, no interest in any of this stuff. But when I was in my mid-twenties, I had kind of a crisis. Things were not going great; my mother had just died, and I had no idea what I was doing with my life. And my grandfather—he was still around—he told me an old family story I had somehow never heard. This man had come to my great-great-aunt's house in Minsk. He was dressed like a rebbe and had a phonograph. He sat in their living room and asked them all these questions, even got them to sing a song they usually sang around the Shabbos table and recorded it. Later, they heard from neighbors who saw the same man, dressed almost like a scientist, going into someone's backyard and spending time with their children and their chickens. I was riveted. Who was this man who had visited my family, going door to door in disguise, with a phonograph? I got so excited when I figured out who he was, I gave my life to the study of him and have never turned back."

After she left Alicja's, Shiva had a couple of hours to spare before she was scheduled to meet with Leora Magid. She felt full with something, but it wasn't the overwhelming saturation she'd felt in the reading room or at the museum archive; instead, it was the kind of fullness whose weight anchors you to the ground. She bought a strawberry ice cream cone and walked with it to Pole Mokotowskie to lie down in one of the public hammocks, where she could turn her attention upward. *Please*, she thought. The sky, open-eyed, waiting.

An-sky's questions had only ever been so leading because he'd meticulously recorded what he'd seen. He'd paid the most intricate kind of attention.

Over her head, the clouds traveled fast, like they were going somewhere.

She, like An-sky, had paid attention. She remembered a quote about attention being a kind of prayer and then thought about whether instead of offering prayers—for which she no longer had much appetite—instead of *please* without any particular direction, maybe she should try offering her own leading questions instead.

Is it true that you harbor those we lose so well that we never catch a glimpse of them again? she tried. *Is it true you can hear us but also that, where you are, you understand us differently? Is it true that your secrets are unlockable? Is it true that your sensibilities are now both evolved and archaic? Is it true that you are at once human and beast, that you are at once hiding from me and watching me, that you want both to take shelter but also to visit?*

•

Leora Magid had given Shiva an address in the Old Town for a small archive where she met Shiva at the door. She was gregarious and ruddy-cheeked, thrilled to meet with a student who didn't yet know about the Maiden of Ludmir, whose given name was Chana Rochel Werbermacher.

She gave Shiva the basics. A woman born in the early nineteenth century, Chana Rochel was a bright Torah scholar from when she was very young. She insisted on following the Jewish laws that were obligatory only for men, but from which women were exempt, and pursued a strict regimen of Torah study like any holy man of the time. When she got a little bit older, she was betrothed to a childhood friend, and this betrothal was said to have distressed her greatly.

When her mother died suddenly, Chana Rochel spent a great deal of time visiting the cemetery. Legend had it that, during one of her visits, she fell unconscious, and when she came to, she claimed she'd been given a new and higher soul and that she would never marry. She'd transcended the world of flesh, she said. She became a community leader and kabbalistic scholar; whatever she claimed had possessed her at the cemetery became license for her to stand up in her power as a woman and rabbinic leader at that time. She never did marry. She was both beloved and profoundly misunderstood.

An-sky, it is told, had heard about her and found her story fascinating. He had a keen eye for the places where ancient tradition and modern sensibilities met, and for him, they met in someone like the Maiden of Ludmir. Someone so uncommon, so devoted to ancient scripture, and so resistant to the constraints that would have told her to stay home and cook for a husband. An-sky had even visited Ludmir, where Chana Rochel had lived, at least twice, and there was both speculation and evidence that she'd partially inspired the script for *The Dybbuk*.

There wasn't much in the way of material on Chana Rochel, but Leora showed Shiva what she had. Some writings, some secondary accounts. No photos. People had drawn and painted her, rendering her from a combination of description and imagination.

"She is so important," said Leora. "There are so many women in our history who were traditionally observant but also completely bucked tradition, and the irony is that the usual modes of narrative don't always have the capacity to capture them. To learn about the Maiden of Ludmir, I've had to embrace less orthodox measures." She laughed here. "You know. But I've traveled where she traveled. I've worshiped where she worshiped. I've followed her, essentially. You could say I'm one of her Hasidim, to this day." She held up her right hand to show Shiva her wedding band. "I *am* married, but for me, study and worship have always come first. Studying someone so unstudiable, you see, it can only be a kind of kinship."

Shiva saw.

She remembered her hushed awe watching Shosh and Amy. She remembered the Messenger, who'd felt like a kind of mirror. She remembered a youth spent quietly, not asking too many questions and mostly looking for clues. She'd felt herself unknowable, at least until she'd stumbled upon the approximate words and fallen into the right kind of tangle.

These scholars were sleuths, shaking out the past for clues. Less like scholars, really, and more like fevered and reverent lovers, just as she was. Chana Rochel Werbermacher's life story, she knew, was unknowable. What they had were clues. There wasn't adequate language to describe her. At least not just yet.

She walked home giddy as a first date, the pink sky blushing down at her.

She sobered quickly, though, when she got back to her apartment and checked her email. Rosen had sent her a note.

Hello. I hope you are very much enjoying Poland and your research. Please give my best to Alicja. How is it going? Focused? I hope. Can you please send me a summary of what you're planning for the conference paper? They're working on the website now, and we'll need an abstract.

She cringed. *Focused.* In a manner of speaking.

She did not email Rosen back that she was dazzled by the assiduousness with which people charted a course of historic study that was also equally and always a love story. She did not tell Rosen that every day she believed more and more that a love story was the engine at the center of anything. Or about the speed at which her idea of what a love story might be was changing. She also did not email Rosen back that she was still hoping to steal away to Ropshitz, to spend some time where her great-grandmother had slept and to see if she could absorb some understanding of what had happened there. She did not email Rosen that she was trying to figure out where she fit, or that she was still worried about her mother back home, or that some days she was worried that she still didn't know what to ask, even after decades of trying. She did not email Rosen that she was still afraid he might be right.

Instead, she emailed Rosen back and told him about the most practical takeaways from her meetings that day. She tried to come up with some earthly promise, something substantial and irrefutably brilliant. She came up empty on that front. She didn't tell Rosen about the hours the next day she was also planning to spend walking, exploring, seeing what the ground or the sky might tell her. *No flying goats yet*, she signed off, an effort to deflect with humor that would likely be lost on her adviser. *Here's hoping.*

———

Because her profession was a solitary one, it is told that the woman on the outskirts of the village was at home often. And because she was at home often, she was there to receive what came and to release what went. Packages and letters, gifts and requests. She lived on the far side of the hill, and so what came to her was often carried by courier, rather than brought firsthand. Sometimes bills and papers, correspondence from far away. Sometimes requests for visits or consultations. Sometimes, rarely, a parcel of delights—cookies or figs or cured meat.

The woman on the outskirts of the village was not particularly sentimental, but her chest swelled whenever deliveries arrived, when she saw a courier approaching. *Stay awhile*, she wanted to say. She knew it wasn't unheard of.

It is told that the woman began to wonder what it would mean to love another courier, someone who understood a life that was neither here nor there but somewhere in between. Someone who could truly understand the sacredness of that place too.

When they tell the story, they tell of a woman.

I, of course, know different.

She was not used to wanting to be seen. In fact, she'd tried to stay mostly invisible, a Jewish woman living where no others lived, keeping company with the wildlife. Sometimes, though, she wanted the couriers to know her. She started leaving trinkets for them in the small yellow box outside her front door. She wondered whether they would notice, or leave anything in return. She wondered whether they would recognize that, even in her current stillness, she was one of them.

———

The night of the queer porn screening, Shiva approached the industrial-looking building in Mokotów that bore the address on the flyer El had given her. Within seconds, she heard the roar of a motorcycle and panicked. The Ghost rode a motorcycle. The Ghost could well be at this screening. And Shiva suddenly realized she had no idea what she would say if, in fact, she was. She had so completely indulged her speculative yearning that she had zero actual contingencies.

She pulled open the heavy black door just as the motorcycle's engine sputtered off in the parking lot. She turned, just long enough to catch a glimpse of the motorcycle's driver: tall and broad-shouldered, wearing lots of black, steel-toed boots, and a royal-blue helmet that obstructed her face. Shiva ducked inside as the driver unstrapped her helmet.

Up a concrete staircase was one gray door. This must be the place. She'd been heartily rained on and was worried about her hair and her makeup and her meager Polish. Dawid had taught her how to ask for soy milk, how to compliment someone's outfit, and how to say, *how are you?* in a casual way, but it seemed rude to ask such a question when you couldn't then understand the answer. *Co słychać?* She practiced it under her breath anyway, just in case. *Cześć!* Hello, hello, hi. If she said it with the right inflection, would she still read as charming? Or even just considerate? She stood for a moment outside the metal door, at the center of which was a little red sign with a pinup-style magazine cutout of a woman she didn't recognize, and then walked inside.

The room she walked into, a stark contrast to the building's facade and the concrete staircase she'd climbed to get there, was a place she instantly wanted to stay in forever. Lush green velvet was draped from every window, and the bar twinkled with firefly lights. In each corner, vintage lamps, red and cream and gold and tasseled, cast warmth in every direction, and crystal chandeliers sparkled dimly from tin ceilings. From the dark green walls hung lavish gold frames, some containing photos and several just hanging there, frames for frames' sake. Along the bar, even from across the room, Shiva could see a moody series of pinup photos strung up under the lights.

A woman in towering heels and an intricately beaded silver dress stood behind a red welcome table at the door. "Cześć," she said, pursing impeccably glossy crimson lips. She pointed to a list of names and asked a question Shiva assumed had something to do with whether she'd registered in advance. Before she could stop herself, Shiva put a hand to her heart, self-conscious about her teeny cherry-red nails. The statuesque woman was holding a pen between two long, sparkly acrylics. When Shiva didn't answer, the woman said something else in the same husky voice, waving her inside.

She headed straight for the bar. The people in front of her ordered something brown and very boozy looking, and she pointed at their cups as they walked away, hoping the bartender would understand she wanted the same thing. Then she shimmied up onto one of the red vinyl stools and surveyed the room.

The crowd was fringed and pearled, sequined and studded and feathered, everyone laughing and talking in quick Polish under their spectacular adornments. Allure here was something wickedly serious. In the spots of luminescence cast by the chandeliers, frenzied assemblies of color and silhouette—dark gold and redbud, chartreuse and amber and ruby red. Along the hardwood floor, a traffic jam of patent-leather heels and wingtips and—oh, there, those steel-toed boots.

Shiva followed the boots up their laces, up the tight black pants to the black leather jacket with the shoulder buckles. She saw the motorcycle rider's face in the dark. The Ghost? She could make out pronounced eyebrows, but from a distance and without more light, it was hard to say. Shiva stirred her drink. She felt underdressed, given this crowd's sartorial enchantments, but pretty enough in a vintage lace blouse with pearl buttons and a butterfly-shaped brooch she'd found in the three-dollar bin at a thrift shop.

"Hi there."

Shiva spun on her stool to see El. They were wearing a floral-print shirt and a dark blue tie and standing next to a redhead in a boxy pink crop top. It wasn't Emi, the tall femme from the other night, and Shiva found herself wondering whether El was dating either or both of them.

"Shiva, this is my friend Anna." El turned to the redhead and said something in Polish. Shiva recognized the name of the bar where she'd met El and Emi a couple of nights before. El leaned in closer over the rising volume of the festivities. "Glad you made it."

"Yeah, me too," Shiva laughed, though nothing was funny.

"What are you drinking?" El's English was impeccable.

"I'm not exactly sure, but it's strong." She was sucking down the drink through a pink plastic stirrer more emphatically than she'd meant to. Behind El, people streamed in by twos and threes. Someone had turned on Edith Piaf, escalating the nighttime glamour into downright opulence, and someone in bubblegum-colored pasties lowered a projection screen. Shiva had briefly forgotten that what she was here to do was watch queer porn with a bunch of strangers.

"Hey, did you find your motorcycle person?" El sat down on a neighboring stool.

Shiva hesitated, toying with asking El now about the rangy motorcycle rider currently in her line of vision, sitting across the room alone, nursing a beer.

"Not yet," she said. Someone was circling the room now, shutting off the lamps one by one, and in the dark, the projection screen filled so rapidly with skin that Shiva temporarily forgot where she was.

———

She is boiling water for tea when she receives the letter, the second one this month. She takes it from the slot, standing very still by the hissing pot, and pinches the envelope too tightly with both hands. This happens every time she gets a letter from the girl. She never feels prepared to read it but also feels starved for it, like she can barely keep her hands from tearing the envelope open.

It is told that the woman on the outskirts of the village doesn't like to get attached. She knows she won't be anywhere for too long, and besides, she's always been happier alone, meeting people only when and where they most need her. She stirs the herbs she grows in her garden into potions and elixirs, and she brings them where they're necessary, and this too is a kind of intimacy. She avoids too much proximity, though, particularly with people willing to look directly into her eyes and see what she'd rather not show them. This strange girl, the one who writes the letters, she sees things most people don't. And it's not just that the girl recognizes her. She also recognizes the girl. It is the kind of mutual recognition, she thinks, that might be flammable.

I, too, know it to be flammable.

She sits at her table and stirs her tea. She looks at the other things first, the notes from people needing her help or wisdom. She sips. Time is slow where she lives. How she lives. Using the utmost care then, the woman tears the girl's envelope open at the seam and slides out the letter it contains. She skims it first for urgencies. And then, relieved, she reads it again more slowly, leaning into the sounds she can almost hear in it, even though she knows the letter is soundless. When she is done, she folds the letter slowly back along its creases like it is something living. She slips it back into its envelope and presses it to her lips, for reasons kept secret even from herself. She finishes her tea and gets up from the table, sinking to her knees and sliding the envelope into the small box that lives underneath her bed—the box where all the girl's letters live—before she climbs into bed and tries, in vain, to sleep.

"The end!" Someone shouted it from across the room in triumphant English. Everyone applauded heartily, appreciative hoots and snarls. A couple of people in boas walked around, flicking the lamps back on and scooping up empty glasses. Edith Piaf returned over the warm din of people milling around.

Shiva had sat through the screening focused on staring at the screen, too shy to look at El or at anyone else. Now, even with the screen gone dark, she had trouble tearing her eyes away from it.

The last film, long and experimental, had featured two naked people in separate but neighboring yards throwing fistfuls of wet mud at one another and then, eventually, breaking down the wooden fence separating them to smear the mud all over one another's bodies. They made call-and-response sounds like foghorns as the mud dried and caked on their skin, and then moaned with pleasure as each, in turn, rinsed the other off with a garden hose.

Meanwhile, in the room, the bodies had begun to close in on Shiva, even if they were actually only sitting still. She'd felt El next to her—El's empty glass, El's dark jeans, El's broad rectangular knee. She had never particularly noticed anyone's knees before, but now, as she tried not to notice the knee, its shape struck her.

"What are you doing after this?" El's voice a sharp thing in the wash of dark, warm cinematic sex. In this room, in this context, such a question could be nothing if not leading.

"I'm not sure," said Shiva, and watery though the answer was, it was also true. She was hungry to be led but not entirely sure where. She looked over at the exposed brick wall across the room, thinking blurrily about who and what she'd followed here, the dumb rigidities of space and time that made it feel impossible to come face-to-face with the people she really needed to meet. S. An-sky. The Maiden of Ludmir. Esther Kreitman. The Ghost. Mira. Syl. Her father. Herself. She wanted to fling herself against a hard thing sometimes, just to prove it secretly penetrable. She knew it might leave her bruised and disappointed, but sometimes she thought the experiment might be worth the pain. Because what if she was right? What if the brick wall split open for her? What if the sky saw her efforts and released something or someone it had been so many generations withholding?

El looked at her expectantly, as if her response had been insufficient.

"I guess I need to decompress from all that sex for a minute before I figure it out." An attempt at a joke she immediately hoped hadn't come off as prudish.

"It was very much sex," El concurred, swigging the very last of their beer. "Did you like the event?" Shiva let herself feel flattered, enjoying the attention, even though nothing was going how she'd expected it to. El was not the Ghost, after all. El was someone else entirely.

"I did like it," said Shiva, not sure whether *like* was the appropriate word to be using. "Did you?"

"I enjoyed it very much," said El. When they spoke, their two front teeth bucked slightly, revealing a small gap between them. Their confidence seemed easy and straightforward but was not without a note of formality. "There aren't always a lot of queer events here in Warsaw, so I love the burlesque. It gives us all a place to go and be ourselves. I don't know how familiar you are with the politics around here, but it can be a very homophobic place. We need these things."

"I'm sure," said Shiva. "It's so great that this space exists. It's really beautiful. And thanks for telling me about it. Otherwise, I would just be wandering the city alone, trying to figure out whether looking at enough street signs might be enough to teach me Polish."

El smirked. "I doubt it." They slid off their stool and put their beer glass down on the bar, making moves to leave. Shiva panicked. She didn't want them to. "You should try to learn a little Polish the next time you come."

The next time.

"Any other recommendations for me while I'm here?" She slid off her chair too. "Things I should be sure to eat or do? More porn?"

El raised an eyebrow. "No more porn until next month, sadly. Unless you want to stay until then . . ."

Someone called El's name from across the room. One of the towering burlesque goddesses, this one in a bandage-tight black minidress. A queer about town, Shiva gathered. She felt something that wasn't jealousy, nor was it quite a longing to be back home, but was something in the neighborhood of both.

"I'll be right back," El said to Shiva, waving to the goddess. "Don't go anywhere."

Shiva re-perched on her stool. She pushed strands of hair behind her ear, sucked down the ice water at the bottom of her glass. Nervous, itchy with the desire to know once and for all, she looked over at the vinyl chair where she'd seen the motorcycle rider. She was still there, standing now. This time, distinctly, the rider looked directly back at her. Eyes dark, like shiny green pinpoints. This person had to be the Ghost.

Shiva stared. She squinted. She couldn't help it. She slid off the stool again. She took just barely a step in the rider's direction. The rider looked back at her for a long beat, unblinking. Then subtly, almost imperceptibly, the rider shook her head. *No.* Another beat then, and she spun on her heels, put her beer bottle on the nearest surface, and walked out.

No.

This place, all whispers and clues leading elsewhere.

El strode back over, burlesque goddess laughter still wafting residually from across the room.

"What did I miss?"

"I wouldn't know where to begin." Part of her wanted to dart out that gray door and down the stairs to catch the Ghost strapping her helmet back and say, *Wait. But why not?* To catch her and say, *But yes.* But the Ghost hadn't wanted to be caught.

"I'm going to head home soon," said El. "What are you doing for the rest of the time you're here in Warsaw?"

"Well," she said. "I'm only here for a couple more days. I have a couple more meetings, and I'm going to see a production of *The Dybbuk* at the Jewish Theater. Otherwise, just going to try to walk around as much as I can." She stirred the ice in her glass, just for something to do with her hands. "I'm not sure this is going to happen, but I'm also going to see if I can get to the place my great-grandmother is from. It's like four hours from here."

"Oh? You mentioned this. Where is she from?"

"She's from Ropshitz. I mean, Ropczyce. Do you know it?"

El's face opened. "I know Ropshitz."

"You do? My great-grandmother was born in the small Jewish village there. She lived there until she and her husband immigrated to New Jersey in 1923."

"Wow," said El. Shiva noticed in the lamplight that they had the hint of a mustache.

"Wow what?"

"Look, it's perfect. I really like driving, and anyway I've been looking for an excuse to get out there. There's something . . ." They trailed off. "I've been meaning to visit Ropshitz for some time now. So I'd be honored to take you. Would you let me?"

It was such an intimate thing to offer.

"But you don't know me."

"That is not entirely true."

"This doesn't seem like acquaintance material." Shiva pushed on. "An ancestral pilgrimage feels so personal. Won't you feel . . . weird?"

"It takes a lot for me to feel weird. I'll meet you tomorrow morning at seven? I have Sundays off. Here, write your address on this." El pushed a bar napkin over to Shiva and lifted a ballpoint pen out of their jacket pocket. Shiva obliged and returned the napkin.

"Are you sure about this?"

"I'm excited," said El. They kissed her right cheek, just like they had the last time they met, and leaving her perched at the bar, walked through the thinning crowd, past the empty beer bottle the Ghost had left behind, and out the large metal door.

For several long minutes, Shiva sat, waiting for whatever whirred frantically inside her to subside. Finally, she took to the dark streets, watchful, letting the shadows accompany her back to her meantime home.

Sixteen

Early the next morning, Shiva watched from the window as El pulled up in a little blue car. It occurred to her to be nervous, but there wasn't time, so she speed-winged her eyeliner, checked her hair, and walked outside. It was sunny, and El looked like a Sunday happenstance in jeans and a sweatshirt.

The first few minutes of the drive were quiet. No whiskey here, nothing post-porn or low-lit. Just a daytime car and a toothy stranger pulling out onto the highway, a French pop song on the radio.

"Coffee?" El tapped a finger on the top of the thermos sitting in the cup holder between them, the piping-hot offering almost erotic. "It's very strong."

The radio announcer's voice bopped over the next song, a lesser-known Beatles track Shiva couldn't remember the name of. She unscrewed the thermos cap and took a slow sip.

"I brought nuts too," said El. "Do you want some?" They nudged a paper bag sitting in the cup holder next to the coffee.

"Thank you," said Shiva.

El drove one-handed, humming unselfconsciously along to the radio.

"So," said Shiva. "Remind me why it is you agreed to drive me four hours at the crack of dawn? We haven't even had a proper drink together."

El smiled at the windshield. "I would ask you out for a drink if you were staying longer. A road trip was the second-best option." On the radio, a glossy 1980s drum fill and the dramatic opening chords of a Polish ballad. "So, it's funny. I actually have a connection to that area. Not to Ropshitz but to somewhere nearby."

"What's the connection?"

"I'm not sure if it's weird to tell you," said El.

"Try me," said Shiva.

"Okay. My great-grandparents, they took someone in." They paused. "A Jewish person."

"Like, during the war?"

"No, way before. She was a youngish woman, and the way my grandmother talks about it, she was very unusual for her time. Lived alone on the outskirts of Ropshitz, which sounds like the outskirts of the outskirts, and worked as kind of an herbalist or folk healer. I don't know what they would have called it back then. But she didn't have any local family and wasn't married. She turned up in Warsaw one night, at the restaurant my great-grandfather owned."

"What happened to her?" Shiva felt suddenly hot with curiosity.

"She ordered a bowl of soup and then sat at a table in the corner the entire evening, reading through a stack of papers and sipping glass after glass of water. I've been told my great-grandfather was the kind of man who would go out of his way to help anyone, and when he found her still there at the end of the night with her suitcase and her empty bowl looking like she had nowhere to go, he offered her a room."

"Do you know what she was doing in Warsaw?"

"I'm not sure. My grandmother was just a kid then, but she says that even when she was young, she could tell the healer seemed restless, one foot a little bit out the door. My grandmother really came to love her and always worried she'd wake up to find her gone. But my grandmother also only tells me so much. I never met my great-grandfather, so I only know bits and pieces."

"I know what that's like," said Shiva. "My great-grandmother from Ropshitz died when I was really young, and my grandmother died the night I was born. In the same house I was born in, actually." She waited for the usual shocked reaction, but El just looked back and forth from Shiva to the road. They turned down the radio. "My mom is pretty private about stuff and also pretty forgetful, so I feel like I don't fully know all my family's stories. Or I only know parts of them, and I have to guess the rest. Which gets frustrating."

"Yes," said El. "I understand that."

"Hence my interest in folklore and storytelling. It's the bits and pieces of people's stories that makes the unknowable a bit more . . . knowable. And even for people who have more access to their families' lore, so many people were cut off from their ancestors, you know, by the war, which has kind of necessitated invention. Inference." *Too much*, thought Shiva.

But El was nodding. "Yes, exactly. You mentioned folklore when you were talking about your research the other day."

"Right." She decided, just for practice, to say it out loud. "My work deals with folklore, but specifically with stories that are really just parts of stories. Questions, fragments, scraps. How those clues get under our skin, individually and collectively. And how so many people from so many fragmented places have worked to make not only a usable history out of those but also a usable present."

"Wow," said El, eyes widening. "This sounds fascinating."

El's almost youthful curiosity made Shiva want to tell them everything: About Rosen, about the fourth Passover child, the one who doesn't quite know what to ask. About her grandmother, her mother, her father, the Ghost. About all the real reasons she loved S. An-sky as much as she did. Maybe it was something about being halfway to the City of Laughter, sun through the window glass, feeling like there was, in fact, something to be found here and like, in this company, she just might find it.

But she held her tongue in place. She crossed one leg over the other, enjoying the length of the road. Slow blooming. "I also particularly like a leading question."

"I'll keep that in mind," said El. "I'm a good lead." They ate a cashew.

"Do you really get away with saying things like that?"

"I don't know," said El. "Do I?"

They turned the music back up. Shiva turned her pink face toward the window. Trees passed, the morning light thin, and everything got sparser as they drove. Periodically, a sign in Polish, but ever fewer as Warsaw faded in the distance.

After that, it was quiet for a long time. Shiva barely noticed when El turned off the radio. Poland sped by, strange. Next to her, El, and a warm feeling up through her legs that disarmed her.

"How did you and Emi meet?" The question was out of her mouth before she could think about it too much.

"Emi?"

"Yeah, that's her name, right? From the bar the other night?"

"You have a good memory," said El. "But it's not—" They fidgeted in their seat. "Emi is one of my best friends. She and I helped each other when we were coming out. It wasn't quite as popular to be gay in Warsaw back then. It's still not, but more than it was."

Shiva tried to mask her relief. "How old were you?"

"I was sixteen."

Shiva couldn't imagine. Levi had also come out as a teenager, but when Shiva was sixteen, it had just been her Jewish school and her *rich inner life*, reading her way through the young-adult section of the library and watching reruns of *M*A*S*H* with her father over late-night cereal. Sometimes, she and Levi spoke in wistful theoreticals: *What if we'd known each other in high school? Would we have been friends? More than friends? Gone to youth Pride together in full regalia and traded angsty zines after school?* It was fun to imagine, but the truth was, it was so far from what her reality had been that it was hard for Shiva to picture it at all.

"That's so cool that you had each other."

"It was important, yeah," said El. "And what about you?"

"Oh, it's nothing like that for me. I came out to my parents really recently." She already illogically trusted El with her more embarrassing material. "It's all so recent that in some ways, it feels like I'm still coming out, if that makes any sense to you at all."

"I think it does," said El.

There was a sign for Ropshitz. They pulled over to use the bathroom and to get snacks at the roadside shop. Shiva bought cheese and bread, and El bought a bag of powdered mini-donuts and a little sack of tangerines for them to share. When Shiva came back out of the shop, El was waiting, the engine already running. She slid into the passenger seat, aware of the distance between her left thigh and El's right and aware that, as intimate as this trip felt, they'd barely touched one another before. There were only those two confident cheek kisses El had delivered at the close of each of their prior run-ins. Shiva wondered how solid their rectangular knee would feel underneath her palm.

The driving, for a long while, was the only sound.

Eventually, El said, "I think we're close."

They'd begun to pass signs that said ROPCZYCE. Around them, Shiva could see vast stretches of grass punctuated with clusters of trees. At the rightmost margin of the highway, a forest. The ground unmarked and unremarkable. No buildings or structures, just land. But not just, she felt. Her insides hummed when she looked at the tops of the trees.

"Where should we stop?" El asked. "Should we try turning here?"

Shiva didn't admit that something had stirred in her when she'd looked over at the treetops. "Sure," she said.

El took the exit off the two-lane road they'd been driving on. They squinted at the road signs and turned onto a street with some restaurants and a motel. Nothing here called out to Shiva at all. She worried that by staying silent about the woods, she'd bypassed a critical clue.

El pulled over. "I'm going to ask around," they said.

Shiva wasn't sure what El would ask but was grateful they were willing to do it. They got out of the car and walked across the street to a café. Shiva watched from the passenger seat as El talked to an older woman with some shopping bags for a few minutes. They came back to the car smelling musky and faintly of vanilla.

"So," said El. "There are a few memorials she mentioned. And there's a Ropczyce museum we could check out if you were interested in that." El looked dubious. "But I think the Jewish community lived more . . . over there." They gestured to the place where they'd entered the town. The trees. The grass, there, and all that quiet.

Shiva felt immensely relieved to hear El confirm her intuition. Three cars passed in succession. "That's my feeling too," she said.

El put the keys back in the ignition. "Let's go back, then. It's quiet over there, so we'll be able to hear better."

Hear what? Shiva wondered, but she didn't ask. They drove back the way they'd come and then coasted onto the shoulder, where they parked. They brought the donuts and the tangerines and the cheese and bread and the nuts and the remaining coffee with them, and walked. They walked past grass and more grass, through groves of trees that thinned and thickened. They walked until the road they'd driven down was behind them, invisible.

———

She has made an uncommon life here, at the edge of the woods, just past anywhere with a name. When she travels, she travels past notice, managing to slip by. Her family, far away or gone. Her body, of the earth. Her body, of something akin to God. Sometimes she lies in the grass, wondering how she's gotten away with so much. This is not what a woman does. This is not what a woman does, so maybe she is not a woman.

She is not a woman.

She is not at home, and she is not passing through. She is not of this world. She is not flawless. She never expected to love. She has not loved much. She has only ever loved the grit and fragrance of dirt on the pads of her fingers. She has loved the work and the silence.

But she loves now.

She has grown in love. Her heart is full for the girl with the animal voice. Her body a message undeliverable.

She has told no one. There is no one to tell.

She has shown the girl in what ways she is able. But she can't anymore. It is no longer safe. For either one of them. In another universe, she thinks, the two of them would be an oceanic collision. The exact alchemy of them something loamy and emergent.

As it turns out, the woman will miss the girl. She misses the girl already. She misses her dearly, and she's not even fully left yet.

———

There were only a few stories about the City of Laughter that Hannah had passed down to Shiva—the badchan who'd been born there, the stringent nature of her great-grandmother's youth, the way the people there had believed in demons who played pranks, who used humor as a weapon—but Shiva's fantasies about the place had always been very particular, lush and sensory.

She'd imagined that if she ever visited, the air would take on a kind of corporeality, and that she might feel the long-gone townspeople breathing, even in the City of Laughter's long aftermath. She'd imagined the rowdy spirits of a whole crowd gathered in a wide wood, the air between them tangy with sweat and wine, forest frantic with the collision of one wordless melody into another. She'd imagined dancing, eyes plastered shut, birds swooping and circling above. She'd imagined hands in hands, or arms outstretched, reaching toward a wide-open eternity no one dared too keenly hope for. She'd imagined smells on the air there still: garlic and onions, chicken and potatoes and stuffed carp, a fire just recently out.

The City of Laughter, however, no longer smelled of garlic or onions.

This part of Ropczyce was flat. Empty of anything, except for its trees.

They walked a little bit more, quiet. Every now and then, a treetop rustled in response to the wind, as the light changed under quick-moving clouds.

Something, then, in the woods. Was it Shiva's imagination, or had she seen smoke in those trees? She thought about Sender and Nisn, the kind of fire that stays and stays, that crackles and burns across time, that even the passing of generations can't extinguish. She snapped around to El and then looked back again at the woods, and they were clear. No smoke, no nothing. And besides, Shiva thought, *If there had actually been smoke, they would have smelled it. Wouldn't they?*

When it became clear the landscape didn't have any intention of changing, Shiva and El stopped. They sat in the grass at the base of a tree. The light changed and then changed again. El lay back, head right up against the tree's exposed roots. Shiva lay back too.

El finally broke the silence. "Do you know about block theory?"

"No."

"Albert Einstein. He says that the differences between the past, present, and future are only an illusion." They angled their face toward Shiva's. "I think about this when I visit somewhere that is completely changed from how it used to be."

"Oh." Shiva thought about this and couldn't decide how true she thought it was. "I guess living in Warsaw, you must think about it a lot then."

A motorcycle whizzed past in the distance, and then the air quieted again.

"Do you feel anything?"

Shiva didn't exactly know what El meant. She felt a lot of things. She felt the air singing. She felt like maybe there was someone here after all. She felt the grass prickling her back and arms, and felt the shape of someone unfamiliar next to her.

"I'm not sure," said Shiva. "I think I do."

"I feel something," said El. "I feel something too."

The light changed again. Something grayer, smokier. Shiva turned her head back toward the thick of the trees, remembering the smoke she thought she'd seen earlier. The whole sky darkening now, getting ever closer to them, or so it felt, and then momentarily brightening again. Even if nothing else here felt alive, the sky certainly did.

Under the restless light, Shiva and El inched toward one another. El's fingertips approached Shiva's in the cooling grass. Their fingers soft and dry. Laced through. Almost accidental. A natural extension of the hours so far.

"Hey," said Shiva. A glazed hush had come over her voice. "I don't think you ever finished your story. About the woman who came into your great-grandfather's restaurant."

"Oh," said El. Their voice had softened too, and their fingers tightened around Shiva's, and Shiva felt the pull all the way down to her ankles. "Well, she was from near here. I'm not sure exactly where, but she told my great-grandfather it wasn't safe for her to go back where she'd come from. She had taken the train from Ropshitz, she said, and the name of this place has always stuck in my mind. I don't know why I haven't come here before."

"You were waiting for me, I guess," said Shiva.

"Maybe," said El. They smiled, but they didn't laugh. "So when they took her into their spare bedroom, my great-grandparents didn't ask any questions. Only much later did they learn she was Jewish.

Probably when she trusted it was safe to tell them. And they kept her identity secret. She stayed on, and in exchange for room and board, she worked as a tutor for my grandmother, who was still really young."

Shiva was fascinated. "What did she tutor your grandmother in?"

"I'm not exactly sure," said El. "Like I said, she was a healer. She taught my grandmother all kinds of things—reading and writing, but also the names for animals and plants and herbs, how to mix a remedy for a sore throat from garden weeds, which foods could improve sleep, things like that. I think my grandmother was kind of a difficult child, and my great-grandmother was just glad someone else was there to help raise her."

Shiva thought about her own mother's inherited remedies. Hannah still made Syl's terrible-tasting cold cure, a tonic of sorrel, ginger, and horseradish root, deriding it all along but brewing it anyway.

"A healer," repeated Shiva. She wanted, without knowing why, to understand everything the word meant.

As the light waned and the shadows above them quickened, Shiva asked the thing she'd been afraid to ask. "What happened to her? The healer your great-grandparents took in? Did she survive the war?"

El turned on their side to face her. "As far as I know she did."

Shiva turned on her side to face El too. She asked no follow-up questions but looked at El expectantly, waiting for more story.

"My grandmother is kind of a healer now," said El. "We tease her and call her a witch. She takes it with mostly good humor."

Shiva shifted closer to El. "My grandmother was kind of a witch too. A different kind. But some kind."

"What kind?" The late afternoon light of the Polish countryside moved like something flying overhead, passing across El's face. Shiva thought of the word *visitor* and then lost her train of thought.

"What I know is that my great-grandmother was from here."

As the words came from her mouth, Shiva was accosted by queasy desire, which she instantly tamped down. This wasn't what this trip

279

was for. How arrogant, to bring her contemporary hunger into this place. How naive to expect that these grounds, long fortified against visitors of her kind, would readily offer up their secrets.

El's hand shifted, and Shiva's hand remembered its texture against her fingers. It was okay. It must be okay. She wouldn't be here, not like this, if it weren't okay.

"I don't know much about her, but I remember that she was very quiet, and that she had this radiant smile, and that everyone in my family is afraid to talk about her. But my grandmother, Syl, she was a character. Really superstitious. Really powerful, I think. She had a lot of power over my mother, anyway. She was known for these odd and cautionary tales she always used to tell, and she apparently loved birds more than anything else in the world." *Syl*, she thought. *Am I close?*

"She's the one who died the night you were born, right?"

"Exactly," said Shiva. "I felt like coming here would bring some kind of great alignment of all these clues I have, but I also know that would have been too simple. It's never that way."

"It isn't," said El. They were looking up again, watching the pale color seep from the sky. "My grandmother won't talk too much about her tutor. I'm not sure whether she doesn't remember, or if she feels protective, or it's just too hard a thing to talk about." El sat up suddenly. "I think my grandparents maybe tried to track her down a number of years ago, but I don't think they were able to find her. I should ask them if they ever did, if there was ever any trace."

"Please do," said Shiva. "I would love to know."

Urgent, like it was her own family she was hoping El could track down and not someone else's. Like it was right now and not some long-ago then she couldn't reach into, no matter how hard she wished she could.

The woman leaving the edge of the woods packs only one suitcase. She has learned to travel light. She does not know yet where she will go. She does not know that she will buy a train ticket to Warsaw and that, hungry from travel, she will end up in the corner of a pub eating a bowl of lentil soup, rich with garlic. That she will feel, for the first time in her life, that she has known some kind of home at her edge of the woods, and with her girl, and that she won't know how to find it again.

She does not know yet that the man who owns the restaurant will be compassionate, uncommon; that he will bring her home for a night of rest, and the one night will turn into two, and then three, and then years with the man and his wife and their young daughter. That she will come to tutor the daughter, a young Catholic girl with a broad and rosy face, who proves to have an intuition about the herbs and other medicines that come from the land. That, eventually, it will come time for her to leave, as it always does. That she will slip out the door in the thick of night, five years to the day after her arrival, leaving a note for the girl and her father and her mother, because letters are her way and because she does not understand how to thank them for becoming the closest thing she's ever had to a family.

Some people never get to know a home, she will think. Soon, she will have had two. One, with the family who will take her in. And one only in her memory now, and in the small box of letters she'll be sure to keep in the bottom of her suitcase for as long as she can carry it.

———

On the way back from Ropshitz, the light was gone, and the air was regular.

"Hi," said El, their voice blurry. The car slowed, and the boxy, dark streets seemed turned around and backward. Shiva didn't recognize where they were until they drove past the big park in Muranów, right near where she was staying.

"Hey," said Shiva. She realized she'd fallen asleep and surreptitiously checked her hair in the dark glass of the passenger-side window. "We're close," she said, testing her own rumpled logic. Saying it out loud felt like sharing something private.

Moments later, they pulled up to the apartment complex where Shiva was staying. El idled the car. "I have something for you," they said.

Shiva looked at El in the dark, disoriented. "What?"

They shifted in the driver's seat, and their keys jangled in the ignition. Out of their jeans pocket, they pulled a small, pearlescent stone. It was so rounded and unblemished, it reminded Shiva of one of those fake gemstones that the science store at the mall carried when she was in high school. She extended her palm, and El put the stone in it. It was almost unbearably smooth. Cool to the touch, but it warmed immediately in her hand.

"What is this?"

El looked down. "I found it there. In Ropshitz. Just right at the foot of that tree where we were. I thought you might want something. Maybe it was weird to take it." They made a nervous sound that was sort of like a laugh. "But I saw it on the ground, just sitting in the roots, and I thought you should be able to bring it home with you."

It was an odd opera's worth of emotions at once: the sweetness Shiva felt in her wrists receiving something from El; the dogged kind of sadness she felt thinking about it being from Mira's once-home, a sentence with no end; the fact that dirt from somewhere so old had yielded something so pristine; that maybe El shouldn't have taken a stone from hallowed ground; that maybe it wasn't hallowed at all; that maybe it hadn't been theirs to take, but maybe it wouldn't have been Shiva's to take either, and maybe they'd both disrupted a cosmic balance as a result.

Thank you was what she managed to say, the stone flat in her hand, lustering still. The opera collected at the base of her throat.

"You're welcome," said El. They sat in the driver's seat, the car still quiet. Nobody made any moves. "You know one of my favorite things about block theory?"

"How do you know so much about quantum physics, anyway?" Shiva suddenly felt urgently curious about her companion.

"It's what I've studied, actually. In college and in graduate school. I love physics, but time and space-time are particular interests of mine."

"What? That's so impressive. You've been holding out on me."

"You didn't ask," El said.

"Fair," said Shiva. She was relieved for a bit of flirtation and a subject change after the unexpected heaviness of that stone. "What's one of your favorite things about block theory?"

"Something called the moving spotlight theory," El said. Shiva watched their face change, imagining them in cartoon-scientist mode, scrawling late-night formulas on a whiteboard in the bowels of some Warsaw university. "It's this one take on block universe theory that allows, like in the others, that the past and future might exist alongside the present. But in this theory, only one moment at a time is absolutely present, and that moment keeps changing, as if a spotlight were moving over it."

Shiva could see it then, in the dark. The spotlight. Moving over them in the excruciating absolute now.

"What should we do?" She wasn't sure, exactly, whether she was asking a logistical question or something entirely else.

"I don't know," said El. In the dark, they looked so soft, their edges all but disappeared.

Somewhere overhead, the sound of flapping. A motorcycle passed, the whir of it muted in the far-off dark.

"I guess you never found your motorcyclist," said El.

Something clenched in Shiva's chest as she remembered the Ghost shaking her head. "I think she just didn't want to be found."

"Hmm," said El, considering. "Does that matter?"

"I'm not sure," said Shiva. "I mean, you didn't necessarily want to be found." Mortified at having implied a finding of any kind at all, she tried to course correct. "I mean," she said. "Meeting you here has just been unexpected."

"I don't know," said El. In their lap, their hands clasped and unclasped. "I think I maybe did."

"Did what?"

"Want to be found."

In the dark, Shiva felt something catch in her lungs. "I should go. I have so much work to finish here. I'm starting early tomorrow."

El leaned in quick, unspooling.

The kiss was sudden and eruptive. No languid lead-up, no steamy windows, no skin slowly discovering skin. No fingers lacing through fingers, no tentative hand-holding, nothing so coy. It was a portal, El's mouth, a hot planet, a magnetic universe behind the simplest lips. It was hungry and fast. Teeth and teeth and all the want behind them. It was not entirely fleeting, but it didn't luxuriate either. It rushed like a thrill that didn't quite want to be caught. It felt extremely right-now. Spotlit.

They blew apart.

Shiva murmured something that wasn't actual words. The kiss was an alien thing. Unrecognizable. It had no referent, Shiva thought, to anything in this world, to anything she'd experienced. It was queerer somehow. More urgent, farther away, closer. Excruciatingly present. Not meant to last any shorter or longer than it had.

El trilled something sweet. Maybe in Polish. Shiva wasn't sure. She imagined the two of them elsewhere, in some other time, on a motorcycle, on a fire escape, around a fire, in the woods, on the run, on some plane she couldn't see. But right now, all they had was the Warsaw dark, the streetlights, the browning night in a place she still didn't know.

In an alley in Muranów, on a perfumed early spring night like this one, S. An-sky met Albert Einstein for a drink.

"I am interested in the impossible," said Einstein. He took a sip from a tumbler of scotch.

"I am more interested in the possible than the impossible," said An-sky. "But I respect you." His goblet held slivovitz. He took a long drink from it, removed a small bag of nuts from his pocket, and offered some to Einstein. "I collect endangered stories."

"In some senses, despite what some may think, I am a very religious man," said Einstein. "Mostly, in the sense that I am subject to wonder. And that I believe wholeheartedly in the thing I love most."

"Yes," said An-sky impatiently. "I know this about you. That's why I invited you here."

Einstein looked surprised. He threw back more of his scotch. "Well," he said. "Thank you. I took you for more of an occult guy."

An-sky was used to being challenged, and he was unafraid of an unexpected response.

"There's nothing occult," he said, "about unbidden love or the persistent work of making a legacy from pieces." He adjusted his thin summer jacket and slid down painted brick, until he was sitting on the ground. "I'm interested in the occult, though. You're not entirely wrong."

Einstein nodded thoughtfully. An-sky extended his long arm, offering Einstein the seat next to him, a gesture too polite and grand for the dirty Warsaw ground, somewhere both outside of and smack in the middle of time. An-sky had commanding eyebrows and a sharply observant face. Einstein, scotch-ruddy, sat.

"You care about belonging," said Einstein. He was good at getting at the heart of things.

"And you," said An-sky, "care about noticing."

"Thank you for noticing," said Einstein. He chuckled. A small beetle skittered past. Outside, the wind sang its intentions. "For example, I notice your jacket is missing a button, my good man."

An-sky looked down. "Right you are," he said. He put his long arm around his companion, getting familiar. "Belonging is a shifting feeling, isn't it?"

"Only with other people," said Einstein. "When I am in the world, I belong. Do you hear that wind? I belong to that wind. And this dirt? I belong in this dirt."

"We are subject to wonder," said An-sky. "I often can't believe how much there is here to belong to."

They sat in quiet for a moment, listening for it, finishing their drinks.

"Look at the stars," said An-sky, though in the alley, they couldn't actually see them. "What time is it?"

"I'm not sure," said Einstein.

Somewhere above them, the wind became laughter, became the weather, engulfed the whole sky. Something folding over, something meeting in some middle, this dark alley the hinge between moments, between somewhere and somewhere else.

———

In the morning, an email from Rosen that was barely even an email:

Shiva. Just following up. Can you send an update?

A stone sank fast to the bottom of Shiva's throat, lodging itself in her chest. Rosen's short missive read like a threat. She shuffled through all the small, innocuous lies she could include in an email back, to fend Rosen off, even for just a day or two. But he would catch up with her eventually. All of this would. She wasn't off track, exactly. It felt more honest to say that she was on some other track entirely.

Her anxiety felt so silly: she had, in fact, been doing research, imperfect and wayward though it had been, and could certainly cobble together something to tide both Rosen and the conference committee over, something that could even grow into a respectable master's thesis. Couldn't she?

But the fact that she couldn't answer the question with a clear yes, she knew, meant that she wasn't ready. Just a little more time, she thought, and she'd understand how to respond to Rosen in a way that justified all of this, that upended all of his expectations about her. That upended her own expectations about herself. That solved the invisible mystery. But not just yet. It would come to her, she thought. She wasn't done here yet.

She washed her face and then, calmly as she could, marked the email as *unread*, giving herself permission to deal with it later. Promising herself she would.

Shiva met Dalia, the Kreitman scholar, in what looked like the world's tiniest archive in a stone building at the end of a dimly lit hallway—a room smaller than her bedroom, lined with tightly packed bookshelves and ancient-looking file cabinets. It smelled like cold coffee, and the only natural light was coming through a dusty windowpane under crooked half-open mini-blinds.

"Mel told me all about you," said Dalia. Shiva had never heard anyone call Rosen by his first name. She also wondered exactly what Rosen had told her. "But you tell me—how basic should I start? Some people have only ever heard of Isaac Bashevis Singer and don't know he had a sister, so with them, I start from square one. But some people have gone deeper in the Yiddish texts and have read Kreitman and just want to better understand who she is, and so we get into it."

Dalia had her sleeves rolled to right below her elbows and a kerchief on her head. She was clearly very religious and also very serious about Esther Kreitman. Shiva found herself wondering if Dalia and her mother would get along.

"Well," Shiva said. "I'm gay and I love *Yentl*, for what that's worth."

"Great," said Dalia, skipping no beats. "So you might already know that Singer got much of the material for *Yentl* from his sister's life. He got the credit for painting the portrait of this character, but in life? He didn't support Esther's career at all. And have you read *Der Sheydim-Tants*?"

Shiva shook her head.

"Mel says you're interested in *The Dybbuk*, and so you must. Put that next on your list. You know, speaking of which, Singer didn't say much about his sister at all, but he did imply that the family regarded her as a madwoman, someone possessed by a dybbuk. He did begrudgingly praise her writing skills, but mostly in light of the spirited letters she wrote home. Typical, right? For a man to relegate her prolific brilliance to the world of domestic correspondence. But also, as we know, letters are where some of our greatest stories live. Anyway, she took her strange and difficult life and became an extraordinary and accomplished writer." Dalia tapped a short, bare fingernail on Shiva's notebook, right below the place where she was note-taking. "You'll notice that Kreitman shares almost none of the sentimentality or nostalgia her two brothers seemed to have had about the traditional Jewish community. It's important, this. It's not some fantasia. Her work is bleak. She was willing to face into the darkness, not because she so much wanted to but because she had no choice."

Not just flying goats, thought Shiva.

"She was a genius, truly." Dalia's eyes shone. She slowed a little, caught her breath. "I love introducing people to her. Some people have a rabbi, something, someone they look up to. For me? Esther Kreitman is a sort of rebbe. You know what she was up against?" Shiva could tell Dalia was going to tell her. "As soon as she was born, she was handed over to a caregiver, if you can call her that. This caregiver, she kept her in a cot under a table. It was so dusty and full of cobwebs down there that she went partially blind. When she was finally sent back home to her mother, she was scarred, physically and otherwise." Dalia shook her head. "What a life. Can you imagine?" She looked Shiva up and down. "I know you're not traditional like I am, but for me, knowing about someone like Esther Kreitman has been so spiritually significant, I can't even tell you."

"Actually," Shiva said. "I grew up Modern Orthodox."

Dalia's eyes widened. "See what I get for assuming?"

"I mean, I'm not observant anymore, but my mother . . ." She trailed off. She wasn't exactly sure how to describe her mother in relation to God or anything God-adjacent. It was complicated.

"Ah, I see," Dalia said. She had an elastic face that made it seem like she truly did see.

"Dalia, where did Esther Kreitman live, exactly? I'm hoping to walk there today. You know, stand where she stood."

"Well, the family lived on Krochmalna Street when Esther was young," said Dalia. "Eventually, she moved away from Poland, though she did return to Warsaw eventually. But you should be sure to spend good time with these archives first." Her expression said that Mel Rosen had called in an academic favor and that it would be bad form to reject it.

"Of course," said Shiva.

"I'll be in the next room if you need me," Dalia said. She got up, smoothed her skirt. "Take your time." Dalia may have been warm, yet Shiva could tell this was not an invitation but an order.

Shiva sat, alone with the files. She flipped through the first, a collection of Yiddish documents. A bit of English, but the print was tiny. She shuffled the papers, trying to orient herself to what she was looking at. They were official-looking documents, and she would need to figure out what they were. She wondered whether it was too soon to go find Dalia and ask her for a bit of guidance.

It was when she was sitting there that something significant began to shift. Not metaphorically. Actually physically shift.

First, she began to feel strange, like there was somewhere else she was supposed to be. She tried to repress the uneasiness, to focus. She felt that, excited as she was about Esther Kreitman, she'd made her way to the wrong place and that, in this small and sunless room, her time in Warsaw dwindling, whatever she was truly meant to find here would elude her. It was so wild and bottomless an uncertainty that she went heavy with it, and then feather light, the feeling she was sinking and levitating in quick succession. The feeling that the room was spinning and she couldn't disembark.

She thumbed through files blankly, trying desperately to reinhabit her head and her body. Yiddish letters swam and danced before her eyes. The room spun more relentlessly then, a carousel speeding up and slowing down in a nauseating, uneven motion. She was a spoke being whipped around some powerful center she couldn't see, thrown with full force, slapped rhythmically against the walls as she spun.

She forced herself to pick up a box of photos and started flipping through them, hoping the images would return her to herself more quickly than words could; that focus would still the circling room. A small, round-faced girl with big, dark eyes. Mouth drawn downward, one hand on her chin and the other pawing through the pages in a big book. A tall solemn man with a beard orating before a group of other solemn bearded men.

She stopped at a photo of two women. She found one of them particularly striking, a crown of braids atop a face so broad and solid, it almost looked like a square. Worried dark eyes under eyebrows sharp enough to signal alarm. The second, so serene-faced as to look sleepy, bright eyes under heavy lids and full lips. Two sets of hands folded into two thick-skirted laps. Did Shiva imagine something about the way these two women looked at one another? The way one set of fingers searched for the other? She looked closely. Did she imagine the way the light fell through the window onto the floor? A straight line, up and down, floor to ceiling. Everyone's eyes gleaming with it.

As she looked at the two women, the room finally stopped to let her off. Shiva closed her eyes for a minute, an effort to reset. There, El's toothy grin. A spotlight, moving from one side of her internal dark to the other. She opened her eyes, closed them again. There, Mira. The strong, stocky legs she'd seen so many times in that photo, but here animated, walking away from the sweater store, from Isaac, walking toward somewhere else, out of the frame. Shiva's eyes fluttered open. She took a breath, closed them again.

And then the feeling all at once, like any hint of it she'd experienced prior had only ever been a preview. That stagger of a bolt through the center of her, sharp and pointed. That ever-present vertical line—the one that ran through generations, through history, through Mira, Syl, and Hannah, and that ran all the way through her still. Wild with the speed of so much accumulated luminescence, it came from somewhere above her and shot lightning-like through the folding chair where she sat, plummeting downward through the floor and through space and time and matter at an overwhelming velocity.

She knew the up-and-down feeling well, but she'd never understood it entirely in her body. Now, though, how vividly she did. Sitting there, she was shot through by something endless in both directions. And there was that wintry blue light, much older now, many more seasons past. Those black birds, only more of them now. And again, as always, that laughter; less a sound, and more an element, something accumulated in the material of the earth. Her eyes fluttered open. She sat, reverberating, her spine especially straight.

Just because she couldn't see something didn't mean it wasn't there. Didn't mean it was wispy or precious or weak. The invisible, in fact, could be quite forceful. Could be stacked eternally tall with the energy of everything that came before and everything that was yet to come. She knew then. The void at her family's center? It wasn't a void. It was a core. It was right here, right at the center of it all. Straight up and down.

Her skin echoed. She stood up, testing her legs. They were shaky, aftershocked. She didn't have a name for what had just coursed through her here, but she did recognize the unprecedented and bodily certainty she felt in its wake.

Mel Rosen, for all his smarts, would not understand the vertical line. Mel Rosen would also never understand this photo of Esther Kreitman and her sweet-eyed friend, nor the spotlight, nor how, at a certain angle, every question was itself a kind of answer. Mel Rosen would never understand, and with a catch in her throat, she realized that she didn't want to explain it to him.

She took a few deep breaths, let her chest fill with the certainty, too. It wasn't that she wouldn't finish. She would. She understood, in the dim of that room, what her conference paper would be about. Everything she'd learned so far—about how an idea or a mythology took hold of a person or their family, how that idea eroded, fizzled, diminished over time, but how in its place remained a sort of patina. Echoes that became new stories. Scraps turned questions turned not quite answers, but something far more interesting. She would give the talk, as terrified as she'd been that conceding to an articulation before she was ready would reflect a kind of investigative failure. But her talk wouldn't be anything revolutionary, and it wouldn't be a culmination.

She didn't want a culmination, after all. It felt so obvious now. For so long, seeking had seemed a liability. The fecklessness of the lost. Time was wasted seeking when there was finding to do. But An-sky had wasted no time on finding. He'd only ever sought. How was she only understanding this now? This was a core, not a void. This was the permission he'd been giving her.

With a passion reserved for lovers and a relentlessness reserved for the possessed, he sought. He sought home and belonging. He sought articulation and a politic and an ethic. He sought friends and love in different shapes and sizes. He sought himself, over and over again, terrified that perhaps there was nothing inside. And when, at any given point, the seeking led to finding, An-sky, burning from the inside out, packed his bags, donned his disguises, and resumed seeking again. His seeking was a way of keeping the world kinetic, keeping the fear of emptiness at bay, fending off the nothing. An insatiable appetite for questions, for seeking treasures where no one else was looking for them. A queer, queer appetite, she thought. A vertical line, live wire, top to bottom, unceasing.

In Shiva, the shift felt electric. She would leave now. It was her story now, and this terrified her. This power was a feeling entirely untethered, as if all her frantic seeking could mean something indefinite, something in and of itself. She was terrified by her conviction, scared it wouldn't hold up once exposed to light and air. Scared, somehow, to walk out of that tiny room and the slab of building that contained it.

She stood anyway. *Please*, she said to the doorknob, and walked out into the sun.

Seventeen

The midafternoon Shiva burst back out into was dewy and possible. Certain. Her even breathing felt like a luxury, and she took one step after the next into the glorious weather as spring people fluttered past like confetti. Teenagers goofing in Polish, someone showing someone else a trick on his bicycle. Tourists consulted maps and phones, pointing upward, putting on sun hats and taking them off. The clouds were shreds, not even hefty enough to be evocative. Everywhere, trees and patches of green.

Could you be new, suddenly, when you hadn't felt new in years? She felt inhabited and also dangerously unattached. At liberty to do whatever she wanted. Doors for the play would open at six, and it was only two.

She ambled around the Old Town, which she hadn't much done yet. Cobbled and ornate, its fairy-tale quality was undercut by the common knowledge that the neighborhood had been rebuilt from unequivocal and devastating ruin. The rest of postwar Warsaw had been rebuilt with a uniform severity, but they'd used prewar sketches, she'd read, to remake the Old Town into a gleaming architectural jewel at the city's center. An opulent gown the city wore, all the deep scarring just one layer underneath.

She walked from turret to archway to alley, until she made her way into the buzzing market square, where hordes of people huddled over lunch and daytime beer under cheery awnings. Dawid had given her a list of his favorite milk bars, including one in the Old Town—the government still subsidized some of them, he'd said, and you could still get a heaping plate of pierogi and a piping-hot tomato soup for next to nothing.

The small space simmered with the smells of frying onion and tomato. It was hot and overrun with tourists trying to overcome language barriers to order their late lunches. Shiva ordered a plate of the *ruskie pierogi*, stuffed with savory potato, cheese, and onion, and a bowl of jewel-pink borscht.

After lunch, she walked for a long time without stopping and without a particular destination in mind. Adrenaline led her, her muscles still taut with it. She walked past the Museum of Warsaw, past monuments and restaurants. She walked past parks and movie theaters and overdone hotels, watched the neighborhoods change around her, and change again. Past the statue of Nicolaus Copernicus, past all the shops on Nowy Świat, bookstores and boutiques and tattoo parlors. She emerged from her ambulatory haze on Mokotowska, not a block from the craft-beer bar where she'd met El just a few nights prior.

She was coming down, finally, and had to use the bathroom anyway, so she would stop in, she told herself. Just for a break.

The bar was cool and smelled of cleaning products. It looked different with sun streaming through its front windows.

"Cześć," said Shiva, to the bored-looking bartender, who stared down at his phone as he vaguely wiped at the counter with a rag. In the bathroom, she splashed cold water on her face as she looked in the mirror, pink-cheeked from walking. She pulled up the English to Polish translation on her phone and practiced it a few times before emerging.

Back at the bar, she leaned in, trying to appear casual. "Szukam kogoś," she said to the bartender. *I'm looking for someone.*

The bartender looked at her quizzically and said something in quick Polish.

"Gabriela," she said. She wanted to say *lesbijka*, a word she'd learned early on, but wasn't sure how that would go over. The bartender stared blankly. "Gabriela," she said again. "Motocykl?"

At that, the bartender's face lit with recognition. He said more, in speedy Polish.

"Angielski?" Shiva looked apologetic.

He looked annoyed but only slightly. "The motorcycle shop on Odolańsk Street. I think."

In the rush of unexpected success, Shiva forgot to be embarrassed. She thanked the bartender and headed to Odolańsk Street.

The motorcycle shop was tiny, and Shiva would have missed it had she not been so intently looking. Maybe it was just a repair shop or a space for someone's expensive hobby. It was wedged between a restaurant and a bar, and there was no name on the door; just the small, spray-painted image of a pair of wings around a motorcycle helmet. The door was red. She shouldn't be here. She should leave, get back to her apartment, and shower before she had to be at the theater.

She couldn't quite tear herself away, though. Not yet. She walked tentatively up to the closed door. She counted to five. No one. She would leave. She would count five more. *Seven, eight, nine.* She heard some rustling and then footsteps.

The door opened to reveal a stocky bearded man in a Metallica T-shirt. He looked at her quizzically. "Czy mogę ci pomóc?"

"Cześć," Shiva replied. "Do you know Gabriela? Does she work here?"

The man squinted, as though trying very hard to remember something. Then his eyes lit and darkened in quick succession. "No," he said. "Not here."

"Does she work here, though? Will she be back?"

The man only shrugged. He looked kindly enough, but Shiva could tell she was interrupting something.

"Okay," said Shiva. "So sorry to have bothered you. Pa pa."

Her body still rang with the certainty she'd felt at the archive—a seeking that was also always an arrival too—but seeking a person like this was different. It had to have an end point. A point at which you needed to accept that there were no clues or bread crumbs. There was nothing holy to be projected on this particular mission, no folkloric underpinnings. She had just let a fantasy grow into something far bigger than what it was. She'd expected wise and generous confluence, easy serendipity. But Gabriela, it seemed, was just a Ghost. Just some queer who'd changed her mind.

She made it to the theater just in time. A lanky teenager with a cap of frizzy brown hair showed her into the theater. The lights already low and the audience hushed; all the day's layers of disorientation and core-shaking recognition and homesick shame melted almost instantly into the cool dark.

The curtains rose to reveal the entire cast standing behind a sheer screen, rendering a crowd of moody silhouettes under the opalescent-blue stage lights. Gravestones jagged up from the stage floor, and at stage left, a creeping pizzicato arose from a small strings section, the only sound for a long while. The music dissipated abruptly, and out walked the Messenger.

She was tall and cloaked, her hair tied back behind a long, pinched face. An unsettling plainness to her expression and yet a near-supernatural ferocity in her eyes. She looked out at the audience, unflinching. When she spoke, her voice sounded milky and thick, uncommonly low. It was unlike any voice Shiva had ever heard.

"Tsvishn tsvey veltn," said the Messenger, a quiet firmness in the Yiddish words. It wasn't a line from the play; it was An-sky's alternative title for it: *Between Two Worlds*. "Tsvishn tsvey veltn," more insistent now. "Tsvishn tsvey veltn," and again, "tsvishn tsvey veltn." Words tumbled into words, and presently, the assembly of silhouettes behind the sheer curtain joined the Messenger in a hypnotic amusical chorus. "Tsvishn tsvey veltn," they said, and the words rose blue from the graves like incantations. The chanting intensified, a collective focused growl, until it sounded certain and piercing, like a rallying cry. "Tsvishn tsvey veltn! Tsvishn tsvey veltn! Tsvishn tsvey veltn!" Underneath the chanting, the strings began to plink and swell again, a melody whose mournfulness was nearly beautiful but ultimately dissonant, displacing, slightly off-kilter.

In advance of the performance, Shiva had read an interview with the director, who'd said she had hoped to create a theatrical experience that was choral. "What do you mean, choral?" the interviewer asked. "Well," she'd said. "Think about something that has captured the Jewish folkloric imagination for as long as it has, nearly a hundred years. And then think about how many people have told this story—have reimagined it, have felt the terror of its proximity in myriad ways. A collective voice—physically, I mean—a collective voice feels important here. To fully immerse in what *The Dybbuk* has become, I found, the experience needed to be vocally cumulative—choral. Something that has avalanched across the generations, picking up speed. Come see; you'll understand what I'm talking about."

The power of the choral in that theater was undeniable, almost indescribable, the room physically full of the vibrations of those projected voices. Surrounded, Shiva felt an intimacy with the people sitting on either side of her that rivaled any intimacy she'd felt at the burlesque. She wanted to bury her face, but also, she wanted to cling to the woman sitting next to her, as if it were suddenly impossible to expect that anyone do any of this alone. Inside a rising scream in a theater that was once the center of a Jewish prewar everyday, she felt sick and then elated and then just heavy, all the way down to her feet.

The Messenger crossed the stage to center, speaking her lines with a flat and somber electricity. She was here to tell a story, to issue a warning. A haunting. The violins screamed and then backed down

298   TEMIM FRUCHTER

again. A possession. She was here to tell a story of a place between two worlds, of something most unholy. We must pay attention, she said. We must not turn away.

The sheer curtain behind her lifted then, and the lighting warmed over the lovers, Leah and Khonen, and over the two intimate friends, Nisn and Sender. The costumes at turns lavish and severe; transporting, nothing spared.

"Der dibek," said the cast. "Der dibek," yelled the cast over a moonlit graveyard, over Khonen's desirous and cataclysmic descent. Onstage, the wedding sprang to life, lace and black silk, the strings section turned wedding band, and a badchan emerged, sagacious and open-armed, to emcee the proceedings. Leah, seized by her dead suitor, spoke in Khonen's voice now, low and anguished, as the dancing turned from cheerful celebration into frenzy. "Mazel tov," the wedding guests screamed and screamed, until the phrase no longer meant *congratulations* but something far more sinister.

As Khonen departed from Leah, as Leah's body ascended, an invisible wire pulled her upward, her arms lifted, inviting whatever sweet death was yet to take her, and the countless layers of billowy white fabric under each of her arms accordioned open, as she rose like a rare bird with the most lavish set of wings. As she rose, impossibly slowly, the wedding guests sang a dirge in Yiddish by way of send-off. They covered their faces and wept, a guttural crying so violent when exponentially multiplied, it almost hurt to hear.

When the lights went up for intermission, no one moved much. Shiva swallowed, feeling something stuck in her throat. A flock of whispers fluttered through the audience, everyone hesitant to unquiet that room. Shiva so badly wanted to stay in the echoes of the first act's trance, she considered just staying in her seat through the break, but she was thirsty, so she extracted herself to get some water.

She couldn't find a water fountain out in the lobby, so she followed a wide, carpeted staircase up to the second floor to see if she'd have better luck. She found a water fountain at the lip of a narrow hallway and then, curious, walked farther, passing several closed doors until she reached an open one. She peeked inside and realized that she was standing in the lighting booth.

"Oh, *przepraszam*," she said. "Sorry."

The lighting tech whipped around.

Shiva's stomach flipped. She fought every instinct she had to flee back into the dark of the theater.

The Ghost.

Jaggy black hair, black T-shirt, jeans. Those unmistakable green-pinpoint eyes. Eyebrows thin-lined, eyelashes a concession to delicacy. *Once when I was a teenager, my sister put mascara on me, and I looked good*, she'd admitted once, amid a late-night text storm.

"Oh no" was what came out of Shiva's mouth. "I didn't know . . . I didn't know you would be here."

Gabriela shook her head vigorously without stopping, as though trying to will Shiva away. "What are you doing here?" Her voice, even agitated, was unexpectedly soft. Her face flushed.

"I'm doing research," she said, her teeth clenching hard as she said it. She almost said, *I was here first*, like a child might, but it wasn't true. "I had no idea you would be here."

A flash of something sad crossed Gabriela's face. "I can't talk," she said. "I'm in the middle of work."

"And I'm at a play," said Shiva. "Wait though. You recognize me?"

"Of course I recognize you," Gabriela said crossly, as if nothing had ever been more obvious. It was a funny thing to say, Shiva thought, for someone who so clearly didn't want to see her. In the window into the theater below, the lights were still up, people slowly standing and stretching their legs.

"Well, I had no intention of finding you here." She didn't mention that she'd had every intention of trying to find her just earlier that afternoon. "I'm sorry to bother you. You knew I was coming, though.

To Warsaw. I thought . . ." She couldn't finish, every apology and qualification a small humiliation.

"You thought what?" Gabriela's soft voice less barbed now.

"I thought I saw you the other night," she whispered. "At the screening at the burlesque."

Gabriela looked down. "You did."

"You told me," said Shiva. "You told me you wanted to meet me. It doesn't make any sense." Her eyes prickled, and she warned the tears back.

"I know I did."

When I meet you we will need to be eating pie so that I'm not distracted by how beautiful you are, she'd texted Shiva just weeks ago, right before she'd fallen off the edge. Shiva had taken a screenshot of the text, looked at it at least a dozen times on her flight over.

"What happened?"

Gabriela looked back down into the theater and then directly at Shiva. Shiva recognized it now, the same look from the dim light of the burlesque. When she'd shaken her head, *no*.

"I wasn't ready," she said, her quiet voice so quickly familiar, Shiva could readily attach it to those fishing trips, the long solitary rides replete with misadventure, the brother and the father, the light and the stars and the smell of bike grease and the Vistula River. She looked at the Ghost's hands over the controls, hovering at the ready, short nails and one simple silver ring. They weren't for Shiva, those hands.

A gust of loss through her whole body. "I wish you had told me sooner."

"I didn't know. Until I did. I tried to disappear. Aleks said someone came by the bike shop looking for me this afternoon. Was it you?" Her voice sharpened, veered into accusation at the question mark.

Shiva's head fell, which felt like the only appropriate response.

The Ghost shook her head again. "I wanted to spare you. But you came, you tried to find me, even though I was already gone. How come?"

Already gone, Shiva thought. Her teeth hurt. The house lights flashed in the theater below them, two minutes to showtime. *Because I missed you*, Shiva wanted to say. *Because I wanted you to teach me how to fish, like you promised. Because I just needed to see what was possible.*

"I'm not here for you," Shiva said, as hotly as she could manage. "I'm here for research," she repeated. An empty chorus. "And today, with the bike shop," she said. "I was just in the neighborhood." This person had a whole life. She was no one Shiva actually knew.

Gabriela said nothing. In the theater below, people were taking their seats. "I have to get back to this," she finally said. "They're going to start in a minute."

"Okay," said Shiva. She turned and then turned back again. "But what weren't you ready for?" Now she looked Gabriela directly in the eyes, silently daring her to look back. It was a rush, confronting her to the adrenaline backdrop of a ticking clock.

For all of her height and swagger in those photos, the Ghost looked small. She shook her head. "I'm working. They're starting."

"Fine," Shiva said. She turned around, back toward the stairs, toward the muffled first strains of violin and cello below.

"Hold on," whispered Gabriela. She attended to the lighting console, adjusting. From the window in the booth, Shiva could see the Messenger take her place again, in front of the sobering tableau of the rabbinic court. Once the stage was lit, the Ghost turned to Shiva again.

"Look," she said. "I liked you." Embarrassment looked so regular on her. "A lot. Too much. And it didn't make sense. You were so far away, and I barely knew you, and somehow I felt like we'd known each other forever. I just couldn't trust it, you know? I wasn't ready for something that made so little sense."

"So you disappeared," Shiva said.

"I disappeared. What else could I do?" Her voice, beseeching. "None of it made any sense."

Sense, Shiva thought. Sense had no place here. Below, the strings zigzagged from the rising chorus of the rabbinic court.

"I'm going to get back downstairs and let you work." She was finally ready to be the one who walked away. The one who left; not the one left waiting. There was a lot to say, but she knew she would say none of it. "I know you didn't want to be found, but really, it was nice to meet you."

The Ghost looked disarmed. Like she'd expected Shiva to linger longer, or like she had more she wanted to say. "Hey," she finally said, her whisper dipping into the entranced darkness and the growing music of grief across the crowded stage. "It was nice to meet you too."

Shiva walked back down the stairs and slid back into the dark of the theater. She didn't turn around once.

———

There is a restaurant on Andersa Street where you can sit in the windowsill. Each sill has room for two, as long as you tuck your legs underneath you. Here, Esther Kreitman and Chana Rochel Werbermacher are having coffee and cake. They are both formidable women, but in this moment above time, the snug sill manages to accommodate them both.

Neither is feeling particularly chatty. Neither really drinks coffee either, so their mugs sit on the sill beside them, getting cold.

"Did you bring it?" Chana Rochel's voice is thick.

"I did." Esther is terse. "I don't know why you couldn't borrow it from someone else."

"You know why, Esther."

Esther pulls a book out of her leather case, hands it to Chana Rochel. Chana Rochel's head is covered. She is wearing so many layers that the book fits tidily inside her clothing. Esther raises an eyebrow. She herself wears a blouse and skirt, no nonsense, plain and simple.

The book, of course, is not a book that was ever published. It is lost to this particular fold of time, and doesn't exist now in any shape we'd recognize. It is a book of stories by women about the haunting thing that clung to them and wouldn't let go. About the thing that they clung to right back. The women wanted, you see, to keep it. It is a guidebook of a kind for the willingly possessed.

"Take care of it, please," she says.

"You know I always do," says Chana Rochel.

For a long while then, they sit together, just thinking. Periodically, one or the other pulls out a notebook and scrawls down a thought or a question. They don't speak much, but every so often, one laughs to herself, pleased with the idea she's had, alone and in company.

Both of them know Chana Rochel won't return the book. It belongs to her now, but Esther has already gotten from it what she needs, the gift of it confirming their unlikely kinship.

At long last, day bending into dusk, the women part ways. They don't hug, but their handshake, as always, is strong and lasts a long hearty time. They leave their mugs and plates behind them, and as soon as they walk away, birds flock like thirsty scholars to peck at the cake crumbs they've left behind.

Eighteen

A messenger's cargo is meaningless without a recipient.
It would be easy to imagine the messenger solitary, reliant on no one. But a one-way transaction would be incomplete. At the end of the day, the messenger does require a kind of companionship: that of a signatory.

But once a delivery has been made, the fate of the cargo is out of the messenger's hands. Imagine, if you will, that the messenger carries something consequential, not only to one individual but to the generations of an entire family. Whether this message is heeded or not; whether the cargo is tended to or buried at the bottom of a pile of socks; whether the letters are treasured or filed away, unread. Recipient's choice: the mutuality of the exchange ends at delivery. Once the messenger is gone, the messenger is gone.

Unless.

Sometimes, what I am delivering feels so important that I—even I—behave differently. I go off script, you might say. I shirk the lore, defy my cosmic calling; I stick around. I watch, I get involved, I become a reminder. I am never too obvious about this—my place, after all, is not of these cities but of somewhere more squarely between here and elsewhere—but I am practiced at camouflage. In all of my iterations, I feel uncommonly moved by other people. Moved by being inside of the world for a time. Never inside of time, though. Time is a thing I am always outside of. It means a kind of forever, and it also makes me largely immune to forgetting.

People, though, are forgetful. Forgetfulness does serve its purpose; after all, an impeccable memory, while enviable, can also be a condemnation. It is enough to endure a terrible thing; it is another entirely to remember it clearly forever.

And while there are times when a recipient simply refuses a message, slams the door in the messenger's face (we are hardy, used to it), and times when it is emphatically received but ultimately ill-used, the most common enemy of the messenger is forgetfulness. A message even received and tenderly nurtured can, eventually, be wholly forgotten.

Families are especially forgetful, adept at the practiced carelessness of leaving things behind. Imagine, if you will, the messenger delivers something of great consequence to a family. But in the family's knowing negligence, what the messenger brought them is slowly dismantled, piece by piece. Generation by generation, each more willfully forgetful than the last, each only receiving and transmitting the diminishing scraps of a message once whole.

The thing is, though: Try as it may, a family will never fully forget. Individuals have bottomless capacity for forgetting. Families, though, have memory outside of the individuals that comprise them, and that memory is wide and long. A message delivered to a family will stay with that family. It will refract and bend, change shape and size, scope and sound, but it is not going anywhere. Once received, you see, what the messenger carried becomes a part of that family's fabric.

It is as simple as this: there was a town, and there I brought my cargo, glimmering and joyous. Call it laughter, if you like. I sometimes call it a kind of desire. From the wilds of that delivery came a family. From the wilds of that delivery, I fell in something like love. With a person, with a family, with the very thing I had delivered. I am not built for attachment, but something in me remembered my own hunger. Once I remembered, I was incapable of forgetting. Or else, like the earthly, I refused to. After all, a love story is the engine at the center of anything.

I am not easily forgotten. Not even after a fleeting encounter. I may shift form, but you won't soon forget me. And once in a long while, I make my indelibility useful. Attachment in my line of work is not only discouraged but unsustainable. But a messenger trades in longing. Without desire, our work would be empty. And I wanted too. I wanted to stay.

When you love someone, I suppose, it becomes important to remind them.

To remind them that desire does not deplete with the generations, and that in most cases, it only gathers a kind of steam. To remind them that there exists a kind of genetics of wanting, and that this, more than anything else, is their inheritance. To remind them that between the unfulfilled longings of each generation rides a determined energy. To remind them that energy doesn't disappear; it only changes shape. To remind them that they come from a line of women made for not strictures but permission. That they, too, have access to the in-between, to a path that curves around to somewhere more possible. To remind them about what families so often don't understand: that the stakes of memory are high. So, I remind. Against my better judgment perhaps, against what all the stories might otherwise tell you, I remind.

And whether you know it or not, you're waiting for my reminder. It is never obvious. It won't be revelation or evidence. It will be back-shadow, skeletal, just past the periphery. Concealed, perhaps, by a notable weather event—a snowstorm, a rainstorm, a fat, presiding moon. It will sit between two yellowed pieces of paper in your musty attic, exactly where you may never find it. It will sit, for as long as you let it, in a box of letters.

•

There is one more thing. Permit me a story.

There was a hungry spirit who took residence in the home of a young woman. This young woman was often sad, but she made excellent soup. She made a different kind of soup every week. Chicken soups, vegetable soups with garlic and bulbous onions, soups that tasted like dirt but were good for you. The spirit would reside in the steam as the woman licked a finger to taste, cried as she stirred the pot. She was lonely. The spirit longed to speak to the young woman, to tell her that it was sad too, that it understood. But it was a spirit, and it could not speak.

One day, the young woman met a young man. Don't ask me how this happened. She was a solitary woman, I know, but this isn't the important part of the story. Let's say she was hanging out the laundry to dry, and there he was, and when her white sheet fell to the dirt, he ran to help her, brushing off the dirt before he rehung the sheet on the line, and this was, unfortunately, the sweetest thing anyone had ever done for her.

The woman invited the man into her home, and he never left. They ate soup together and had one child, a girl, and eventually, many years later, they grew old. The man died, and then the woman died, and the spirit was sad, because he would miss the woman (and, begrudgingly, the man too) and the fragrance of her soups greatly.

But not for long. The woman's child had grown older, too, and was not bad at making soup herself. The spirit hovered over her stovetop too. It was a more modern stovetop in a more modern place and time. The spirit was sad still. It could only smell the soups, not taste them. This daughter specialized in more complex flavors—tangy, sour-sweet, rounded spices and sharp surprises. When this woman, too, grew old and died, the spirit found its way to her daughter. And, as time is predictable and relentless, this daughter—whose creamed soups and purees, the introduction of the immersion blender into the equation, were not to be missed, said all the friends and neighbors—grew older too. The spirit was still sad, its tongue swollen in its spirit-mouth and its fingertips electric with the things it couldn't touch.

In the fourth generation, the spirit waited for the young woman's great-granddaughter to come of age. She was seventeen, eighteen. Finally, she moved into her own apartment right next to a train track that rumbled every twenty-two minutes. She bought firsts—her first set of matching dishes, her first milk-glass nesting bowls, her first champagne flutes.

The spirit was patient, haunting the fire escape until it came time. The young woman opened her laptop and put on a song. She took off her jean jacket and threw it on the small red couch. She turned on the burner and cracked an egg into a small nonstick pan, let it sizzle. Then, as though she had just heard something alarming, she spun around to face the spirit.

"Who are you?" Her face pale, bewildered.

"You can see me?" The spirit was just as shocked. The women had sensed its presence before, it was certain, but no one had ever seen it, acknowledged it, looked it in the eyes. Its hunger roiled in its chest. It had waited for so long; maybe the time had finally come. It straightened its rumpled spirit-shirt and smoothed its wavy spirit-hair. It balked a little bit at the depth and vibration of its own voice.

"Yes, I can see you. Why are you in my apartment?" The young woman began backing away. She picked up her first spatula and held it in the air as she walked backward.

"I just wanted to know if I might have some soup."

"Soup! Are you crazy? What's happening? Are you a ghost? Is this a dream?"

"I know your mother." The girl stared, wild-eyed. The spirit pressed its luck and continued. "And your grandmother. And your great-grandmother." When it mentioned the great-grandmother, it felt a tiny flock of longings flutter through its chest.

"I don't know what you mean," said the girl. "But you're scaring me."

The spirit sighed aloud this time, giving up any fantasy of being understood here. "Look," it said. "I understand. I don't mean to frighten you. I'm just a simple spirit who's been waiting for some soup for a couple hundred years."

The girl softened a little, lowered the spatula. She moved a half step closer to the spirit, sizing it up. Then she looked at the floor.

"I'm sorry," she said. "I don't really cook."

What I mean to say is that even if a messenger breaks the rules and sticks around to make sure their message stays intact, the cargo they've delivered no longer belongs to them. That sometimes, at a certain point, somewhere down the generational line, there is someone ready not only to receive the message but to run with it. To barrel out the door so ungently, so moved by the memory of everything so willfully forgotten, that they flip the messenger in their wake. They flip the messenger upside down—*at last*, I think, *at last*—never to be fully righted.

Nineteen

Hannah entered all ten digits from Riva's cryptic business card at least a dozen different times before she finally managed to press *call*. As it rang, she held the phone away from her ear like it was something rotten.

"Hello?"

"Hi," said Hannah, bringing the phone close again. "It's Hannah. From the funeral home."

"Oh, hi." Riva sounded like she was in the middle of something. "You called."

"I did," said Hannah. Internally, she sped through her options: *I'm calling to ask for a meeting; I found your earring and then lost it again; I think we've met before; we've definitely met before; I know this sounds weird, but I think you're beautiful; this is a butt-dial.* "Do you want to have a drink with me?" It was just what came out of her mouth. "Before you leave town? I figured, just since I had your card, I might as well ask."

"Right in time," Riva said. "I leave tomorrow."

"Oh," Hannah said. She wiped her clammy palm on her jeans.

"Meet me at eight? There's a little dive bar nearby that I love." Riva gave Hannah the address and hung up, hurrying back to whatever she'd been doing when Hannah called.

Hannah fell backward onto her bed, slick with nerves, Riva's card still in her hand. It was raining outside, and she tried to even out to the rhythms on her windowpane. *Jon*, she thought. Oh god, she thought. Oh god. She would wear black. She would wear jewelry. She would wear *something*. Let her hair down all the way, how Shiva was always saying she should. Her special-occasion lipstick, the deep plum color, and the gold hoops that made her feel *youthful*. She would go, she would keep on listening to that one senseless impulse amid all of her sense, that shred of intuition that had come to stay when she'd turned sixteen and never quite left. *But I called*, Hannah thought. *I found her, and I called, and she said yes.*

The bar was small, with tin ceilings and a little chandelier draped in Mardi Gras beads. On the jukebox, something noisy with lots of juicy guitars, a female vocalist Hannah didn't recognize. She couldn't remember the last time she'd been to a bar. She spotted Riva instantly, sitting at the bar with a glass of water, in jeans and a black vest, thin gold chains hanging from her ears. Hannah came up behind her.

"Hi." She let her voice be indeterminate. She wasn't yet acquainted with her own intentions.

Riva spun on her stool. "Hi," she said. She looked bright and unbothered. "What can I get you? Let me guess. A cider?"

Hannah's eyes flew wide open. "Cider? I come from strong Eastern European stock, okay? We take it stronger than cider."

Riva laughed. "*I'll* take a cider," she said to the bartender. "The dry pear. I'm a lightweight." She looked at Hannah, those green eyes friendly and almost regular. "And for the lady, a Laphroaig, neat." Riva raised one eyebrow at Hannah, who nodded and sat.

"So," said Riva.

"So," Hannah said. She wasn't ambiguous date nervous. She was thirty-nine years' anticipation nervous. She thought about her quiet home, maybe a cup of ginger tea and a *Golden Girls* rerun. She halfway wanted to bolt. But a small, keen part of her wanted to stay inside this dive bar forever. "Thank you for meeting me."

"My pleasure," said Riva. "Okay, listen. Let me get one thing out of the way."

"Okay," said Hannah. The bartender handed her the tumbler of scotch. She sipped at it. It was strong and peaty, smokier than she liked. She couldn't remember the last time she'd had hard liquor.

"I'm not going to talk about my work or where I'm from. Or why I'm here."

"What? What kind of an opener is that?"

Riva laughed. "I promise, it's just easier this way."

Hannah's bafflement and annoyance fought each other for prominence. "Why?"

Riva looked at her very closely then, unflinching, like someone she had known for a very long time. "Just go with it?" It sounded like a request, but it was a demand. Hannah knew this much.

"Do I have a choice?"

Riva raised her glass. "L'chayim to the people we're all meant to meet in the bowels of funeral homes," she said.

Hannah touched her tumbler to Riva's pint glass. Even just there, a quick crackle. Was it possible for someone's hands to look familiar? Her own hands were trembling, and she couldn't quite stop them. "I'll be right back," she managed. She slid off her stool and headed to the back of the bar.

At the bathroom sink, she stared into a mirror hung under a neon-pink light, the only light in the room. In the smudgy mirror, her eyes looked big and dark and her lips pointed. Not half bad. She reapplied her lipstick even though she didn't need to.

Tonight was the first night since Jon's death that she hadn't worn her wedding ring. *Of course you shouldn't be wearing your wedding ring,* Shiva would say, and Marla, and everyone. *He's dead over a year now.* She knew people talked but she hadn't cared enough to stop. Tonight, though, for no reason that she felt ready to explain to herself, let alone to anyone else, she'd pried off the ring and hidden it at the bottom of her jewelry box. Then she'd hidden the jewelry box in her sock drawer—*just in case*, she thought, though she instantly felt silly about it because, *in case of what?*

Here, now, the mirror was behaving itself. She was just out with a woman. A beautiful woman. A woman she felt like she knew. A woman. She couldn't formulate the words quickly or slowly enough. She re-reapplied her lipstick. *It's just what's happening*, she said to no one. *Go with it.* The last time Hannah Margolin had just *gone with* anything, she couldn't remember. There probably was no last time.

She walked back up to the bar, steadying herself on the stool, and taking another throat-scalding sip. "So," she said. "If I can't ask you about work, what can I ask you about?"

"Basically anything else," said Riva. "Try me."

"Okay," said Hannah. She felt so hot. Her body remembered before she did—the night of the fire, the night Shiva was born. It was that kind of hot. Unnatural. Like an actual burning. "Tell me three things you really love to do."

Riva smiled. Hannah noticed that when she did, her eyes stayed open; they didn't get any smaller. "One, I love boats. I'm working on fixing up a boat right now."

"Boats? Like sailing?" It wasn't what she'd expected. She had no idea how to make small talk about boats.

"Yes. I mean, not sailboats particularly. But yes, boats."

"Okay. What are two and three?"

"Well," said Riva. "I like making things with my hands. I sculpt." She took a swig of cider. "I can peel a potato in one fell swoop."

Riva's hands were unadorned, Hannah noticed. She cupped her glass with one, and the other rested on her knee.

"And?"

"Hmm," said Riva. "Well. I enjoy traveling. I travel a fair bit." She did not then elaborate. Riva the consultant seemed unbothered by long stretches of quiet.

"Are you going to ask me a question?" Hannah was nervous, impatient. Wrecked.

"Yes, just one," said Riva. "I'm going to be blunt. I'm in town for one more night. Are you going to ask me home with you?"

Hannah reeled. She became a pile of boulders, a gnarling. The floor and the walls vanished, but there she still was, that knuckled and tortured minute between wondering and knowing. Who. And how. It didn't matter. Here they were, just right here. Hannah didn't understand. She wouldn't understand, maybe ever. But her entire body remembered what the mirror had told it those countless years ago.

The words turned to dark every time they reached her lips. The letters turned to chaos. *It wasn't. It's not. I can't. I wouldn't. I won't.* "It's so hot," she said, wishing she hadn't.

"Is it?" Riva drank more of her cider. "I hadn't noticed."

"Yes," mumbled Hannah, not certain which question she was answering. Her thighs, operatic. Tops of their lungs. "Yes." The second time, she said it with her whole tongue.

As Hannah drove home, Riva driving a small black car directly behind her, she said nothing to the dashboard, nothing to the windshield, nothing to the steering wheel. She prayed to no one, she cried to no one, she texted no one, she called no one. She was alone. Alone, she thought, in a way she felt like she was supposed to be in this particular moment. Stripped of language. Of control. Of any resident dead. Just the extra-quiet engine of her car in the suburban night, getting her from one place to another. *Don't think too hard*, she thought. *Don't think.*

While Riva parked, Hannah hurried into the house to make sure it was presentable, though it usually was, even when she didn't plan on visitors. The last time she'd had someone back to this house was never. She and Jon had bought it in 2002, an upgrade from the first house they'd been able to afford, pooling all of their young savings. Sixteen years later, the entryway still lit by a fixture Jon had chosen; the kitchen, still flanked by the window seat he'd built; and of course, in the corner of the living room, still his reading chair, like a very old friend. All over the place, remnants of a husband.

Riva slipped in the door quietly behind her. "Nice house," she said. "Have you lived here a long time?"

"I have," said Hannah. "About sixteen years." Willing Riva's eyes away from the framed photo of her and Jon in Kauai, taken by a friendly stranger, both of them laughing as a rowdy wave licked at their waists.

"Who's this?" Riva pointed to the photo.

Should she say *ex-husband*? *Dead husband*? *Widow*? "That's Jon," Hannah said. "We were married thirty years. He died last February. Cancer." May as well get it out of the way.

"Hmm," said Riva. "I'm sorry to hear that." She looked genuinely sorry but not like someone who would dwell on it.

"Thank you," said Hannah. "Do you want anything to drink?" There might be an iffy half bottle of chardonnay in the fridge. Maybe some seltzer.

"Nah, I'm okay," said Riva. Her eyes were wandering, curious, and Hannah watched as this stranger took in her home. She walked over to the mantel, where Hannah had framed photos of Isaac and Mira, of Syl and Robert, of her and Jon, of Shiva all dressed up for a fancy gala Hannah could no longer remember the occasion for.

"It's a really nice house," Riva reiterated, as though she'd understood something now more clearly than she had before. "Can I see your room?"

Her bluntness was unnerving and perhaps unearned. Hannah wondered what Riva thought was happening here. Hannah certainly had no idea, only knew that her body was vivid with attention to Riva's every move. She was at the total and incapacitating mercy of a stranger.

"Yes," said Hannah. "Though it's not much to see." She led Riva upstairs, feeling the walls on either side of her adjust to another presence in their midst. She opened the bedroom door, almost expecting something or someone to come out and greet them. But it was quiet, serene as it ever was. Her large bed, a wide linen island piled with pillows. Bare dresser and nightstand. The most vocal thing in the room was the large grayscale painting above the bed with the splashes of blue and yellow across the center, the one she'd once told Jon made her feel like she was inside a Smiths song.

Riva stood in the center of the room and spun slowly around, taking it in. She looked up, and then over at the nightstand, where under Hannah's lamp, there was a small pill bottle (her thyroid), a rumpled tissue (she grimaced), last night's glass of water, and a tiny vase of dried flowers from Shiva's two-years-ago Mother's Day gift.

"Wow," she said.

"Wow?"

"Some energy in here."

Hannah bristled. She didn't need anyone reading her energy—or her house's, for that matter. She worried, instinctively, that she'd made her home vulnerable to something she shouldn't have. Her home and still, somehow, Jon's.

What would Jon think? She'd alluded to the mirror woman several times during their life together and, on one or two occasions, had nearly caved in and told him the whole story. But something had always prevented her from coming fully clean. From admitting what, deep down, she thought it all meant.

Hannah only nodded, collecting her unruly feelings.

Riva looked like she had more to say, but didn't say it. She walked over to Hannah's dresser, picked up the lone dried esrog she kept there, turned it over in her hands, and put it down. She certainly seemed comfortable. Hannah watched as Riva looked at herself in the mirror, just for a moment, swept her bangs to the side. Did the room get darker then? It was impossible to tell.

Then she walked over to the bed, sat at its edge. Hannah sat too, abruptly, like someone had told her to. Riva smelled like skin, another person's. She smelled a little bit windy.

"Hannah," said Riva.

Her name out of Riva's mouth sounded torrential, nearly leveling her. She turned to Riva, who put one of her hands on each of Hannah's shoulders. They stayed like that: Hannah shivering, and Riva still. Then she moved her hands up so that they cupped Hannah's face—one on one cheek, one on the other.

Inside and outside and everywhere, whipped silence.

Through the window, the sound of a late-night bird. Had she left the window open? Hannah was hungry. No, she was starving. She had never felt her feet so precisely. She had never felt her tongue, the tender insides of her arms. Parts of her warm that hadn't been parts before. She wanted to be fed. She was afraid.

Riva was close. Hannah felt breath on her lips, sweet and dark and musical.

"I," said Hannah. "I." The stutter not only in her words but in her jagged breath. Her lungs working faster than they had in thirty years. "I," she said. The one syllable that would successfully and succinctly locate her on earth, in her body, in this room.

It was only when she felt Riva's hands slide easily down her cheeks that Hannah realized she'd started crying. She was embarrassed, but Riva seemed steady and unbothered.

"Close your eyes."

"What?"

"Close them."

And Hannah did.

"I want," and Riva paused. She sounded not nervous, exactly, but focused, like she was finally about to tell Hannah what she'd really come here for. "I want you to feel me."

"Feel you?" Hannah was whispering now. She opened her eyes. The dark was ever darker. The mirror, she thought, ever bigger behind Riva's radiant face.

"Yes," said Riva. "You've seen me. Now I want you to close your eyes and learn my body." She paused, waiting for Hannah to understand.

Hannah's frozen face. "Not with your eyes but with your hands. Just for a minute." Her voiced hushed, almost pleading.

Hannah clamped down her teeth to stop the chattering.

"Just for a minute." Riva repeated the prompt, and Hannah, impossibly slowly, reached toward the person sitting next to her on the bed. She fumbled until her hands found the two sides of Riva's waist. No vision in a mirror now, but a real body. Her vest was thin, and Riva, too, was thin—Hannah could feel her ribs. She moved her hands very slowly upward, afraid to be bolder than she'd already been, until she heard a small sigh escape her guest, one that could signify nothing but pleasure. She traveled farther up Riva's body, smooth, smooth, straight-up smooth, until the tight curves along the sides of her chest, and then back down again, where she felt for fleshy and round, where she dragged burning fingers across curves and divots, feeling Riva tense and suspend under the sensation of her fingernails, where she let her hand slide all the way up to Riva's face—traced the jut of her lips, the wide angle of her nose, those lashes. Her hair was thinner to the touch than Hannah had imagined. Her ears. Her neck. The slope, the slope, and down again, accumulating speed and hunger. The warm insides of Riva's thighs, the worn denim there smooth as a memory, and Hannah could feel Riva's entire body arching up toward her. Down and down to the ankles, prostrate, to her feet, flexed and waiting, boots kicked off.

In the process of Riva, Hannah had lost track of her own body. She felt only her hands burning. Only her eyelids sealed shut. Only the entire middle of her, queasy and tight with want. She was only avid for Riva, starved for the fact of her skin. She didn't know how to stop. From the backs of Riva's legs and back up and up again, until she felt Riva's hands on hers, until she slowed, she slowed, she sat, and she opened her eyes.

"Hello," said Riva. Her face looked dazed.

"Hi," whispered Hannah. Her palms were screaming, and something pounded in her thighs.

Riva sighed again, a sound less waiting and more complete. She seemed undone in a way she hadn't all night. "Yes," she said, as though only to herself. "This is a good start."

"Start?"

Riva tucked some strands of Hannah's hair behind her ear in a way that felt drunkenly intimate. "Yes. Start." She kissed Hannah, soft and quick, directly on the center of her lips. "I'll see you again."

"You will? But I thought—"

"I'll be back," said Riva. "Before long."

The room sharpened back into quiet.

Overhead, an airplane hummed its monotonous way across the sky, and right then, as though on cue, the night leaned back, settled into its most final and blackest dark.

After Riva left, and Hannah walked back into her bedroom, it felt like someone else's. The bed and the dresser and the windows looked generic and unfamiliar. She floated back to the edge of her bed where she'd just navigated the universe of Riva's body. Where she'd newly understood the meaning of the word *encounter*, weeping in the brazen face of mutual recognition.

Mechanically, Hannah began to take off her clothes. Was this what being outside of your body felt like? Or was it more like being inside? She didn't generally like to be naked. Even with Jon, she'd preferred to be covered by sheets and blankets. But now, her skin so tender it physically hurt, naked was all she wanted. She collapsed onto her pillows, wild with an adrenaline so palpably uncontainable it threatened to become sound. With Riva gone—with Riva having been there to begin with—everything suddenly felt unbearably quiet.

She needed music. Her body was firing at speeds her brain couldn't keep up with, and so she picked up her phone and pulled up the only album she could think of: *Songs from the Big Chair*. She connected it to the Bluetooth speaker Shiva had bought for her a few years back and put on "Shout."

The opening snaps, little dings, and mini-hoofs, synths like jangling keys revving up to go. And then the leap: SHOUT. SHOUT. It kicked in louder than Hannah expected, and it was late, but she lived alone now, so she didn't turn it down. She let the glossy production wash over her, the men's laden voices so familiar they felt like family. That throaty longing at the edge of the chorus—the jumping for joy you shouldn't have to do—that would always remain Hannah's first memory of real adult desire. Men in the 1980s always sang like they were crying; like it was there that they had real permission. It was the kind of crying you could only do inside of a song.

She curled up in the middle of her bed and brought her knees to her chest, letting the sweet thick of the sound reach inside of her. She felt vast and needful, snorting and giddy with an excess energy she'd always thought reserved for the young. Hannah cackled. She couldn't stop laughing then. It wasn't reserved for the young, she thought. It was for her after all. The sense that every haunting song is for you. That the whole wide road is for you. That the weather and the weeping sky are for you. That it is all for you and only you.

May 10, 1921

Dear L,

You seemed different today. I hope it is okay to say that. After what happened in the woods several weeks ago, I feel changed, so maybe I'm imagining it, and of course I mean no disrespect. But your forehead looked creased, and your eyes heavier with worry. I can't tell if the worry makes you seem closer to me or farther away.

I hope nothing has changed because of what I have told you. I saw you smile when you noticed the esrog on my bedside table, the one I told you I had found in my clearing. Each week you come with such tenderness into my room, and each week, it makes me feel that you believe me. That you will not betray my secrets. This is more valuable than anything in the world. If you'll allow me to call it friendship, then, from the gladdest part of my heart, I will.

I have been so eager to write you, L. Yesterday, Mama sent me again to the market. I have been practicing walking at a quicker clip so that I have enough time to stay in the forest for a little bit before I have to be back out in public. Voiceless as I am now, my hand no longer flutters to my throat as if to say I am ill, because everyone believes that the reason I am not speaking is much stranger than a sore throat. And they are right. It is far stranger. And so, to the woods. I go to my clearing, and I stand in the center, and I speak to the rough brown bones of the trees in my new animal voice, the one that makes sounds I still don't recognize or know how to harness but that makes me feel more familiar to myself than ever before.

This time, I stood there for a little bit longer. I thought I heard a creature approaching, responding to my call. For a moment, I worried, but Papa was at work and wouldn't suspect I would come back to the woods, not after what happened there. Then I felt a nervous thrill—what if my new voice brought me closer to the foxes, the bears, the creatures of the woods? I opened my eyes and saw no one. Please, I said to the woods. I didn't know how to finish the prayer.

And then again. In the belly of the tree where last time I found my esrog, there was something small and gleaming, something that caught the light. My heart started pounding furiously. I was not alone in this place. My conversation with the woods was not imagined; it was real. Slowly, I approached the tree. The object, a small stone, was smooth and shiny as glass. Someone had cleaned it, and it glistened like an amulet. It fit perfectly inside my fist, where I carried it with me all the way to the market. When I got there, I tied it up in a handkerchief, just in case, and pushed it deep into my skirt pocket. I brought the fish and the bread and vegetables home just in time.

I have to confess: I am excited, but I am also a little bit nervous. I wonder who is on the other side of these gifts. I wonder who knows where I go, and who finds me there without finding me. Do you think it is someone I would recognize? Do you think your earthly magic is making me snarl instead of speak, my voice now recognizable to the panthers and the wolves? Be honest with me, L. What or who do you think I am?

Before I end, before I lose my nerve, I need to say one more thing. I am not sure how to say it, but I am learning that most of what really needs to be said in this world doesn't easily translate into human language. I will tell you that I think about you sometimes when you are not here. More than sometimes. I am shy to write it down because I don't know what it means, even as I write it. I always want to show myself to you. It has never been safe for me to show myself to anyone, not fully. And maybe it is because you are kind, and because your hands are strong and warm, and because your neck is wide, and because your brows are thick, and because your nose has the beautiful angles of a sculpture. Your voice is calm, and you tell me what the earth has told you. You tell me the truth.

I heard a story once, from Sarah the neighbor, about a strange woman from a neighboring shtetl who never married. She wasn't like me, exactly—she spoke, for one thing, and she didn't laugh like a hyena—but she stood notably tall and long-nosed and did not, it was said, enjoy the company of men. She was wise as a sage, but she did not study. She was towering and sharp and behaved strangely, moving in solitude as a wild animal might. Despite this, she had many suitors, who couldn't help their curiosity about her uncommon beauty, but it is told that she refused them all. Sarah said she might have been the most beautiful woman in the town had she not kept her hair shorn close to her head. She wore a scarf to the market and to synagogue, but at night sometimes she walked bareheaded to the cemetery. People who saw her pass wondered who she visited there, why she wore her short hair uncovered, and even, at times, whether she was a woman or a man.

I want you to understand, L, the things I can't say.

I can't speak, but I think you see what is in my eyes.

Yours very truly,
Mira

Twenty

Here the ground is soft, which is how we know we're somewhere we can stay. We land quietly. The moon never notices us, so few of us and so slight. We wear the same curves it does, after all. We collect with rigor. We take our hunger seriously. If you don't see us, it's because you aren't looking.

———◆———

You called me Gabriel, and I let you. It was an unspoken arrangement. It's not always my name, but I have never been that attached to names. You, though. You loved names. You named the birds, and you said my name just like I was one of them. You had no idea how close you were to being right. *Gabriel*, you said, your face broken open by a smile, and I knew you were calling me *messenger, archangel*. You could see what I was. I felt, in those moments, incomparably holy, like when you wrapped your arms around the center of me, you were holding pure light. I wonder if you felt it too. I had never been pure light before, anyone's. *Gabriel*, you said, your cheeks pinking so wholly it looked like they were trying to catch up to the red of your hair. *Gabriel*, you repeated, and I could see how much you liked my name in your mouth.

———◆———

Curloo-oo. We against the wet blue, we, and otherwise it is quiet. *Curloo-oo.* We announce ourselves, but sometimes it isn't enough. Does our one voice sound like anything to you? In our language, the word for *cry* is the same as the word for *hello, my name is.* Is the same as the word for *something is wrong, something is too true.* Sometimes we wait for you to hear us, to call us back. But sometimes we leave before you have the chance to miss us at all.

———

I don't usually tell strangers our story. Other stories I tell, but this one I keep close. It's ours, after all, not theirs. Though sometimes I want to tell them about us, because of how telling makes a thing more real, even as it recedes. If I did, I might begin with how, at first, you didn't know whether I was a man or a woman. How, back then, you weren't used to this kind of confusion. How your eyes first caught my suit— burgundy, three pieces—and then, only afterward, the bend of my nose, the angular clip of my hair. You watched me from your upstairs window as I moved past, the fast and incognito walk of a courier. From that height, you knew no better. You fell for a gentleman.

That brisk day you finally came outside to say hello, you were dressed for something, a plum pillbox, sharp white blouse tucked into a swirl of olive-colored tweed. Your lips a doubtless crimson. *Excuse me*, you said. I stopped. *Hello*, you said. Your voice was sharp, decisive, like you'd been considering saying it for some time. When I answered you, finally made myself known, the high tenor of my voice didn't feel to you like a betrayal; it only peeled away the shapes you thought you knew, only drew your peripheral vision nearer the center.

The days that followed became our days. I walked past your window, and you came down. You began to walk with less composure, and I could sometimes hear you hopping down the stairs in twos. You finally had permission to call things by their most unexpected names. In your parents' small Brooklyn garden then, you put a sign that said TOMATOES in the zucchini. You wrote CARROTS and staked it in the curls of parsley.

You were ecstatic, told me breathless one frosty night on the corner beneath the streetlamp that you had never kissed a woman, that nothing looked the same anymore. Besotted, I didn't mind being your watershed. *I am no woman*, I said. We are both in disguise now, I thought, but I'm not sure I said the thing out loud. The world can fall away easy, clumps of mud from a ready wet hillside. You drew in your chest as if to make space for me to come closer than physics allowed. The lamplight diluted us, and the street was quiet but for the birds. *Curloo-oo*. How badly I wanted you to know me right then, and for this reason, I was afraid. How badly you seemed to want me to know you, and I know this frightened you, too.

Quiet nights, we tell love stories about places we have landed, even places that were unkind. It is easy to remember a place as though we were whole there, as though our plural felt singular, as though we flew with ecstatic speed over ghostless terrain. It is easy to remember lush grass, night whispers, a hot kind of yellow buzzing *yes*.

I might begin with me, a collector. I hunted treasure, adorned with abandon. It is true that I have always had a strange tenderness for objects. That this is uncommon for my kind. In the mid-1950s, my work as a courier took me to Marcus, the dispatcher with the curlicued mustache and perhaps the longest lashes a man has ever worn. We were all in disguise, interlopers of one kind or another, rushing unmarked packages from place to place, collecting signatures from important men and avoiding eyes.

I have always loved my work. Delivering the needed thing to the person who needed it. I relish fleeting. I get to be one person when I leave and another when I arrive. I never have to speak my name, or I can speak a new name daily. We are all so many names; why do we

narrow ourselves so forcefully to one? Nights I lay in bed, haunted by
the heart shape of your lips. Lips had never mattered to me before.
But yours. That lost and hungry season. So much true at once. This
world so full of truths, it never fails to stun me, even still.

I might begin with you, observer. Storyteller. Your eyes perpetu-
ally upward, fixed on the flights of the crows and the sparrows and
the hummingbirds, as if each contained a promise. You could watch
for hours, chin in your hands. When you laughed, you laughed loudly,
and when you let down your hair, it was a kerfuffle.

Stories were your most fluent language and mine. We traded them,
night after night: one of yours for one of mine. Our stories began to
bleed into each other, to become one another's until it was difficult
to tell where one ended and the next began. Sometimes, they were
only middles. Our stories betrayed our desire and our grief more than
anything else. Stories, I knew, would one day become the magic you
would use to stave off the fear we had briefly postponed. Our stories,
remnants from another time. Our stories, the most intimate kind of
travel. We peddled in stories. We peddle in them still.

You were to be married to a history professor, but you were unsure
about it. You were less sure every day that season. Your skin was hot,
even on the coldest winter days, anticipating. The time before you
married was supposed to be a stilling time, but we flew mad circles,
walking everywhere we could until you were half sleeping, holding
each other like the only alternative to drowning.

You told me about the curlew, your favorite bird: shy, nocturnal,
homebody, impossible to sex. Curlews move together, one collective
musical organism. You smiled shyly at me as if to translate, though you
weren't ordinarily shy. When a group of curlews cries, you told me,
the birds know something you don't. When they cry, it is a warning.
When you cried, it was secret, a kept room. You warbled, and I pre-
tended not to hear you. I couldn't help but listen, though, mesmerized
by such an uncommon sound.

There was something you'd always felt, you told me late one night, your eyelids heavy. Felt it almost like knowing, the sensation of a line that went straight from your feet to the top of your head and back down again. You weren't sure what it was, what it meant to feel this way, but I knew. I knew it had something to do with what allowed you to smile at me so openly the first day I spoke to you, even though I was something much more uncommon than you'd ever laid eyes on. Or maybe, in fact, you were the uncommon one.

It was the lavish party your friend had, the sort of affair you only read about, or that appears in dreams from which you wake immediately nostalgic. It felt like we'd been transported to another time, though it was only December of 1955, and it was only Manhattan. The wine was poured by men wearing bow ties, from decanters into shallow polycrystalline goblets. Everything was characterized by a clinking, winged laughter, tremors of breathless chandelier. Fruit and cheese appeared on platters, briny olives in tiny silver bowls, small round cakes on tiered glass stands. A dripping elegance that made me lusty and brazen. I wore my lushest finery—my bronze cuff links and my favorite jacket, a midnight blue.

You wore a wine-red dress that flared at the bottom, and introduced me to everyone you could. *This is Gabriel.* You didn't touch me, exactly, but you were close enough for me to feel the warmth emanating from your arm. Close enough for me to know you wanted to touch me and that you might if you didn't think it dangerous. I knew this danger well, felt it chasing me even as I eluded it. Admittedly, I also liked the danger. I liked watching people see me, their faces furrowing and expanding, at first a blank curiosity, and then that flash of terrible desire, and finally, a spill, the quick pink shame that so often morphed into rage.

At the party, I ended up alone, as I tend to. I watched you talk, gesturing brightly, hot-cheeked. I patrolled the buffet table, the ornate silver spoons now scattered, little beads of citrus floating at the top of the diminishing taffy-colored punch bowl. I ate a cucumber spear with my fingers, then another. A couple, linked at the elbows, approached the table to refill their glasses, and I saw their faces change when they noticed my hand in the crudité, followed my arm up to my angular shoulders, to my face. I dared myself to look at them, and they didn't recognize me; they weren't sure to whom I was giving the bad name. They hurried away, and I receded, leaned into an armoire, where I immediately found the bird, my souvenir. It was made of a colorless and translucent glass. The smoothness of it so unbearable that I lifted it to my lips and slowly brushed it back and forth. Then I slid it directly into my pants pocket. So small, it fit perfectly there.

———

We hear your songs. We feel your hot glass windows. We invest in your unfoldings despite ourselves. When nothing is lost until the last scene, is it still a sad story? What about the fat and joyful middle? Why do we always leave with only aftertaste? We can fly with mud in our mouths, and so, for expediency, we do. Place to place, heavy, mouths too full with ending to try to remember anything before.

———

After the party, we tumbled down into the marbled lobby and spilled out the front door onto the street. My lips prickled with cold. Your warm fingertips to my mouth, and we pushed into an alley, launching a spray of pigeons upward. Seasons condensed in that moment—the musky radiator heat of the fancy apartment into ice-frosted streets, the sidewalks steaming and the leaves blowing hard in all the wrong directions. You put a hand on each of my cheeks and pulled my face to yours, told me a small, quiet story about how New York came to be so full of pigeons. You, storyteller. Your powder-blue coat the same color as the lamp-wet sky. I told you a story about the color blue, how it came from the glass at the bottom of the ocean, but then I couldn't hold it back any longer. I told you I loved you. I had never. I would never. Not like this.

My words hung in the air with the cold smoke between our faces. You, who noticed color, you, who knew the names for things that flew. I pulled the small glass bird out of my pocket and offered it to you. I wanted to give you something, and it was what I had. You began to reach but then changed your mind, pulling your hand back and stuffing it into your pocket. Your eyes darkened, and you looked at me for a long time; so long, the quiet rang like a question mark.

———

We rest before a long flight. New moon nights we make room, we nest together, bring each other tidbits for the journey, preparing. We can't stay anywhere forever; no one can. We see you move in circles too, around your rooms, making space for one another in farewell beds. Maybe you, too, are preparing, or maybe you are unprepared. Sometimes, leaving is just the truest thing: a contraction, a wrenching. What's next. You don't always understand this, but we do.

———

You were too superstitious to let a thing go unnamed. When there was a bird whose name you didn't know, you simply pointed and said, *There*; not generically, as in, *oh, there*; more like *There* was a name in and of itself.

Together, we had one tight and rollicking season, but I like to imagine it was four. The truth is that I wanted to switch the sheets from flannel to linen with you, to go from scotch to gin, from long walks to movie theaters, to pick fresh flowers or spruce boughs for some warmly laid table. Winter would be for chickadees, woodpeckers, and nuthatches. Spring for hermit thrushes, woodcocks, great egrets, and black-crowned night herons. Summer for starlings, waxwings, and nighthawks. Fall for spotted sandpipers and greater yellowlegs.

Once, in Brooklyn, by that curious elm whose name I knew was Camperdown, you saw a hummingbird, such a rarity, you wept. We had one season but loved urgently in the night pockets we had, and in this way, the season stretched long.

It is true that I liked you looking at me, and I liked you looking away. It is true that I wanted nothing more than to stay, and that I couldn't possibly stay long. I stayed for a time, though. I wanted to remind you. I wanted you to remind me, too.

Some afternoons, I delivered documents to your father's office. I kept my eyes down when he signed for them and handed them back to me, a stranger standing before his great brown desk. Sometimes I worried he suspected something about me, if only because of the fever that inevitably crept up my neck as I stood before him. Over his desk, a family photograph I longed to study more closely. You had his nose, I noticed, but didn't dare notice for long.

Your parents hosted dinner after dinner for you and the history professor. Your mother, long quiet, served you brisket and parsnips, stewed onions and beets and hot bread, foods over which to linger. You spent long evenings there and came to find me in the late afterward, somehow famished still. I wasn't used to being anyone to come home to.

We were temporary. We stood trembling in the place between stillness and movement as long as we could. And then we were out of time, but not in the way it sounds. We were outside of time, let's say. Still are. That's the closest I can come. That's how I'd tell it to the strangers, the ones I don't usually tell.

Where will you go? I asked you. Secretly, it was a kind of pleading. *There*, you said, and you weren't pointing. Your hair brushed into submission. Your voice thick with something like fear, and you took my hand to warm it before letting go.

I left that night while you were sleeping. The moon was wide and high, I remember, and how quiet the sky. Most distinctly, an absence of birds.

The night I left I buried the tiny glass bird in Prospect Park at the foot of the Camperdown elm, that tree whose branches grow parallel to the ground. It felt like it belonged to a time, no longer to me, and besides, I have no shortage of souvenirs.

It is true, too, that I wanted to leave a clue. Something to mark a place we'd once stood, just in case we ever wanted to remember our way back. I like to imagine that the ground everywhere is full of treasures buried by lovers out of time. I always know how the story ends, and with you, it is no different, but I like to imagine that you did not marry the history professor, and that you ran off with his handsome and equine sister, that there is a name you call her now, still, that no one else knows.

I like to imagine that you've traveled to see the rarest and most storied birds and live where the sky is spacious. That you've stopped letting fear tame you. That you are aflight. That, sometimes, on wet nights, when the curlews remind you, you still fly mad circles looking for clues. That you'll be sleepless and go walking one night, that you'll slip out of bed, leaving the history professor's sister sleeping there. Somehow, you'll know where in the vast and squawking city to go, and you'll walk all the way to the park, where you'll kneel in that pliant dirt. You'll dig easily and without thinking, and your generous fingers will unearth the rounded glass almost effortlessly, and without even seeing its contours. And when you brush off the dirt and press the cold smooth thing to your lips, you'll know for sure.

I have loved well, and I have had many names. I do my cackling and my crying in transit, and take small things from the places I love most. Mostly, I am solitary. But sometimes I wake up sweating, that one indecipherable season in hot relief. It is true that I like to imagine that you'll follow the clues and, impossibly, find your way to my door. I like to imagine you'll take my arm, your uncommon and irrational certainty unfaded. I like to imagine that we'll walk to some bar somewhere, a room full of strangers, and yes, I'll tell. We'll tell. But first, I'll introduce you by name. I'll say, *Hello, meet Syl, this is Syl, my Syl.* I'll relish it on my tongue, a reunion. Your name in my mouth. Pure light.

May 23, 1921

Dear L,

I thought you were to come this week, but you haven't.

I must confess to you how disappointed I've felt. I look forward to seeing you, to feeling your hands on my shoulders, often the only touch I experience in a given week. I look forward to the herbs and spells and stories. I feel like I have learned enough from you that I can do some of the incantations on my own by now, but I wish you were here, still. It's different when you're here.

I am worried I have scared you away with my honesty. Things I haven't even said. But you are wise enough to understand the unsaid, L. Even I know this.

You didn't come this week, but I am still writing. As is our tradition.

And I needed to tell you that this week has broken my heart, in more ways than one.

First, I'll not wait any longer to tell you—Isaac asked my father for my hand in marriage. My father, no longer certain what he is supposed to do with me, gave his consent. Isaac is not wealthy, but he is a working man who can support a household. I do not know what a man wants with a wife who does not speak. I am not beautiful, and though I do believe my eyes have fire in them, that fire is not for Isaac. And my reputation is accursed among men in this town. Maybe he simply needs a wife, and sees that I might willingly become that wife. Isaac is kind enough, but he speaks to me with a flatness, a sense of obligation. He speaks about nothing I love. I cannot speak to him, and I cannot love him. This I know already.

I do not want to marry Isaac. There, I have said it. I do not want to marry anyone. I have never known anything so completely as this, L. I know I'll not have a choice, but when my parents told me that Isaac and I were to be married, that they'd scheduled the tanoyim already, I nodded my assent and then walked up to my room, sat in the place where I was born, and wept silently, the grief coming in gulps like wind in the wrong direction. My life no longer belonged to me. It never had. I wish I could bare my teeth and let the beast that has replaced my speaking voice come out here, but it cannot. It will not. It knows, as well as I do, that this place is not safe for the wild.

After a long time, I came back down the stairs. I walked up to my mother and put out my hand for the list for market. If she knew why I wanted to leave then, much earlier than I usually went, she didn't let on, but in some show of pity or kindness, she gave me the list and let me go.

This time, I ran. I ran all the way to the woods without stopping. My lungs were forgiving enough, because every part of my body understood the urgency in my speed. I needed to get to the only place I could truly be. My sanctuary.

When I got to the clearing, I stood in its center, opened my mouth, and unleashed the ferocious thing I had been holding inside. It was immense, alarmingly loud, much louder than before. The sound that came from me had teeth and fur, a sound that bit and caught at the air. It filled the clearing. It filled the sky. It didn't care who heard. It was the sound of the grief I felt, being handed from one man to another. Afterward, I stood in the echoes of what I'd released. The woods shook with me. I was more powerful than I'd ever been. I reminded my body of this as I prepared to walk back into a world where I felt powerless.

I looked across the way then, into the sweet nook of the tall tree, the one that always had something for me, something from the earth that seemed like a reminder I would be okay.

But there was no offering. In the tree, just a tree. There was nothing.

My disappointment sharp and cold, like metal on my tongue.

No visit from you, L.

No gift from the tree.

It is hard to write this, knowing you might not reply.

It is hard to lift my heart up off this ground.

Yours,
Mira

June 30, 1921

Dear L,

What does it say about me that I still wonder whether you will return? After all these endless weeks, I think it's clear that you will not, but I don't understand it. I know this will sound strange, but your unexplained absence saddens me even more than a death might. I think this is because it is less certain. Even if you have decided you can no longer face me or my shameful thoughts or secrets, I wish you would send a sign to let me know that you are okay.

Mama says that I am strong enough and no longer a threat to myself or others, and that I no longer need a healer, and that she doesn't know where you are either.

Jacob got married. The wedding was beautiful and joyous, but I felt subdued as my brother and his Hinde stood under the chuppah without me. I danced but did not sing. I smiled but did not laugh. The badchan was funny, but he was not as funny as my brother, whom I will always love best, even if I have mostly lost him now, as he is further away from me than ever, belonging to his own family and no longer to me.

Soon, I will marry Isaac.

You know how I feel about this.

I am scared of what I am losing, though everything already feels lost.

I miss you, L. I miss what felt true between us. What, in some other place or time, might actually have been.

                                                             Mira

July 13, 1921

Dear L,

I mean to stop writing to you. I don't know whether you receive my letters. I only know for certain now that you won't be returning here.

But yesterday, I went back to the woods. Stood in my clearing. The place I can hear myself and be heard.

I looked at my tree, and this time, there was something in its nook. Cautiously, I approached and found a tiny vial containing a liquid of some kind. I unscrewed the vial, whose contents smelled earthy and looked thick.

Thank you, L.

I know you are okay.

I know that I will be okay, too.

If I could tell you with my lips, press them soft against your ear, tell you in the voice I don't show anyone else, the voice I know only a rare few and the forest can bear, then I would tell you that way. You, my dearest L, are the rare few. You are the person to whom I want to show my teeth. And even though you're gone now, even though you've run from me, I feel certain that in a different world, in a different time, you wouldn't run, L. You wouldn't have to. You would stay.

I won't find you, I know this, but if you want to find me, you know where.

All my love,
Mira

Twenty-One

Shiva waited until the last possible moment before she left War-saw—after sitting on and trying to zip her suitcase, after calling the cab that would take her to the airport, after stuffing the bedsheets into pillowcases and speed-tidying her rental apartment—to hit *send* on the email reply to Rosen.

She'd composed it the night before, but sending it seemed to require more bravado than she thought it might. To the email, she'd attached the briefest of abstracts about her talk. *"It Runs in the Family"* will be a talk about both S. An-sky's ethnographic work and the choral cultural phenomenon of The Dybbuk, she'd begun. *It will be about how a family itself can become possessed by something, and how the shape of that possession gradually changes shape, generation to generation. About how past generations send clues into the future, and how, for so many of us, the present is mostly comprised of clues.*

Composing the long-avoided email, she'd felt euphoric with doubt. What could come next for her could be anything. *This trip has been illuminating*, she finished. She deleted *illuminating*; *luminescent*, she typed. *I can't wait to see what comes next.*

She'd need a new adviser, of course. She'd need more grant fund-ing, more time, more space. She'd need boxes and boxes to hold all the stories. She'd need a word for what she was going to become. A word for wholehearted submission to what was equal parts exorcism and ancient possession. *Seeker*, she thought. At her core. Not exactly the right word anymore, but she'd wear it for now. One life is a lot of time, and a person could have many names.

In the cab, she pulled the stone El had given her out of her jacket pocket. In the light of morning, through the car window, it looked ordinary. Just a shiny stone, not much larger than a pebble, flattened by water or by time. She rolled it around in her hand, letting it warm to her touch. Out the window, a stretch of road rolled out behind her.

From the airport, she tumbled back into Brooklyn's blunt spring humidity, bleary-eyed and sleepy-haired. It was the kind of fragrant evening that felt so still when you walked through it, you started to worry it was something lying in wait.

On the train home, Shiva held her luggage as close to her body as she could. Everything sounded different here, and the language people spoke—her own, her first—was at once comforting and intrusive in her ears. A man in a grungy Nets sweatshirt carrying a mandolin walked through the sliding doors. He edged his way through the crowd, stood by the center doors, and launched into a sweet and wordless melody, the intricacies of which made Shiva feel softer, happier to be barreling home. While he played, he closed his eyes.

She walked in the door to an apartment that smelled empty and unfamiliar. She hadn't been gone that long, but it felt like long enough for her Vanderbilt Avenue bedroom to have forgotten her. She dropped her bags in the entryway and proceeded directly to the shower.

She came out to a stack of texts from Hannah.

Call me.

Are you back yet?

Let me know when you're home?

She called her mother.

"Ma," she said. "I'm home. I'm back. Hello."

"How was it?" Shiva was surprised to hear how changed her mother's voice sounded, how energetic and curious. "Tell me everything."

"God," Shiva said. "I'm exhausted. It wasn't at all what I expected it to be. But also it was incredible."

"Welcome," said Hannah. Her voice sounded thick with a warmth Shiva hardly recognized. "I'm so happy you're home. You must be exhausted, so I won't make you tell me everything right now, but . . . any highlights?"

"The light," said Shiva. "And the park benches, and the trees, and the alleyways. Everything is . . . it's not haunted. It's just almost alive. There's so much life there. It's just teeming." Her mother was quiet. "Hello?"

"I'm still here," said Hannah.

"Ma," said Shiva. "I went."

"Went where?"

"I went to the City of Laughter."

Between them, a vivid humming across state lines.

Hannah cleared her throat. "Shiva. I have to tell you something."

"Okay . . ."

"Actually," said Hannah slowly. Her voice sounded bright, certain. "I have to be more honest with you and tell you a few things. Do you have a little time?"

Shiva sat down on her bed, still in her robe, her wet hair wrapped in a towel, a light rain pattering on her window as if it had waited for her to begin falling.

"I do," she said.

The way Hannah told her was orderly, like packing a suitcase, like she'd been thinking about it for a long time. How Hannah's father had found two of Syl's notebooks and sent them to Hannah, and how they both suspected she'd had an affair with a mysterious lover. How Hannah's dynamic with Syl was even more fraught than she'd ever let on, and how she was willing to tell Shiva everything she could remember. How Hannah was sorry she didn't know more about what had happened to Mira, but that it was bad, really bad, and she was so sorry she'd kept Shiva so far away from her great-grandmother as a baby, how she wished they could meet again.

Shiva wanted to tell her mother it felt like they almost had. She could feel herself holding her body still, too afraid that if she moved, her mother would stop talking.

"I'm sorry," Hannah finally said. "There is so much I haven't been able to understand. So much I haven't known how to say, not even to myself. Not even out loud alone in a room. But I'm going to try to say it. I'm going to try to learn how to say it."

"I understand." Shiva felt awash in something. She felt keenly aware of her mother's fallibility and sort of reverent of it.

"So, there is one more thing. Forgive me for not telling you sooner. I promise you, I'm trying."

"What is it?" Shiva couldn't believe this was her mother she was talking to. Hannah's manner was open, her voice direct, like somebody sure of something. Something must have happened in Shiva's absence, though she couldn't imagine what.

"Shiva, your great-grandmother had a brother."

"She did?"

"He died," Hannah said quickly. "A long time before Mira did. But . . ."

"But what, Ma?"

"He has a granddaughter." An endless pause. "She lives in Brooklyn."

Shiva couldn't form the words to say *what?* or *thank you.* She listened to the silence in the wake of what her mother had just told her. It was odd—since she'd been angry with Hannah for so long, in so many different ways—that she didn't feel angry now. Shocked, but there was a calm, like a landing. Like her mother had been listening. Like she might have the capacity to make different decisions from the ones she'd been given.

"I'm sorry," Hannah whispered.

"Thank you," said Shiva. "Thank you."

She wrote down the number as her mother spoke it on the other end. And she hung up the phone.

Shiva met Chani Lieber on Friday at noon in Prospect Park. Chani said she liked to walk in the park at some point every day, and this way, she could do two things at once. Shiva waited by the Grand Army Plaza entrance until she saw a petite woman in a large hat approaching, white sneakers shuffling briskly under a long denim skirt.

"Shiva!" Voice high as a teenager's, face youthful, though she had to be in her mid-sixties—Shiva had done the math. The hat covered her hair entirely, so it concealed any grays, and aside from the smile lines around her eyes, her face was virtually wrinkle-free.

Chani threw her arms around Shiva without hesitation. She smelled like hair spray and pound cake. "Oh, bubeleh, I can't believe it, it's so nice to meet you. I'm so glad you got in touch. Should we sit for a minute? Let's sit."

"Thanks so much for meeting me," Shiva said. "I would have gotten in touch sooner. I just didn't know . . ."

"I know," said Chani. "I hadn't been in touch with your mother in a long time either. I was so surprised when she called me to say you might be reaching out." She sighed. "We just weren't ever close, you know? My grandfather died so many years ago, and I know your great-grandmother died when you were little. We just didn't stay on top of it." She shook her head. Around them, joggers and cyclists and all the easy energy of a Friday afternoon. "It's silly, no? We all live right here. We're mishpocha."

"Right," Shiva said. There had been some kind of code, Shiva now understood. With Syl. Things Hannah felt like she could say out loud and things she couldn't. Things she'd willfully forgotten and things that had just been lost along the way. It felt like the code was beginning not to crack but to melt away. She could only hope. She put her hand in her pocket, touched the little Ropshitz stone. Touched where she'd been.

"I knew Hannah had a daughter, but I didn't realize how grown-up you'd be, or how beautiful!" Chani looked at Shiva like a doting grandmother. "You must have a boyfriend. Do you have a boyfriend? A husband?"

"I don't have a boyfriend," said Shiva. "Or a husband."

"Oh, that's okay," said Chani, brightly.

"I'm gay," said Shiva. Maybe Chani was one of those funky ultra-Orthodox Brooklynites who had a gay friend or an outspoken progressive daughter, and everyone still gathered around the cholent on Friday nights anyway.

"Well," she said. She looked surprised, not alarmed. "It doesn't matter. We have a lot of children. I've seen almost everything. And now you're family." Chani stopped, making some kind of decision in her head. "So, gay, okay. We'll have to have you for Shabbos sometime. You and your mother. I make delicious challah."

"I've never turned down challah," said Shiva, relieved.

"Good," said Chani. "How is your mother anyway? I was so sorry to hear about your father. Baruch dayan emes. He seemed like a wonderful man."

"He was. He was the best man." Shiva wondered what Jon would have thought of Chani Lieber. Had he known about her? The question stung, and Shiva filed it away. "My mom is okay. She's still sad. And lonely." Chani was family. She could be honest. "I think she's also trying to figure out a lot of stuff about her own life, and there's more time and space to do that now that my dad . . ."

"Oy, of course," said Chani.

"I think that's why she reconnected with you," said Shiva. "When my dad died, it was like, we both realized how disconnected from family we were. How important knowing family can be to knowing yourself. You know—family in the bigger sense. I think it's good for us to be in touch again. With whoever we've still got."

"Absolutely," Chani said. She was nodding continuously as Shiva spoke, like a patient and very religious therapist. "When someone dies, it makes us remember. It's interesting, Shiva, your name. I've never heard of any Jewish girl with such a name. But I bet it helps you remember."

"I never thought about it that way," Shiva said. "Chani, do you remember your grandfather? Jacob?"

"Very well," said Chani. "He was very special to me. He was very pious; he was a pulpit rabbi, you know? But also—and not many people knew this—he was hilarious. And how he loved your great-grandmother. I know they were estranged when he died, but I can tell you, he always missed her."

Shiva tried to process what she'd just heard. "Estranged? Do you know why? Or what happened between them?"

Chani looked at a thin gold watch on her wrist. "Oy, I have to get back to my cooking soon. We're having a lot of people tonight." She looked at Shiva, her face neutral. "I don't know too much, dear. What I know is that Mira was very important to my grandfather, and that he had always tried to protect her. I get the feeling they didn't have the happiest childhood, and something terrible happened to Mira, something my grandfather refused to talk about. *Let the past be the past*, he said. I'm no expert, and I'm not sure, Shiva, but I get the feeling my grandfather felt very bad, that there was something he didn't want to think about. Maybe he thought he could have prevented it, or protected her better . . ." Chani waved her hand then, dismissing the theory. "Oh, but this is all just modern guesswork. It could have been anything."

"They were completely estranged?" The thought of it made her want to weep. Two Jewish siblings who both got out of Europe before the war but managed to lose one another nonetheless.

"Well," said Chani. "He was working as a rabbi up in Albany; he wasn't down here. And then your great-grandmother, she moved to Florida, right? I think she did go to see him at the end of his life. It was odd. She didn't like to travel, is my understanding, and you know about her voice, of course."

"Her voice?"

Chani's eyes widened. "Your mother never told you?" She clucked and made a *shhhh* sound with her teeth. "Oy, I wonder how much your mother knew. The things families don't talk about." She paused, considering, and played with the strap of her purse. Then she looked back up at Shiva. "Your great-grandmother—my understanding is that she lost her voice when she was very young."

"What do you mean, *lost*?"

"My grandfather didn't talk about it much, but I know that whatever happened to Mira, she stopped being able to speak for a very long time."

"What?" Around Shiva, the park spun, and the joggers seemed to her to be glitching, running in place. Mira had died when she was just a toddler. Shiva remembered Mira's smile. Always the smile, the one that took up her entire face. She remembered warmth. She didn't remember a voice, but she didn't remember no voice. *Your great-grandmother was very quiet*, Hannah had told her. But *very quiet* was not a lost voice. *Very quiet* was not *something terrible happened*. *Very quiet* was not *estranged*.

Chani simply nodded.

Shiva's voice came whispery and sad from her throat. "I wish I could talk to her. I wish I could have met your grandfather, too."

"I know," said Chani. "I'm sorry to tell you so much. Maybe it wasn't my place to tell."

"No," said Shiva. "Thank you. I am so grateful to be told."

Chani stayed quiet a moment. Then she shook the dark out of her eyes and looked at her watch again. "Before I go." She pulled a rumpled manila folder out of her cavernous pocketbook. "When I got your call, I started going through some old boxes to see if I had anything of your great-grandmother's. I'm not sure how this ended up in my possession. I think maybe after the funeral. There are a few articles, a couple of my grandfather's speeches. They're in Yiddish. Do you speak Yiddish?"

Shiva shook her head.

"Well, more reasons for you to visit. I'll have to translate. Also, in here, there was some kind of letter or something. Maybe from a friend? It's in Polish, so I don't know what it says, but I just wanted you and your mother to have it. Just a little something."

"Thank you," said Shiva.

"I really do have to go," said Chani. "The brisket takes hours." She stood up, and her long denim skirt fell back around her ankles. "Promise me you'll come for Shabbos soon?"

"I promise," said Shiva.

"And promise you'll bring your mother sometime too?"

"I'll do my best," said Shiva.

Shiva watched Chani walk back up toward Eastern Parkway with a bounce in her step, and Shiva wondered, as she sometimes did, whether the kind of devotion required by orthodoxy also fueled a particular kind of vitality. It hadn't ever looked that way on her mother, but on the phone yesterday, Hannah had sounded livelier than she had in years, an awake quality to her voice Shiva didn't remember being there even before Jon got sick. She wondered again what had shifted. What had prompted Hannah to call Chani Lieber? And how was it possible Shiva had not been able to touch even the tip of the truth about her great-grandmother until now?

As Chani became a dot on the median strip, shuffling at high speed back to Borough Park, two joggers half stretched and half gossiped on the bench to the right of hers. And on the bench to her left, someone ate lunch, one-handedly turning the pages of a Dean Koontz novel.

Shiva wasn't ready to walk home yet. She took the envelope out of her tote, her wrists shaky. Her body knew so much more than she did, she now understood.

She let her body lead. Let it walk her into the park, like it had walked her all over Warsaw. Let it take her around the curve of the bike path, onto the green, past a couple of hippies on a homemade tightrope and a group of friends on a blanket trying to force a cork out of a bottle of wine with a ballpoint pen. Someone from somewhere shouted, TIME FOR THE SECOND CHORUS. Her feet worked, her feet worked. The sky, bright, looked on like someone receptive, waiting—nothing too dramatic but nothing absent either. Past an older lady napping in a floral cape, an open book of sudoku on the sheet next to her. Past an outdoor yoga class and a couple trying not to look like they were fighting. *I didn't*, said one of them through clenched teeth. *Stop trying to rewrite the story.* She let her body lead her to the base of a tree, where she sat, dropping her tote to the ground.

Her fingers went to her phone. Levi had texted her about drinks at Felix's on Saturday night with Aria and Marv, saying that no one could wait to drain a bottle of bourbon as Shiva regaled them with tales of her time in Poland. Hannah had texted her to say that she should book a bus down to Maryland soon, and maybe she could show her Syl's notebooks and they could talk a little. Did she want to text Dani? Shiva scanned her fingertips for clues. Dani felt like a distant ache now, a previous era. Texting her no longer felt necessary. She opened her message history with the Ghost. The Ghost was definitive, an ending. A small certain sting at what could have been, but what could have been had now become what *was*. She, here, in Prospect Park, having just met her great-great-uncle's granddaughter.

And there was El. *Yes*, her fingers said. She didn't know what the protocol was for texting after you've been to another time with a person, a whole different universe. After they've given you the object that's been keeping you on the ground. She slowly released her phone back into her bag and, instead, touched the rock for the hundredth time that day.

Then, she opened the envelope.

There were Jacob's speeches, the ones Chani had mentioned, wrinkly Xerox copies and handwritten Yiddish scrawl. There were a couple of printed articles about Ropshitz, one about a badchan Shiva had never heard of, not the famous Rabbi Naftali Tzvi of Ropshitz but a man named Baruch. Shiva wondered if he too was a relative.

And at the bottom of the envelope, folded in half, was a thin, translucent piece of paper. Shiva pulled it out, holding her breath. She unfolded it. Each side of the piece of paper bore a short handwritten note in Polish. The Polish was difficult to read, and each of the notes was written in distinctly different handwriting.

That settled it. She hesitated for only one moment before messaging El.

Hi, she wrote. *Would it be weird for me to ask you for a favor?*

No, texted El, just moments later. *Ask away.*

I need someone to translate these. She photographed the letters and texted them to El. *Thank you*, she wrote. *Xo*, she typed. And then she untyped it. *Xo* didn't quite capture it. *I miss you*, she typed, and hit *send* before she could reconsider.

She sat under the tree and waited. She let her fingers play with the dirt. It wasn't muddy, but it wasn't bone-dry, and it felt oddly nice under her fingertips. She touched roots and rocks, picked up twigs and returned them to where she'd found them. Her fingers found a matchbox. She slid it open. It was from someplace called Nickleby's Pub in midtown, and it was full of matches. *It's weird*, she thought. *How much the ground holds.*

She thought about Dani's lizard. How she'd never found it, and how Dani had sworn it was buried somewhere in Prospect Park. Was there some kind of queer sixth sense that would have helped her, had she wanted it to? The ground was vast and regenerating, and it seemed more likely that if someone someday found it, it wouldn't be her.

Hannah was particular about objects, too, mostly because Syl had been. Rabbis wrestled with one another over the power imbued in beds, stones, pots, shrouds, tools, pottery. So you couldn't mess around with just any old object. Some objects required certain kinds of cleaning, replacement, maintenance. Others did, in fact, require burial. Objects could take the shape of something humans were otherwise unwilling to see. Objects passed from hand to hand, making their haphazard way through the felt world.

Objects carry the energy we give them.

And that energy doesn't disappear.

It only changes shape.

A few minutes later, El texted the entire contents of the document in translation:

May 13, 1988

Dear L,

I realize that it may seem silly and maybe even delusional to write after decades of silence, so I will keep it short. I doubt that this letter will find you at this address, but it is the most recent address I could track down for you, so I had to try. I don't know where you are, or even whether you are still alive, though the thought of you being elsewhere pains my heart, even still.

I live in Florida now, though I lived in New Jersey and New York for many years after we left Poland in 1923. In Florida, I am happy. I live near swamp and woods and have spent countless hours in those overgrown places. This is important to me in ways only you truly understand.

Isaac died some years ago. He had a weak heart. We had a daughter, Sylvia. I insisted we pick a name with the letter L in it. It's a small tribute, but I promise, it has always been for you. There is so much more, but I don't know how to put it in a note to you, one that you will probably never read.

I am only writing to you now because I am not well. I am very unwell, in fact. And when I am not well, you are still the person I want to tell about it. Is that ridiculous? I am trying to be strong, but strength, as I see it, has been elusive and overrated.

I wish I could see you.

I miss you. I have always missed you.

I wish I could know whether you had ever been mine.

Whether you had ever been.

All my love,
Mira

And the second translation, underneath:

My dearest Mira,
Don't go yet. Please.
I'm sorry I was gone so long.
I'm putting this letter in the mail, and then I'm coming to you.
I'll see you soon.

And yes, I have always been yours,
L

The sun, dazzling. Ambient shouts and something that looked like a red kite. Shiva's throat caught with questions. *Decades*, her great-grandmother had written. A deathbed plea, a reunion, and love. Swamp and woods. Actual love. A letter and its response. Someone named L. Like El. On the other side of Warsaw, her questions had teeth. On the other side of Warsaw, and here was Mira. It wasn't a culmination, after all. It was an opening.

That name is some coincidence, texted El. *Yeah*, Shiva said, and her skin prickled everywhere as she said it, as she waited, the cross-oceanic dots taking their time, until El finally said, *Or even better: maybe not.*

What did one do next, then?

Across the green, a family was playing a sloppy game of soccer. The mother, it seemed, kicking the ball, over and over again, at the command of the daughter, who was in a soccer uniform, trying to teach the mother how. Two men entangled in one another, one of whom had a sapphire-blue notebook in which he was lazily writing. The other, chewing on a long blade of grass. Distantly, the sound of a motor. And bicycles, piles of them, across the grass. A queer couple holding hands, great sneakers on the both of them, and one of them really pulling off a skater dress. The sky swinging under all of its weight, too full to stay still.

And then, sharply, right in her line of vision, a tall redheaded woman built like a sculpture walked across the field, swaying at the hips as she moved. She practically glowed, spotlit. She looked like she'd emerged from a scene in a movie or, Shiva realized in her gut, an old photograph. Unseasonal leopard-print shrug over her shoulders. Sharp white blouse tucked into a swirl of olive-colored tweed. She strode, certain, heels clacking on the concrete that cut through the grass, like someone with someplace important to go. For one moment, right around the center of the park, the woman stopped, turned slightly, like she was looking for someone. Shiva could plainly see her face—those clear and searching eyes, and lips the shape of an impeccable bow, a slight smile and a matte crimson red.

Her phone dinged. Even the *ding* had a different quality to it. *I miss you*, said El. It was the opposite of an afterthought. Shiva's head filled with something warmer than singing, and she felt herself slowly lifting off the ground.

Hello, she said to the beautiful mystery woman she knew by heart, the one disappearing into the trees at the park's very edges, a small cluster of birds following closely behind her. *Hello*, she said up to the sky, as though finally truly introducing herself. *Hello there.*

Epilogue

It is told that the day of Baruch and Bluma's wedding, everyone awoke to rain. Bluma's mother wept in her long yellow dress, while her father in his special prayer shawl pleaded with God for just a sliver of sun.

Bluma, though? She liked it. It made a kind of sense that the sky should crack open on the day she married her love, her very own badchan. She thought she might crack open too. She put on her blue cloak over her wedding gown and wore her boots instead of the pointy wedding shoes her mother had picked out for her. They walked out of the house—Bluma, her mother, and her father—and they could already hear the klezmorim tuning their instruments in the distance. The even-tempered rain allowed them through.

They arrived at the edge of the woods where the wedding was to take place. Bluma wasn't nervous. Under the cloak, she was cool and dry. She had loved Baruch since they were children in cheder. She had no idea what to expect—not from marriage, not from this life, not from this uncommon man she had come to love—but she preferred it this way. To have no idea. The men were setting up the badeken, the women winding vines around the legs of the chair meant to serve as her bridal throne. The violin swelled as the klezmorim began to play in earnest, kicking off the day's festivities.

Bluma wrapped her cloak tightly around her and let the rain guide her across the green, ducking down as she passed through the assembling crowd so that no one would notice a bride leaving her own wedding. They'd be there late into the evening; there was time. She walked past the crowd and into the thicket of trees, pushing shiny leaves and thorny branches out of the way and forging a path through the growth. She rounded the bend, to a place where the gray daylight washed freely over a clearing. And in the clearing she stood.

The strangest thing: she had seen Baruch come here several times in the last year. She'd followed him here on three different occasions; she hadn't ever meant to, but her curiosity had gotten the better of her. What could it have been that drew him to these woods, the ones that felt like the edge of the world from the small village where they made their lives? She'd watched him navigate his way through the thicket, around the bend, and into the clearing. She hadn't followed him into the clearing, though. Unusual though the recurring outing, she could tell that whatever he sought here belonged to him and wasn't for her. She hoped that, one day, he'd choose to tell her about it.

One evening, he'd been in the clearing a whole hour, emerging teary-eyed and softly humming. She'd run home, chest thumping the entire way, and couldn't sleep that whole night, consumed by wondering what or whom Baruch might be visiting in those woods.

But now, these months later, both the clearing and its arboreal encirclement—how the trees gazed down, held her in their midst like a group of kindly dancers—belonged to her alone. The rain fell lightly through the treetops, and breeze licked at her cheeks. From the field, faintly, she could hear the klezmorim start to play a tune full of longing, slow as a chant.

Across from where Bluma stood, one extraordinary tree rose out of the ground—tall and broad, strong branches like open arms. There was a crook in its center that looked like a perfect place for a bird or a squirrel to perch. There was something, Bluma thought, about looking into that crook, that felt almost like looking into the tree's eyes. Something about the presence of this particular tree felt almost like another person here with her, a person who might want to listen. It made her want to sing, or pray. No, to laugh. Bluma was overcome now with the desire to laugh.

From the field, the violin soared, held its note so long the air vibrated with it. Bluma was enraptured by everything she hoped would come next. Even in this life, sometimes hard and humorless as gravel, wonder could still find you if you were paying the right kind of attention.

And here, it had found her. Bluma moved closer to the tree. She touched it, first with one palm, then with the other. And then, careful not to catch her hair to the bark, she brought her ear close to the tree's trunk.

It is told, then, that a man in his finest blue jacket emerged from behind the tree.

When people tell the story, they tell of a man.

I, of course, know different.

"Hello," said the man.

"Oh my," said Bluma. She hadn't expected company.

It is told that Bluma's eyes were a brilliant slate gray and looked like no color at all in the light of the sun. They widened expectantly, waiting for the blue-clad interlocutor to introduce himself. They narrowed as Bluma noticed the brown leather bag slung over his shoulder.

"Are you a visitor?"

"Yes," said the man. "Just passing through. I wanted to pay my respects to the bride and groom."

"Do you know my Baruch?"

"In a manner of speaking, I do," said the man. He paused, stroking the clean-shaven place a beard might otherwise be. The man, thought Bluma, was beautiful. Could you think such a thing about a man? Too late, she supposed. "I work as a messenger," he said plainly, indicating his shoulder bag. "I once left something in his care."

Bluma was wild with curiosity. What had this messenger delivered to Baruch, she wondered? Why was he at her wedding, and how had he known to find her here, and now, and just like this?

Then the light caught the eyes of the stranger who stood before her, revealing their uncommon color. His eyes, it is told, were a dazzling green—a green made from sea moss or emeralds or thick verdant grass—like no green she'd seen in anyone's eyes before. Like no green she had a name for.

As Bluma looked into his eyes, the man in the blue jacket began to gleam, to grow in scope. There, where he stood, he looked less and less like a man—at least not the kind of man Bluma recognized—and more and more like someone else. Someone familiar, thought Bluma, though she wasn't sure why or how. The stranger's smooth cheeks, his moonward lashes, the sway in his hips when he came around from behind the tree and approached Bluma. His hair thick and wavy, mimicking the ocean or the wind, his lips soft-looking as her own, and his hands, Bluma couldn't help but notice, uncommonly strong. The afternoon light was as clear as water. Was it still raining? Bluma felt a trembling in her ankles, her knees, through the thick of her middle to the top of her head, where something radiated.

"I've never seen anyone like you," Bluma breathed. She was honest.

"I know," said the man who was not a man.

Said the man who was me.

"What's in the bag?" Bluma drew closer. She needed to know.

"Not much today," said the stranger. He was simply here to offer his blessing, he told her. Baruch and Bluma's love, he said, sown in laughter, had been a beautiful thing to witness, and he wanted, at last, to meet her. There was someone else also, he said. A woman he loved from another time and another place, whom he hoped he might find here too.

"Another time?" Bluma couldn't understand. And how did this stranger know anything about the laughter that lit her and Baruch both?

The stranger smiled. "Time works differently than most people think it does. And there is nothing like a great love to fold time over on itself more completely than anything else can."

Bluma nodded, eyes wide, unsure how to respond. Time, at once abundant and brutally brief, engulfed her.

"Would you mind standing here, against the tree?" Bluma knew which one. She obliged without question, leaning back into the towering oak, the one with the arms that looked like they might actually be capable of holding her. The stranger put his strong hands on Bluma's head. She could feel the warmth of his palms through the hood of her cloak. She closed her eyes.

When she opened them, the stranger was gone, messenger bag and all.

Bluma couldn't explain why she felt like crying.

Slowly, she turned to face the crook of the tree. It is told she was barely surprised to find the sand-colored stone there. It stood out like a visitor, shone smooth as the messenger's cheeks had been. Bluma touched the stone, and it warmed in her hand. She laughed then, first a private sound and then a louder one from her stomach, a raw, unvarnished noise that surprised her. A laugh meant for the sky to hear, and the wolves. The violins soared in the distance, as though in response.

"Let this place protect you." She spoke the words aloud to the clearing, which felt anything but empty. To whom was she speaking? To the stone? To the messenger who was neither man nor woman and now gone? To the tree? To herself? To someone she had yet to meet, or perhaps never would?

She put the stone in the pocket of her cloak. Then, a gust of rain, and she changed her mind. She turned around, walked back to her tree, and knelt to the ground in her wedding finery. She picked up a stick and dug a small hole at the base of the tree, never mind the mud around the hem of her dress or the grassy spots on her knees. As she dug, she thought about what might be underneath her. What would happen if she kept digging, she wondered, straight down through layers of earth and even time? She put the stone in the hole, and patted a handful of wet dirt back over it. It would be here now, for whoever needed it next.

It is told, then, that the weather changed, sun warming the faces of the guests. It is told, but that's not how I remember it.

I remember it stayed gray and rainy the entire day. That the wedding was soon to be watery and wild, all mud-stomping exuberance, no difference between the joyful tears, the longing ones, and the rain itself, how it poured down the people's faces.

Bluma was reluctant to leave the tree, the one that stood guard over this small, hidden place. She wished with all of her body to understand the language of the tree, to know whether it had heard her supplication. Finally, after a long while, Bluma began to back away, never taking her eyes off the tree's crook.

And no one could hear it—not even me, and not Bluma, who stood, finally, and walked, mud-streaked and smiling, back toward the milling crowd to celebrate her own wedding—but as the story goes, right then, on that small sacred day, inside lifetimes of millions of other small sacred days, the tree gave its word.

Author's Note

In the summer of 2018, I went to Warsaw for a month, where I studied Yiddish and took lots and lots of walks. I owe much of this writing to the time I spent there. Specifically to the International Summer Seminar in Yiddish Language and Culture at the Center for Yiddish Culture in Muranów; my Yiddish classmates and their local friends who showed me around and helped translate for me; the truly joyous queer evening I spent at Madame Q; the baristas at Fat White Coffee who were always so kind and taught me Polish vocabulary daily; and the motorcyclist who was gracious enough to respond to the note I left on her motorcycle seat in the parking lot after the show.

I don't know much about Ropshitz, the shtetl where my great-grandmother was born. I do know that it is perhaps best known for Naftali Tzvi Horowitz, the storied badchan who hailed from there. Much of the rest of the Ropshitz in this book comes from my imagination. But for some of its foundations, I looked to the translation of a book called *There Once was a Shtetl Ropczyce*, edited by Ita Rosenfeld and translated by Aryeh Wanderman, available at jewishgen.org.

Some of the folktales and superstitions in this book are drawn from life, and many others are invented. Some fall somewhere squarely in between—the "mirror trick," for example, is a suburban legend I heard somewhere in my Modern Orthodox youth that never quite left me.

I don't remember the details of it, so I've handsomely embellished it here. The folktales I've written anew here are a kind of homage to my rich Ashkenazic Jewish oral tradition; how folktales are created and recreated in kitchens and around fires; how they shift shape. These invented stories are lovingly wrought from the expansive spirit of the folktales my parents read to us on Friday nights: the lore that raised me.

For Shiva's idea about the transgenerational impact of Nisn and Sender's love in *The Dybbuk*, I am indebted to Naomi Seidman's scholarship in her remarkable essay "The Ghost of Queer Loves Past: Ansky's 'Dybbuk' and the Sexual Transformation of Ashkenaz," from the book *Queer Theory and the Jewish Question*.

Finally, gratitude to Gabriella Safran for her book *Wandering Soul: The Dybbuk's Creator, S. An-sky*, a treasure of a resource for getting to know An-sky better, and for more deeply understanding my kinship with him. And to Nathaniel Deutsch for his invaluable translation of An-sky's questionnaire in *The Jewish Dawrk Continent*. I relied on both of these works in writing this novel.

Acknowledgments

Here, some profound gratitude:

To my extraordinary agent, Stephanie Delman, who has championed this book tirelessly, who makes actual magic, and who I simply adore. You are a bright star and I am so thankful. And to Michelle Brower and Khalid McCalla for their vital wisdom and support across the finish line.

To my brilliant editor, Amy Hundley, who has always understood how much more deeply itself this book could become. And to the entire team at Grove Atlantic, for treating my book with such great care, generosity, and dedication. I am delighted and honored that my debut novel is in your collective hands.

To the disparate and expansive raucous dinner party of dear friends—in DC, in New York, and beyond—who have cheered this story on from its very beginnings, and who will find their influence in these pages. Countless people made this novel possible, in both direct and indirect ways. The writing itself may be solitary, but nobody gets through this creative process alone, and I am very lucky to be so well held.

To my once and future writing group: Rebecca Novack, Laura Laing, Molly Gallentine, Rahne Alexander, Luke Dani Blue, and Jennifer Audette. To my workshop at the University of Maryland MFA, who gave me feedback on early portions of this book, and to my MFA mentors Maud Casey, Gabrielle Lucille Fuentes, Emily Mitchell, and Howard Norman. To Garth Greenwell, in whose master class on style I received indispensable feedback on the book's direction. To Lidia Yuknavitch, in whose 2014 online class I remembered how to write fiction. To my first forever writing group, Tanya Paperny and Fid Thompson. To Jami Nakamura Lin, for vital companionship in the book-publishing process. To my dear friends in the Delman-hive, for always cheerleading with such gusto; and to Trellis, for cultivating such a radical sense of belonging among its authors.

To every writer and editor who has believed in my work, shown me kindness, or offered literary friendship. To every generous literary citizen who has made the room spacious enough to accommodate ever more of us. To the queer ancestors whose stories I touch with my imagination, and to my queer kin, in whose abundant presence I have learned myself.

To Sarah Zarrow, who thoughtfully read this manuscript as someone who has known both Warsaw and S. An-sky far longer than I have, and has been a kind and patient consultant on both.

To Emily Bernard, for believing in my work: I'm so excited to pay it forward.

To Vermont Studio Center and Monson Arts, where fellowships and time made it possible for me to write and revise large portions of this book.

To the Rona Jaffe Foundation for honoring me with an award in 2020. It was a life-changing kind of surprise, and a boost to both this project and my spirit that made all the difference in the world.

To my original besties, the apples and bananas: Dasi Fruchter, Ora Fruchter, Yoshie Fruchter. Your friendship and our antics are the foundation of any story I've ever written. To my dear parents, Rena Fruchter and Harold (Chaim) Fruchter, who raised me on the best stories and have always asked, *How is the novel going?* with genuine love and interest. To my beloved and wildly inspiring family: Leah Koenig, Max Fruchter, Bea Fruchter, Bradford Jordan, Gideon Jordan, and Daniel Krupka. And to Willow and Moby, obviously.

To my cats, Kermit Frances and Oscar Anelna, who have taught me more about love and kinship than I ever believed teachable.

To Eli Oberman, my spiritual chavruta; the Toonces to my Toonces, in whose company I dreamed up so much of this world, and to whom I raise a thousand glasses of champagne.

To Erin Anthony, whose unwavering support and kindness and humor made this writing possible. A bouquet of lizards for you. You are a great adventure.